Paradise
Park

THE DIAL PRESS

Paradise Park

A NOVEL

Allegra Goodman

THE DIAL PRESS

Published by
The Dial Press
Random House, Inc.
1540 Broadway
New York, New York 10036

The Dial Press® is a registered trademark of Random House, Inc., and the colophon is a trademark of Random House, Inc.

Library of Congress Cataloging in Publication Data

Goodman, Allegra.
Paradise park : a novel / Allegra Goodman.
p. cm.
ISBN 0-385-33416-8
1. Jewish women—Fiction. 2. New age movement—Fiction.
3. Young women—Fiction. 4. Hawaii—Fiction. I. Title.
PS3557.O5829 P37 2001
813'.54—dc21
00-049376

Book design by Jo Anne Metsch

Manufactured in the United States of America
Published simultaneously in Canada

March 2001

10 9 8 7 6 5 4 3 2 1

BVG

For Paula and Ernest

How long will I go on crying "tomorrow, tomorrow"?
Why not now?

—AUGUSTINE
Confessions 8:12

1

Honeycreepers

ALL this light was pouring in on me, and I started to open my eyes. I didn't know where in the world I was, and I reached over, but no one was there. The room was empty, and I didn't even know where the room was—it was all just floating in empty space, and I couldn't say what planet or star I'd landed on. All that was running through me in that one second was the loneliness of being this tiny insignificant particle in the universe, and how a life weighs nothing in all that light. And what is that light compared to God? Then I woke up and it came back to me. That the guy, supposedly my boyfriend, who came out with me to this joint, a fleabag in Waikiki, was now gone, run off with a chick on her way to Fiji, and he—actually they—had left me with the hotel bill, which since I had no idea how to pay I was avoiding by just staying in the hotel and not checking out. But you know, the vision I had before, when I was just half awake, that was the important part. That was like the angels talking, when they speak to you and teach you right before you're born, and then they put their fingers on your lips—Sh! don't tell! You almost forget, but somewhere inside, you remember. At the time, that morning, I just lay there and had no idea what to do, not to mention I had never as far as I knew even believed in the existence of God. But in my subconscious, and my unconscious, and everywhere else, I had all these questions and ideas about this higher power and this divine spirit, and maybe I would have been dealing with them if I hadn't been so broke.

Finally I got up. I sat on the edge of the queen-size hotel bed. The bedspread was halfway off, sliding onto the floor, and the spread was green, printed yellow and orange with bird-of-paradise flowers so enormous they looked like some kind of dinosaur parts. The headboard was white rattan. So was the dresser and the mirror frame and the desk. There was no chair. Everything that could be nailed down was.

THERE I was all by myself, yet it wasn't exactly like I'd had some kind of one-night stand! We were folk dancers. That's how my boyfriend and I had met a couple of years before. Gary and I were two of the original dancers that danced in Cambridge at MIT. Balkan on Tuesdays. Israeli on Wednesdays. This was in the seventies when the folk scene in Boston was just starting, and there was a group of us—it was our life. We'd gather together at night—guys in cutoff shorts and girls in Indian gauze skirts, tank tops. In winter we'd strip down out of our parkas and ski hats and wool socks, and unzip until we were barefoot. I had long straight hair, light brown, and I wore it loose down to my waist, and I lived to dance in Walker Gym with my hair flying around me and my shirt against my bare skin, and the smooth gym varnish on the floor like syrup to my toes.

The music came from a tape recorder mounted on a little wooden cart painted gypsy colors, yellow and red, and stenciled in fancy green: MIT FOLK DANCE CLUB. The names of the dances were scribbled in chalk on a green chalkboard wheeled in from one of the classrooms. Then, from seven to eleven at night, we circled and wheeled and flew. We would dance like this for Balkan: twenty at a time together with our arms linked in a line, and our legs kicking and feet moving to rhythms like 7/8 or 11/16. Like this for Israeli: in concentric circles, feet flying, every other person off the ground.

Gary and I were such a pair that everybody watched us. When we left the gym it was like after a performance, all those admiring eyes. We'd walk outside in winter, and shuffle through the snow with the heat still on us, carrying our coats for blocks before we started to get cold. Just wandering in the slush and barely noticing that gradual little bit of freezing cold water that starts wicking in through the seams of your boots. We'd get home to Allston and run up the stairs to Gary's apartment—a real find on top of a doddering Victorian house. We had a kitchenette wired up in half a hall, and a dormer bedroom, where we curled up in blankets. I used to sit for hours in bed playing my guitar, the radiator like drums behind me, bang banging away.

Originally he was the one with the traveling bug. Gary was one of those Vietnam-era graduate students, thirty-five at that time, which was '74. He was still working on a government public health grant at Harvard, and he used to cart around boxes of those manila computer punch cards. Every once in a while the profs would fire up the old computer, and they'd input their data with a clicking and a clacking till the oracle spoke, spewing out numbers on that wide paper with pale-green and white stripes. Then Gary and the other grad students would all go back to their shared offices adorned with shag carpet remnants and cork bulletin boards, and they'd ponder the numbers. Gary had been doing this for years; and since it was a longitudinal study, which meant it didn't ever end, he was getting kind of restless. But I, on the other hand, was really busy, since I was just twenty—in the middle of stopping out of college and getting seriously into dancing and my music—folk stuff on my guitar. I listened to Joni Mitchell and Carole King and Jackson Browne. And of course I was writing my own stuff, too, all in their same styles. I was biking over the BU Bridge to Central Square, where I was working for this antiwar, antinuclear couple, Vivica and Dan, who I'd met from dancing, and who had originally come from Berkeley. We were holed up, the three of us, in a little one-room office trying to put a stop to military spending. To me bringing peace about was pretty good. But Gary, being fifteen years older, had bigger ambitions for the planet. He started talking about how he wanted to go west.

The thing was I loved him. Not that he had a face to sink a thousand ships. He had fair skin, blinky brown eyes, shoulder-length hair, a Fu Manchu moustache. But he had beautiful feet, elastic arches. He had the longest arms of anyone I knew. And when he jumped! He could have been a pro. He could have traveled the world leaping in the air. That's the way I pictured it, him leaping and me spinning at his side. I still hadn't gotten over it, being so much younger than he was, and him choosing me to be his partner—because my dancing was so good. And getting to live with him, which meant getting out of my dad's house and my stepmother's hair. And just realizing that Gary thought I was beautiful! It wasn't like I was plain. I wasn't plain at all. I was slender and had big black eyes, sleepy with eyeliner, and that shimmery loose hair, so when I danced I looked like a ballerina down at the hem. But I was young—not even one-and-twenty like the guy in the poem—and I couldn't believe Gary with his long arms and his gorgeous feet and hard muscles in his calves actually thought that I was beautiful.

He had ideas about the environment and about the world and basically about cleaning up the oceans and saving the forests. He thought we'd go to Portland, Oregon, and fight the loggers and clean the rivers—finding big pipes sending poison into the fresh water—and we'd camp and explore all along the way. At that point in my life I was not much of a camper, and I'd never explored any strange places besides Cambridge. But I thought the oceans and the rivers were my causes too. And I knew Oregon wasn't far from Berkeley—and since the couple I worked for, Vivica and Dan, had always described Berkeley to me as nirvana, I figured we'd get to Oregon and then go downstream to Berkeley and I'd work there for a while and get my California residency and continue my education at the university and on the streets. So we went.

We drove a Plymouth Fury, a cursed lemon that sputtered and spit its way across the country and probably vomited as many pollutants as some of those companies Gary wanted to go after. Starting in January, taking I-80 west—by Toledo the transmission was shot. Just past Des Moines the fan belt slipped. Then through Iowa our muffler was dragging. We had a slow leak in our front driver-side tire, so half the time we were stopping at service stations for air. It was more like biking cross country than driving. We spent all our money on repairs, including some we didn't need. Those roadside mechanics looked at the two of us and my guitar in the back seat, and saw we were such a cliché we were begging to be ripped off. When we got out to the coast after three weeks, and we drove up to the Pacific Ocean, and we really saw it roaring all gray and restless in the rain, I almost cried with relief that there was nowhere else to go. We were stiff and filthy from sleeping in the car, from breaking down and hitching rides for help and getting towed and getting lied to. I really thought I'd seen it all.

We bummed around Oregon for a while and did some contra dancing in Portland. First I waitressed, and then I got a job cleaning rooms at a seniors residence—two twin towers with distant views of the Willamette River—and we lived there in some cement-block staff quarters in the back. I really really wanted to get to Berkeley, but Gary was going house to house for the Sierra Club. It was actually very old fashioned in a way, me scrubbing floors, and Gary like the Fuller brush man going door to door, peddling clean air and meadows blossoming with wildflowers. I started thinking it wasn't just a figure of speech, that you could die of loneliness.

Finally, after eight months or so, I convinced Gary to drive down to Berkeley and check out how activist the campus really was, and if the place was all it was cracked up to be. I was sure once he got there he'd want to stay, because it would all be so much his thing. I was just bereft of my bookstores and my coffeehouses and the folk dance club and little twisted streets in Boston, and I thought in his heart Gary was too.

We drove south, not right along the coast, but through the mountains on I-5, to take the faster route. We'd poured so much money into the Fury it was running for days without trouble, but we knew it was just a matter of time before that car broke down again. Mountains towered over us, all covered with pine trees, and desolate ranches came up, yellow bluffs and only cattle. Not a single rancher in sight. Then trucks would thunder down on either side of us and wall off the view. We broke the trip into two days and spent the night at a camping ground just outside Yreka, and then we drove through that little town, and past all the roadside dealerships for farm equipment, new and used. We drove all the next day, down, down, down, till the land was flat and we got to Vallejo, which was so flat it seemed to seep right into a blue haze at the edges, and then we got tangled in those steel bridges and highways that shoot out all over the bay.

What a relief! There was dancing every night in Berkeley, in the churches and the classrooms; and, since it was spring now, we'd dance practically all night in the parks on the grass. Gary and I danced until we hurt. We took razor blades to slit the blisters on our feet. The two of us showed off East Coast Israeli dances, steps Berkeley had never seen before. Everyone was talking about us. Everyone was gathering in circles in the evenings to watch us dance in Cedar Rose Park.

I spent my days working in Moe's, where the books were piled up on musty shelves and orange crates. I combed through the library closeouts, when the public libraries would dump books by the box load. Books in library bindings, all sensible colors like for ladies' winter purses: crimson, forest green, and navy blue. Between customers I used to stand around and read old tomes about Nature and Art. Books on microbes with black-and-white photographs, art-history textbooks with color plates—dark prints of oil paintings veiled with tissue-paper pages to protect them. Evenings, Gary and I went home to a vegetarian cooperative house of environmental people in South Berkeley where we slept on a futon high up under the roof. We had some silly weekends there in the house, dropping acid in the common room on these big vinyl sofas. But really mainly we were dedicated to turning people on to the plight of the marshlands around the bay. We had a ditto machine we had liberated from a basement office in Tollman Hall and we were busy putting out newsletters with that wavy lavender printing and trippy inky smell that dittos have.

Still, Gary had that traveling bug. "I want to go out and see some islands," he told me one night in bed.

And I said, "What kind of islands?"

"In the Pacific," he said. "I want to get out there before it's too late."

"Too late for what?" I said, being kind of sleepy.

"Before they're spoiled."

"I thought they already are spoiled."

"Did you know," he said, "that almost half of Hawaii's endemic birds are now extinct?" And he told me how forty percent of the known native bird species were now wiped out, and sixty percent, which I guess was all the rest, were on the endangered species list. And he told me how he wanted to go out there and see those birds, and work on saving them.

I lay there, my head in the hollow right beneath his shoulder. He was so big his whole body warmed me easily from head to foot. Being twenty, I figured I was past the escapades of my teenage years, and now settling down. I didn't want to go anywhere. I was something of a homebody for an activist.

But Gary had got started with this reading group from the geography department at the university. It was a very small odd radical group of graduate students. They didn't just study maps and charts. They were into geopolitics and the history of colonialism, and invading peoples warping ecosystems, and that's where Gary got this bee in his bonnet about going out into the Pacific and trying to do some good in Hawaii. There was this guy who was a legend to the reading group, this guy out in Hawaii, named Brian Andrew Williamson, who was saving endangered birds. He was the world authority on some of the rare species, and had actually seen a pair of elusive vermillion iiwi birds that had been thought at one time to be entirely extinct. Gary went and read all Williamson's papers in Doe Library, which he got access to as a "visiting scholar" from Harvard. He got hold of everything by Williamson in *Pacific Science,* all his articles in *Atoll Research Bulletin.* "Birds," Gary said. "They're like a key to the whole ecosystem. They're the bellwether, did you know that?"

"No," I said.

He looked at me as if I lacked feeling. "When the birds go, it's symptomatic of the whole habitat's decay!"

Gary was already starting to get this Gauguin thing going. He was obsessed with seeing the birds of the Pacific. He got antsy; he gave me grief—which at the time I didn't really understand, since we'd been through that big journey west, and all that time in Oregon. I thought all that had brought us closer together, all that history between us. But Gary was getting quieter and moodier and full of plans.

Inspired by the ornithologist, Williamson, Gary got an idea he would go out and work on saving the endangered bird species in what was left of the jungles in Hawaii. He talked all the time about goats eroding the hillsides and wild boars uprooting trees, and the invasion of the white-eyes, these little green finches from Japan wiping out the native honeycreepers, which were Hawaiian finches. He just had to fly out there; he just had to see those raped islands for himself and do something about them. For money he was going to sell the Plymouth. He was going to find some guy, some automotive virgin, and sell him the Fury from hell. Then Gary would take off. So, of course, I said I would go out to

Honolulu with him. I figured I'd go see the place too; and I cared about the native finches. And I think somewhere in me I knew that if I hadn't gone with him he would have gone anyway.

HERE'S what I took to Hawaii: my guitar, and my backpack with my name on it in black laundry marker. In the backpack: six panties, and a bra. Five T-shirts of different colors, a pair of shorts (I wore my jeans), two Indian gauze skirts wadded up in little balls, and a macramé bikini. A notebook and a ballpoint pen to write down my feelings. My wallet, my hairbrush, and toothbrush, and, from the free clinic, a good supply of the pill. I had a watch, a big silver man's watch that had been my grandfather's. Grandpa Irving's watch had a creamy face and bold black roman numerals. The crystal was scratched, and when you opened up the watchcase there were pawn marks inside, stamped in the silver. The watch was battered up, but lucky. Grandpa had kept it during the flu epidemic of 1918, when he holed up in his room for two weeks with a bottle of wicked germ-killing brandy, and he'd carried it through all his union organizing. It was his talisman—at least that's how it was told to me. He even brought it down to Mexico, when he'd tried to organize the tobacco workers in Yucatán. So of things of value I had that watch and my guitar.

It was raining when we got to Oahu. Everything was gray and white and windy, like an old movie as we came down closer and closer, and out the airplane window I could see these little palm trees waving around hysterically by the tarmac. I couldn't take my eyes off them. My face was just pressed against that cold airplane glass. In the airport there was slack key guitar music and such a strong sweet scent of flowers I thought at first that everyone was smoking weed. There were servicemen, and tourists and honeymooners, who you could tell right away because they were all dressed up, everything about them new. And then there were scraggly folk like us, some with hiking gear. We all got free paper cups of pineapple juice.

The two of us piled into a station wagon taxi—which wasn't really necessary, considering how little luggage we had, but we laid our backpacks and my guitar in the back and we got in. All the car's windows were open in the rain, and I couldn't believe it, the air was so warm and soft and damp. We drove on the shortest freeway I'd ever seen. It was like it was foreshortened, and there was Honolulu coming up so fast, just a few tall white buildings, a little clump right in front of Diamond Head. We'd got a two-week deal in Waikiki. Our hotel was not on the beach; it did not have views, its rooms were not equipped with many towels, but it was cheap. We figured it would be our launching pad.

The rain cleared up by the next morning, and we hopped a city bus, which was painted turquoise and had turquoise seats too. The windows were half open, and outside the colors were spectacular. I couldn't get over it. The greens were so green, the blue sky so blue. The leaves, the clouds, even the mock orange bushes. It was like everything on that island had just come out of the wash; it was like the trees were hanging out to dry. I just wanted to ride around all day. I just wanted to go out to a park bench with my guitar and write a song. But Gary had a look of disgust on his face. He hadn't come to ride buses and feel like he was still in the United States. He never said anything to me unless it was some kind of critical comment about tourist traps and raped ecosystems and the scummy bars in Waikiki.

We got off at the university, which was full of trees. There were trees that launched these seeds just like brown golf balls, dimples and all. And there were trees with big saggy phallic seed pods hanging down, just obscene looking. The buildings were all a mishmash, lots of dirty cement and glass. There was a tubular sculpture, bright orange, house high, with enameled pieces of metal bent into cones and big pointy curves. The top looked like lipstick scaled for a giantess. I loved all this. I was gawking at everything, but Gary just strode over to the zoology department. He was focused on digging up that ornithologist, the hero he had come all this way to meet and work with and learn from and basically get involved with his cause. There was real drama about it, the way Gary walked into Spaulding Hall. It was like it was going to be: Dr. Williamson, I presume? And Gary would be Stanley.

Well, as it turned out, Brian was a very down to earth feet-on-the-desk type guy. He was about Gary's age, mid-thirties, but shorter than Gary, and stockier. He had a lot of sandy blond hair and a beard, and basically looked like a mountain man. His eyes were dark and steady, his nose was peeling. His arms were thick and freckled, and his shoulders broad, as opposed to Gary, who was so tall and sinewy and fleeting. At the time I just thought Brian looked bluff and bland, and not as sharp as Gary. I thought Brian didn't have a lot of rhythm to him. Still, when it came to birds, he seemed to know his stuff. He thought it was cool Gary had read his articles. He said why don't we all have lunch. So we went to a lunch wagon on the street and bought big white dumplings with pork called *manapua,* and meat sticks, and that sweet cold *inari* sushi in a brown sugary-vinegary cone.

We sat out on the grass and Brian talked about his new project that he'd just got funded. It was a study of red-footed boobies, which were a very gentle lovely bird that traveled all through the Hawaiian Islands to breed, even to certain tiny islands way northwest. They were one of those species that were indigenous to Hawaii and they weren't used to having any predators. They had no idea how to protect themselves against goats or pigs or mongooses. On Tern Island and various atolls they were being slaughtered by the jeeps and machinery the military was bringing in. They were flying into guy wires, and being sucked up the intakes of jet engines, which tended to crash the Air Force's precious fighter-bombers. Naturally, grunts had no sensitivity to this rare bird. In fact they liked driving around mowing boobies down when they stood in the middle of the road. Brian had been ridiculed by the Coast Guard when he'd gone out to defend the birds on island bases and installations. The government's official position was that the birds were dumb for getting in their way, while in fact it was the boobies' innocence and trust that was getting them killed. But now the Coast Guard was pulling back from a lot of places in the northwest, so Brian had a grant to sail out there and take a census of the boobies and other seabirds that were nesting happily on the islands the military had left. In particular, he was making plans to go out for three months to observe a bunch of red-footed boobies that he'd banded on Kauai when they were just chicks.

Gary listened closely all during lunch, but he didn't say much. I think maybe the Berkeleyites had made Brian out a little larger than life. Gary was becoming a little bit downcast.

After lunch when Brian went back to his office, Gary and I walked through campus.

"Where are you going?" I asked. "Isn't the bus the other way?"

Gary kept his eyes on the ground. He just kept walking. I looked over at him. He was making me nervous. What should I say to him? That I was having a great time? That those meat sticks and pork dumplings had made my day? It had been months since I'd had meat, and I wasn't exactly a vegetarian, even though in Berkeley I'd been living in a vegetarian co-op house. I just walked and walked along. It was hard to keep up, Gary's legs were so long, and he was so deep in thought. Finally I said, "Gary, could you just stop for a minute?"

He stopped.

"Don't you want to work on Brian's project?"

Gary looked at me like he'd never seen me before. I guess I should have realized the very suggestion was an insult. He'd come to Hawaii planning to work in the jungle looking for those endangered honeycreepers being driven out. He wasn't here to sit and watch a thriving seabird colony!

"How come you don't like it here?" I asked.

He didn't answer.

All of a sudden I lost it. "Well, what the hell *do* you like? What do you want? We've been traveling together all this time and nothing is good enough for you. Nothing is clean enough or wild enough; nobody is radical enough. Just what exactly are you looking for?"

He set his mouth, and still he didn't answer.

"You are the most selfish person I've ever known!" I raged. "I've come all this way with you and you are never never satisfied. I'm not going to take it anymore. I'm not going anywhere else with you. I'm not walking with you; I'm not dancing with you, I'm not following you from—"

Then Gary floored me. He said, "Fine."

I couldn't believe it. I should have known. But it just hadn't occurred to me. I'd been too young and green to understand that Gary's goal in life wasn't just being with me! It hadn't occurred to me that we were different that way. I still had in my head some idea of symmetry, that since I loved him, he loved me the same way. And since I was all wrapped up in him, he was also all wrapped up in me. And that was the way it should be. I'd probably written too many songs.

He left me there right on campus with those ridiculous golf-ball trees, and I walked around and around, and my face twisted up like crumpled paper as I walked.

Finally, I went back to the hotel room and gathered everything that belonged to Gary. There were some papers, and his good hiking boots, and some extra clothes. He had his backpack with him, but I took everything he'd left in the room out onto the balcony. And if we'd had a room looking out on the ocean I'd have flung it all into the sea. As it was, we were on the tenth floor overlooking the street, and not far from an open-air shopping bazaar called the International Marketplace. I didn't want to kill anyone with the boots, so I left them on the balcony. Then I hurled Gary's shirts with all my might, so that they fell all the way down ten stories to the ground and flopped all over the sidewalk and draped on bushes far below. I wadded Gary's papers individually into little balls, and I tossed them too. All those balls of letters and notebook doodlings blew back against the building, and so did his socks, so they probably landed on the balconies below me, but Gary's jeans went straight down over the side, flapping in the breeze. And his underpants had a good wind behind them. Some hit the street, and some landed on the sidewalk, where the tourist couples in their matching aloha wear looked up to see what was going on.

But even after I did all that, I couldn't believe it. I couldn't see how Gary would want to shake me off—I who not only had loved him, but who had been such a good sport.

I started looking for him. For days I looked. I called Professor Williamson and I searched all through the university, and went back to the lunch wagon on the street. I walked through Waikiki and peeked in the lobbies of the hotels, the pink Royal Hawaiian, and the Halekulani, which had this whole library in the lobby of old novels and mysteries, and the Moana, which was a rickety old white-frame colonialist building from the twenties with a banyan tree in its courtyard. I searched the Pacific Reef Hotel. I stood like a zombie in front of their oceanarium—a humongous fish tank where they used to send a girl down in a bikini and scuba gear to feed all the bug-eyed fish with pieces of lettuce. I looked in the restaurants and the bars, like the Tahitian Lanai with its paintings on black velvet of Polynesian maidens and topless hula dancers. I didn't realize at the time that those paintings were world famous, being artworks by *the* master velvet painter, Leeteg. I just figured they were pornography.

I walked to Ala Moana Shopping Center and spent hours looking for Gary in the shops there. I wandered by the marina where the sailboats bumped against the dock. After five days my anger had almost all turned into sadness, and my energy was gone. Poor me, with my long hair and my callused feet. I was actually getting frightened because I didn't know anyone, and I only had a few traveler's checks. Then Gary showed up again. He walked into our hotel room in the evening like he'd never been away. I almost jumped off the bed where I was sitting with my guitar. I almost felt more relief than actual despair.

"Hi," he said.

I put down the guitar.

"I came to get my stuff." He started opening up the rattan dresser drawers.

I said, "Your stuff isn't here anymore."

"None of it?"

Then I remembered his boots. I got up and opened the sliding door onto the balcony. The boots were sitting there all covered with pigeon poop. They were all mottled with little black-and-white turds and runny green.

But Gary picked them up and took them inside and began cleaning them off in the bathroom with my one hotel towel. "I've met up with a group going to Fiji," he said.

So I looked at him and I was going to shriek: You selfish clichéd opportunist pig! You shallow self-serving piece of scum! Yet I was still gasping for air. I took the boots and I dumped them in the bathtub and turned on the shower till they were soaked. I wanted to kill Gary's stuff for good—although I should have known you can't destroy good hiking boots—meanwhile I was shouting, "Who's in this group, Gary? Some girl who wants to see the world?" And I screamed all kinds of other stuff at him, and I tried to hit him, and I think I did scratch him a fair amount. I screamed, "Don't lie to me, asshole!"

"I'm not lying," he said. But when I let go of him and we went back into the bedroom and talked a little but not a lot more calmly, it turned out the group of three he was taking off to Fiji with did include a girl named Katrina. He'd managed to hook up with this German chick who was an anthropology student with a huge fellowship to write her diss on quilt making in the Pacific Islands and she was traveling all through the South Pacific photographing quilts and taking oral histories. But the main thing I gathered was she had all this money. So she must have been enjoying herself, having a great time partying along the way.

I was numb by then. My face was all dried out from crying. Gary didn't once say he was sorry. What could he say? He was sorry he was tired of me? He was sorry our relationship wore thin as time wore on? I guess there was no good way to put it. I told him to get the fuck out, which was pretty much what he was waiting for. He turned tail and closed the hotel room door. And he didn't forget his sopping boots, which he carried by the laces.

After he left, I lay on top of the bed and I thought and thought how just two years before in Boston this same guy was practically begging me to sleep with him. How he'd picked me out from all the dancers as his partner to teach with. How we'd walked out after dancing in short sleeves in the winter, and all down the street we didn't even notice the slush and the cold.

2

I Shall Go A-Wanderin'

THERE are all different famous kinds of sleep. The sleep of the just, and the sleep of the good—but there's nothing like the sleep of the totally devastated. Nothing so sound. Nothing so deep. You hit the pillow and your eyes shut, and your whole body sighs with relief. You don't want to wake up, ever.

The night Gary left I slept that way. I slept and slept far into the morning, and that was when I had that vision about light, and space, and God, but, as I said, the whole thing dissolved as soon as I woke up all the way. I just couldn't make myself sleep any more. Then I sat on the edge of my bed and tried to figure out what I was going to do.

The hotel bill was half paid, because Gary had paid half in advance. But the other half I was going to have to come up with, and that was about all I had in traveler's checks. I tallied up the bill, and I counted my money a few times. Every time, I saw that the hotel would just about clean me out. I guess I cried a little bit more. I saw myself in the mirror crying, and then I felt strange doing it, but I couldn't help it. I watched myself crying. I began to feel like I was watching some girl in my situation. And that feeling was the worst of all—that I was hanging around watching myself. That was the feeling of being alone.

I got up and started washing my face, but the towel was filthy lying there on the bathroom floor. Who knew when housekeeping would come with another one? Probably never. Especially not for me, who they wanted to check out already—settle my bill and split. I went and dried my face on the top sheet of the bed.

Then I did something odd. I made the bed and smoothed out the bed-spread on top until it was perfectly flat, hideous bird-of-paradise design and all. I took my guitar and my backpack and all my things, even my toothbrush, and I laid them out on the bed around me very carefully one by one. And I got on the bed and sat cross-legged with my back to the mirror and looked at my stuff. I sat there on that green bedspread like I was a castaway doing an inventory of the things left from my wreck, spreading them out to dry on my little bed-size island. There were my T-shirts. There was the wad of string that was my macramé bikini. I looked at everything I'd packed to see the world. I picked up Grandpa Irving's old silver watch and I held it in my palm and rubbed it with my fingers like a worry bead. I looked at the little dime-store notebook I'd bought back on Shattuck Avenue. There wasn't a single word written in it. I turned over Grandpa Irving's watch in my hands, and I looked at the pawn marks like tattoos inside the cover of its case. I wished that some of the luck in that watch would rub off on me, or maybe that some genie or ghost of my grandfather would pop out from the winding stem to grant my wishes—except what would those wishes be? I was almost too de-moralized to come up with anything besides Gary's plane crashing in the ocean on the way to Fiji, and a tiger shark coming in to eat Gary limb by limb, leaving a long trail of blood in the water. For myself I guess I could only wish I had money for the hotel and also some breakfast, which I really needed, since I was so hungry. Beyond that I didn't even know what I'd wish for, because the last five days had pretty much destroyed any confidence I had.

But there was one little voice inside of me that kept speaking to me. I wish I could say it was the voice of reason, but to tell the truth, at that stage of my life reason didn't speak to me very often. I really wish I could say I heard a still, small voice. I love when there's a still, small voice! But nope. My voice inside of me was more of what I would describe as en-raged and terrified yet squeaky, but it kept on talking till I couldn't help listening, and it kept saying— It's not fair. It's not fair! That was the one thing I kept telling myself. Because, why did Gary get to go off to Fiji while I had to stay here? How come he got to pursue his causes while all I got to pursue was him? Why was that?—apart from the fact that I'd been in love with him? Why were all his harebrained schemes so important? I mean, what about my journey, and my odyssey? Where were my poems that were supposed to be written down there in my notebook? Where were those songs from my life experiences that I was going to write? Of course nobody had forced me to become the long-suffering girlfriend of this jerk—but I wasn't thinking about that—I was thinking how it was just so unfair. Angry and sulky and with a wounded pride, I sat on that bed and looked at my little array of clothes laid out there. I looked at my guitar, and my scrunched-up gauze skirts, wrinkly as tissue paper. And then my eye fell on my return ticket to California.

I could go back, I thought. I could always go back. That probably should have comforted me, but it made me feel worse than before. Just the thought of coming all that way and then giving up! Retracing my steps so defeatedly. Just letting Gary have the whole Western hemisphere—when he didn't even deserve it. Leaving him to sail the Pacific, when he was the one who dumped on the whole ocean and all the islands in it! Even Hawaii wasn't good enough for him. Even Oahu wasn't paradisiacal enough, not to mention me!

I hopped off my bed and ran over to the balcony and I stood out there and saw the crowds of tourists down below, yet that didn't bother me. There were fast-food joints, yet that could be a good thing, not bad. I've never understood this: Just because you are on an odyssey, is there something wrong with once in a while having a hot meal? I looked down from the balcony. I leaned way over the edge—not that I was going to jump or anything, but I leaned. I called out, "Go to hell, Gary. You can take Fiji and shove it!" And I screamed some other things, mostly swear words, I admit, until I was tired, and I felt like an idiot.

Then I went back inside and just sat on the floor for a couple of hours, until I was very very calm. With great deliberation I picked up my plane ticket from the bed. I knew I could do one of two things. I could stay in Hawaii, all bitter and heartbroken, feeling sorry for myself and drifting aimlessly, just wrecking my spiritual compass. Or I could retrace my steps, rethink my actions, fly back to San Francisco, and then make my way back to Boston—trying to learn from my mistakes and grow, reconcile with my dad, return to school, and live my life. So that was easy.

I ran down to the hotel lobby where the desk manager guarded probably the hotel's only copy of the Honolulu phone book.

I called a ticket broker, and I walked all the way down to his office near Hotel Street, and I sold that guy my ticket home.

Having sold the ticket and decided I was going to hang out in Honolulu and just be an abandoned aimless folk dancer with a broken compass, I felt much better. I went back to the hotel. No one had cleaned up the room. The dirty towel was still lying there, but I took a shower anyway, since who knew when I'd see a shower again. Then I packed up, went downstairs, paid my bill, and checked out. I walked off down the street just like in the song: "Oh, I shall go a-wanderin', my knapsack on my back. . . ."

All around me the hotels were crowding up to the beach. The whole day was ahead of me. So what should I do? I wandered around for a long while before I came up with something. Laundry.

I found a coin-op Laundromat just off Kuhio Avenue and I put all my clothes and also the hotel towel in the wash. Everything was dirty, even what I was wearing, so I went across the street and bought some breakfast at a noodle shop and used their facilities to change into my bikini, so I could get even the clothes I was wearing into the machine.

I was sitting on a rusty old folding chair with my bare feet up against one of the dryers. I was holding a tall foam cup and eating my first saimin, which was this warm salty soup swarming with noodles, vegetables, and pink-and-white discs I later found out were fish cake, and I was all absorbed in my thoughts and in my saimin, but I guess because of my attire some of the other coin-op clientele might have gotten the wrong idea about me. A couple of guys approached me, and one even asked where I was staying. Of course I didn't even look at them, since I was off men.

When my load was done, I put on my shorts and T-shirt, all warm and clean, over my bikini, packed up the rest of my clothes, and took the bus to see the only person in Hawaii that I knew, Professor Williamson at the university.

I went straight to the zoology department, and when it turned out

Williamson wasn't in his office I waited out in the lounge, which I realized smelled really peculiar, now that I was spending an hour there. The place smelled nauseating, like cats had got into the green carpet—not that I had anything against cats! Probably the being I was closest to in my whole childhood was my cat, Clarissa, who I raised from when she was just a tiny ball of fluff and who became admittedly so obese, you would have thought she was pregnant if she hadn't been spayed. Yet she was beautiful that way. She had heft. She had stability! She would sit and sit. What I'm saying is—that comment wasn't meant as derogatory that the department smelled like cats. Just I was surprised to smell cats in that context!

So while I was waiting, a couple of zoology graduate students, Rich and Geoffrey, wandered in, and we went down to the candy machines in the basement level of the building and the two of them got some snacks—and I almost did, but then I thought, I'd better not. I was afraid to blow any excess money.

I told Geoffrey and Rich how I'd come out west from Boston. And they told me about the smell in the building. It was actually from chickens that were kept upstairs and experimented on, which kind of turned your stomach. Still, I didn't leave. I kept looking up the stairwell, and finally I saw Williamson sauntering in, dragging his bike after him up the stairs.

"Brian," I called out.

He looked around, confused.

"It's me, Sharon." I ran up the stairs.

"Hi." He looked nervous to see me, since I guess a few days earlier I'd sounded hysterical and maybe suicidal on the phone when I'd called him looking for Gary. "I still haven't seen him," he told me.

"Oh, well, that's okay," I said hurriedly. I'd resolved to myself in the reception area never to speak of Gary, so that way I would avoid crying. "I didn't come about that," I said. "Actually, is this an okay time to talk? Are you busy?"

"Well, yeah. I am."

I felt my eyes welling up when he said that, but I held the tears in. "Do you have just one minute?"

"All right," he said.

I followed him into his office and sat down in a rush. "I wanted to come talk to you about the census project and find out if you still have an opening on it, because I'd really like to work on something like this—"

He leaned back in his swivel chair, back, back, till I thought he might fall over, and he put his feet up on the edge of the desk. He wore frayed old leather sandals. "I thought Gary was the one who wanted to study bird populations."

"No, no," I said, "Gary was just a bullshit artist. Really. He never cared about birds at all—especially not red-footed boobies. He might have said things to you about how he loved endangered animals and how he wanted to help the native honeycreepers, but it was just like a fad with him—it was just a passing thing." I choked up a little there, but I was worried any second Williamson was going to say he had stuff to do, so I kept talking, making up whatever I needed as I went along. I said, "The truth is it was my idea to come out to Hawaii, because for years I wanted to come here and I wanted to be a tropical naturalist, but there weren't any good courses in that at BU, so I came out here wanting to transfer to UH. And when I made that decision Gary got all interested and decided birds were his thing, too, but when we got here and he saw the reality of living in Honolulu, and also when he realized how much work the booby census would take, I think he got just—just—"

"You're an undergraduate at BU," Brian said.

"A junior," I said, which was almost true, because if I'd been back in Boston and in school I would have been a junior.

"Uh-huh," he said, and he looked at me blankly like he'd almost rather I was some kind of bird, because then he wouldn't have to be po-lite and have a conversation with me. He could just count me or some-thing. "Sharon, we won't even be starting the census until next May. Remember what I told Gary? The observation time is from mid-May until September."

I was just crushed when he mentioned that. When the birds actually laid their eggs hadn't occurred to me. I'd just figured I was going to convince this prof to let me on his boat right away and he and I and the rest of the team would be sailing off to the northwest islands far away. But the project wouldn't even start for almost a year. A lot of the charm of the whole census idea wore off right then.

Much subdued, I said thank you to Professor Williamson and trudged

off to the campus center, which was practically empty. But I got a sandwich and talked to the guy behind the counter about cheap places to
stay. I found out about the YWCA on University Avenue, and I went
there and checked it out. It was an old beige brick-faced five-story
rooming house with a restaurant-cafeteria downstairs called The Breadline. What was neat was, the restaurant had almost all special-needs employees. The downside, I discovered later, was, there was this chili-like
gruel, like if Charles Dickens went to Mexico, and it just kept coming
back at you every day. The Breadline was the kind of place that had
stainless-steel milk machines and a few bugs in the corners, but hey. I
gave the superintendent a deposit and I got a room on the third floor
with a bed that had sheets and a pilly blanket and a pillow so flat you
had to fold it over to rest your head on it. There was a table and chair
and a splintery dresser with little mounds of sawdust in the drawers,
which later I found out were termite droppings. There was no rug or
telephone. There was a pay phone in the restaurant. At the end of the
hall there was a bathroom with showers. It was good I'd brought my
own towel from the hotel.

WELL, the next few days were bleak, because I didn't actually know
anybody, and here I was across the street from the university, and the
summer session was starting, but, of course, I wasn't registered. And it
wasn't like being unregistered at BU, where I knew people on campus,
and could walk around looking disaffected and too cool for everyone
else. Here, I'd never been a part of the scene to begin with, so there
wasn't anything to be disaffected *from,* which, if you think about it, is
the whole point of being cool, the whole raison d'être.

However, pretty soon I got out and started hanging at the campus
center, and befriended some people—not so much the young under-
graduates, all my age and cute and perky—but the older crowd, the
graduate students, a lot of whom were from the Mainland like me, and
the postdocs, and some of those zoology students I mentioned before.
They were a rowdy group with great parties off campus, usually on the
North Shore, and a lot of times they'd take me along, being very hospitable. They shared everything they had—food, drink, drugs. I remember a couple of times lying out on the beach in a white and pristine

cove—about twenty people, including Brian Williamson and his girl-friend, Imo, and Brian's colleagues Ron and Christian—all eating chips and smoking dope, just getting a pleasant buzz, just softening your edges a little so your self wasn't all hard and separate from the rest of the world, but sort of dissolving. It was like becoming all crumbly, and cracking your outer shell—but not in a crazy way, not like turning into some kind of volcano spewing red hots, but rather, feeling your mind and your whole spirit becoming porous inside, like a malted milk ball.

One of the zoology students I hung out with was Rich, the guy I'd met at the department. Rich was short and hairy with bright brown eyes like a squirrel's and faded T-shirts and cutoff shorts, and a love of birds, seabirds especially, and also a love of oceans. He'd spent his child-hood landlocked in Arizona. He was lighthearted and laid back. He could have been a real heartbreaker if he'd put in the time. Truthfully he was just too sweet and lazy.

At the end of a few parties we stayed after, camping in this old army tent, and fooling around in the dark, and I have to say he felt good after Gary's melancholy, and his sad little smiles and pretentious hair, and that abstracted look he had—like he was thinking of higher things than you. Rich was always right there with you. With Rich it was never what would happen next, and where would we go, and if he would be happy when we got there, it was just him and me drawn up to him when the ocean was calm. Just us swimming together in shallow water and lying down on towels warm from soaking up the sun. And not all that ego, not to mention all that undressing and sheets and beds like there used to be in Allston, and being careful not to brush the silver radiator, all clang-ing hot as a teakettle, but instead, being naked to begin with and already wet inside and out. It was just for fun, nothing serious. Apart from a few weekends Rich and I had pretty much a platonic relationship.

The money thing was a problem, but I did manage to earn some cash as an emergency substitute secretary around campus for departments and programs that were in the middle of fiscal belt tightening, scandals, sanctions, firings, and other crises. I used to come and fill in when needed—always purely as a temp worker, officially a "casual hire," since, of course, it was a state university, and only state employees could be real permanent secretaries—which meant wearing dresses to work and hav-ing candy dishes on your desk and photos under the glass of your desktop. I just came as is and did filing and phone answering and hunt and pecked a few letters, as the case may be. My favorite gig was the Women's Studies Program, which had digs in the back of Crawford Hall, so you actually had to climb up and down a rickety metal fire escape to get to and from the parking lot. It was just a few lady profs and a department library with metal shelves and floor cushions, and a desk for a receptionist, which was a lot of times just me at the black rotary dial phone. We used to cool the place with World War II–era oscillating fans with putty-colored rubber blades, and I loved it there because, as I said, it was just femmes, and very egalitarian. We were all like sisters. There was a southern lesbian English prof named Corinne who would give me poetry books to read, and there was a psychologist, Margo, who used to tip me off about jobs at the medical school where you could get cash for sleeping in a lab or being a patient for students to learn on— not getting operated on or anything like that, but just undergoing physical exams. Women's Studies was my home away from home. There was a poster on the wall above my desk, a black-and-white picture of Golda Meir with a caption that read "But Can She Type?" That was very empowering to me when I worked there, because I'd never learned.

RICH and the zoology guys, even Brian, liked me a lot, and when May rolled around they mentioned that if I still wanted, I could go out and lend a hand on the booby census. I could go with them to French Frigate Shoals—as a volunteer. They didn't have funding for me, but I could come along with Brian and Imo, and Rich and that other graduate student named Geoffrey, who was a weight lifter but also a very religious person who had dedicated his whole life to Jesus Christ, so to him, studying boobies was for the glory of God.

It was such a great group of people, I said I'd go. I wouldn't earn anything on the trip, but I'd get room and board, so to speak. Free beer and good dope, I figured—judging from the department parties—moonlit swims, and my name on an article, not to mention just being on some island where hardly anyone had ever been before.

The downside was leaving my guitar. Everyone said that where we were going, my guitar would be toast. So I wiped it clean and put it in its case and took it over to Corinne, the English prof from Women's

Studies who lived in a gorgeous old moldy house in Manoa with saggy wood floors and lots of pictures on the walls, botanical engravings warped in their frames, and faded frayed books and furniture covered with white hair from Corinne's cat, Jane.

"Oh! I miss my old cat," I said as soon as I saw Jane lying on the couch. I put my guitar down by the door and I went and sat on the couch and stroked Jane and, God, my fingers had almost forgotten how good it was to be stroking a cat, just knuckling that wiry body under that soft soft fur. Oh, wow, I missed my cat so much, my cat Clarissa. She died when I was seven and no one let me have another one. This cat Jane was all white, except she had a black nose, just the tip, like she'd dipped it. She was so sweet and she felt so good, so knobby.

"Let me get you some tea." Corinne went to the kitchen and put on the kettle. She was a very literary southern gentlewoman, and she had short silver-gray hair and willowy arms, and gray eyes and this melodious voice. I'm sure back in Nashville once upon a time Corinne had been one of those girls in white silk and organdy in cotillion balls. She, of all the people I'd ever met, I could imagine wearing white kid gloves with buttons at the wrist. We had raspberry tea and English tea biscuits that came out of a tin, and I told Corinne about the expedition. All the time I knew her, I loved to confide in Corinne. She was what I would describe as a wisewoman. Full of reason, and gentleness, and self-respect. She always gave me good advice, except I never followed it, which proved to be a little bit of a strain on our relationship. That and Corinne's girlfriend, Rae, who was fierce and short and spiky, with a buzz cut and heavy black eyebrows that she would knit when I was around.

Anyway, Corinne was a scholar of American women's literature, and she showed me her own original Alcott books that she'd kept from when she was a little girl and taken with her after she broke up with her original husband. She had *Eight Cousins,* and *Rose in Bloom,* and *An Old-Fashioned Girl,* and everything. "Oh, I *love* that book," I said, when I saw *Little Women.*

It seemed like Corinne couldn't help smiling at me, loving *Little Women* and sitting on the couch in my shorts and my tank top that I was wearing without a bra. Not that I was one of those bra burners at that time, not at all, but I had to wear one to work, and this was my day off. I put *Little Women* on the stack next to Jane. "When I was little," I said, "I always wanted to live back then. I wanted to live in the old days."

"Well," Corinne said, "all girls like the old days when they're little, and then they grow out of it."

"Not me," I said. Because suddenly, the old days seemed like the epitome of shore, and those March girls in Concord, Mass., seemed so cozy sitting at the piano—singing songs and knitting, and putting on plays. And I, on the other hand, was all alone, and I was sailing out that Tuesday. I couldn't help feeling sorry for myself, going six hundred miles away to the northwest islands, and without women friends or music, when it was so cozy in Corinne's house with Jane—who was named after The Jane. Austen.

In two days I was going to be adrift with no home at all. No piano, no sisters, no singing. And the ocean was all shifty and impersonal and so lonely. I blinked back a few tears.

So then Corinne got alarmed. She said I shouldn't feel like I had to go to the northwest islands. She could help me get home to my folks in Boston, and if I felt I couldn't go back there, she'd help me find some job, or some better place, and I could stay with her, and register for classes in the fall. But I said, no, no, I had to go because I'd promised, and she asked me if I felt pressured in any way, and if I felt I was going to be used on this trip, since I was going for no money, and if I was sure it was the best thing to do.

But I said I couldn't stay with her there in the house, even though the house was so great and I would miss my guitar so much. Admittedly, it felt good to have someone feeling sorry for me besides myself, but after a while it was like I was getting a crick in my neck from being so droopy and being so mothered, and I pulled myself together and went and put my empty tea mug in the kitchen sink. I didn't mention it, but I had a feeling Rae wouldn't be crazy about my staying with them. As for my parents, I really didn't want to get into them. Mom wasn't in the best shape. And Dad—this was ironic for an economics professor, but true—he had this serious pathology about money. He tended not to spend any, except on himself, which had made childhood and college and stuff somewhat difficult, and I guess had led to a little bit of stealing from him, and check forging on my part. Not to mention some minor drug dealing in high school and college—purely as a middleman—but which he couldn't forgive me for, since the one time I got hauled up by the authorities I was a BU student, and it so happened my father was a dean at the time. My defense, which was later published in the *BU Bridge,* had been that Dad was such a dickhead, he wasn't even paying my tuition hardly, and I had to live off campus, and even there I didn't have money for food and rent. All of which was true, yet truth was not what the police and university were after. They were after punishment, like community service, and leaving school. And Dad, of course, had to come out against me hardest of all, given his position and his feelings toward me in general. All this being relatively fresh in my mind, the idea of going back to what Corinne called my folks really dried my eyes.

"I should get going," I said. "I have to pack."

"Take this with you." Corinne gave me this fat little Norton anthology of English literature (volume two) bound in green with INSTRUCTOR'S EDITION NOT FOR SALE stamped on it. I stuffed the book in my bag, and Corinne told me my guitar would be waiting there with her safe till I came back. I left with one longing look at Jane.

3

French Frigate Shoals

IN the clear morning light with not a wisp of cloud I stood on the dock and stared at *Gaia,* our so-called research vessel from the Hawaiian Oceanographic Institute. She was a thirdhand donated yacht loaded down with equipment, like sounding devices and fathoming weights and cables and specimen tanks and rusty old chains. This is it? I thought. It was just she looked like such a piece of crap. Still, when we lifted anchor and set her loose, I forgot any first impressions I'd had. I forgot everything, even being cozy in the old days, since I was so excited to be starting out and actually sailing. We were on a voyage! We were going to be out on the ocean for six days! All the time we motored out of Honolulu Harbor I was just jumping around on deck and watching the whitecaps and feeling like a crazy sea woman.

Then that night we hit rough water, after which I was lying below doubled over. All the others were busy running around on deck, back seat navigating, and shooting the breeze with *Gaia*'s crew, whose name was Sean, and her ponytailed captain, David Abernathy. Captain Abernathy was paunchy and permanently freckled, and his face was covered with tiny wrinkles, either from laughing a lot over the years or from squinting too long in sun, you couldn't tell which. He had once been an

ocean sciences professor at the university but was one of those profs
who never cared for publishing, and therefore flunked a department-
wide post-tenure review and ended up becoming emeritus when he
was just fifty. Now he piloted *Gaia* full time, which apparently he'd
been born to do. Abernathy was an academic sea dog. All around the
Pacific he ran *Gaia*. He sailed her as a long-distance research taxi, and
enjoyed her as if she were his own yacht.

I was the only seasick person on *Gaia*. I missed out on the views, and
the waves, and the sun, and I missed out on most of the food, since what
I did eat I couldn't keep down. After a while I was lying below, too
weak to move, practically, and with my eyes closed wishing I'd never
come along, I was so nauseous, and so embarrassed being this way my
first time. I'd pawed through my clothes, and got Grandpa's watch, and I
was holding it, clutched in one sweaty hand, while my tongue was
heaving up into my mouth. The others came down and glanced at me
with either pity or disgust. "You okay, Sharon?" Rich asked, which was
one of the most asinine questions I'd ever heard.

Brian was the one in charge of the whole grant and expedition, and I
thought he would be worried, or feel a little bit responsible for me. That
was what I had left over from being a registered college student. That
was that little feeling of entitlement I clung to. I mean, wouldn't Brian
be in trouble with the National Oceanographic and Atmospheric Ad-
ministration, or wherever the hell he got his money, if I ended up dying, and Abernathy had to bury me at sea?

When Brian came below, I managed to croak to him how I thought I
was hallucinating. I was dehydrating. I couldn't even keep one sip of water down. I'd take a drink, then run up to the deck and puke over the rail.

He looked me over lying there, and his eyes crinkled up. I wanted to
beat him over the head. He was trying not to smile.

"Well, you'll get over it," he said.

Then along about the third day, late in the afternoon, I got up. I lifted
my head and it stayed up. I swallowed, and I didn't gag. I staggered to
the stairs, and hauled myself up onto the deck. The wind hit me, and the
dazzling water foaming up; the waves slapping *Gaia*. There were dolphins playing all around us, and I laughed out loud. I felt like I'd risen
from the dead.

Mostly people treated me like I was some kind of servant, like I'd

signed on for cabin boy, since I was an unpaid volunteer with no experience. Rich and Geoffrey had been out before on expeditions, so they
laughed at me—although Geoffrey was a little nicer to me than Rich.
He was what they called a local guy, meaning born and bred in Honolulu. He was part Hawaiian, part Chinese. He'd just recently fallen in
love with an undergrad at UH named Julie Liu, and the farther west we
sailed the lonelier and gentler he became. He told me he was going to
write her every day—even though there was of course no mail service.
As for Brian's girlfriend, Imo, she just seemed to assume I'd come because Rich and I were sleeping together, even though we'd evolved so
far beyond that. Imo was, so to speak, a full-fledged ornithologist—a
distinguished visiting lecturer at the university. She was from New
Zealand—Imo was her nickname, because her real name was Imogen.
She was dark from the sun, and thin and nervous-looking. Her hair was
curly and cropped short and she had dark brown eyes and she was so
crisp when she was talking with that colonial-English, New Zealandish
accent of hers, that she made you feel limp. Imo really took the expedition part of the trip to heart, like we were going out there onto those
shoals and we were going to land on those beaches and risk health and
happiness to get those birds observed and counted, or God help us all.
She was brilliant and fit, and on top of all that she kept a bound journal
with pure white unlined paper where she printed her entries in black
India ink, and made these drawings with crosshatchings of everything
she saw, like of our boat, and the dolphins, and the flying fish that
jumped onto the deck. When I saw her journal, I didn't even dare to
bring my notebook out.

I didn't realize at first that we'd arrived at French Frigate Shoals. I
couldn't make out anything because the islands lay so low in the water.
But the winds were behind us, and when we swung in closer, French
Frigate Shoals came clear. The islands were tiny—so much smaller than
I had expected. Just clumps of rock and sand atop a coral reef, and with
a little scrub brush in places. No trees.

David Abernathy and Brian and Rich got out the charts and started
amending them in pencil, because in French Frigate Shoals, what with
the shifting tides and currents and sand deposits on the reef, you never

know how many islands there will be. In the time since Brian had last visited, two of the islands, Whale and Skate, were now joined by a sandy isthmus. And Big Gin had shrunk, so that Little Gin now dwarfed it. Several islands had disappeared and had to be crossed off the maps, and on the charts in the column for elevation above sea level, Abernathy had to write next to those islands, "Awash." But there were also new islands that had risen up, and while at last count there had been nine islands in French Frigate Shoals, now there were eleven. The largest of the new islands we called Tonic, since we figured there were already two Gins. Tonic was full of sticks and debris and, it looked like, nesting birds.

LET me tell you about red-footed boobies. They are white with long pointy bills and pouchy necks like pelicans'. Their feet are bright scarlet red, and they lay one egg, and they hold that egg with their two scarlet feet, and I learned right away that if you come in close to take a look at them, those birds rise up flapping and open up their beaks and scream at you, and sometimes barf squid vomit on your head. They are not small birds, and they are not tame, and you have to creep up slowly and tiptoe around them. Once you approach them with the proper attitude of respect, however, the birds stopped screaming and just glare.

The work was hypnotic. We mammals all went into a trance there on those islands, while from sunrise to sundown we tracked and watched and stalked those nesting birds. And I know it sounds strange, but the birds became almost like people to us. Although they were only two feet high, they did not seem short. We were crawling around at their eye level, and so, to us, the birds had almost human stature. We thought of the boobies that way—just as if they were these white sharp-eyed aristocrats who happened to have red feet. It was as if we'd arrived on these islands inhabited by bird people. And there we were trying to interpret all their screams. What were they telling each other? What were they trying to say to us? We were like bird disciples, we were straining so hard to understand.

That was a magic time among those disappearing islands. I knew it even then, down on my knees among the bird people, the boobies. Their black eyes absorbed me, and their small heads, just the way the boobies held themselves against the wind, and took turns on their nests in twenty-four-hour shifts, mates flying in with wet feathers and food nipped from the sea. Their calls to one another, as much as the waves, filled my ears. That was a place of great teaching; that was really an open university. The lectures were all from the birds, the research was all done on foot, and the learning wasn't done in words, but all by hand.

I remember one day I was working with Brian observing on a rock ledge. The sun was beating down. There wasn't anything to break the wind or absorb heat there on those barren rocks. Brian and I crouched down, and there was a booby, and we were close, but quiet, and I saw something stir, and the mother bird was moving and shifting, and she opened up her wings a little like she was flapping a white parasol, and then Brian touched my arm, but I already saw that Mom's chick was hatching, and I saw that in the hot sun she was shading the chick with her body and her wings. She was her baby's own awning. "Like a beach umbrella," I whispered. But Brian put his fingers to my lips, and then we watched together and we didn't say a word.

We almost forgot ourselves in deference to the birds. It stopped mattering who was a professor, and who a student, and who might have been the girlfriend of a student. There was this mystical silence that grew up among us, because we were all listening and looking so hard at nests. And that was my first glimpse of the world, I mean, the creation: the heavens and the earth, and the birds in between. In the mornings we all sat up and saw the sun rise, all of us, the humans unzipping tents, and sitting up in sleeping bags, the birds, alert in their nests, built up just off the ground from bracken. In the morning light the ocean spread out around us and you felt how the land was just a speck out there in the water, the ocean tides sucking, sucking the teeny shore just like the island was sucking candy. You felt out there under that blue sky and in that sea you might actually be resting in the palm of God.

What broke the spell was, we all got mites. Tiny red mites lived on the birds, and those mites started hatching in our hair. Then everyone forgot about the birds and the work and the ocean and we cursed and jumped and screamed and were just about ready to murder each other, until Brian rationed out the expedition's official mite-killing shampoo. We washed our hair with the primitive shower we'd rigged up. Just a plastic bag we filled with salt water. You held it up above your head and squirted the water down at you, which left your hair sticky—but since we'd brought all our drinking water with us, we couldn't exactly afford to waste it on our hair.

Unfortunately for me, what the bugs really went for was my long straight hair. Everyone else had short hair on that trip, which now I could understand, because even after I shampooed, I had mites' eggs all up and down my scalp, and bugs nesting in my roots. That shiny smooth slippery hair that used to sweep around when I was dancing was crawling with mites. Everyone else was rid of them, but I couldn't wash or comb or pick all those bugs out. Rich took his sleeping bag out of our two-man tent and moved in with Geoffrey, because, obviously, he didn't want to get reinfested. That's when Imo said to me, all crisp, "You've got to cut it off."

"My hair?"

"Of course, your hair," Imo said. "What else do you think I'm talking about?"

But this just goes to show my vanity or foolhardiness or something like that. I waited a whole day after Imo spoke to me before I could face cutting off my hair. I waited and waited, hour after hour, even though I felt like I had a Medusa head and all the tresses of my hair were writhing snakes. I kept limping around while Imo rolled her eyes, and Geoffrey had a horrified but fascinated look in his, like he didn't want to stare but he couldn't help it. Like in his mind he was already composing a description for his next letter to Julie. Rich wouldn't go near me or any of my stuff. Still it took me a whole day to go to Brian and ask for the scissors from the first aid kit.

I don't know what it was—the way I asked for it—or the fact that he didn't want me using the good scissors. Brian had been working on his notes, squatting down with his clipboard, but when I spoke to him, he jumped to his feet, as if to say, I've had it! He got the big old shears he used for cutting rope, and he gathered all my hair in one hand and he cut that whole thick pile in one stroke. He kept cutting bunches and fistfuls as short as he could, until I had nothing more than tufts and stubble on my head and a whole pile of hair on the ground, more hair than you would have imagined, like the kind of mess you make when you're husking corn.

"Hey, Sharon," Rich called out. "Look, you've contributed new nesting material." And he pointed to my hair scattered around on the ground. Now the island was littered with scrub and sand and broken eggshell, bird feathers and bird poop, and long strands of my own hair. "I'm gonna have to write you up," he told me.

"Fuck you," I said. I was not very philosophical at that time of my life.

That night I got into my tent all alone and I lay down and zipped myself inside. I felt like such a worm. You're such an imposter, I thought. You don't even know how to deal with mites. Then I thought, We're all imposters. No wonder the birds look at us like that. The boobies' faces were like kings on coins—so noble, but also so disgruntled. Who do you think you are? they asked us. How dare you? I lay awake in my sleeping bag, all alone, and all around me in the dark I could feel the birds staring with unforgiving beady eyes.

I was so blue. I was claustrophobic with loneliness. My tent was suffocating me. I unzipped myself. I burst out and gulped the air. I struggled out of my sleeping bag, and took some steps. I felt the sand under my toes and I knew the other tents were all around me, but I couldn't see them. I couldn't see anything on the island. I looked up and the dark was huge. The sky was so deep and the island such a slip of a thing. The stars showered down; they spackled the whole universe down to the ground, like roman candles flickering to earth. The sight of those stars froze me in my tracks. I watched and watched. Finally, I got so cold I had to turn back. But then I saw a tiny red star near the ground. I came closer to the red speck and I could smell it now—the ember of a pipe.

"Sh!"

It was Brian sitting there smoking.

A wave of relief swept over me. I crouched down next to him. He was warm. He had a jacket.

"What are you doing?" I asked.

"What does it look like I'm doing?" he said.

"Why're you always snapping at me?"

"I'm not."

"Yes, you are, it's like you have it in for me."

"Sharon, I don't have it in for you."

"What about when you cut my hair?"

"Somebody had to do it," Brian said.

"Yeah, so you attack me with the pruning shears—what the hell was that?"

He didn't say anything. He just sat there smoking. It was too dark to see his face.

"You're really into power," I told him.

"Power?" He seemed genuinely surprised.

"Yeah—it's like your little island kingdom here and we're your minions," I said.

"Oh, will you please shut up," he whispered. And then what surprised me—he handed me his pipe.

I breathed in that warm toasty poisonous air and I blew it out again. He let me take a long turn.

"How many people," Brian said, "get a chance to see this many stars?"

"It's scary," I said.

"It's not scary. It's"—he was searching for the word—"it's really really fun."

"Fun?" I started coughing. The smoke went down the wrong way. My eyes were watering. "That's the word you come up with?"

Brian thumped me on the back.

"Look at the size of the sky! Look at the majesty! Aren't you scared sometimes out here?"

"Nope," he said.

"I just feel like—the universe is so huge and it just dwarfs us. We're like ants. We're like dust."

"So what?"

"You mean you don't even mind? I mean, here we are, and this island might not even be here a year from now. Here we are right on the edge—it's like the edge of the world."

"You know," he pointed out, "the universe is no bigger here than it is anywhere else."

"But it *is*," I said.

"It's really not." He got to his feet, and he pulled me up too. "Go to sleep." With his flashlight he guided me back to the tents.

"You never worry about anything, do you?"

"Not about the size of the universe, I don't."

"You think since you're a scientist it's beneath you to even think about stuff like that," I said. "It's this whole male scientist thing, like you've got the world under control."

"You've got it all backwards," he said. "Scientists observe. The whole point is to watch! The whole point is to stay out of the way."

"So then where's the awe?"

"The awe?"

"Where's your whole sense of the wonder about what's out here?"

Like an usher in a movie theater he was pointing to my tent with the ray of his flashlight. "Sleep."

"Okay, okay, I'm going."

I felt his hand brush my stubby head. He roughed my hair and then he smoothed it in just one caress. And it was the strangest thing how that touch warmed me. It wasn't as if I'd never been touched before in my life. Twenty-two years old, I'd been touched all sorts of ways. But that one brush of Brian's hand was so much better.

After that night I stopped feeling sorry for myself. I forgave everybody, even the mites. I just got back into the work we were supposed to do out there, meaning observation of the boobies' chicks coming out of their shells and stretching out their scrawny necks. Incubation graphs, and census plotting, and these social behavior experiments, where you'd see if the birds would incubate two eggs instead of just one—they wouldn't. Or whether they'd incubate some foreign object like a can or a rock or even a brick—they would. Or whether they'd go and incubate an egg that we moved outside their nests—about half would and half would not. When you concentrated, all the work was full of joy. The problems of humankind were far away. Everywhere I looked, even in my Norton anthology, the universe belonged to birds. That book was full of bird poetry! For example, William Blake's poem "Milton." It was all a bird's-eye view of the universe. The cosmos was this eggshell; the earth was called "mundane egg." I'd never understood Blake before, but on Tonic it all made sense. And there were the great bird poems by William Butler Yeats, like "Leda and the Swan" and the one about the falcon "turning and turning" who leaves blood sports behind and just flies up into the sky.

Admittedly, nobody on the expedition took the literary bird connection seriously. One time when I was reading my anthology I said to Imo, "Dig this—there's a whole poem about an albatross in here!"

> At length did cross an Albatross,
> Thorough the fog it came;

As if it had been a Christian soul,
We hailed it in God's name.

Imo raised her eyebrows.

"They killed it!" I burst out after I turned the page.

"I've read the poem," she said.

"Really?"

"I read it in school."

Then I felt stupid. Imo was practically English, after all. Probably everyone in New Zealand read *The Rime of the Ancient Mariner* in school. "Oh, we read it in school too," I told her. There I was all of a sudden defensive about the American school system. "I'm pretty sure we read it in eighth grade, right, Rich?" I called over.

Rich shrugged.

"Help me out," I said. "Hey, Geoffrey. You read *The Rime of the Ancient Mariner,* right?"

"Nah, I don't think so."

"Well, I think we did at my school," I said to Imo. "Maybe I was stoned that day."

She looked at me like I was some kind of moron.

"Just kidding!" I hated when she stared at me like that. As if she could see inside of me. As if she knew that I was starting to get just a little bit of the wrong idea about Brian. I ducked down and kept on reading.

That night I crept out to smoke with Brian. It was the only way I could talk to him alone.

I confided, "I really want to stay here with the birds forever."

And he, being Brian, said, "Well, since you have to drink fresh water, that probably wouldn't be such a great idea."

And I said, "But don't you wish you could?"

"No."

"I'd really rather live on uninhabited islands—"

He put his arm around me there in the dark and leaned in close to me. But all he said was, perfectly logically, "You can't live on an uninhabited island."

"I mean, uninhabited by other people!"

He was laughing at me. His beard brushed my face. I felt him hesitate for just a second. It seemed to me that just that one second lasted about a day; I felt him almost kiss me—and then think better of it. Close to him in the dark, I was holding my breath wishing. But he never did kiss me. He was a terrible flirt that way.

WHEN *Gaia* came for us I was dragging my feet, I wanted so much to stay. Geoffrey and Rich almost had to pry me away. And I was moody and moony on the boat and hung over the rail with the breeze flapping in my face just looking back at the island until it was a dot, which didn't take much time since it was less than two miles long. On *Gaia* everyone was jolly, talking about taking showers and peeing indoors and stuff like that, but I got quiet and didn't talk to anyone. I thought I was too sensitive to speak, too brokenhearted about leaving the birds, and just leaving Nature in general. Then the wind changed and started running from the north.

It was evening when the waves came up. Where they'd been small and choppy they started to whip up higher and slap *Gaia* around. It was getting dark, and the sky cloudy. And then suddenly all the light and glassy blue went out of the ocean and it turned black. *Gaia* pitched up higher and higher on the waves, and every time she reared up, the water below seemed farther down. And she was heavy to begin with, her deck weighted down with all our gear, and all the equipment she tended to freight around in general, other people's electronics that Abernathy was commissioned to drop off on islands to the south, and camera equipment, and spare parts. It was all piled high, so *Gaia*'s weight in that rough water made her bob and dive like she was in a game of chutes and ladders. Everything was tied on, but she was straining and rolling in the water with all this scientific scrap on her back.

At first it seemed like an adventure, sails down, battens locked, all of us cooped below, but the rolling kept getting worse. *Gaia* started pitching at higher and higher angles; and, while before we'd laughed and gasped like we were on a ride, one huge slam-down ended all that roller-coaster stuff and punched the laughter right out. And our own captain, Abernathy, looked scared, and all of us started cursing. It was like a party getting ugly; you watched it happening, but it wouldn't stop. *Gaia* was top-heavy. And we all crouched there, seven of us in life vests,

Abernathy and Sean, and Brian and Imo, Geoffrey, Rich, and me. Each of us knew that at this point a wave could knock *Gaia* so she'd roll over, and then she'd be too heavy in this surf to right herself.

I felt for my silver watch in my pocket, only this time *Gaia* was the one who was seasick, tossing and retching. We heard her straining in the tempest. She was like an old chair, and it was as if the ocean was one enormous fat person determined to sit on her. She was splintering under the weight. There was no light. All the darkness was howling. The water started coming in and seeping up, and we took turns pumping by hand, because the electric pump was dead. Abernathy and Sean were up on deck. They had ropes tied around their waists, and they were trying to unload the heavy stuff up there, and slip it off. The rest of us were down below and Brian and Imo were pumping, and Rich was swearing and Geoffrey was praying. Everyone was doing his or her thing except for me. I didn't know what my thing was. I was just holding on to the side of my bunk, trying not to fall.

The boat rose and rose, and then it fell, and water came in on us from all sides. We were wet and shivering and the ocean drove at us. It was strange, but in the troughs, in the ravines and alleyways between the giant waves, there would be these moments of calm, because, ironically when the waves rose up on either side they sheltered us from the wind. In the seconds before the boat got swept up high again there would be still moments where you could hear and see, and you checked yourself and felt your racing heart and how cold you were. I would catch my breath and obvious yet intense ideas would occur to me. Such as: My life was shorter than I thought.

We tossed and whirled. Tilt-A-Whirl, like at carnivals, only higher, only deeper. Down we dove, and each time we swooped down lower. This was drowning. Like an underwater Ferris wheel. We were still wheeling up and around, but soon it would be our turn below. Down, down, down.

Now Geoffrey was pumping, and as he pumped, he was chanting prayers. Another wave and I knocked against him hard, and I heard him repeating like a broken record: "The Lord is my Shepherd, I shall not want. He maketh me to lie down in green pastures." And I thought, That isn't right. That's a land poem; that's not relevant to oceans. And I wanted to yell and scream, Think of something else, damn it. Except no one would have heard me. The rain was beating down; the wind was so loud. And then that calm moment would come right before we smashed back down; the calm inside the storm—just enough to fall back in your skin again. And I thought, But I'm still young. I thought, I haven't done anything—besides internships and getting thrown out of school and that one trip cross country, which was a sham; I was just along for the ride; he didn't love me. I thought, Please, please, please, there's so much I could do workwise. For the earth, or for women, or for peace. I haven't even had a chance hardly. Please. If I'd known it was going to be like this, I wouldn't have wasted so much time.

SOMEWHERE in the night the in-between times got a little longer. The waves dropped back, and then calmed down, and quieted. When the light came up over the water, the sky was clearing. We lifted up our heads and looked. The cabin was all wet; our stuff was sopping, but Abernathy had the pump running again. To tell the truth, in the height of the storm he'd saved us by pushing all the oceanographic gear over the side.

On deck the sun came up and warmed and dried us and turned the whole world gold. The water was so calm it was thin, almost transparent. Then almost green. We wrung out our clothes. We opened up the logbooks in the sun to dry. I sat and stared at Grandpa Irving's lucky watch and I looked around the boat where we were huddled up, and I thought, Here we are with our lives.

4

Find a Pearl

THE noise was a shock. The cars, and the car horns, and the buses, and the pedestrians scurrying around to get out of the way. Honolulu was riddled with people. My ears were ringing; my eyes were tired from looking up and down and everywhere. All those colors and all those trees. What was I still doing here? I kept wondering. Wasn't I supposed to be lost at sea? I should have been dragged under the boat! Who, at the last minute, reached out and saved me? Nobody. Only good luck. Could that be? I couldn't sleep, I was so jangled. There I was, safe—yet not sound, way too confused to be sound. At night the streetlights shone through my window from University Avenue. My brain was flooded with that milky imitation night you get in cities.

The worst of it was realizing: if I had died, nobody—except maybe Corinne—would have even cared. If I'd drowned, nobody would have noticed! Especially since my closest friends would have drowned with me. And now, the irony was, having almost drowned together, the whole experience was driving our little group apart. Rich and Geoffrey were back in the department crunching numbers from the trip, and they didn't want my help, they made that clear. Brian and Imo were not exactly available. They were obsessed with showing the university and their granting agencies they had done nothing wrong. The two of them were sweating it, since it turned out some of the equipment Abernathy had to toss over the side was not officially supposed to be on *Gaia* in the first place. They swore about three hundred times that they had no idea he'd been overloading *Gaia*. They'd been completely unaware that he was sailing her unsafely. And I thought, Wow, slandering their own friend and colleague! I even came to Brian and asked him how he could say things like that. And he put his feet on his desk and leaned back in his chair and totally evaded the issue. He looked at me over the tops of his leather sandals and he basically said, "Sharon, this ain't any of your business." None of it was my business anymore. Not the boobies, not the research, not the data analysis, not the storm at sea.

The fall semester was starting. Brian was teaching and writing up results with Imo, and no one even thought to ask me to help. I caught Brian in Spaulding where he was picking up his mail. There he was, coming from class, all dressed up, wearing a shirt.

"Sharon." He stood there by the mailboxes holding his letters.

"I feel like I've been dismissed," I told him.

"Why?"

"Because on the islands—I mean, I worked out there and I lived out there—I *lived* this whole bird study and now it's like my contribution didn't even exist."

"Your contribution did exist," he said.

"Not if I'm not helping with the paper! Not if I'm not part of the journal article! I thought I was working alongside all of you. I thought I was on the team. And now I'm not even going to get any kind of acknowledgment!"

"Oh, no, we'll definitely include you in the acknowledgments," Brian said.

"You mean down at the bottom? In a paragraph at the end? Brian, I was on the *team*. I want to be an author."

"An author of the journal article," Brian said.

"Yes!"

"Sharon," Brian told me, "you are an unregistered, unfunded, unaffiliated—"

"So what?" I said. "What does that have to do with anything? That's nomenclature."

"Sharon, look . . ."

"What?"

He pulled me out into the hall. "Come on, this whole conversation—"

"What?"

"Sharon, that's just not how journal articles work. You were an intern, you had a great experience, and you learned a lot over there on the count. But you know that was all that was going on there. And this thing about authorship—full authorship—it's just not done in our community."

"What community?"

"The scientific community. The community of Pacific ornithologists. I think if you just sit down and—"

"Brian, I think you're full of shit," I said. "And you're talking about all these protocols and affiliations, but you know that on Tonic there was equality, almost the whole time. You know I was working with you. I was living with you guys. Smoking with you. Observing with you. Practically getting drowned with you! *That* was full participation in the study, okay? That was the reality of the whole trip, and that's what you're betraying now."

Then he just sighed and he looked at me like he was trying to be really patient, and like he was full of regret, since it was his own fault I'd ever stepped aboard *Gaia* and come along and got into his work, and he said, "Sharon—"

But I turned away.

"Sharon, you don't need a publication. What you need is to go back to school and turn on your brain and get an education."

I whirled around. "But that's what I've been doing. That's what I've been doing all this time! What do you think I was doing in French Frigate Shoals? I was working my ass off *learning*. And I'm asking for some credit for it!"

"Well, it doesn't work that way," he said.

WOUNDED and resentful—sure I'd never speak to Brian again—I limped back to my splintery old room at the Y and tucked my head under my wing. I lay there on my bed with the shades down, just trying to process all I'd been through. Just sitting in the shadows, trying to create a little darkroom for my soul.

I had my guitar back from Corinne, and my fingers tried to make music, but they were stiff and out of practice. They still had their positions and their chords inside of them, but they were like old-lady fingers trying to get where they were supposed to go. So I wrote some sad, slow songs about the sea and stars falling down. I put down the lyrics in my notebook, but then I ripped out the pages and crumpled them up. None of the songs was doing what I wanted. I was trying to capture how big the whole universe was around this earth. And how the earth seems so real but is really nothing more than sand in the hourglass, and how hope and love are dashed to pieces in an instant. But I wanted to say all this in new fresh ways; that was the problem.

If I could have afforded it I probably would have nursed my wounds for longer, but I was out of cash again. I didn't have the heart to work at the university anymore and see all those people from zoology. I couldn't stand that anymore: academia. I couldn't stand Honolulu. The place was such a scam. You got there, and you were so excited, and the sky was shining; the beaches were pure white sand; the streets lined with glossy trees. And then it turned out the only thing anyone cared about was rules and regulations. You needed cash and affiliations. If I'd kept my return ticket, I would have been on the next plane. As it was, I couldn't afford breakfast cereal, let alone a ticket out of there. I remember actually sitting down and writing a letter to my dad.

Dear Dad,

You probably aren't even reading this, considering how we ended up (on such a bad note), yet I am writing you anyway from Hawaii, where I am doing research on ornithology. The reason I'm writing is not to apologize, since there is nothing to apologize for, or to ask you to apologize to me, since you'd never do that anyway, apologies not being in your vocabulary. The reason is to tell you I'm OK. I feel you have a right to hear that and not find out I was drowned through some third party—all of a sudden getting a telegram after a shipwreck in the northwest Hawaiian islands and therefore the shock of your life, that your one daughter is gone. You think I'm gone now. Yet being gone far away is one thing and being dead would be another. And I'm saying that because I almost did die—which made me realize you have a right to hear I'm OK—especially since we were not on good terms. Having bad blood would be a weight on your conscience if I were killed. Then you would have to live with that.

You were not the kind of dad who I could talk to since you were off doing your own thing or else hurting me. You were not exactly easy to communicate with since you were so busy yelling and ordering and putting me down throughout my life. You have to admit, the major thing you have done to me is punish me, from kicking me out of your house to kicking me out of school. It was because you are restrictive—that is who you are. Yet restrictions caused a lot of my behavior, e.g., the house party, the dealing, the thing in the swimming pool, the exposé of you in the student paper. If restrictions had not been your way of life and punishing the central part of your vocabulary then maybe I would not have felt compeled to do some of the things that I did to you and to your property. You thought you could treat me like something less than a human being, Probably you would have locked me up if it was legal. Yet stifling can only excaberate one's feelings.

Therefore, it was tempting to never write or speak to you again, but I am. You are my father. You cannot and I cannot change that. Nothing can. That is why now that I have lost almost all my belongings on the ship (and almost my life) I am writing to you. Despite you forcing me to leave college and actually denying me an education—even though you are an educator!—I have been working my way through college attempting on my own to slowly get my BA. My plan was to go back to school in California where I was doing my research at Berkeley. However, my plane ticket is gone and the semester will be starting without me. If I do not find the money to return, then I will lose my chance and my registration at the school. I am not asking for tuition, only for $500 (one way) ticket money to return. I do not want to lose the thread of learning. I do not want to forgoe my second chance I had worked so hard on. $500 would only be a LOAN. I would pay INTEREST. I would promise to pay that from the first paychecks of my first job as soon as I got back there. This amount of money which is not a lot to you if you think about it would be huge to me. It would be not just money but the chance to regain my education. I hope you can see what that would mean. I am sure you could, being, that, after all you are a Dean of a university yourself. $500 can be wired straight to Honolulu through Western Union. All the instructions are on the back. Please turn the paper over. Please do not stop reading. . . .

I wrote the letter and took it to the post office and mailed it. Then I waited and waited. I figured on five days for the letter to get to Boston. Then, five more days for a response. Rationally speaking, I knew Dad would never send me any money, yet my heart said you have to try, because who knows? There are lotteries all the time, and people struck by lightning. The chances are infinitesimal, yet somewhere right now lightning might strike, and people might be transformed. They might fall on their heads and turn into someone else. They might discover something, like a letter from their daughter, and then a feeling would awaken in them, something they have never felt before (or maybe that had lain dormant) like love or sorrow, or even a paternalistic instinct. So how can you not try?

At last, a good nineteen days after I'd mailed my letter, this typed note came from my father.

Dear Sharon,

I have received and duly noted the news that you are "OK." If you are indeed OK after your ordeal at sea, I'll assume you have the strength to find your own money for a one-way plane ticket from Honolulu to San Francisco, which I'm sure you know costs less than $500.

You might also be interested to hear that the registrar's office at Berkeley does not have any record of your enrollment. In fact, there is no record of your enrollment in any college in the UC system.

As so often in the past, I might have found your activities more compelling had you not felt it necessary to lie about them.

I won't comment on the rest of your letter, except to say that before you make any other accusations, you should learn to spell.

Sincerely,

Dad

I probably read that letter two hundred times. It stung my eyes, but I kept rereading, and rereading, and all I wanted to do was race to Berkeley and take every class offered in the place. I wanted to work double time and graduate and give a speech at graduation in the stadium. I wanted to fly to Berkeley and become valedictorian of my class. I wanted to take my dad on *Gaia* in a storm and see *him* toss his cookies out at sea. Well, I wanted a lot of things, but without money I couldn't even begin to get them. That was always Dad's main point—and his trump card, being an economist. Since I had to work, and since I was always hungry, I started working full time at the Manoa Zippy's.

My uniform, which needed tender care at the Laundromat and air drying, was an orange short-sleeved polyester, flame-retardant dress with a brown full-body apron and matching brown hat. And I had a badge: HOW MAY I HELP YOU? SHARON. I worked the counter registers, took orders for yakitori chicken and rice, tempura shrimp, saimin, and all the local fast-food specialties. I called the numbers back to the kitchen with a mike.

The guys in the kitchen turned out to be great friends to me. They were all local and loved to tease me, since I was what they called a "haole," which was an affectionate way of saying intruder and outsider and interloper. Actually, I didn't understand a lot of what these guys said, because they liked to talk in pidgin English, putting on these accents that tilted all their sentences into questions. One of the cooks was named Kekui, and he was twenty-one—a couple of years younger than me—and also stopping out of school for a few years. It turned out before he left, he'd been a star football player at St. Louis High School in Kaimuki, but was kicked off the team for a combination of too many failing grades and a bowie knife. He was heavy, and half Hawaiian. He had black eyes and a broad nose and a barrel chest. Big shoulders, and big arms, but this was what blew me away—his voice. Kekui had this pure sweet tenor voice, and he was so musical he could sing anything— pop, gospel, Hawaiian songs. He used to sing in the kitchen, and we were all in awe of him. A lot of times, after the customers had gone, we used to beg him to sing, and he would sit up on one of the wood-grain laminate tables, and sing Hawaiian music, like early Beamer stuff, or even covers of Cecilio and Kapono. And I started bringing my guitar and accompanying him, and if the time was right, he'd do a whole act, this pidgin Elvis imitation he'd dreamed up, and everyone would shriek and squeal, even the manager. I'd hit the chords, and he'd start crooning: "I get some t'rill / On blueberry hill. . . ."

Kekui had an uncle who owned a Find-a-Pearl stand down in

Waikiki at the International Marketplace right near my old hotel, and Kekui would help out there on Saturdays. A Find-a-Pearl stand is a booth with a cash register and a barrel filled with pebbles and briny water, and a plastic tube bubbling—an aerator, as in a fish tank—and then, in a big heap on top of all this, a pile of black-and-gray oysters, all different sizes. Your customer comes up and picks an oyster out and pays for it, and then you take a knife and split the poor animal open. You take your knife blade and turn the oyster's flesh, and ta dah! your customer finds his pearl sitting there, shiny and new, where it had been planted back at the aqua farm as a grain of sand. The customers take the pearls home in little white boxes along with the clean oyster shells.

I started going down on Saturdays to keep Kekui company while he worked the morning shift at the booth. We sat on stools and opened oysters for the customers. Sometimes the pearls were white, and sometimes pink, or silvery gray, or even green. You never knew if you would get one or two or even three pearls. That was supposed to be the fun part, although, obviously, for the oyster it wasn't. Kekui had a garbage bag in the booth, which was where he dumped the bodies.

The International Marketplace was fringed with booths selling puka-shell necklaces and bracelets, and Hawaiian dolls that did the hula. The central court was filled with a giant banyan tree strung with lights. Day and night there was music blaring on loudspeakers. Tourists strolling through. Couples and teenagers red from the sun, old ladies in their pastel double-knit pantsuits, would-be hippies, who may not have been hip but were shaggy for sure, probably a lot like Gary and I had looked a couple of years before. I said to Kekui almost in a pidgin tone, "Look at all them—"

And Kekui teased me, "Eh, Sharon, you gon' be local now?" He was like Corinne with her southern accent. He could turn his pidgin up or down. He was such a sweet guy, and he was out of school like me, out of the mainstream and just drifting in his own little eddy. He had a baby son his old girlfriend Janelle's mom was raising, and who he used to visit and bring presents. His wallet was full of pictures of his baby and his brothers and his sisters and his thirteen nieces and nephews, not to mention photos of his mom and dad. His wad of pictures was thicker than a pack of cards.

Kekui turned me on to what was happening in Hawaii—and not just what was happening to the birds, but what was going on with the native Hawaiians who really owned the land by rights, because they'd been there first. Hanging with Kekui at Find-a-Pearl I could see Waikiki and the whole city through his eyes, all those servicemen and honeymooners, and I saw that the place wasn't real to haoles at all. It was another Disneyland, as far as they were concerned, and not an actual Land that belonged to a People. All these visitors treated Waikiki as if it were some amusement park, some campy tame adventure, just a little over the top. And they liked it that way. That was the scary part. That's what they wanted. You know how the famous line goes: "There's no *there* there." You gotta know it was a tourist who said that, a tourist just loving the surface of some vacation spot and then denigrating the place for being shallow!

So while we split those oysters open, I told Kekui all about the northwest islands, and the quiet there except for the birds, and the way the sun rose, and how you sat up and watched, because that was the great event of the day—the sky being all the art in that place, the light changing and the moon rising. The stars pouring down. And I said I felt like those islands were some of the last good places left, but they were restricted and they were owned by the government. And that was when Kekui told me about his sister Lani and her boyfriend Joseph, who were actually living and farming out on Molokai all hidden in the rain forest on U.S. Government land.

"Did you ever go out there?" I asked. "Just to visit?"

"Nah," said Kekui.

"Why not?"

"'Cause it's not too easy to get in and out, and Joseph and Lani don't have phones, so you can't warn them when you're coming."

"Oh, I get it," I said. But I didn't really.

I decided early on with Kekui that I wasn't going to be his girlfriend, since I liked our relationship just the way it was: work buddies. There I was all ready to fend him off, but it turned out Kekui was actually a very straight, restrained kind of guy. In fact, apart from Geoffrey, he was the most religious person I'd ever known. I mean, I came from a background of staunch secularism. Nominally my family was Jewish, but we didn't belong to anything, or do anything. For holidays we went by the decorations in the stores. We did Halloween and trick-or-treating, and then

Thanksgiving at a restaurant, before Mom had her first breakdown, then Christmas—but not as a religious festival or anything, just presents and a tree—then New Year's Eve, which, after the divorce was kind of cozy, with Mom drinking quietly at home, curled up with me and my brother, Andrew, on the couch, and giving us sips and watching old movies, especially *An Affair to Remember,* on TV, which was how I learned the word *corny.* "That's corny," Mom would say, toasting the television screen. Later on, Mom couldn't hack New Year's Eve anymore—actually none of us could—since that was the holiday Andrew got killed on, drunk driving and not wearing seat belts and the whole deal. And when it was just me and Mom, I guess it was too sad for her, which is one of the reasons when I was thirteen she had to take off. And she was in MacLean, and I had to live with my dad and Joanne, my stepmom, and had feelings of abandonment, which was the genius insight of Mr. Firefag (né Frietag), the shrink of Brookline's Runkle Middle School.

After New Year's, in my family, that was pretty much it for the rest of the year as far as holidays. I never did Easter baskets or egg decorating, except at my friends' houses—and that was sort of Jewish, that we didn't do that stuff at home, but it was also because, to put it mildly, Mom did not do arts and crafts. As for religious services, we never ever went to a temple or a church of any stripe. But now, here was Kekui, and every single Sunday he went to Makiki Gospel Church. He and his whole family went and sat there for four hours and sang hymns, and Kekui sang in the choir, and then they all went home and celebrated the Sabbath, which meant no one worked all day. No one in the family could even smoke on Sunday. And, in fact, Kekui and his brothers and sisters weren't supposed to smoke or drink at all, or have children out of wedlock, except sometimes they did. Still, Kekui didn't sleep around, and even after we were buddies he was reserved with me. He would look at me, but that was all. A lot of what made him so wary of me was our religious differences, I being from out in left field and never baptized, which more than once he asked me about—if I was nervous. Since if anything happened to me and I died, I'd be stuck in limbo at best, and in the worst case, I'd plunge straight down to hell. But I had to say I wasn't nervous. I could say this for my family, despite being its own little version of hell, none of us ever had a hang-up about the *hereafter.* To me the whole idea of God watching over you and caring about all the little things you did seemed like something from the

old days, or actually from some Hollywood movie of the old days where
there were clouds and heavenly music, and the Lord turned out to be this
white Republican male like Charlton Heston.

BEING so religious and devoted to his family, Kekui wanted to introduce
me to his parents. And this was when we were still just friends. My gosh,
I thought, this family is tight knit. He hadn't even kissed me yet. And actually, we'd been buddies for so long, I was starting to kind of want him
to kiss me. So what did this mean? Was he intending something? If this
had been Gary we would have beaten the whole subject to death, and if
it were Rich, we'd have been done by now with the whole relationship,
but Kekui was somebody totally different, and he didn't explain anything. He just mentioned that his niece Kehili was having her one-year-
old luau, and he wanted to bring me to meet his family.

I still remember when Kekui and two of his brothers drove up outside the Y. It was Saturday, early in the morning, and they had a beat-up
station wagon, the kind they used to make with fake wood-grain panels
on the sides, an imitation woody. I squeezed in between them on the
bench seat in front. The entire back of the car was piled with food. Picnic coolers and foil trays and about three thousand paper napkins, and
jumbo Tupperwares. It turned out for this one-year-old birthday luau,
Kekui's family was having two hundred people.

We drove to the other side of the island, the North Shore, where the
flanks of the volcano were wet and craggy, and covered in some places
with green fern, and in other places with tangled forest. There were
steep patches of banana plants on the mountain slopes, and wet valleys
planted with taro, and hardly any buildings at all. Only in the distance
you could see the occasional apartment building or old-age home, like a
watchtower of the enemy.

When we got to Makaha, there were still tents up from some of the
family camping the night before, and there were cars rolling in, and
people bringing and fetching and carrying, and there was music, a
whole band with ukuleles and guitars and hollow gourds, some big and
some small, to thump with your palm. The sand was white powder, and
the view was blue as far as you could see. Just blue waves in front of
you, and at your back, those tall green cliffs.

There was swimming all day, and the guys surfing in the waves, and there was food spread out over the picnic tables at the beach park near the shore. Trays of *lomi lomi* salmon with sea salt on top, and a whole pig, pink and juicy from cooking all night wrapped in ti leaves and buried underground. There was rice, and also *huli huli* chicken, which Kekui's aunt Georgiana brought from a fund-raiser for the Kaneohe High School Band. The chicken had been marinated and then roasted on spits over an open flame in steel drums, so it had this special bitter-burnt-sweet flavor.

In the beach park Kekui's parents sat in chairs in the shade of the ironwood trees that grew there. So when you approached them you walked up from the ocean onto this thick carpet of green pine nee-dles—and the occasional tiny prickly pinecone that stabbed your bare feet. I was yelping, "Ouch!" when Kekui brought me up to his parents. But they did not smile.

"This is my mother," Kekui said to me. "This is my father."

His mom and dad looked at me, but they didn't stir. His mom wore a palaka muumuu, which meant it was checkered. It was covered all over with little plaid squares in red and white. Kekui's dad wore a white shirt with white embroidery, the kind imported from the Philippines. And they were big people, really big people, and they sat on their chairs with regal faces, unsmiling. They had some incredible gravity about them.

And I said, "Hi, I'm Sharon," and Kekui's parents didn't answer. I turned to Kekui's mother and I smiled at her, a little bit anxiously. I said, "What's your name?"

And his mother looked at me and said, "My name is Mrs. Eldridge."

I felt like I'd done something wrong, but I didn't know what.

However, Kekui just led me to the picnic tables to meet his aunties as if everything was fine. Then he took his surfboard, and his brothers took theirs, and they went back down to the ocean and paddled out on their boards, and left me far behind, which I thought was rude, since his aunties and I had already run out of things to say to each other! I ended up going swimming, but without a board, and without anyone to help me. The waves were taller than me, and I'm five foot seven. They were colossal. When you got up close, they rose up in front of you, massive thundering walls about to fall. If you didn't duck and swim under them, or turn and learn to ride them, the waves would crash down on your head and jerk you underwater, head over heels in spiraling somersaults, and you would open your eyes and see the sand swirling around you in the aquamarine until at last the wave would cough you up on shore and leave you in a heap. I tried and tried riding those waves, yet every time they rode me; they trampled me down to the ground. They filled my bikini bottom with sand, and I kept losing my top until I tied it on with double knots.

When the sun set there was more music, and there was a dessert, cool to your tongue, and tall in your mouth—coconut cake topped with this creamy coconut gel with arrowroot in it, and iced with coconut icing and then sprinkled with coconut flakes—haupia cake, which is what I would define as angel food, since this is probably the stuff that real angels eat. The band of relatives stopped playing. Just one aunt sang and one uncle kept time, slapping a gourd. Then Mrs. Eldridge and two of Kekui's aunties stood up, and everyone hushed. They stood up and danced a hula, these big ladies, who when they moved had this suppleness—this enormous grace, slowly turning and dancing with their hips and feet and hands. And that was the first hula I ever saw—I mean the first real hula outside of the Saturday-afternoon shows in Waikiki, where an emcee took you on a journey through the Pacific Islands from the plastic raffia skirts of Tahiti all the way to the Saran-wrapped white poi balls on braided black and red yarn that the Maori girls were supposed to swing. After the hula there was a bonfire. You couldn't see the green cliffs anymore above you, only the white foam rushing from the sea.

The party broke up when it was almost dawn, and Kekui took me home. "How come you abandoned me all day to your relatives?" I complained, but then I put my arms around him, because I'd missed him, and I put my hands under his shirt.

So I turned out to be the impatient one. I remember the first touch of his hands. He touched the tan lines where my bathing suit had been, and he whispered, "You're so white! You're so white."

We were best friends. We went hiking out in the Hawaiian Homelands, where Kekui's tutu, who was his grandma, lived. It was so wet out there, water was always trickling, and a lot of times there was so much mud you took off your sandals so you could get a better grip on the trail with your toes. When we went hiking, the plants and trees were always tangled up, and there would be fruit hanging behind the leaves—guavas, and *lilikoi,* which were passion fruit and grew on vines. Later on I found out the fruit got their name from these little red spots inside that were like the wounds of Jesus in his passion. Back then, though, I thought calling *lilikoi* "passion fruit" was odd, since the actual fruit were so hard and tart. I mean, you'd think passion fruit would be soft and wet, and easy on your tongue. But that was just me.

Mainly we used to pick guavas for Tutu, so she could make guava jam, which the church sold at Christmastime to raise money. We did another thing too. We caught cockroaches, big flying ones that lived out there in the jungle, and we would bring them back alive to town. Kekui had a high school friend who worked in a not very upscale bar, and he had a special box he'd built like a miniature track with dividers for lanes, and a clear plastic cover with ventilation holes, and he'd race those roaches. Guys would come in and place bets on which roach would win. My conscience I think told me a few times that cockroach racing was not a respectful way to treat members of a species that had been here on earth so much longer than humankind, but at that time of my life my conscience didn't speak very loudly. Being twenty-three was so loud it drowned out the conscientious voices in my head.

The problem was, Kekui's parents didn't like me, and actually none of his family did. This was for a few reasons. One was that I didn't share their religion. Another was that they still thought he should marry his old girlfriend, Janelle, and take care of his child. And finally, they didn't approve of me because I was a Mainland haole—white—which, no matter how you looked at me, you just couldn't get around. After a while Kekui's family started feeling like I wasn't going away by myself, and they started worrying about my intentions, even though I didn't have very many. In any case, Kekui's mom, Mrs. Eldridge, refused to let me see Kekui in her home, and she and Mr. Eldridge told Kekui they didn't want me coming to the family get-togethers as if I was part of the family, because I wasn't. And they said they'd raised him to be a good Christian man and to be responsible, and what about Janelle? What about Luke? Luke was the name of Kekui's baby.

While Kekui's family was giving him grief, one of the cooks at

Zippy's told him about a sideline he had as a supplier for a place down near the airport that did gold electroplating. This was in the days when gold electroplated jewelry was huge. You would take a leaf, for example, a nice green little marijuana leaf, and you would electroplate it so it was now a nice shiny gold little marijuana leaf suitable for wearing on a gold chain around your neck. Well, the latest thing was electroplating cockroaches—not the big fliers Kekui and I caught for racing, but daintier, under an inch. People loved gold cockroaches. You could get them on stickpins, sort of a roach broach, or you could just buy them as collectibles, big as life, just as detailed, and better than any model cockroach could be because you'd have the genuine article there encased in fourteen-karat gold. Those insects were in such demand, Kekui and I could get a finder's fee for collecting them. So we started supplying this place on Middle Street with small- to medium-sized roaches. We brought the creatures to their doom.

Probably the most grisly part was that the roaches had to be alive for the electroplating. If they had died a natural death, they would have rolled over onto their backs and lain on the ground with their legs waving in the air, and then when the end came, they would have folded their legs peacefully to them, like Medieval Christians on top of tombs. But what the public wanted was gold roaches that looked alive, and ready to crawl right up your arm, so the bugs had to be up and breathing when they got zapped and turned to gold, caught in the moment, just like the people of Pompeii. The guys on Middle Street had a refrigerator in the back, and they kept ether in there, which I'm not sure exactly how they got, since it's a restricted substance, but I guess they claimed they were scientists. They had ether in glass flasks, nice woozy stuff, and they used to administer the ether to the roaches Kekui and I brought in. Very carefully they dosed each cockroach with an eyedropper. Just one to two drops on a cotton ball per insect, just enough so they held still for the procedure. If you gave a roach too much ether, then he or she might overdose. If the poor thing OD'd, then the roach would spread his wings like a little angel, and that wouldn't look lifelike at all. So the guys dosed all our roaches just enough to put them out while they were still standing on their own six feet. And then they went ahead and immersed the victims in a saltwater bath with the gold in solution and zapped these electrical charges, from cathode to anode and back again, and every little particle of gold migrated to the submerged body of the bug, so the cockroaches turned to gold.

Kekui and I started collecting about once a week. Mondays we'd take the swing shift at Zippy's from early morning to three o'clock, and then we'd borrow Kekui's brother's car and drive out to the Kailua dump and basically go prospecting there in the mounds of garbage and broken-down appliances. We'd catch young roaches, ten, twenty at a time, just by looking under old stoves rusting out, or picking through the kitchen waste sitting there and putrefying. We hardly ever ran into anybody there at the dump, or if we did, we kept to ourselves and just left with our catch, which we took home in old clean mayonnaise jars with the lids screwed on tight and punched with just a few tiny pinholes for ventilation.

Then one week we came up against a couple of local guys harvesting auto parts. I was collecting in an old wreck and I'd found a beauty right in the front seat of the car, antennae just poking out from the ripped upholstery. Boom! The whole car starts rolling and pitching. I see these two guys prying open the hood and pulling out the engine and transmission, right from under me. In a flash my roach was gone. "Hey!" I screamed. They couldn't have had any trouble hearing me since the car had no windows or doors.

They just kept on working at that engine.

"Hey!" I jumped out of the wreck and ran around the hood to face these guys. "What do you think you're doing!"

"Eh, bodder you?" one of these guys jeered at me. He was probably just a kid, but he was bigger than I was.

"Yeah, it bothers me!" I hollered right back at him.

Then the other guy pushed me so hard he knocked the wind out of me. I heard Kekui calling, "Sharon! You all right?" And I couldn't even answer, but already he was running over, and he was carrying a pipe he'd dragged from somewhere, and he flew at the first guy and the second one, both of them at once. It was the most chivalrous thing anyone had ever done for me. I was really touched, in addition to being scared shitless. But it was two against one, and not a kung fu movie, so Kekui got beaten and cut and scraped, and his nose broken, before we managed to run out to his brother's car and I could get it started, my hands all shaking, and these two bullies pounding on the doors and windows and basically hounding us out of the dump and promising they'd kill us if we ever came back.

Kekui's whole family was up in arms about this. His mother was beside herself, which you could understand. But the unbelievable thing was she and Kekui's father both blamed *me* for the whole incident! They didn't care that I was the one who took Kekui to the emergency room and made sure he got stitched up and had his tetanus shot. They didn't care about that at all. Instead they blamed me for being the cause of the fight and getting their son into danger, since presumably if I hadn't shown my haole face and provoked these people none of this would have happened. And they told Kekui that having a haole girlfriend was going to get him beat up more and more, and having a girlfriend who wasn't Christian was going against his faith, not to mention I was wild and setting him a bad example.

I wasn't there at Kekui's house to hear all of this, but Kekui told me about it. How his parents were going to disown him if he kept seeing me, and kick him out so he'd have nowhere to go. Kekui and I were sitting together at the Find-a-Pearl stand when he told me this. The customers kept coming by, and Kekui kept slitting open those poor oysters. In between times we asked each other what we should do, and sat looking into the oyster barrel with downcast eyes, like we were the original star-crossed lovers. Suddenly I shook myself. "Oh, for Godssakes," I said. I mean, did we think we were living in the Middle Ages? Romeo and Juliet had been obsolete for years.

"What?" Kekui asked me.

"If your mom and dad don't like me, then tough. And if they feel like kicking you out, then go."

"Go where?" he asked.

Then I got inspired. "We'll get out of here, and go to Molokai," I said, "to that government land, and we'll live out there in the forest with your sister."

Kekui grinned at me.

"What do they farm out there, anyway?" I asked.

And he said, "You never figured that out?"

5

Eden

THE government-land jungle out on Molokai was the most ruth-
less place I'd ever been. Philodendrons choked the trees. Vines
strangled the philodendrons. Every plant put out its leaves and tendrils
like grappling hooks; its stems like stilts to catch the light. Every day
those trees and ferns and roots were jostling and pushing each other to
get by. And since in rain forests there isn't any limit to how far living
things will go, they just grew and grew till they were giant size. The
philodendron leaves would be three, four feet across, and the ferns
would grow the size of banana plants, just unfurling more and more
fronds, sending up more flags. The lichens and the fungi would grow till
the tree trunks were soft and leprous. And there were these vines called
kauna'oa—orange parasites that had actual suction cups to suck the life's
blood out of any tree or plant they could latch on to. *Lilikoi* vines were
so thick they grew into whole arbors. The place was festering with fruit,
so you couldn't eat it fast enough. The guavas shone like yellow eggs,
and they were so sweet, so good, but you had to watch what you bit
into, because these special fruit maggots used to nest in them, and you
couldn't tell from the outside, unless you turned the fruit all over in
your hands. The bugs could enter through a hole small as a pinprick and

leave the fruit's skin pure and smooth, while on the inside, ten thousand swarming black maggots would be feasting and pillaging on the pink guava flesh. The insects were obscene. At night the moths thumped like bats. The roaches were the biggest fliers I'd seen. Their antennae were longer than my index finger. But they were lean, not broad like rubbish-fed city roaches, and they bit in the night. They were always hungry. There were rats, too, running and climbing in every crevice of the place, and it was nothing to them to shimmy up a tree and eat out an entire nest of fledgling birds. Then there were pigs running rampant, with tiny little eyes, and they ate everything in front of them. They'd eat the rats, and the birds and the fruit off the trees and the trees themselves, and if they got hungry enough, they'd eat their own piglets too.

But as human life went it could be quiet there. It could be beautiful. It was very physical earthy work, farming. Kekui's sister Lani and her boyfriend, Joseph, and I were just working that rich humus and growing *pakalolo,* which was marijuana. This was, of course, before the helicopter patrols. It was the golden age. Every day we got up and we tended our green plants and cleared away space for them and weeded them and personally picked off the slugs and parasites, because the whole operation was organic. We nurtured every crop by hand in a network of little patches among the trees. We were raising a secret garden.

Lani and Joseph had an incredible place they'd fixed up where the jungle and the runoff water ran down to the sea. It was a weathered old hut with a corrugated iron roof. The glass in the window was broken when they moved in, but they stapled up fresh screening on the window frame so it was like new. Kekui and I lived farther in, meaning a little bit closer to the crops. We also had a gem, an abandoned field station—needless to say, rent free. It was only slightly termite eaten and surrounded by trees, or actually one banyan tree that was the size of a herd of elephants with its roots hanging down like tails and trunks and legs on all sides. There was a door that closed, and hooks inside to hang your stuff, and a great table Kekui scavenged. It was a giant spool that the telephone company had used once upon a time to reel out cable. When you set it on end, it turned into a round table. Around harvest time our distributor would come out and he'd bring us stuff—money, kerosene, batteries. But it was amazing how the so-called necessities of life turned out to be so forgettable. Like newspapers, or plumbing, or cars. None of that mattered. And that's what I loved. We had mountain apples, which were these small fruits just blushing red, and you bit them and they were completely delicate with the slightest crunch, just sweet enough. We had waterfalls with clear sweet water running down the forest slopes into a little stream, and we had fish in there, gray tilapia we used to fry up on our smoky little hibachi and eat right in their curling skins. And of course we had the fruits of our labors, the best home-grown *pakalolo* there was, so in the evenings or the afternoons, or any-time at all, you could roll your own, and sit back and blow some rings.

On the one hand it was a very simple life, and not a lot of thinking or wrestling with questions in your mind, but putting your mind to rest, and letting the days just carry you. On the other hand, farming was a huge effort, cutting off other plants that every day tried to move in and strangle your crops. You had to be vigilant about the rats eating your supplies. And it wasn't like at any point you could let up, because there was no winter to hunker down and hibernate, mend the nets and oil the traps. But there were patches of pure pleasure, just sitting around, or swimming in the stream when it was swollen up after some rain, or just enjoying the absence of society, ditching all those clothes and rules that went on out there. I was at a time of my life when I was not into clothes very much, and when I was alone, or just working with Kekui, I ended up being naked, just feeling that warm air with my skin, just opening up all my pores. My hair had grown long again, and I liked to feel it hanging down against my bare back, because it was so soft and heavy. I liked to swish it all around me.

Kekui's sister Lani always wore at least a bathing suit, and most often a Hawaiian-style *pareo* wrapped around her and tied at the waist. She had thick hair she wore loose and purposely roughed up when she brushed it, because she liked it to look thick and Hawaiian, being so proud of her heritage. A lot of the reason she and Joseph had come out to Molokai in the first place was to live a purer Hawaiian life, in nature, without having to deal with haole civilization. She and Joseph were both half Hawaiian, and since their culture was in danger, they wanted to raise their kids to know who they were. When I first met them they had two little ones, and then the next year they had a third, and they had natural births every time. Lani birthed all her kids at home—actu-ally outside. Those kids had the longest, most poetic names I'd ever heard, but, of course, they went by nicknames. The youngest baby was called Kananipuamaeole, which meant beautiful flower of something or other. But she went by Kanani.

Since Lani and Joseph were trying to raise their kids pure, I was worried at first about what they'd think of me, but actually they didn't mind my living with Kekui so much, since we weren't having children or anything, and I used to baby-sit for them, and Kekui and I both tended the crops, so they liked having us help out. The area was pretty sparse as far as people went, and this was on an island that was rural to begin with—a place where if you were running for public office a good campaign tactic would be to paint your name on the side of a cow.

The strings of my guitar rusted out so badly I couldn't play anymore, and there wasn't anyplace to get new strings. I missed playing, but for music we could always sing. On Sundays we sang hymns, which Kekui taught me, like "We Gather Together," and other nights we'd sit back with Joseph and Lani, who had a lovely alto. Just hymns or rounds or newish local music, like "Brown Eyes" or sometimes Peter, Paul and Mary, like "Puff the Magic Dragon" or old songs such as "Good Night Irene," in harmony like the Weavers. Joseph didn't sing, but he beat time, clapping. Our music was our voices, and our hands and feet, and at night the rain concertizing on our metal roof. Kekui and I would lie awake listening, and the rain would be drumming and thrumming, and nothing was better—unless the rain blew so hard it came in those cracks between the sheet metal and the walls and we got wet. Sleeping in wet sleeping bags tended to ruin the experience.

We had no clocks, just a radio that was broken half the time. I still had Grandpa Irving's watch, but I didn't bother winding it. You could look around you and tell the time of day, and you didn't have to be so precise, making hours and fractions of hours. You could take your mornings and your afternoons and nights all in one piece. Apart from Lani's Bible, the only book we had was my Norton anthology, which got wet and swelled up so it wouldn't close, and its thin white pages turned puffy. I skipped around among all the authors, but the one I loved was John Keats. His writings were so vivid to me, the "Nightingale" and the "Urn." What blew my mind was John Keats had created all this poetry when he was my age, and then he died, and his whole voice was lost to the world like Buddy Holly, and Richie Valens and the Big Bopper. He was just an unbelievable talent. I used to walk around with his lines humming in my head, like "season of mists and mellow fruitfulness." I used to say to Kekui, "Where did he get the gift?" We'd be sitting in our rusty old lawn chairs, which we dragged outside in the afternoons, and I'd have my book open on my lap and I would say, "Oh, my God!"

"What?" Kekui would ask.

"Oh, my God, listen!

> And still she slept an azure-lidded sleep,
> In blanched linen, smooth, and lavender'd,
> While he from forth the closet brought a heap
> Of candied apple, quince, and plum, and gourd;
> With jellies soother than the creamy curd,
> And lucent syrops, tinct with cinnamon;
> Manna and dates, in argosy transferr'd
> From Fez; and spiced dainties, every one,
> From silken Samarcand to cedar'd Lebanon.

"Doesn't that make you hungry?"

The Eve of St. Agnes. I used to read it all the time. The page got ripped. I used to walk around chanting it: "St. Agnes' Eve—Ah, bitter chill it was!" That poem had everything I didn't have out there on Molokai, not that I missed it in real life, but I got a charge from the idea of those things: bitter chills, and gargoyles, and all this repressed sensuality. Repression was something I was definitely lacking. And the words just made my mouth water. I mean, lucent syrops! Kekui didn't really see it, though. Poetry wasn't his thing. If he were hungry he'd rather do something about it.

In a lot of ways our life was what I would define as paradisaical. There wasn't even a single serpent, because there are no snakes on Molokai or on any of the Hawaiian Islands. There was just one thing. One bad thing. That was Joseph's gun. I was against having a weapon from the beginning, but there wasn't any choice. Every once in a while, even though we were remote, people would come through and try to steal from us. We actually had a lot of money growing there in those green plants.

I hated that shotgun. There was a special box for it under the floor-boards in the field station, and I always stepped over that spot on the floor, like I was superstitious. It just seemed like an evil thing to me, harboring a firearm. I mean, there were some things that were illegal, like growing *pakalolo,* and homesteading on government lands, and being illegal wasn't bad, and a lot of times it was good, since laws were all about artificial rules being imposed on people's freedoms, and imperialist feds appropriating the Hawaiian way of life and locking people into lot lines. But then there were some things that were actually just *wrong,* like weapons. I just felt people should live and let live, so having a gun in the house alarmed me, especially since our lifestyle was otherwise so edenic, and in general we had such a good time. Whenever Kekui or Joseph had to go out and chase someone off the land, usually just a lost hiker, and they had to intimidate these people and act like they were trespassing onto our property, I got upset. I didn't want there to be any property at all or any ownership getting in the way. I didn't even want the money for our crops, I wished we could be subsistence farmers and wouldn't need a distributor at all—but wishing didn't change anything. We lived a pastoral life with capitalist interruptions.

We were in our second year out there when the intruders got to be more of a problem. One morning when Kekui and I got up we went out to one of the patches and found all our plants stripped down, and the leaves stolen. They were so badly trampled I thought at first some animals had got into them, but Kekui said no, it was people. We were just shocked. It was like the plants had been raped. Some had been brutalized so badly that their main stems were broken. Kekui and Joseph started taking turns watching at night. Kekui would go out on patrol with the heavy-duty emergency flashlight and the gun and I would lie awake inside. I couldn't sleep, I was so nervous. I felt like we were all turning into members of the police state we were supposedly here to get away from! "Z, Y, X, W, V, U, T," I recited in my bed. That was a trick my brother had taught me when I was little. Sing the ABCs backwards if you're trying to get to sleep. "S, R, Q, P, O, N, M, L."

I said to Kekui in the morning, "Can't you stop all this guarding?"

And he said, "Those folks'll come back now they know where to get their stuff from."

And I said, "I feel like we're turning into the whole system we were running away from."

But he said, "Eh, I wasn't running away."

That hurt. Looking back, I can see Kekui was simply pointing out that ultimately, despite being his girlfriend, when you came down to it I was a white interloper trying to impose my pacifist ideology on him and his sister, when they, who were truly embattled, and truly endangered by my own dominant culture, did not have the luxury of giving up guns. And I guess he was suggesting that I should get real rather than continually try to turn our lives into a formal utopia that would have to be not only for things—like living the mellow life—but also against things, e.g., violence. But at the time it just hurt.

Life was better when Kekui and I didn't reflect too much on the differences between us. Life was better when we just focused on the matters at hand, singing, sleeping, smoking, making love. Our tolerance for pleasure was really quite high. Our pleasure threshold was way up there.

One day we were outside sitting in our chairs with a couple of joints. The sun was setting so the green forest was rosy and warm, and in my lap I had my book, so puffed out its pages were exploding all over my legs, and I was reading to myself this very sad yet lovely poem about getting high—"The Lotus-Eaters." I was just feeling the words, just getting a little bit numb and feeling the syllables riding up inside of me, and repeating them to myself like they were a mantra: "Rolling a slumbrous sheet of foam below. Rolling a slumbrous sheet of foam below." And every time I said it I saw different things, like big white sheets blowing in the wind, and giant rolling pins beating the white sheets, and beaches foaming and panting to meet you.

Night came, and I had to stop and put the book away because I couldn't see. Still, for a while we sat in the warm darkness. You couldn't help it, the way it melted around you—sweet and sticky like melted chocolate. Then all of a sudden we heard a noise. Footsteps. Breaking branches. Maybe the trespassers were coming back. Maybe even the police. Someone was moving out by our *pakalolo* patches. Kekui went and got the gun. He called, "Who's there?"

There was no answer.

"Who's there?" he called out again.

Then out of the trees came Kekui's sister Roslind, and her husband, Michael.

Kekui threw down the gun. He said, "What you guys doing here?"

They'd flown in and then taken the bus as far as the line went, which in those days was Kualapu'u. When the paved road ended, they'd hiked in, and we'd had rain, so they had to wade some muddy gullies where you never know when a flash flood might come up, just a wall of white water that can rise and carry anyone, crush you in an instant, or suck you all the way down to a roaring runoff stream and out to sea. But they'd made it out to Lani and Joseph's place, and now to ours, and Roslind said, "Dad is dead."

No one could take it in at first, and especially not Lani and Kekui, since their dad was such a young guy, only fifty-four. It was true he was diabetic and he had a heart condition, but he'd had all that for years. No one ever thought about him dying. I put my arms around Kekui. I tried to comfort him, but he shrugged me off. He wouldn't even look at me, let alone touch me.

Early the next morning we all washed ourselves in the stream. We brushed out our hair and we dressed in clean clothes, and the grown-ups put on sandals. And Joseph got our money, and we hiked all the way out to the road, which took half a day, and we got up to the dirt road, which was just a track cut from the velvety red earth, and we followed the road cleft out of the forest, so on either side you could see the ba-nana plants and the tangled vines and the great trees sinking under the weight of all the greenery they carried. We each had a bag of some sort, and I had my backpack on my back, but since it was too much to carry, not my guitar, and we walked, this sad yet clean little procession, until we got to the paved asphalt. We took turns carrying the baby.

We rode the bus into town, and then we waited for the bus out to what you would call a one-horse, or maybe single-engine, airport. No one was too surprised there in the terminal when Joseph went to the ticket counter and peeled off our fares from this wad of twenty-dollar bills. I guess they could see we were country people, so that was how we had to travel.

THE next morning we were standing at the funeral service at Makiki Gospel. We were all gathered at the cemetery, and Kekui and his sisters and his brothers were the coffin bearers. The minister spoke and spoke, and Mr. Eldridge's children lifted that coffin and eased it down gently into the freshly dug earth. It was baking hot, and there was hardly any breeze. I think it was the hottest fall day they'd had in years. But we stood there, it seemed like hours—all the relatives, and Mr. Eldridge's descendants, eight children and fourteen grandchildren. In front of everyone, and not crying, probably just willing herself not to cry, stood Mrs. Eldridge—such a big woman, not fat, big like an opera singer, big like the photos of Princess Ruth when she sat at the Summer Palace on her throne.

At the end of the service, when everyone else just about collapsed weeping and embracing and falling onto one another, Mrs. Eldridge still stood strong, and she lifted up all the grown children caving in on her, and she looked each one in the eye, from the oldest, who was named Minnie, down to the youngest, who was Kekui, and when she looked at Kekui she said the first words I'd heard her speak all day. "KK, you're coming home."

"What?" he said.

"Roslind and Michael have the back room, Minnie and her kids are in front, Earl and Matthew have Minnie's room, Leilan and Mitchell are upstairs," she said.

Kekui just looked at her, just all hollowed out with grief and guilt.

"We cleaned out your room," Mrs. Eldridge told him.

"Excuse me?" I ventured.

"Keep quiet, girl," she said, but she kept her eyes fixed on her son.

In a funeral caravan we drove up to the Eldridges' house in Aina Haina with its two plumeria trees in front. Mrs. Eldridge had six of her eight kids living in the house and, one way or another, a whole bunch of the grandchildren. There were add-ons in back of the house, and a second story above the garage. Mr. Eldridge had been a contractor. And there were something like seven cars in the driveway, plus a boat and a tour van. We sat down inside, everyone low from the funeral, not to mention bathed in sweat, and some of the babies were crying. Mrs. Eldridge took a couple of them on her knee. She looked around like she was ready to take everyone on her knee. But for what? To rock us? To hit us? "KK," she said, "you've come back home to stay."

"Excuse me?" I began again. I was trying to be polite.

"Quiet, girl. I have an application for you," she told Kekui, and she reached down in front of her over the babies to the coffee table, and picked up a bunch of white forms. "West Oahu College," she said. "I brought up all my children to go to college. Okay?"

Kekui looked down totally crushed. His entire immediate family, which was at least forty people, was sitting there in his mom's living room and out on the lanai. He couldn't even look his mother in the eye.

"Everyone in this family is a worker," Mrs. Eldridge said. "You filling this out?"

He didn't say anything.

She just waited.

"Yeah," he said to his own callused feet.

"Goddammit, Kekui!" I burst out.

Then Mrs. Eldridge turned on me. "Get your mouth out of my house," she declared, standing up in her full dimensions. "Hippie girl, just 'cause you washed up here on Oahu you don't need to come invading my family. Go back to where you started—California, England, Holland, or whatever nationality you are. And don't you dare walk around taking the Lord's name in vain blaspheming my husband's funeral. Get your *pakalolo* face away or Earl'll take his badge out and arrest you!"

6

—

Civilization

I never got my guitar back. I used to dream about it lying there in the field station in the trees on Molokai. I dreamed termites were marching on the guitar case, chewing the black cardboard away. I dreamed mynahs came and plucked tufts of the guitar case lining, which was fake fur the color of papaya, and the birds carried off all the fur for their nests. Rats sniffed to see if the guitar was dead. They scrabbled over the top and thrummed the rusty strings.

Kekui, however, was studying at West Oahu College and working nights as a fire-eater at the Hilton Hawaiian Village. He was busy being a father to his son—returning to his values he'd ditched two years before. I used to come sometimes to the Hilton to see him in his loincloth and grass anklets after his act, when he was packing up his jar of fire-retardant jelly and his three torches, which he used to juggle when they were aflame. At first when I came by we'd have conversations and arguments, and sometimes tears. But even then we both knew, although it took us a few months to admit it, that this wasn't a short visit, or even a couple of years at home for college; Kekui was home for good. And I missed him; it made me sad, because he had been my best friend. I was just a little bit hurt to realize that in the eyes of his family I had been his wild oats and his fling. Back there on Molokai I'd kind of assumed we'd been sowing our oats together, and flinging each other. But no. To his mother I'd just been a bad influence all along.

Kekui was that one hundredth sheep returning to the fold, the one that everyone loved even more than the other ninety-nine. He had his whole life there around him, his mother and all his relatives and his church. He actually started a children's choir there. He loved children. He ended up having two more sons by his new girlfriend. But as for me, not being a sheep from a fold, I came back to Corinne's sofa. And I had my backpack, and my, by this time, kind of minimalist clothes, and my puffed-out book of English literature, and Grandpa's silver watch, which I have to admit, more than once I thought about selling.

After Corinne I stayed with Rich and his girlfriend, Kathryn, for a while. Then I came back to Corinne's couch, and stayed so long, and lavished so much attention on the cat, that Rae accused me of driving a wedge between her and Jane, and Corinne said she threw up her hands. So I found a job at the concession stand at Sea Life Park, and moved back to the Y.

Every morning I took the bus down the short gray freeway past Kahala and past Wailupe, just rattling down Kalanianiole Highway, on the left all the little valleys full of tract houses like ticks on the furry flanks of the volcano, and on the right, the ocean shining. I just stayed on the bus till I got all the way to Sea Life Park right on the rocks by the shore, with its open-air paths running past outdoor tanks, its seal pens, its pretend lagoon, where twice a day a local damsel in an aloha print skirt and bikini top paddled in a canoe to a cement-and-lava-rock island covered with sea grapes and exactly three coconut palms, so she could throw fish prizes to the dolphins when they did their synchronized swimming and leaping. I worked in a little store with a roof thatched, Hawaiian style, with pili grass, and I sold film and candy and killer-whale key chains, and various plastic windup toys and clear plastic snow globes, except these were tropical so they had glitter that swirled around miniature palm trees.

I got to know some of the guys who took care of the dolphins, and some of the vets who watched over the sick and injured animals that came through—dolphins with big bites taken out of their dorsals, and little orphan seals, and a baby humpback whale, who was resting in a holding tank before getting towed out to sea. And I loved those animals, especially the dolphins—just the way they rolled slightly on one side to look at you, and the way they chirped when you spoke to them, and clucked and laughed. The dolphin guys, Jason and Neil, would let me throw herring to the dolphins sometimes. They'd let me stand on the platform that extended over the dolphins' tank, and I'd toss out fish, and sometimes beach balls that the dolphins would bat back to me.

There was one older dolphin named Leilani, one of the stars of the park, who used to get off work the same time I did, meaning she finished her afternoon show when I went off shift at the store. I used to sit down on the platform by her private exercise tank, and tell her all my troubles—for example, how I missed Kekui, and the quiet back on Molokai, and Leilani would really listen. She would glide right up and cock her head and look at me with her wise black eye. I'd ask her questions, like "How do you think I can ever get back to living in a more natural place?" and she'd swim very deliberately around the tank, like she was thinking it over, and then she'd come back to me and roll so she could look at me with her other eye, so penetrating, but yet so sympathetic. I really considered her my mentor, and I told her everything, even things I'd never dream of telling anyone else. She always listened to me. She always had time—and, of course, since she was far more intelligent than any human, she always understood. Actually we had a lot in common, because we were both so isolated. Leilani was an Atlantic dolphin, and she'd been imported five years before for some comparative scientific experiments on echolocation. So she came from back east like me.

"The thing is," I told her, late one afternoon, "the happiest I've ever been was out where it's still wild. Where people haven't spoiled the land yet."

Leilani bobbed up in the water and sat back, head and neck out of the water, which was one of her signature tricks. That was when, in the shows, Neil or Jason would toss a lei around her neck.

"Civilization," I said, "is such a scam. It's all about affiliations, and school. And pleasing other people."

Leilani bobbed up and down, yes.

"Living your life for your mother, for Godssakes! You think you know someone," I said, "and then he goes home, and he's completely different. It's almost like the person he was when he was with you didn't exist at all!"

She clicked.

I trailed my hand in the briny water of her tank. "Do you ever wish you were a wild dolphin again?" I asked.

Then she dove down into the tank and swam around deep. I was crestfallen. How could I have asked such a tactless question? I should have known it would offend her.

Leilani put up with a lot from me. I used to come read my poetry to her in the tank, and she used to glide up right near me and listen with her invisible ears. And I used to sing her songs I had composed back when I had my guitar. But now I sang a capella. One of my best songs was titled "Hey!"

> *HEY!*
>
> *I said, hey, did you see the sky today*
> *Did you see the sun shining down?*
> *Hey, did you see the sun today,*
> *Warming everyone?*
> *Hey, all of you,*
> *Did you thank the land today*
> *For supporting us for free?*
> *Well there's a lot of giving in the world*
> *No thanks to you and me.*

I used to ask Leilani what she thought of her keepers, and what she thought of animal rights—whether people leading that movement was actually a contradiction in terms. I told her how I was over Kekui. How could I respect somebody who would just walk away like that? I was going to find someone else. He wasn't the only one who had other people in his life! I had other people too—I just hadn't found them yet.

I even used to tell Leilani about my family. I said, "When I was a kid I was an orphan—I mean, not technically, but to me I was. It was like everybody had left me behind. We started out and we were the most regular, most normal family. Mom used to get up in the morning. Dad drove home every night in his car. I took ballet, for Godssakes. I was in *Hansel and Gretel.* Then Dad left and got married to Joanne. Then Andrew was killed. Then Mom took off. And then there was one—I was the last of the Spiegelmans. What do you think of that?"

Leilani was perfectly quiet, listening.

"I had a plan, though. I was going to take the train to New York and audition for the School of American Ballet and star in the *Nutcracker*. But nobody let me. I had to move in with my dad and Joanne instead."

"Clik!"

"Yeah, everybody thinks performing is so great. You get out there in front of an audience. They throw you a fish. People don't even realize how hard you're working. But I was thirteen. What did I know?"

"Clik. Clik."

"My brother had drums. Andrew got a complete drum set for Christmas when he was ten. He let me play it, too, even though I was only five. He let me do a lot of things. He was really generous for a brother. He was the one who got me into music. He was going to have a band, and when I was older he was going to let me in—or at least help set up and be the stage manager."

Leilani looked at me with her beautiful smooth face. I didn't have to say it, the next thing, which was that Andrew never had a chance to get his band off the ground. She knew. Her mind was tremendous. The way Leilani thought, she was always three steps ahead of you. People from the university were always evaluating her intelligence, yet the essence of it was impossible to pin down in some academic test—because her intellect was all intuitive. I even introduced her to this guy, Wayne, who was a Marine I was dating at that time. She got his number right away. Just tisked at me. "Tk, tk, tk."

I'D met Wayne at the concession stand where he was with some buddies and buying batteries for his camera, and we'd got to talking. He was a tall, blond, slightly sunburned, chivalrous guy. Incredibly strong, and thick necked. He had blue eyes, stunningly clear and bright. His nose bridge had a bump in it, because when he was growing up in this ranch place in Colorado, he'd got into a fight one day with some other kids. Wayne came home with his nose broken, and his dad, who was naturally much bigger and stronger and tougher than Wayne, was really proud of him, and he never let Wayne go to the doctor and get it set right. Wayne's dad said there wasn't anything wrong with a broken nose that wouldn't heal naturally.

Wayne would bring you chocolates, and he would bring you flowers—real florist flowers—even if he couldn't afford it. Really, he would do anything for you—the downside being, if you talked back or provoked him or made him jealous, he'd just as soon slam you against a wall. The first time he ever took me out he brought me a dozen long-stemmed coral-pink roses. I had to borrow a vase from my neighbor. And he took me out to dinner—not for drinks, or to a club, but for dinner at Horatio's in Ward Warehouse, with candles on the table, and a basket of fresh rolls, and medium-rare steaks and crème brûlée for dessert. On the way home I stepped off the curb before the light changed and a car shot out at me. Wayne pulled me back. He said, "Sharon, don't go off endangering yourself, now!"

I leaned in against him. He put his big strong arm around me. Even the way he did that—he didn't drape his arm over your shoulders like Gary used to, or just give you a quick hug like Kekui—he held you close, and you felt like you were the most treasured, most delicate thing in the world.

The first time he kissed me was when he walked me home that night. His lips just brushed my cheek and my ear. It was almost a shy kiss, as if he were afraid to presume.

The second time he kissed me was in Waikiki on one of those warm crowded Saturday nights when people were streaming out of the movie theaters and every store window was lit up to sell. Wayne had wanted to buy me something—a necklace made out of coral beads, or a little glass figurine of a bird, or a batik dress, or at least a stuffed animal—and I wouldn't let him, because all this idea of buying stuff for me made me nervous. Like he was determined to turn me into his princess. And I stopped right on the sidewalk, and I said, "Wayne, stop it. I don't want anything, and I'm not going to want anything. Presents just aren't my thing. They aren't."

And then he put his arms around me and kissed me right on the sidewalk with the people streaming and eddying around us, and he said, "I'm sorry." He tried too hard, which scared me sometimes, and embarrassed me, but was also charming in a way. He was clumsy, and shy, falling over himself trying to be some kind of gentleman. He was trying to be as good on the inside as he was on the outside, and sometimes he succeeded.

THANKS to the military Wayne and I had an actual courtship, like from my parents' era—when there were such things as parietals, and people went on dates. We couldn't live together, and a lot of times we couldn't even see each other, because Wayne was stuck out at KMCAS, which was Kaneohe Marine Corps Air Station. He was living in the barracks with the guys and doing that enlisted-man thing. No women after hours and all that. Those rules were harder on Wayne than they were on me. He was dead serious about us right away.

"Sharon," Wayne said to me at The Chowder House, "someday we'll get a bunch of land, and we'll build our own house. . . ."

And I'd be thinking, Oh God, can't we just enjoy our meal here? The current meal—the lobster in front of us, as opposed to the banquets we would eat on our great big farm in Colorado with the kids sitting around the table and our horses running around outside.

"I like pipe dreams," he admitted to me.

"Well, I don't," I said.

"What do you like?"

"Just being here now," I said.

He took my hand. "Why can't we think about the future?"

" 'Cause I'm not sure about the future," I said.

He said to me, "Sharon, you've never been with any guys who treated you right. You don't even know. But you're my lady. . . ."

I choked on my drink. I was laughing so much; I couldn't help it. "Did you just say 'you're my lady'?"

So he got furious and stormed out and left me there at the table, and he didn't call me for days. I guess we broke up for a while. And then he called me up again and we went out camping on the beach and we were back together again. We went out to dinner, and we went for drinks, and we even went to Paradise Park, which was a whole bird zoo with walk-in aviaries and daily parrot shows. You drove up to this jungly place in the back of Manoa and you paid your money and got stamped on the back of your hand, and then you could wander through the great aviaries where parrots swooped and called, and if you were unlucky pooped on you as you strolled along. You could see the brilliant flashes of macaw wings, scarlet, and blue, and golden yellow. The birds were all flying up into the rain forest canopy that soared upward, until they hit the high wire-mesh roof.

"You think they're happy?" I asked Wayne.

"Sure," he said.

I looked around; I craned my neck as we stood there on the walkway. I was trying to catch sight of those birds' faces.

"They've got the good life," Wayne said.

"You think so?"

"Yeah; they've got no predators whatsoever. They've got all the food they'd ever want to eat. Plenty of room to fly around."

Tourists with cameras were thronging the walkways. The birds were shrieking louder and louder.

"What's wrong?" Wayne said.

"Nothing," I told him. Then I said, "It's not the good life. It's parrot prison, that's what it is."

"What do you mean, prison?"

"I mean, these birds were born to fly, not to be photographed! If you've got a pair of wings you're supposed to shoot for the stars! Not bump up against cyclone fencing every day of the week."

"Sharon," said Wayne, "I guarantee you these macaws don't know the difference."

"By now they're probably brainwashed," I said. "They probably *are* happy. They don't even know how to live free anymore. Put them back in a real rain forest and they'd be looking for the chopped fruit station. They'd be trying to find the mixed nuts."

All during the open-air bird show I was stewing about trading in your freedom for happiness. We were sitting on riser seats and the park bird-wrangler was talking about his bird performers, putting those captive spirits through their paces. The African gray parrot was bobbing his head up and down three times when his human asked him what was two plus one, and a cockatiel was pedaling a tiny unicycle across a teensy tightrope, and I was thinking, maybe the birds didn't even know how to want to fly away anymore. Maybe they didn't even care about seeking for themselves. Yet they seemed cheerful, and so attached to their humans. They seemed so tame, by which I mean, eager to please.

Maybe they did enjoy their role as educators, maybe that was fun for them, reaching out to the community. There they lived in their giant aviaries in total harmony—since all their basic needs were taken care of. But if the structure is imposed from the outside, how can a place be a true utopia? A real paradise, that would have to come from inside the birds themselves; that would come from their own hearts. A real paradise, that would mean undergoing a paradigm shift in your very soul. And how can you even begin to have a breakthrough when your forest canopy is all you have, and you can never rise above it, due to the roof of your glorified cage?

I guess the whole place brought home to me how I'd lived in paradise myself (on Molokai), and how little it seemed like I'd got out of it. I'd been good at dropping out, no question. But when it came to tuning in, just what frequency had I been on? As a lotus-eater I was a natural, but as a learner? As a flyer? I looked down at my lap. Look at yourself, I thought. I looked at my shorts. Just look at yourself! Can you honestly say you are the seabird you always thought you were? Or are you actually just a parakeet? Do you travel on the wings of gulls? Or do you chirp?

Everyone was clapping hard for the African gray's rendition of "Yellow Bird," but I walked out.

Wayne was annoyed as hell. He took offense a lot, because to him it always seemed like I was either making fun of him or acting like I was deeper than he was. But he kept pursuing me anyway. This went on at least a year, because I was his lady and his princess in his mind, and because he imagined that I loved him—and sometimes I did. It was complicated. It was like we were playing from different rule books, and mine was, to be honest, more about lust, and his was also about lust, but more about romance.

Wayne was always protective of me, although my old friends called it jealousy. He always walked with his arm around my shoulders or my waist. My long hair floating over the two of us. And people like Corinne and Rae, and Rich, and Geoffrey, would look at me and Wayne and then later they would say, "Doesn't that guy ever let you go?" or "Does he ever let you out of his sight?" I took offense when people commented like that—as if it bothered them that someone cared that much for me.

Then there was Brian. I'd brought Wayne to a party in honor of

Geoffrey and Julie's engagement. It was a beach party at Rich's place out on the North Shore—a great big all-day bash like the old days, except there was no booze or dope, in honor of Geoffrey and Julie's Christian morals. Wayne and I didn't even come for most of it. We arrived at the end when there were just crumbs of chips left in the bags, and empty soda cans; and the towels and tatami mats spread out on the sand were hot from baking all day in the sun. So we rolled up in Wayne's rusted-out station wagon and we walked over to the remains of the feast, where Brian and Imo were sitting. Imo was wearing small, dark sunglasses.

"Hey, Brian!" I said. I bumped into him every once in a while at these kinds of celebrations, and I was by this time truly happy to see him, having forgiven him for leaving me off his precious research paper. Academic credit wasn't exactly important to me anymore. "You've met Wayne, right?"

"No, actually, not," Brian said, and he scrambled up and shook Wayne's hand. "Howzit," Brian said, politely. Wayne was a head taller than he was.

Wayne and I sat down on the sand, and I told Wayne, "These guys were the ones who took me out to French Frigate Shoals."

"Man, someday I'd love to go out there," Wayne said.

"Well, you know, you can't just *go* . . ." I said. "You have to be doing research. They're restricted islands—just for birds."

"I love birds," Wayne said. "I used to go bird watching all the time when I was a kid."

I shook my head at him. He sounded so ignorant in front of Brian and Imo. What was he going to tell them next—how much he loved to go to Paradise Park?

"What's up with you guys?" I asked Brian.

"Well, we got married," Brian said.

"No kidding!" If I'd been drinking something I would have choked on my drink. "So now you're living in the same place all year long?" For the last couple of years they'd had one of those academic commuter relationships. Imo had a position in Auckland, so she had to go down under like Persephone every year for their winter semester, which was our spring.

"No, I'm still at Auckland," Imo said.

"We gave up waiting till we lived in the same place," Imo explained.

"Congrats!" I burst out, which sounded so phony. Congrats? When in my life had I ever used that word?

"See," Wayne was telling me. He put his hand on my bare thigh. "Everybody's doing it."

Brian looked at Wayne's hand on my leg.

"Well, give me seven years." I jumped to my feet. "I'm going to say hi to Geoffrey and Julie." I practically ran off to find the guests of honor. I had to get away somewhere—just to take in the fact that Brian and Imo were now permanent. I just had to get used to the idea. So I left Wayne there with Brian and Imo, and he tried to make small talk with them, and there they were humoring him, being polite, only he didn't realize it. They were observing him, but he didn't get that. He actually knew a ton about animals, but it was all in the area of raising, breeding, and hunting. He didn't understand about making observations.

That's what I thought. Actually, as it turned out, he observed just fine.

"Why did you do that to me?" Wayne asked me that night in my room.

"I didn't do anything to you," I said.

"You pushed me away in front of all your friends."

"I just wanted a chance to talk to them," I said, "without you breathing down my neck. That's all."

"If you're embarrassed of me, then why did you bring me?" Wayne said.

"I'm not—why would I be embarrassed of you? I just wanted for one second to see them without you touching me all the time. It just bothers me, that's all."

"Why shouldn't I touch you?" Wayne said. "Is it because I'm not some professor? Is it because I'm not some scientist?" And he put his hands on my shoulders and shook me. There I was in his grip, and I couldn't pull loose. He was way too strong.

"Stop it!" I screamed. My teeth were rattling. "Wayne, what is your problem?"

He stopped. He was in tears. He yelled, "My problem is that I love you, and you don't love me back."

7

The Whale

Now I seemed to be, in the classical sense of the term, in something of a rut, since here I was on an island in a dead-end job, and in the middle of this tempestuous relationship with the wrong guy. Maybe if I'd been smarter or stronger I would have seen how to get out—of the rut, the island, the job, the relationship, what have you—but probably then I wouldn't have gotten in there in the first place. Somebody else with just a modicum of sense would have up and quit a job selling miniature surfboard key chains. Somebody else would have looked at Wayne and said, You're big, needy, and overbearing, and I love someone else. We're through. Yet I was not somebody else; I was myself. That was the whole problem.

I mean, here I was, twenty-six already, and what had I done? I'd already been in Hawaii five years. I'd never intended to stay that long; I'd intended to keep traveling through the entire Pacific. I'd intended to circumnavigate the globe by this time, yet I never had. That was the terrible thing I was discovering about myself. Gary got to be Ulysses and what did I do? Hunker down like Penelope. To put it another way—in gender-neutral terms—maybe some people think they're buffalo, but when it comes down to it, they don't actually roam. When it comes

down to it, some people are really more like cats, who like to curl up—
who actually seek out the smallest spaces. Yet even in the smallest place I
peeked out, trying to find, or at least know, something bigger. Even
with my flat little cat eyes I was always looking. I was always on the
lookout for a better spot. Maybe I didn't see my way out of my problems, but I was always ready for a solution to come along. That's huge:
readiness. As Hamlet once said, it's "all." You have to be open to ideas.
You have to be ready—you have to be on your toes—then, boom! Your
whole life might be transformed. All of a sudden you're looking at a
whole different picture. To me it happened on a whale watch.

It was the first time I'd ever been. Wayne and I sailed out from Waikiki
on the whale-watching boat, and it was a gorgeous Sunday with puffy
clouds, and we'd had a few beers, and we were good—we were having a
ball. He had this camera with a timer on it and we were running all over
town setting up the camera and then racing in front of it and photographing ourselves. So we got onto this whale-watching boat that was
about to leave—a dilapidated boat stuffed with tourists, and with some
nautical tour guide at the helm who carried on about how there were
ample snacks in the galley and rest rooms for our convenience. Wayne
and I were cracking up. He was saying, "Ample snacks, ma'am?"

Then when we finally sailed out to where the whales were supposed
to be, it seemed like they'd heard us coming. The tour guide kept announcing things like "At two o'clock you can just see . . ."

Thumpity, thumpity, thumpity, all the passengers ran to two o'clock.
The boat tilted down from the weight of everyone running and pushing and shoving to one side. Then, "Well, it looks like she's gone down
for a dive. We'll wait and see where she comes up. Oh, there's her friend
there—nine o'clock. . . ."

Thumpity, thumpity, thumpity, everybody was running back the
other way. The boat was starting to tilt in the other direction, and everyone was fighting for the railing. But now it looked like the whales had
gone down again.

Wayne and I were already in a rambunctious mood. There we were in
the thick of it, running around, making more commotion, laughing our
heads off.

"It looks like a case of stage fright today," said our announcer. He was
starting to sound somewhat resigned. Everyone on board was getting

impatient—like, we've sailed forty-five minutes out here already—where the hell are the whales? And some people said how could we be so unlucky? It was only something like one trip in a hundred that there weren't any sightings. And other people said clearly the whales were out here but they didn't want to show themselves. And then one big guy with an aloha shirt that was too small for him, and the buttons were straining against his belly—he said the whale-watching cruises were guaranteed, and we'd all get our money back if we didn't actually see any whales.

But this other guy said, "You don't get your money back. You just get tickets for another cruise. And if you read the fine print," this guy said—and he opened up his brochure—"dolphins count as a whale sighting."

"No way!" I said, pretending to be scandalized.

"Yup," he said. And he said it so smugly—like, I have looked into the heart of this scam.

There we all were, maybe fifty people on this little boat idling in the ocean—and somewhere in the distance, or deep down where we couldn't see, those whales were hiding. Everyone was milling around, and people were starting to get grumpy. We were starting to sound mutinous. And I was standing near the bow of the boat with Wayne, and I was staring at the water, and I got kind of quiet. I looked down at the green sea, wistfully, as in, Just my luck. As in, A watched ocean doesn't boil. I stared and stared. "I can see how you wouldn't want to reveal yourself."

"What?" said Wayne behind me.

"I was just mumbling," I told him. I leaned over the side of the boat. I sent my thoughts down into the water: "I can see how you wouldn't want to come up with all these people around. Why should you? It's crass. It's worse than that. It's the descendants here of the folks who killed your ancestors. What a sick little world." But I was also thinking, Please, please come. I was thinking, Whale, please show your face here, because we need you. We do. I was thinking, Please, whale, come out, because there are some people here who miss your presence. There are people out here on this boat who can't even imagine staying under water for twenty minutes at a stretch. There are people here who can barely hold their breaths at all, and, honestly we are surface dwellers. We like our dolphins in tanks, and our birds in aviaries. We're very trivial. Yet we have so much respect for you when it occurs to us. Whale, I kept thinking, please come.

Then I saw them. Two clouds coming up from underneath the sea, and they were two whales, big ones, and they came up like these black clouds from underneath, enormous but swift, from right under the boat. And suddenly everyone was on top of me and Wayne; they were pushing and squishing us against the railing, and there were cameras and the announcer was talking, but I didn't even notice. I was just about flattened there against the rail and Wayne was somewhere, but I'd forgotten about him. The shadows were melting back under the water.

Then one whale came back. The whale's flukes began to lift. Our boat was still. The whole vessel was frail next to her. She was massive as a building, and almost close enough to touch. In a rush her flukes came up. Our boat rocked backward. It was as if the whole ocean slid back for an instant, the surface of the water sliding off and opening as that tail reached and tipped itself. It was as if the whole ocean was sliding open. And I saw something there. The world was big, not little. The place was deep. The sky swung back in liquid gold, the air mixed with the water. I saw something. It was a whale, but not just the whale. It was a vision. It was a vision of God.

I was shivering, just in pure terror; just in shock—because all of a sudden I'd seen it—all the power under the world, all this presence and wisdom that wasn't human.

"Sharon!" Wayne was calling to me. "Sharon, are you okay, hon?"

I was just looking and looking at the green ocean. The whale was gone.

"Get off of her. Get off!" Wayne was yelling. He was shoving people back away from me—just peeling people off me and the railing. And I remember feeling grateful to him for doing that. I remember it occurring to me briefly that it was very sweet of him—but I was already in a completely different place.

AT first Wayne thought this vision was just a passing thing with me—a bad reaction to the crowds and the choppy water. Just a serious case of seasickness on the boat. But days and weeks went by—and I was still dazed. I wouldn't go out anymore. No dinners, no movies, no more Kailua Drive-in. No more bar-hopping in Waikiki. I wouldn't even sleep with Wayne anymore.

Wayne tried to be patient with me, but I was not back to my old self. I was just not the same. Two months later we went for a walk on the beach. It was a moonlit night and we walked along, and I tried to explain it to him. I pointed out to sea, all the way out to the horizon, where the ocean slipped over the edge of the world. I pointed to that place and said, "Wayne, I saw a vision of God there."

"What do you mean, a vision of God? What does that mean?" he kept asking.

"I can't explain it," I said. "I saw Him."

"How long is this going on for?" he asked me.

And that made me mad. "What do you mean, going on for?" I said. "What? Do you think I'm coming off a bad trip or something? You think I have a cold?"

Wayne yelled back at me, "What's your point?"

"I don't *know*! Stop bothering me so I can find *out*!" I stomped off.

He ran right after me. Sand sprayed up against our legs. He grabbed me and he wouldn't let me go, which ordinarily would have frightened me, but I looked into his face and I had no fear at all. A jealous boyfriend was all I saw. A guy I'd been with at one time. That was it.

"I saw God, and I'm going to find Him," I said. "I'm going to search and search until I find Him again. I'm going to look everywhere. Every single place there is."

He started shaking me. "Snap out of it! Snap out of it! Who do you think you are, Joan of fricking Arc?"

And I started laughing at him. I couldn't help it. He was so helpless there with me, like a kid with a broken toy, shaking me, trying to make me work again.

He pushed me as hard as he could. The sand burned as I fell. My hair fell all around my face and I just lay there in a heap. "Don't *ever* laugh at me."

"Okay," I said. "I'm sorry," I said. "Wayne, I'm so sorry."

He came over to me. He helped me up, and I put my arms around his neck. "Wayne," I told him. "It's not personal. It's nothing about you. You were great—don't get me wrong—and I'm sorry all of a sudden . . . it's just that—it's like all of a sudden I'm not available anymore—not through my own choice. It's not that at all. It's just all of a sudden I see—I *know.* . . ."

"You're breaking up with me," he said. His voice was sullen and at the same time desolate.

"I'm sorry. I'm so sorry. I don't want to," I told him.

"Sharon. You're making me crazy! You can't tell me this stuff. It doesn't make sense. You're breaking up with me, but you don't want to? Then who's making you? What're you, listening to voices in your head? Hearing God talking to you? The whale is telling you what to do? *What?*"

"All I know is I saw Him. I know He's out there, and I've got to find Him." I kept saying that, over and over.

"Why?" Wayne asked. "Why?"

"It's just—when you see Him, even for one second—you have to get back to Him again."

I didn't just break up with Wayne, I changed everything else in my life as well. New house. New job. The works. My new place was a room in a house with a couple of guys, Baron and Thad—who everyone called T-Bone. I'd met them at some zoology parties years before. They were not zoologists, but they were partiers, that's for sure. They were two extremely big, basically decent yet rowdy local guys. Baron was a former football player—he'd been kicked off the university team, the Rainbow Warriors. He was heavy now—out of shape and depressed about it. He was trying to get into music and his dream was to start a band, except he wasn't very musical. T-Bone, however, was a comer. He lifted weights, and was a player in the bodybuilding scene. He had a girlfriend named Christina, who was lifting too. The two of them, when they were together, they bounced when they walked.

Baron and T-Bone were a little wild at times, but also generous and open-minded. When I said I was on a quest for God, they said okay. When I wanted to adopt a cat, they told me no problem. So I brought home a kitten an Ecuadorian grad student named Miguel had found at the university. Just a little black fluff ball with white feet, and he was so soft and sweet. But after a few months he grew into a black slinky outdoor teenage cat, and he went out at night and fought all the neighbor cats, and it turned out he wasn't cuddly at all, yet he was my new companion. I named him Marlon, after Brando. All the neighbors hated him. You could hear him screaming at night.

Our neighborhood had bungalow homes with teensy tufty mondo grass lawns in front and borders of hedges manicured every day by these older Japanese couples, mostly second generation off the sugar plantations. However, our place was not exactly manicured. It had once been

used for cockfighting and then boarded up by the cops, and then converted into a rental. The bugs were plentiful, but, given my experiences,
to me it was no big deal. The house swayed a little in the breeze, since it
was mostly termite eaten. Baron and T-Bone went to school some days
and sold restricted substances on others. Yet when I moved in with
them I barely ever took a hit. There I was, searching for God, and caring
for Marlon, and it wasn't as if I had a lot of time for smoking dope.

I got my new job through Geoffrey Wong's fiancée, Julie Liu, whose
aunt and uncle owned Paradise Jeweler in Ala Moana Shopping Center.
And one of the main reasons I took the job was that Mr. and Mrs. Liu
were very religious! They were, in fact, evangelical. At the store the Lius
would stop everything they were doing just to talk to me about the Lord.
They were always open to discussion. They got me my own copy of the
New Standard Annotated Bible to study and mark up, and they invited me
to pray with them whenever I wanted to, and also to go to their church.
Telling it now, it sounds a little bit wrong, like mixing church and state—
me praying with my new employers. Yet at the time I couldn't get over it.
Just when I was looking for divinity, this highly spiritual couple was look-
ing for a salesperson! It was like all along they'd been waiting for me.

I had been to church a couple of times before with Kekui, but the Lius
had a different house of worship. They went to a place in Manoa called
the Greater Love Salvation Church, which was a Pentecostal millenarian
revivalist congregation. The gist of the church was there was no greater
love for mankind than that of Jesus our savior, and he chose to die for us
in order to save us. But since there was still sin in the world he was coming back. He could be coming any day, so we had to get ready, because
when he arrived there would be an Armageddon and a rapture, and those
who were saved would rise up on eagle's wings, and those who were not
would go straight down the chute to hell. I admitted up front I was skeptical about these concepts of the faith, but the Lius were fine with that.
The idea was that someday I'd get so bowled over, I'd get the big picture
all at once. It would be like a circuit of the philosophy of Jesus and my vision of God. The two would click, and zap. I'd get the charge, and then,
like one of those gilded roaches, there would be no looking back.

The Lius' Pastor McClaren loved to preach and read from his scripture
that he'd selected for the day and extemporize and tell anecdotes about
what he'd seen and heard during the week. He had a big cross, maybe five

feet high, hanging up above him, and a smaller one on his lectern, and a cross on his robe, and he had about two hundred people filling the pews of the funny old cement-block building. Little kids passed around polished monkeypod wood bowls to take collection, and Mr. and Mrs. Liu used to sit with me and look up front with their gentle faces, and Geoffrey and Julie used to sit together holding hands. As for me, I sat on the edge of my pew. I was on tenterhooks. I was just trying so hard—not so much to understand, but to believe. I was very ignorant, so a lot of times I didn't get down beneath the beauty and the poetry of what the pastor said. I only perceived the surface, and the shape of the words, rather than all the connotations he was assuming everyone knew. The rapture, for example, didn't have a lot of technical meaning for me, but just sounded very sexy. Sort of like Christ and the Church finally getting back together after they'd been apart so long. I was reading in my annotated Bible the Lius had given me, and I'd found this Song of Solomon, which the annotations said was all about Christ and His Church being lovers. And the Church was this beautiful virginal girl who had taken up with all these men who weren't good for her, but just the same, she ran everywhere searching for Christ who had been her first love, and better for her than anyone she'd been with since. And that really touched me, having this whole ballad with these two beings, the Church and Christ, who longed for each other constantly and searched for each other, and just so wanted that rapture of being together again. "Oh that I could kiss your lips; your lips are sweeter than wine" or "Oh that his left hand were under my head, and his right hand embracing me!"

Music was the high point of the service. There wasn't any choir or organ, but everybody sang the hymns. All that harmony was soothing after a sermon where you had to seriously get your head around Ezekiel's wheels with wings and wheels with eyes and everything spinning, so that picturing the scene just about blew your mind.

I had so much trouble with the concepts that the Lius wanted me to take formal instruction from Pastor McClaren and also to join their Bible study group. So I did. I appreciated it that they were trying so hard to mentor me, even though I didn't have the understanding to start moving toward conversion. I hadn't heard Jesus speak to me yet, but the Lius weren't worried, since they relied on faith. I wasn't worried either. Not yet, anyway. My vision was still fresh in my mind. And in terms of religions I was just starting to look at my options!

8

—

Revival

Quite often in Greater Love I would feel it—this greater love shining down upon me from the Bible study class and the altar and the cross overhead. This gentle warmth would fill me—the whole idea of gentleness and mercy; and I could feel just a brush of this incredibly tender holy spirit that wasn't far away or out there at all, but dwelt in me, in my own personal tabernacle—my heart. And I would leave Saturday-night Bible study with my Bible in my arms and I'd step out into the Hawaiian winter night, which was so mellow and warm, and I'd walk along, and my whole being would be relaxed and happy, and I'd take the bus home to Kaimuki humming hymns. But then when I got to my house there would be cars packed together all along both sides of the street, and the house would be rocking and shaking. There'd be another party going on, and the whole place streaming with Baron and T-Bone's friends, and their friends' friends, and their acquaintances. And, it wasn't as if I didn't enjoy a party, but right after Bible study it was not the atmosphere I was looking for.

Having envisioned God and moved, and started a new job and all, I have to admit, all of that got old pretty quick. Now I felt this longing to move again! Up and go to Molokai, or Walden, or Inisfree! Or west, to the western islands. To go somewhere with no boomers and woofers vibrating the floor at night, and no gold earrings to sell. To go off alone—or even better to go off alone with someone. Except who would that be? It was kind of self-defeating to keep thinking of Brian.

A lot of times I just stood around at work and sighed. "I wish I could go somewhere just to be with my thoughts," I told Mrs. Liu at the store.

"Somewhere you can pray," she said.

"Yes!" I burst out. I flung myself down on the counter. "Where I can pray in peace."

"Not on glass," she chided. I was always leaning against those glass jewelry cases, and Mrs. Liu was always wiping off the smudges. The Lius were very neat. Mr. Liu wore aloha shirts, and Mrs. Liu wore cotton muumuus, but they were always pressed.

"You need a retreat," Mrs. Liu said.

"I *wish*."

"Our Father," she murmured, "please make Sharon a retreat."

"Amen," I said.

Then the very next day, boom! With that kind of beginner's luck that people sometimes have when they first start praying for things—I got this great opportunity! It happened like this. I strolled by the Women's Studies Program to see Corinne, and there I ran into the psych prof Margo who used to tip me off on gigs at the medical school where you could be examined or studied for extra cash, and she started telling me about her Mind-Body-Spirit Exploration Seminar, which she and her husband, Harrison, held at Christmastime as an annual couples' retreat. See, Margo and Harrison were scholars who didn't feel totally fulfilled in the ivory tower. Every year they organized this great big workshop for couples about self-realization in relationships. They had actually written a book, *Our Partners, Ourselves,* and this was their chance to open up their research to the community. They had about one hundred couples coming out between Christmas and New Year's, for a teaching and learning vacation, a vacation exploration where couples could relax at the Hilton Hawaiian Village and swim and watch the hula shows and eat, drink, and be merry and have the time of their lives, but also have an opportunity to learn about each other and grow together, and basically just remember what they saw in each other in the first place and catch up on where they were now at. But the program had grown so successful that Margo could use some help. So she told me I could man the registration desk and be a troubleshooter. For this they would *pay* me, while I was participating and learning as much as I wanted about how to realize myself and enhance my relationships, et cetera! So of course, I saw immediately that this was not exactly what Mrs. Liu had been praying for, but it wasn't too far off either! I signed on.

ROLLING up to the hotel in tour buses, the one hundred couples looked a lot older than I'd expected, and tireder, which was understandable, since they'd been on long flights. They got out where Margo and Harrison and I stood to greet them; and they looked like moles blinking in the sunlight, surprised out of their winter slumbers. We had to guide these folks along and help them through the shops that fringed the bottom of the hotel and into the hotel proper, all beige stucco and adorned by a mosaic rainbow.

The main thing about this hotel was it had its own lagoon carved from the beach and enclosed with cement pylons topped with lava rocks to look more natural. There were guaranteed no waves inside that lagoon. Still, it was pretty in a greenish way. And when I saw my room, man, I wasn't disappointed. It was a far cry from the hotel I'd stayed in when I first got to Hawaii. There was a dresser with a television, and a bathroom with towels. There were two queen-size beds, just for me! There was even a balcony looking out on the ocean. I'd come up in the world! At least temporarily.

Then there was the food. We had these buffet dinners that were part of the package deal, and there were salads, and beets, and steamed asparagus, and potatoes au gratin, and cauliflower, and did I say soup? and fish in cream sauce, and spicy chicken wings, and broiled tomatoes topped with bread crumbs, and then right at the end of the line, there was roast beef carved by a chef, and you could get this humongous slab, only there wasn't any space left on your plate to put it, so the chef would have to lay it right on top. I was in heaven. At breakfast the next morning we had omelets and bacon and hash browns in silver dishes covered with silver domes on top, and glazed pastries, and toast cut in triangles that came prebuttered. I ate as much as my skinny bod could hold. I could have stayed all day at breakfast, but we had to start the morning session.

Everyone trooped into the Prince Kuhio Ballroom, which was set up with these lovely yet quite uncomfortable gilt chairs. Margo and Harrison presided at a table with a white skirt.

"Aloha," Margo said.

"Aloha," said everybody.

"You can do better than that," she said. *"Aloha!"*

"Aloha!" said everybody.

"Now one more time. ALOOOOOHA!"

"ALOOOOOHA!"

"Welcome to Hawaii," Margo said. "And welcome to the first day of the rest of your lives together."

Everyone applauded.

Then Harrison gave the introduction on the Body, Mind, Spirit triangle, which led to the day's first Our Partners Ourselves exercise.

"Body. Mind. Spirit," Harrison said. He was tall and originally southern, although he'd lived in Hawaii for years. He just had a little bit of a southern accent left, so his voice had sort of a soft center. He was actually a little younger than Margo, I think, and he had a lot of brown hair, and a moustache and deeply sympathetic brown eyes. Even in his aloha shirt you could picture him as some kind of Civil War cavalryman. He was really a very handsome man. The women in the group totally responded to him. "When we love," Harrison said, "what do we love? Do we love the whole person? For what they truly are? Or are we attracted to one facet? Are we attracted to one side of the triangle? And if it is one side, then which side is it? Can we truly identify which is the single part we've come to see?"

Body, I thought, somewhat ruefully, since that was the facet Wayne and I had got stuck on. I was standing there on the sidelines, in my dress that I had worn for the occasion, which was one of those tank-top T-shirt dresses; basically a tank top that extended down to the floor, and was the color of orange sherbet.

"Pass out the affirmations," Harrison told me. "Yoo hoo, Sharon?"

All of a sudden I woke from my reverie and passed out all the photocopied affirmations. And I thought, "Please" would be nice. I thought, Jeez. But I did understand that Harrison had to focus on trying to get these folks to rethink their whole entrenched attitude about each other. "Turn toward your partner," Harrison instructed. "Look at each other. Really look. Look as if you are seeing each other for the first time." And he turned toward Margo and he took her hand and looked deeply into her eyes.

So everyone turned toward his or her partner. For a long long time everyone looked deeply into each other's eyes. Then a few minutes passed. Then a few more. People couldn't help stealing some looks up front, but Harrison hadn't moved. He was still gazing at Margo. So everyone kept on gazing, and some people took each other's hand. And some people tried to hold both hands, but then they had to put their affirmations on their laps, so they settled for just one hand the way Harrison did it.

And Harrison read, "When I love you, I love the whole you."

"When I love you, I love the whole you," the couples echoed back.

"Not just part of you, but all of you."

"Not just part of you, but all of you."

Then Harrison paused for another long pregnant pause. There was actually a beautiful silence in the ballroom, and I looked up at the modern chandelier and saw it throwing these neat prism rainbows on the walls, and I looked at the carpet and saw the pattern was hibiscus flowers, bloodred flowers and green leaves. What startled me was suddenly Harrison broke the silence and said in this firm, yet totally loving and compassionate voice, "You are a hole."

"You are a hole," the husbands and wives said to each other.

And I thought, Huh? Because I'd handed out all the affirmation sheets and hadn't kept one for myself. But what I found out later was they were all saying, "You are a whole."

All around the room, the husbands and wives were gazing at each other so earnestly. I tried to imagine gazing at anyone that way. Just knowing anyone that well—so you'd look and look and you'd never burst out laughing. I looked from one couple to the next and they were all perfectly serious, and their eyes so earnest—tender and unblinking. It was such a landscape of commitment I felt like I'd traveled to a completely different place. The Land of Eyes.

Working in small groups turned out to be the killer. Once talking was permitted again, peace, serenity, and wordless love went out the window. Three to four couples clustered their chairs together and discussed the values Margo put out to them, and I had to walk around and not just hand out supplies, but comfort people as well, because the rules were everyone had to be totally honest—so naturally that opened up some floodgates. Like, for example, when they had to work with these open-ended statements that began, "Sometimes I feel . . ." and one wife would say, "Sometimes I feel like a maid," or something like that. And then there would be countercharges and recriminations and lots of tears, and I'd have to help with hugging. There was so much honesty in that room that Harrison and Margo couldn't spread themselves around fast enough. At one point I thought there was a pair that was going to come to blows. It was a case where it got to be the husband's turn and he was this ornery old guy and he said to his wife right there in front of his small group, his face getting redder and redder, "Sometimes I feel that you make me come to these things to punish me." And he got up and said he was going to walk out.

And his wife, whose name was Barbara, started screaming bloody murder and pulling him back, and then he turned on her and yelled into her face. "Damn it all, I'm getting some fresh air!"

And Barbara said to the small group, "You see the way he talks to me?" and she was crying.

Margo came over and she knelt down next to Barbara and I handed out the tissues, and Margo told Barbara we had to let John, who was the husband, go and have some cooling-off time, and that this had happened before, but there wasn't any reason to panic, because it was just that the emotions were sometimes so strong. Sharon would be a stand-in for John, and Barbara should take all the time she wanted and vent to me.

So I ended up having to play the part of John for a therapeutic exercise. And I had to listen to Barbara vent at me for half an hour and I couldn't say a word, because those were the rules. And I mean, I tried not to take it personally, but I couldn't say a thing to defend myself while this woman hurled invective and curses on my head!

THE next morning I got up real early, just around dawn, and I put on my new bikini, which was crocheted of turquoise string. I took a bath towel and my suntan lotion and padded down to the beach. The only guy down there was a Filipino groundsman who was raking the sand. I spread my towel and lay down on my stomach and just zoned with my eyes closed. Not exactly asleep, but at rest, and with my mind free of voices, I listened to all the little early-morning sounds. The mynah birds calling to each other, and the rumbling sound of the ice machine at the poolside bar. I was actually almost in a meditative state when suddenly freezing cold drops of water started falling on my legs. "Hey!" I yelled. I looked over and saw Harrison standing there in his wet swim trunks. "You're dripping on me!"

"Oh, I'm sorry." Harrison stepped back and dried off and shook himself like a wet dog.

"How's it going?" he asked me.

"Well," I said, "the small groups were rough, but they made me reflect a lot."

"On what?" he asked.

"Just on life. Just the way two spirits can drift apart. How can you avoid that? When your soul is going one place and your partner's soul is off somewhere else? It's communication, right? That's the key."

He'd knelt down next to me, and I guess he was looking at my back, because he said, "I can see exactly how far you could reach with the lotion."

"Really?" I had a thing about getting an even tan. I had my bikini top untied so I wouldn't have a line across my back.

"You can see on your back how far your fingertips could stretch," he said. So then just to help out he rubbed on some more lotion, and I guess at the time I thought he was doing a pretty thorough job, but what's some Tropic Sun between friends? He gave me a pretty terrific back rub.

"Wow," I said, and I propped myself up on my elbows, and I said, "You're good!" and that was when he slid his hands around the front of me, and to my breasts. And I said, "Whoa!" because I didn't know what to think—I mean, not being a prude in any way or feeling uncomfortable with my body, or with his, but in the context of the situation, I have to say a little warning bell went off inside my brain. I said, "Um. Harrison! Um. Wait!" and I pushed him off and flopped down with my chest against the towel and said, "Don't you see just a little tiny contradiction here? Since we're here like counseling married people? I mean, since you and your wife are here doing that?"

And then, you aren't going to believe this. He laughed at me. And that really pissed me off. And I just stood right up and wrapped my towel around me, and picked up my bikini top and my lotion and I said to him, "Harrison, you'd better apologize."

And he said in his southern velvety yet ever so slightly mocking voice, "Sharon, I'm deeply sorry."

And I looked at him and I said, "Yeah, well, you really are a hole." But I don't think he got it.

Of course, I was going to tell Margo, but frankly, this being her husband we were talking about, I was worried about how she'd take it. She might believe him over me if he denied the incident; or she might just turn on me, assuming the whole thing had to be my fault. So I just thought very briefly about running to Margo. I admit, I wanted badly to get paid for my week's work, and that was mercenary. I felt like a worm. And a disillusioned worm at that! Because I mean, what was really going on here? What was happening at this so-called workshop? We had this couple of so-called counselors in front, a lecherous male sociologist, and a psychology prof—who was also a clinical psychologist on the side—and these guys had either some pretty major deceptions going on in their marriage, or some massive cynical scam going on, I didn't know which. Then there were all these people from the Mainland who'd read the book and had come out here to learn from these total marriage gurus. And suddenly I began to wonder, as I walked around holding people's hands and passing out dittos and values-clarification worksheets, was I participating in a genuine attempt at understanding that was actually leading people somewhere? Or was I actually engaged in highway robbery? I couldn't figure it out at all. The only slightly encouraging thing was that about three quarters of the couples seemed to be really making strides in the togetherness arena.

By Saturday night when we had the luau and evening show, a lot of the couples—with some notable exceptions like Barbara and John, who were barely on speaking terms—were sitting at their tables under the tiki torches, and touching each other, and making eye contact, and even wearing matching outfits they'd bought. Muumuus and short-and-shirt cabana sets all made out of the same wild aloha-wear material. Brown-and-green block print designs. Or white and orange. So they weren't just husbands and wives vacationing together; they were like theme couples. And I couldn't help looking at all of them and noticing that I was alone, not even part of a dysfunctional pair. I couldn't imagine any boyfriend of mine, not even Wayne, wearing matching clothes with me, let alone holding my hands and making goo-goo eyes at me at a luau. The hands, maybe, *or* the eyes. But not both. Did Brian ever do all this stuff with Imo? I'd never seen the two of them stare deeply at each other. Of course, why would they do that in front of me? Brian was far too sensible, and Imo—I just couldn't picture her melting at all. She was way too prickly. Still, they had each other, in ways I'd never know.

At the buffet I stood in line behind Harrison and watched his back. I'd come to the retreat so optimistic, but now I felt like the only one without a date at the prom, or like some modern-day Cinderella in a story where Prince Charming would be happy to feel you up. The end.

I loaded up my plate and ate like a pig. I tried to cheer up, since the food was so good. I drank a couple of chi-chis. Just slurped them up like milkshakes. But then lights went down for the show. Tears pricked my eyes. This luau show was the one Kekui had worked when he was putting himself through college as a fire-eater. And I thought I'd been lonely then, losing Kekui to his mom and his girlfriend and his whole extended family. But now, sitting there with all the married couples and the luau feast glowing in the light of all those citronella candles—now I could have put on my own workshop in the art of loneliness. I was so sad. And I was so angry at myself for coming on the retreat in the first place, thinking it might be some sort of twofer: learning plus a resort vacation; contemplation together with all that extra cash. If I'd come with someone else we would have laughed. The whole thing might have been an adventure, or at least a humorous scam. Alone, I couldn't help noticing that my motives were crummy, and the whole retreat so phony—despite the sincerity of the couples in it. I put down my drink. And that was when it hit me. God was not here. On the whale-watching boat I'd felt his presence. In the water I'd sensed him, through the ocean and the whale, through my own imagination. But not here. So I skipped out to catch the Upper Manoa bus. I figured I'd go hear the message at Greater Love.

This was in the days when the Saturday-night services at Greater Love Salvation Church were just beginning. Pastor McClaren got the idea, I think, from the popularity of the Easter sunrise service, where the congregation would stay up all night praying, almost in a vigil, and then celebrate Christ's rising with the sun. Well, once a month McClaren had a service at night that was really for the young bloods in the congregation, and for the people with potential who had not yet been saved, like me. And in fact he called it his revival service. There was a fervency about it that was just catching. Everyone prayed harder, and everyone sang louder, and everyone stayed longer too. I had come once before at night, and been moved by the experience, and especially the singing and the stomping. Still, that time before was nothing like this night when I came in, because this time I was aching in my heart.

There was a crowd inside—more people than I'd ever seen in church. There weren't even enough seats for everyone and I had to stand in the back, because it turned out Pastor McClaren was doing a special Christmas-week sermon. McClaren was standing up in front at the pulpit and he was already speaking, and not from notes, not once looking down, just preaching and exhorting, as if he were inspired. His eyes were just shining behind his wire-rimmed glasses. Our pastor McClaren was a local guy, despite his name. He was Scotch-Irish-Hawaiian-Japanese-Portuguese, and he had dark skin and longish straight black hair, and Oriental eyes, and a sharp hook nose that along with his glasses gave him a scholarly look. I stood in the back, and I craned my neck, because a lot of other people were standing too. But the craziest thing was, as he spoke, he wasn't just talking to the group, all those maybe three hundred people crowding around at his feet and up the aisles and in the back—no, he was actually talking directly to me. It was like he was saying, "Sharon! Listen up!" Of course he didn't really use my name, but he spoke to me.

Pastor McClaren was saying, "Why? Why do we spend our time involved with things that are not right? Why do we spend all our days around people who are not people of God? Why? There's a very simple reason, and his name is Satan. Now, you folks say to yourselves, 'Not! Satan neva' live on my shoulder. Satan neva' live ova' here. Satan is some kine haole guy.'" Everybody chuckled, hearing Pastor speak in pidgin. "'He live over dere, bra. He live on da Mainland, far away from here.'"

The pastor paused. Then he asked, "Now, where does Satan live fo' real? Right over here, man. Right on top of you and me. He's living right here on our shoulders, and you know what he does every day? He whispers to you and me what isn't right. He goes, 'Eh, no worry, no worry—tomorrow won't nevah happen, man. Eh, lie down, go sleep some mo'. Christ's Kingdom nevah gonna come.' Or he goes, 'Jus' make some money, man, jus' get me some good food and some wine. Jus' make me feel good, man. Jus' go eat and drink and have one good time.'

"Now, who here in this room has heard Satan's voice?" McClaren asked, and you better believe I, and everybody else, too, raised our hands. "And who here felt like it was wrong, but couldn't stop listening?" I had to raise my hand. "And did you ever feel like you were all alone at the mercy of your desires?" McClaren asked.

It was just something about that question, just the way he put it. That
was what set me off. That was where I started crying. Because it was
true. I really felt how true it was. That was me, just a bundle of desires,
and all for myself, all about me and what I wanted at the moment,
whether it was food, or guys, or what have you. I was all alone. I was
wandering all alone thinking only about myself and hardly anyone else
in life except if that person was someone I could use, just a floor to
sleep on or a pair of arms or sympathetic ears.

It was like McClaren could read my mind. He asked me, "Do you wish
you had someone to share your troubles, and support you when you fall?"
And then he answered, "Well, you do have someone, and he's coming to
get you; he's coming to lift you up, and his name is Jesus, our Lord."

And McClaren told how Jesus had been tempted just like all of us,
from his childhood on. He'd chosen to live in this world of ours, even
though he didn't have to. And he'd felt all the pleasure and the pain, so
he knew exactly what each one of us was going through. And he'd even
been tempted in the desert by food, and drink, and sex, and been tested
by every delicacy Satan could devise, but he'd triumphed over all of
them by his spirit. And he'd been persecuted and even killed, but still he
triumphed over all of that and rose above it. Nobody had forced him to
live a human life, but yet he did anyway for our sakes. And now he was
gearing up to come back again, and when he arrived, just the breath of
Jesus was going to make all the world's sinners shrivel up and writhe in
agony, just one little move, and the sinful ones of the earth would be
blown away into everlasting punishment. But the good and virtuous
were going to zoom straight up to heaven. And you'd better believe
Christ would know which was which, and who was set to go where.
He and all the angels behind him would see into every heart, and to
every heart that was pure he would say, "Follow me!"

"Do you feel alone?" the pastor asked. "You *are* alone, because you
are not yet saved. Do you feel lonely? You *are* lonely because you are not
consecrated to your Lord. But did you know this? You are the one Jesus
loves most. Did you know? You are the one, the lonely one, the alone
one, the person without a friend. The man who has no one to lean on.
The woman who has lost her way. The person who has no home. Jesus says, 'I am the one for you to lean on. I am the way, the Truth, and
the Life. I am your guide. I am the one who will lead you home.'

"Come home," Pastor McClaren said, "come home." And it was the strangest thing, but this woman from about the middle of the church got up and walked forward right to the pulpit, and she knelt down and Pastor McClaren put his hands on her head, and she rose up and her whole face was lit up smiling. More people started to come forward, and they got in line to kneel down, and more and more. And it wasn't a big crazy moment where they jumped up and screamed and yodeled, "I'm healed! I can see!!" or anything like that, but it was just this moment where they knelt down. And Pastor McClaren said, "Do you accept Jesus Christ as your personal savior?" and they said, "I do!" And so they received His love through their shepherd, just like the sheep coming gently into their fold to stay. And there was this feeling in me—this unbelievable longing that made me want to go up there and kneel down and receive Jesus too—but I was afraid, and I did not. I just stood there where I was, and I watched everyone and my eyes were full of tears, because it was right, what our pastor said; it was true. It was the most true comment on my own issues that I'd ever heard. But still something held me back, and maybe inside I thought I wasn't good enough to receive the blessing, being maybe tainted by the past several days, and all the marriage counseling Sinner Harrison had been giving out, while I assisted, egged on by my desires for free food. So my eyes were full of tears; I was practically sobbing, but I couldn't move.

The people kept on coming up, until at last it seemed like Pastor McClaren had blessed everyone, and he got out his hymnal, but before he opened it, he said, "There are some of us who feel ourselves unworthy. There are some of us who wish we could come to the front to receive the Lord's blessing, but Satan has beaten them down, so they cannot rise. They listen, and they want to draw near to your presence, O Lord, but when the time comes—at the last minute—they say, 'Eh, I go stay here. I no stay go.' Jesus, help them to receive your blessing, help them to feel your touch. For they are like dead people, and yet in your eyes, the dead awaken. They are like prisoners, and yet in your hands the prisoners are set free. Dear Jesus, give them the gift of your love; extend to them your tender mercy. With your power *revive their souls*."

And when he said that, he set me free. My feet moved; my lips opened. "Excuse me; excuse me," I said. I got over to the aisle, and I walked forward and the people hushed around me, and patted me and nodded to me as I went on, and the lectern and Pastor McClaren blurred, because there were such tears in my eyes, but I sank down on my knees in front of him. The pastor said, "Do you accept Jesus Christ as your personal savior?" And he put his hands on top of my head and I felt a thrill shudder through me.

I felt something; I really did. It was an electric thrill right through his fingers all the way down to the tips of my hair, and all the way down my spine. I felt all that mercy and all that love just surge through me, and I said, "Yes!" and I said "Yes!" again. I said, "Yeah!!!" And I said, "Yippee!"

And when I stood up and I backed to the side to sing, it was "Amazing Grace," and there were the Lius, and Julie, and Geoffrey, standing there in the second pew, just beaming and shaking their heads, having prayed for me so long. And everyone was so happy in that church our voices lifted up to heaven, and all my tears of guilt turned into tears of joy.

And I'd heard the expression before of walking on air, but this was the real thing, because when I left that church, my feet were so springy that as I walked, they barely touched the ground. It was like my head had floated up and my neck had gone all long and slender like a giraffe's so my face was a little giraffe face up there, bending and bobbing in the breezy night air. And I walked all the way back from Manoa to Waikiki, back to the hotel in the darkness, and smelled the flowers and just caressed the whole world with my eyes. The soft round beauty of the monkeypod trees, and the mock orange bushes, and all the plants, and the pure white never-cracked-by-ice sidewalk under my sandal feet. I got to Waikiki, and the lights of the hotels and the bars didn't faze me, not in the least, and police were speeding down Hotel Street, but I didn't even notice. It was as if I'd been dancing all the way from church back to the Hilton Hawaiian Village. It was as if I was waltzing away down Kuhio Avenue, and I waltzed into the hotel and took the elevator up to my floor and waltzed some more around my room. And then I got onto one of the queen-size beds and I jumped on the bed for joy. And I jumped from that bed to the other and back again and then just leapt up into the air and down, and up, and down, and grazed the little sprinkler heads in case of fire. I jumped and jumped and whirled around, and all of a sudden, for the first time in five years, I was dancing again. I had been reborn.

9

Picking Up the Rug

WELL, I don't know how it happened, but at some point in the night I must have fallen asleep, because the next day I woke up. All of a sudden, not even daybreak, I threw off the covers and sat up just like that. I wasn't dreamy at all, and I got up in the dark, and my feet were right under me loving that soft green hotel carpet. I marched into the bathroom and used the facilities and hopped in the shower. Man, I was starving. I couldn't wait for those omelets and pancakes and pieces of prebuttered toast. Then it hit me, right there with the water streaming down my face. That whole experience, that whole birthing the night before! What was going on? Good grief, what kind of hedonist, selfish, egomaniacal person was I? It was already wearing off! I mean, not even a day, not even twelve hours, and I was back to my breakfast and my hotel carpet, and Satan's creature comfort ways, and I felt like such scum that when I got out of the shower I really expected to look in the mirror and see him—Satan—sitting on my shoulder like the slime bag he was, exhorting me in pidgin. But all I saw was this thin wet girl, bony with her shoulder blades sticking out. This person with dark eyes and long hair and this anxious look on her face. My tan, I realized, actually *was* pretty uneven. So I had to admit Harrison wasn't putting me on about that. But then I shook myself, because, wait, what was I doing—staring at myself in the *mirror*? After my life had been changed? Oh God, oh God!

My first impulse was just to run back to Greater Love as fast as I could and get help. Except it was only around five-thirty in the morning, and Sunday-morning services wouldn't be starting for another four and a half hours. My second impulse was to kneel down and pray. So I did, right on the bath mat, for as long as I could, until I started repeating myself, going in circles. Then I got dressed and read my Bible for half an hour, but I couldn't concentrate, because I was just so incredibly hungry, and the breakfast buffet didn't open until nine, since it was Sunday. I was at my wits' end! So finally, I went out onto my balcony and stood there looking out at the ocean. The sun was rising, in a rosy-tipped dawn, and the water glowing, and the sky all pink and rose and golden orange, like eggs over easy and syrup and French toast. But I made myself focus. I tried some affirmations.

I said, "Lord, dear Jesus, I love you body and soul."

I said, "You are my rock, and my redeemer. My healer and my home."

I said, "You lead me not into temptation. You deliver me from evil."

Then I stood there and wondered if that last one was really an affirmation. Because the thing about affirmations is you aren't supposed to say anything negative in them. That was one of Margo and Harrison's main principles. And "You lead me not into temptation" was sort of negative, because it had "not." But it was one of those tricky biblical phrases where being negative could turn around into a positive thing. I just didn't know. So I scratched that one, and I just said, "You deliver me from evil."

But then for some reason I felt dumb saying that, so I went inside. Because, I mean, how exactly was the Lord going to deliver me from evil? He hadn't ever delivered me before. So all my doubt and skepticism seemed to bubble up to the surface again, not to mention my stomach growling. I paced around my room. I said, "Jesus, sometimes I feel like you aren't there for me."

And I said, "Lord, sometimes I feel like you aren't really listening."

I said, "Jesus, sometimes I think you don't give a damn!"

Then I said, "Sorry."

I said, "Sometimes I feel like I don't know who you are."

I said, "Sometimes I feel like you make yourself unavailable to me."

"Sometimes I feel that you aren't really attentive to *my* needs."

Then I sighed, because, what was the use. What was I trying to do here? Who was I to start up couples therapy with Jesus? Just who did I think I was? Not to mention His issues, being a holy spirit made flesh, and still living with His Father. Trust was the key, right? Trust was the foundation of all relationships. So if I was going to hang on to this relationship I began last night, I was going to have to let go first. If you're really going to trust, you have to give your spouse, or lover, or other, his space. And then once you have space, you can try dialoguing. But how did that work in my situation? I tried and tried to get my mind around it, but in the end I just flopped on the bed, because I was so tangled, I couldn't think straight.

AT the dot of nine I was downstairs in the Ilima Ballroom loading up my plate. A lot of the couples were down there, too, a few of them wheeling suitcases, since they were checking out right after the morning session.

I have to say, that last day of the retreat was pretty good. Maybe Margo and Harrison really did have some insights into relationships. Or maybe my whole rebirth and morning-after thing had swept away my cynicism of the day before. I still don't know, but at that session Margo and Harrison got down to the nitty-gritty. The personal statements and resolutions that everyone had to do two of. 1) *This Is What I Want to Do for Me* and 2) *This Is What I Want to Do for Us.*

Everyone got busy there in the ballroom once brunch was cleared away, and it was a happy busy, not a tense recriminating feeling like there had been in the past. Everyone was writing statements, and then sharing them with their spouses, and also with their whole group of five couples. And there were some statements that were absolutely beautiful. Especially the ones from the older couples. Like: *Dear Harold, This is what I want to do for me: to cherish each moment of every day. This is what I want to do for us: spend each moment of every day with you.* Or just incredibly romantic, like the guy who wrote: *Dearest Betty, This is what I want to do for me: learn how to make you the happiest girl alive. This is what I want to do for us: put that knowledge into practice!*

But, of course, like there always are in any group, there were some people who didn't completely get the assignment. Like the guy who started writing about his long-term childhood dream. *Dear Linda, This is what I want to do for me: take early retirement and apply to Clown College. This is what I want to do for us: go to Clown College with you.* He kind of pissed his wife off when he shared that.

Somehow, though, by the end of the session, when Margo got up and did the closing remarks, people felt really good. And when Margo read some of the statements people had written to the whole assembly, there was a lot of applause, from the participants for each other and for themselves, and a lot of hugging, because really, they had come through this all together.

I distributed dendrobium orchid leis, and sitting at the white-skirted table, Margo and Harrison thanked each other, and everyone gave them a standing ovation. And then Margo and Harrison stood up and clapped for all the participants, so in the end, everyone was giving everyone else an ovation.

We all checked out of the hotel, with me facilitating, and I got paid, and while Harrison was going out front to tell the valet guy to bring their car around, Margo told me I'd done a superduper job and she hoped I'd do it again next year. And that would have been the perfect time for me to speak up about Harrison, but I was still so overwhelmed from being reborn, and now having this weird rejection, or reaction, to the whole experience, that I didn't say anything.

WELL, the next few months a lot of praying went on for me, a lot of concern and pleadings from not only Mr. and Mrs. Liu, and Julie and Geoffrey, but from people I didn't even know—for example, all the people at Greater Love, who even formed a prayer chain on my behalf and united to ask the Lord to bring me back to that holy state where I'd been at for just a few short hours after the revival service. And it wasn't just them, I prayed too; I prayed for my soul, and I studied. I went to Bible study every single day, and I studied on my own at night, and highlighted just about all of the Gospels, as well as Ephesians, and Paul's Epistles in their entirety. I met privately probably five times with Pastor McClaren, and he told me he knew I'd get there, but I wasn't sure. I was in the clutches of this horrible doubt. Because I just couldn't get back

to that feeling I'd had before; that unbelievable feeling of joy and ecstasy. And I'd been so close; it was like I'd finally pushed over the crest of
the hill, and then all of a sudden I'd rolled back to where I was.

One night I poured out my heart to Baron and T-Bone. We were sitting in the living room, and I was in the La-Z-Boy, which was forest-
green Naugahyde with some rips in the back, and I had my feet up on
the footrest and my Bible in my lap. Baron was having a few beers, and
T-Bone was doing a few reps. I said to T-Bone, "Hey, you're Christian,
right?"

"Yeah," T-Bone said.

"And you've been saved, right?"

"I was already saved when I was a baby!" T-Bone said. He curled his
arm, up and down. He was very focused on his biceps.

"How did you do that?"

"I was baptized!"

"Oh," I said. "But it didn't wear off, right?"

"Sharon," T-Bone said, "it doesn't never wear off!"

"You believe?" Baron asked T-Bone from the couch. He sounded
surprised.

"Yeah, I believe."

"Not!" said Baron.

"I'm a Christian," said T-Bone. "What?"

"I don't believe," said Baron sadly.

"How come?" I asked.

"Because," he said, "I feel like Jesus forgot about me."

"He never forgot about you," T-Bone said.

Baron just shrugged. I guess he felt bad because Jesus hadn't come
down and healed him from his injury so he could have a shot at a football career.

"Well, if you're *really* saved, it won't never wear off," T-Bone told me.

"But it just lasted a few hours," I said. "It's just like for a few hours I
was up there and I was flying, and I could see everything so clearly. It
was like my brain was on fire."

"What were you doing?" Baron asked.

"I was in church!" I said. "What do you think I was doing?"

"Coke."

"Oh, c'mon," I told him.

"Eh, Baron's right," T-Bone said. "That's not religion you're talking about."

I said, "Then what is religion?"

"Church," said T-Bone. "Gospels. Catechism."

"What's catechism?"

"You don't know what catechism is?" said Baron, incredulous.

"Just what is it?" I demanded.

And Baron said darkly, "Theology. How else can religions get around without theology?"

Then I sighed. He'd put his finger on it right there. In two seconds Baron had got to the heart of the matter. The thing was, I didn't really get theology. Pastor McClaren had been working and working with me, but it was almost as if my mind didn't go deep enough to understand the theology of Christianity. Pastor McClaren said my faith and God's deliverance would carry me through, but apart from that vision I'd had on the whale watch, and that one rebirth I'd had at Greater Love, my Faith seemed to be nonexistent, and God's deliverance way behind in coming. It was just that coming from such a secular family, and never having any religious instruction as a child, I was so ignorant. The Trinity with the whole three-in-one, one-in-three thing went whoosh right over my head. The more I thought about it all, the more confusing it became. And actually, the truth was, I didn't want to think at all. I just wanted to feel it happen again, God putting out His rays to me, just lighting me up, my soul all charging up with His holy fires. I just wanted to skip right to the ecstasy and the voices, and Saint Joan, and Saint Teresa—as if they hadn't sat and studied *so much* before they could get to the level of sainthood they achieved! But needless to say I was in a rather deluded frame of mind. I was just taking up all these real Christians' time when what I was really after was becoming some kind of dervish, rather than a permanently saved citizen soldier in the on-coming army of Christ. Definitely I was hung up on a lot of the bride-of-Christ imagery I had read, and just being his lover, like in Solomon's song, just having Him come to me in my tent, and wanting it to last on and on. I think I was a little bit mixed up between grace and orgasms.

So the upshot was I spent so much time venting to Baron and T-Bone that they couldn't stand listening to me anymore about wanting to get back there to that place I'd been. "Sharon," Baron said, "you know what your problem is?"

I nodded. "I'm on the verge of—"

"No," said Baron, "you know what your problem really is?"

"What?"

"You need a fix," he said. He looked at T-Bone, and T-Bone agreed.

The guys went into their stash and got me some incredible stuff. But at first I wouldn't accept anything. I said, "No. No. I'm clean."

They said, "Oh, come on."

And I said, "It won't solve anything."

And Baron said, "Oh, yeah?"

And Thad said, in joking pidgin, "Why your brain wen' so uptight?"

Which you had to admit was a lot of my problem, an uptight brain. Still, I told them, "This is the kind of stuff you have to do on your own, guys. This kind of stuff you have to figure out on your own."

"You aren't getting very far by yourself," T-Bone pointed out.

Finally I sat back in my La-Z-Boy and relaxed. I lay back and started dropping acid. Just lay back like that, tripping out. And it was the most amazing thing, because I started to feel all those theological conundrums loosening in my head. It was the most spectacular thing, they were untying themselves and flopping all around me like noodles in soup, and I was watching.

It was just such a show. It was all this light pouring from my inside windows, in all these gorgeous rays—like stained glass, and sectioned pineapples. It was like fireworks gone all soft and juicy. It was like this whole synesthesiatic sound system, because there were so many dimensions to it. I was all of a sudden seeing in stereo all my former preoccupations, so I could taste this incredibly smooth Bible music. O that I could kiss you with my lips. O your lips are sweeter than sunshine! I saw right there in the La-Z-Boy chair leaning back with my feet up and all my neurons set free—I saw all the ideas I'd been struggling over. And I could see them fully. It was like the proscenium arch was crumbling down, and the fourth wall blown away, and I was actually in this theater in the round. And every single person in the audience was in the round, too, because everyone was flies with just hundreds and millions of these lovely iridescent eyes. So of course I saw then that three in one was no biggie at all and actually three in one and one in three was fine, and all the other numbers too. It was just like, hey, any number can go into any other number as many times as she wants.

And I saw loaves and I saw fishes, and all of them multiplying. And I saw my bird teachers—they were there, too, and they were flying upward with their slender beaks and their crimson feet, and actually I realized for the first time what they were, and I couldn't believe it had never occurred to me. But those bird people were actually angels dipping into the wind and sky—and they were laughing, because I'd never noticed before. I'd never seen the glory of their wings.

I laughed, and I cried, and I saw all this wisdom I had inside of me, whole planets in my mind. And I could just taste all the joy I had locked within me, just these big pots and jars that probably for years had been bubbling and simmering, but now had a chance for the first time ever just to jell. I was now for the very first time getting to a place where I could fructify.

And I guess I was in that happy place where there weren't any minutes or hours bugging me, so I can't really put a fix on when I thought of it, but partway in I saw that I had this whole cathedral of spirituality right inside of me. And a little ways farther I could just touch all the abstract problems of theology and they would all melt before me and caress me and want to make love to me. And farther still I came on the biggest, baddest insight I'd ever had, and that was that Jesus Christ the Savior was actually me! And that I, Sharon, was the ultimate incarnation of the whole entire Trinity: Father, Son, and Holy Spirit. I in my womanness and my birdhood. I with my sooty wings. Then that understanding illuminated my soul and I heard the whisper of my own gentleness. I just wanted to touch every one of my creations with my feather tips.

I ended up staying high most of that week, and gave Baron and Thad all my money for the means of doing so, and also slept with them, which didn't bother me at all, because I was so focused on my inner life. But other people I knew were wondering about me, since I wasn't showing up anywhere they expected me to be. Pastor McClaren was trying to get in touch with me, but he never got through. Mr. and Mrs. Liu were

looking for me all over, and in the end did track me down by coming to
the door of the house. And I guess they looked inside when I answered
it, the two of them in their glasses and their cute little clean clothes.
They weren't too thrilled when they saw me, who was supposedly their
employee, and also their candidate for life everlasting. I told them I was
back at the place that I'd been looking for. I tried to reassure them that
I was unbelievably great and that I was on a journey, but inside my
mind. I think if she hadn't been so polite and self-effacing, Mrs. Liu
would have slapped my face.

As it was, she and Mr. Liu told me they would keep praying for me,
which actually really touched me, and made me just reach out to hug
them. But the two of them practically ran down the street past all the
mondo grass lawns. They looked scared to death. Or maybe it was the
smell from the living room.

You know how the back of a bakery smells sometimes, out by the
Dumpsters? Just this rancid smell of spoiled doughnuts, and grease
poured off, and curdled custard. Weird to say, but that was what I got a
whiff of when Mr. and Mrs. Liu turned tail and ran down my street. I
got this little jolt of nausea there, and I went back inside and looked
around our home for a second, and fogged as I was, I thought, Wait. I
thought, Hmm. And a day later I stopped, by which I mean, all the substances I'd been taking, by mouth, and through my skin like an acid-
loving amphibian. I didn't stop because I was sated, but more because
for some bizarre reason I could smell myself, and I reeked. Even now I
couldn't tell you whether it was my conscience kicking in, or just having a good nose.

I took a shower and cleaned myself off, and then I got into a clean
T-shirt and shorts, and tied my hair back, and as best I could, began
cleaning up. I scrubbed the putrid kitchen that we had there, and also
the black mold growing in the bathroom. We didn't own a vacuum
cleaner, so I tried to borrow from our next-door neighbors, but they
were very reserved people and wouldn't open the door. They peeked
out at me with their door opened just a crack. Oh, well, I thought, and
I went home and sat cross-legged on the deep green shag carpet in the
living room, and I picked out the crumbs and specks of dirt and hairs by
hand, until Baron wandered in and wanted to know what the hell I was
doing. "I'm picking up the rug," I said. I still had that aura of heightened

common sense. I was coming down just very gently, like a balloon you bring home that eventually starts sinking down below ceiling level, and then drifts down to the floor, sighing out its helium incredibly slowly, just shrinking and then dimpling up and wrinkling, and getting all soft and finally squishy, like the balloon equivalent of old age.

Around evening of that day I took a walk around the neighborhood. I could smell all our neighbors cooking dinner, but I didn't have my appetite back at all. I tried to think back over the past few months, and I tried to think way back to my rebirth and that joyous feeling I'd experienced. Then, I had to admit it to myself, on drugs, joy felt better—and so did peace and love and hope—at least to me. And I could see by that—anyone could see—I hadn't been saved in Church at all. Because a saved person would never feel that way—closer to her God on acid. When you got down to it, a saved person would never have given up on Christianity's teachings after only a few lessons either. So the truth was, I'd let Jesus down, not to mention letting myself down with my behavior. Essentially, I'd been offered eternal life, and I'd decided to go on roller-coaster rides and see movies continuously and eat Sugar Babies all day instead. So what did that say about me? I was not exactly the worthiest person in the world. Still, it did not once occur to me that God in his wrath would strike me down, or that Jesus would wreak vengeance on me. I just knew they wouldn't. Despite Pastor's teachings I felt, somehow, God and His Son weren't those types of guys. It was true I'd been unfaithful to Jesus, and essentially run out on Him just after we were wed, but jealousy was not Him, not Him at all.

So I was decided about two things. One, I was not saved. Two, that was okay, because that was just not where I was at right now. I was going to find God again, I knew it. Plenty of other options were still out there. If one didn't work, I'd switch. Visions, Bible study, hallucinatory trips. I had a fickle soul, but I couldn't see it that way. The only thing I can compare it to is that time in your life when you'll sleep with anyone, but you think you're doing it because you so believe in love.

10

Speechless

I dedicated myself to cleaning, to the point that our shack of a house was the prettiest it could possibly look without repainting and ripping out the carpeting and furniture, and evicting my housemates. I took wet rags and filled the plastic wastebasket with water for a bucket, and I washed the glass louvers in all the windows. All the gray, linty dust washed away. The water in the wastebasket turned black with dirt. I washed the mirror in the bathroom and then dried it clean and sparkly with pieces of ripped newspapers. I even cleaned out the oven and the stove in the kitchenette, and it turned out they both worked, which was good to know.

Heading back to work at Paradise Jeweler was on the agenda, too, but after a while, cleaning house, I thought, You know what? Better give it a rest, and the theology too. I just didn't want to disappoint any more people, doing all that Bible study and then not going the extra mile. So I got a new job at The Good Earth, which was where I tended to buy my food anyway, and where people knew me, and thought I was a responsible person—I mean, on the day-to-day, if not the religious, level.

The Good Earth smelled like sawdust and wheat germ, and had every kind of vegetable grown organically on the island, and also bins of ancient grains, and refrigerator cases where you could get big blocks of rennetless cheese. There were vitamins, and powders, and protein mixes, and loose teas, and at the register for impulse buys we had honey straws for sucking, and garlic tablets, and carob-coated peanuts, and copies of *The Herbalist*, and *Vegetarian Times*, and *Boycott Quarterly*. I started working there full time at the checkout counter.

My manager, who was a semiprofessional surfer chick named Kim, actually lent me a yogurt maker and I bought yogurt starter and started culturing my own at home, because it occurred to me, maybe I should start working on my diet again. Since it's practically a truism that whenever you clear up your diet you also tend to clear up your mind. And God knows I needed that.

I was still so fogged I didn't know what I believed anymore. I hardly saw any of my friends—and didn't even want to see them really—except I missed them in a hopeless sort of way. I barely had a chance to see Brian, what with his teaching and his marriage and all. I'd trudge to work, and then trudge back home again. On weekends my housemates would be partying away, but I didn't join in. Music and drinking and getting high. None of it mattered to me anymore. In fact, the noise bothered me. At the age of twenty-six I was growing crotchety. Like how dare you party all night when I'm trying to sleep? How dare you trash this place yet again? Instead of a fun little haven, the house seemed to me like a druggy little dump. I felt so world weary. No, that wasn't it. Actually I was afraid the world was weary of me. Could that happen? The world getting so tired of a human that one day it blows her away like a caraway seed? I wouldn't have been surprised. I had imagined that once you have a vision you were set for life. I had thought once you were saved, you were saved. And if you were born again, then you would be better organized than you were the first time. So naturally when it didn't turn out that way I was a little bit disillusioned.

One day while I was at my Good Earth register, I started watching the monks who used to come and deliver lettuce to the store. There were four of them who came every week. They grew hydroponic butter lettuces, and they used to carry them into the store on cardboard flats. Soft green lettuces on pure white stems, their little brown tendril roots like pubic hair. The monks wore orange robes, and they had fuzzy

shaven heads. They were small spry men, although after a while I realized one was a woman. They had this beautiful sexlessness about them.
They looked like local people, tan, and somewhat Oriental, and they always came on the city bus. But the thing I noticed most about them
was that although they murmured to themselves, they did not speak to
each other. They did not even glance at me.

After they left, I couldn't get those monks out of my head. I stood
there ringing up bulgur, and cashew butter, and weighing plantains, and I
imagined the monastery where the monks must live. It would be way
high up in the Ko'olau Mountains, right up there in the crags. And it was
all tile roofs and secret courtyards, like the Hidden Fortress, cloaked with
mist.

I began to wait for the monks to come every week. I'd watch for
them, and when they came, I'd strain my ears, but I never understood
what they were murmuring. I wanted to ask them a million questions. I
wanted to ask them about their lives, and about their devotions, and
if they ever taught people who were seeking God. But, of course, I
couldn't approach them, because they were so silent and looked so
peaceful. I envied them that. Peacefulness. When in my life had I ever
even come close? Monastic quietness. Man, I loved the thought of that.

"Kim," I said to my manager, "I wish I could be a fly on the wall at
the monastery, just for one day."

Kim shrugged. "Why don't you go on a retreat at the center, then?"

"What center?"

"Consciousness Meditation Center. That's where they all live. It's in
Kailua. They have weekend retreats every couple of months."

"You're kidding me!" I was shocked. You just didn't have weekend retreats at the Hidden Fortress.

"They're not bad," Kim said.

"You've been?!"

"Sure."

"How many times?"

"Just once," Kim said. "They're two hundred bucks."

"Two hundred bucks! For a weekend? No way."

"Yup." She got a kick out of my sticker shock. "But it clears your
mind," she said.

Well, yeah, maybe, I thought, but I'd already been washed white as the driven snow for free. Except then I couldn't stay clean. "Do they have work-study or something?" I asked.

Grumble, grumble, but for two months I saved up. I wrote a check. I went.

I took the bus out to Kailua and got off and followed Kim's directions, and I got to the center, which was surrounded by a high white wall. Some other people were arriving in cars. About ten of us waited at the gate, and the robed monks ushered us in.

The place was a spacious ranch house with add-ons. An enormous 1950s Buddhist ranch. The floors were white tile, and the walls in a lot of places were made out of those glass bricks that let light in, but you can't see through. I remember it was raining, and the garden was full of orchid plants, whole hedges of orchids, which the monks grew, and there was a pond with goldfish and a tiny bridge, and no grass, but white gravel, and some larger black stones.

Instead of a living room there was a meditation room where we all sat with our instructor. He was a tall heavyset haole man, although a monk just like the others. He wore an orange robe and had peach fuzz on his head like them, but he was about six foot four, and he had blue eyes, and wire-rimmed glasses, and he actually talked to us. Each day in addition to our meditation, and our breathing exercises, Michael told us about himself—the path that he took in his life, and how he had come to that path, and how it was right for him. He said, "Ten years ago I used to be totally caught up in my desires. I had an addictive spirit, so even though I was a lawyer in New York, and I seemed like any other suit, inside the only thing driving me was alcohol. All my spirit knew was what it wanted," he told us.

I just looked at him and shook my head. You couldn't imagine this man wanting anything anymore. He seemed so at peace, in his robes and his shaved head, so stripped down, and, I don't know, ergonomic. He had such a gentle voice, and such calm blue eyes that seemed out of place at the beginning, being so haole, but you got used to them. And really he was one of the most quietly inspiring teachers I'd ever seen, just sitting on the floor in front of us talking with such simplicity, and not only telling us, but being what he was telling, being in his speech and in all his tiniest movements so mindful and just so in the moment with all of us. The way he spoke about Tibet, you could tell it was his true home country. The way he showed his understanding, you could tell he was a person who had found not so much his calling in life, but his listening. He was so open; his whole body and breath were so big. I thought, he is so at home in his skin. You couldn't imagine he had once been in such a mundane state, with all those bourgeois appendages, an apartment, and a car, and dress shoes and cuff links, a marriage, and a divorce.

Yet, after a while when you got to know Michael, it turned out you really could imagine him as a lawyer wearing a suit. Despite him being essentially a cleric and, you know, a black belt in meditation, he was one of the most uptight people I've ever known. For example, if by some chance you were late for meditation, he got all tense, and he looked at you, and he glared this unmistakable glare, like all the neurotic New Yorker was coming out in him, and he was bringing it to bear on you. And if you happened to interrupt him in class because suddenly a question or a burning insight came to you, he'd blow his top! And he would say, "Sharon!" in this sharp tone of voice like the crack of a whip, like the tone my own dear dad would take when I was thirteen and reeling around in my pubescent fumes. "Sharon!" As in, How dare you. You couldn't help but flinch. Yet I didn't get to know Michael that well until later.

What we did with Michael was Dzogchen practice, which was this very basic no-nonsense silent meditation with your eyes wide open. And we did it in the morning and we did it in the afternoon, and in between we walked. We walked up and down the street, which was a quite lovely quiet suburban-type street. We walked like monks and we spoke gathas to ourselves, which were mindfulness prayers, like this: I feel my feet walking. I feel my legs moving. May I walk gently. May I tread lightly on this earth. We just followed Michael in our shorts and T-shirts, like we were these spiritual ducklings and he was our father bird. We all ate together and slept in one sleeping room and meditated together, but yet, I had no idea where anyone else came from or what they did for a living or any of that, because we didn't have any discussions or conversations. We respected the silence. We listened to our own minds. We were busy remembering who we were.

And I sat, and you know what? I didn't think about anything. I just looked straight ahead, and I breathed, and I focused, and I thought about absolutely nothing. I just emptied my mind, foosh! of all the clutter. Just shut down my hyperimagination, until there I was, totally blank. Just white, like a big white unfurnished room. Just plain vanilla, without a cone, without a spoon. I sat and I breathed. I was so focused, the only distraction I had in the whole two days of meditation was every once in a while thinking, Whee! I'm good at this! Because it was true, I was a natural!

I was so good that by the end of the weekend I was an inch taller than when I'd started, just from all the tension melting off my shoulders, and from being mindful of my posture. And I was so good at it that my lungs grew, I'm sure, from getting a workout for once and giving up that shallow breathing that I'd been doing for years. All my perceptions were sharper. Everything about me was more expansive. And I saw that this was where I needed to be right now. This was what I needed to be doing. And the most amazing thing was that Michael and all the other monks saw it in me too. I started coming to the center every chance I got. I started coming just to breathe, just to get some oxygen, just to return to myself. I started practicing; I started seeing the way before me, and every day and every retreat, I grew more calm. And then one day, about three months after my first weekend, I brought all my money and valuable things, including even my silver watch, and I gave them to the center, and I attached myself to Michael as his student, or groupie, or what have you, and I stayed.

All my connections to the outside world—like balloon strings—I just let them go. All my valuables—just gave them up. And the giving didn't mean a thing. I didn't feel a single pang. Except for Grandpa Irving's watch. I have to admit, I almost kept it. I almost hid it in my clothes. I'd rubbed and rubbed the silver case until my hand was worn from rubbing. What would I do now to rub away my worries and my fears? But that was the point—I was giving up my superstitions. I was sacrificing my attachments that weighed my soul. So when I thought of keeping back the watch, I knew right away I should give that thing up first, because it was more precious than the others. And when I mourned its loss, I thought, Well, that proves it was just a big distraction.

I stayed at the monastery, and for months and months my soul just grew. Not from experiences or hard knocks or from revelations that were at hand, but by itself in the meditation room, just hydroponically, like the lettuce heads in their tubs of water, without any roots in the ground. I stayed, and my mind opened. My spirit hummed to itself; it rose and fell on my breath. I walked and I breathed. I sat and I simplified. I ate only lettuce and fruits and a few grains. I drank only water. I took almost nothing from the world, and the world took nothing from me. I wasn't running around looking for some Western conception of God—as if any day I'd turn him up under some rock. I'd exchanged that whole crusading questing Holy Grail hang-up for something so much better; this smooth stillness.

So of course, that was too good to be true. Pretty soon, deep into my stillness, like a guy you've broken up with who can't believe you aren't still attracted to him, my imagination came around to tempt me. My imagination started whispering at me, "Sharon! Shaaaron!"

And I'd hiss inside myself, "Stop that, you fool."

"Shaaaron! The color blue."

"No colors."

"Purple."

"Sh."

"Periwinkle, lavender, plum, oregano."

"Oregano? That's a spice."

"Made you look."

"Sh!"

And then all would be quiet, until he'd start up again, my imagination, and now he'd take some other form, like of a little kid, "Sharon. Sharon, can I touch the Buddha? Can I touch him? Is he real gold?"

Because there was a benevolent gold Buddha sitting on the table in the meditation room, and he was so soft and rounded he looked like he was cut from pure buttery gold. But, of course, I would never dream of touching him, except this little voice inside me kept bringing it up. I began to have some very hard days. I began to feel like Satan was inside of me trying to subdivide my spaciousness.

I started oversleeping in the mornings. Instead of getting up before dawn with Michael and the rest of the community, I'd be fast asleep having these wild dreams. I'd dream about Molokai and the guavas hanging down from the trees, and I'd dream about Tonic and the birds, and they'd be speaking to me with their intelligent beaks. They'd be speaking to me in tongues, yet I'd understand them. "Where are your feathers?" they'd scream at me. "Feathers! Feathers! Where is your chick? Where are your wings?"

Ding! Ding! The little wake-up bell would ring far away, yet my eyes just would not open. I kept lying there. And being my own personal mentor, Michael was pissed.

Four months into my stay I was sitting in the meditation room with the monks and teachers, and the visitors retreating on that weekend. We were observing three days of silence. The whole community was round and still with listening. The ears of every human in the place were open; every pore was awake. Now. Now. We are breathing now. We are living now. That was the rhythm like a drum inside of us. But all of a sudden I felt myself about to speak! My hand flew up to my mouth to cover the words before they spilled out. I was so embarrassed.

We rose up and went walking through the neighborhood. There were about thirty of us, and I was walking next to Michael, and I felt the words burbling up inside of me, and again I had to cover my mouth with my hand, like when you're trying to stifle hiccups, but the words kept coming, and they were question words, like "How come? . . . How come? . . ." All of a sudden my whole being was itchy with questions; I was just growing questions all over my body. It was as if I were three years old again, when everything you see makes you ask why. Like "Where did the stars go now that it's morningtime?" Only, my questions were about our medita-tion practice—like "How come you guys chose this day to be a silent day? Why this day and not a different day?" And "Why is it important for us all to walk together now as a community?" And "How do you main-tain your focus when sometimes everything seems to be distracting you?" And "Why, all of a sudden, is this stuff not working for me?"

We walked along through the neighborhood, which was damp and misty and green. We walked past these pretty tract houses with lychee trees in their yards, and mango trees laden with purple mangos, and oc-casionally little decorative ponds with teensy arching Oriental bridges, and once in a while a Shinto shrine. I started to pull at the sleeve of Michael's orange robe. He averted his face from me. He was absorbed in his own steps. So I tugged a little more. "Michael," I whispered.

He looked at me, aghast. I'd said a word.

I started gesturing at him like this was urgent. I made the time-out signal with my hands. I looked at him imploringly.

No good. He was furious. He began walking faster. I ran along trying to keep up. Yet the New Yorker in him was starting to come out. Even on those side streets off Old Pali Road you could see it happen. His pace was quicker and quicker. His eyes glazed over. He was striding through the community to the front, just to get away from me. Like saffron flowers the monks drifted to the edges of the road as Michael marched through. Like a hyper Scotch terrier I ran after him, worrying the edges of his consciousness. Faster and faster, he kept walking. His legs were long; his mouth was set, until finally we left the rest of the community behind.

"Michael." I panted. "I'm sorry. I really am. I tried not to speak. I couldn't help it. I'm probably not ready to be this quiet. I'm probably not even deserving to be your student. But I have to talk. I have to say something. This silence isn't working on me. My brain is going haywire. I'm hearing voices. My imagination and my ego and everything else. My whole subconscious is out of control."

He stopped walking and turned on me right there in the street. He said, "You have broken my peace."

I threw up my hands. Now, all of a sudden, no words would come.

"How dare you," he said to me. His face was turning red. "How dare you!"

My voice came back. "How dare I what?" I shot back at him. "And since when is it *your* peace? I thought it was all of ours."

"You said you came here to learn."

"I am here to learn. That's what I'm trying to do."

"And I was trying to teach you!"

The monks had caught up to us, but in their serenity they didn't bat an eye. They walked right by us, and the weekenders followed—except they turned back to stare like rubberneckers at a traffic accident.

Michael's hands twitched against his orange robe. His jaw was working. "I've tried to put up with you," he said. "I've tried to be patient with you. When you interrupt. When you start with your questions . . ."

"You are not patient," I told him. "You haven't been patient at all! You're an anal-retentive control freak, that's what you are!"

He breathed in, and he breathed out, and he said between clenched teeth, "I am expending every ounce of energy right now not to wring your neck." And he glowered at me, huge in his robes, and beads of sweat stood on his brow and on the stubble on his shaved head. He looked like the Jewish-Tibetan version of Friar Tuck.

"Learn to listen," he said, and he left me standing there on the gray asphalt, and all the car ports on the street blurred together, each with its own copy of the *Honolulu Advertiser* rolled up in a rubber band.

"But, but . . ." I called after him. Michael was gone. And one last question died on my lips. The one I really wanted to ask. Which was: How could you devote your life to contemplation and practice meditation for so many years and still be such a tight-ass?

Yet I calmed down by evening, and Michael regained his cool. The truth was, this guy was teaching me a lot. He was just understandably protective of his inner space. So over the next few weeks I respected his boundaries and stifled my own nagging curiosity. I realized I and only I could put to rest those nagging voices inside of me. I focused, and I practiced. I lived in the present and did not bother the community or the day students or weekend visitors around me.

Once I'd stopped irritating Michael so much, and showed I could live without constantly breaking the peace around me like I was a bull in the meditative china shop, he began to work with me again. He talked to me once a day, and instructed me, and he mentioned something to me which I had forgotten, which was that I had a lot of detritus inside of me from my former life. And I considered how I'd lived, and what I'd eaten, and in turn what had consumed me, like my love of beer and pot and acid, not to mention men, and there were a lot of toxins in my system, to say the least. So with Michael's guidance I went on a course of fasting, during which I drank water and some juice, but ate nothing, and that helped a lot. That really restored me to myself, and quieted me down. My body was lighter, my head was cooler, and it was like I bid each of my wandering selves good-bye, like I sent each one on pilgrimage with a pilgrim's staff. The child in me, and the wild girl, and the mixed-up traveler. Good-bye, good-bye. The house of myself was empty, and I had two days of perfect peace.

On the third day I saw something about myself. Just very clearly, and without a mirror. I saw that I was starving, and it wasn't just my bones sticking out and my hands and arms all skeletal. It was my mind; it wasn't bright and spacious anymore; it had turned all thin and brittle, and all I could see when I looked inside myself was sludge and darkness. I was so disappointed I couldn't even tell my teacher. I lay down and I slept for a day, because I didn't know what else to do.

I woke up and lay on my sleeping mat, and Michael came to me and said, "What's wrong?"

And I said, "Hey, Michael, I'm sick."

He put his hand on my forehead.

"I don't think I have a fever. It's just inside of me. I'm all hollowed out. It's like, the more I look inside myself, the less I see."

Then he smiled at me—a real appreciative happy smile, like Now we're getting somewhere. He said, "That's right."

"It's right?"

"Yes," he said. "The more I look inside myself, the less I see. That's true."

I said, "I look at my body, and I look like I'm dying."

"Yes," he said, "you were before, but now you see it."

"I don't get it."

He didn't answer.

"My practice seemed simple before," I said, "but now it's not."

He said, "It is simple."

"I don't know what to do."

He said, "I think you do know."

And I sat up on my sleeping mat slowly, trying to figure out what I knew.

And wouldn't you know my imagination came around again in my distress, just to plague me, and I was so weak it was hard even to argue in my head. My imagination just swaggering around like he was so hot and knowing any moment I'd have to give in. "Sharon! Shaaron!"

"What?"

"I'm hungry."

"Go away."

"I want something."

"Go away."

"I want something."

"What?"

"Sprinkles on top."

"What is that supposed to mean?"

"Garnishes."

"Stop that."

"I'm bored."

"Tough."

"I'm so bored."

"So, life isn't about being entertained all the time."

"Yes it is," my imagination whined to me; and then he said, "How long is this eightfold path, anyway?"

"It isn't about distance!" I said.

"Well, where's it going?"

"It's not about going anywhere," I said. "It's not about going, it's about being."

"Being is a drag."

Then I closed my eyes tight and covered my ears. I tried to go back inside of myself, but I just started babbling, to my imagination, "Do you know how spoiled you are? Do you know what a total pain in the neck you are? Instead of joining me in mindfulness, you are dividing me and just forcing me into this Western duality and just making some kind of schism inside of myself, and driving me mad in the process! You are so shallow! Haven't you ever heard of the possibility of peace?"

And my imagination said to me, "Yeah, I want peace."

"Good."

"But with music, and dancing, and ice cream and song!"

Well, all I knew was that everything that had been working before had stopped working now. My hungers were starting to return to me, my body was crying out for meat and eggs and cheese, and, believe it or not, milk. It seemed like all my blood and flesh was crying out to eat the products of other living creatures and to forget about being holy. And my lips and my hands were starting to yearn and feel sorry for themselves, because they so wanted to be touched. It just seemed like my whole body and my imagination and my memory had decided to rebel and conspire against me. I breathed and breathed and tried to give my spirit space enough to open up again, and my poor spirit tried to open, but whenever it did, it was like an umbrella pummeled by this horrible inner wind, and all its little wire spokes got bent, and it would turn inside out.

Then—remember; how I bade good-bye and let go of all my wandering selves, and gave them pilgrim staffs to go their own way? Well, they all
marched right back inside of me again. The child and the wild girl and
the mixed-up traveler. And the child was crying she was tired, and the
wild girl was complaining I never let her go dancing, and the mixed-up
traveler was just making all these demands like "What the hell is happening here? Are you on the verge of enlightenment here? Or are you just
really screwed up? And how do you know which is which? Because it
seems like there's a fine line between purification and starving to death."

So of course, I tried to compose myself. But still I could not. And I
just got more and more irritable and grouchy. And finally I realized, This
is not productive here. You've achieved some real peacefulness and had
some awesome spacious days, but that time has passed, and it's too bad,
'cause you still need so much more teaching, but until you can get
yourself and all your inner voices to shut up again, that isn't going to
happen. So you'd better take the good and absorb the knowledge, and
live the Way at the level you're at.

I had some broth, and I ate some flatbread, and got some of my
strength back the next few days. Then I bowed to Michael and to all the
other monks who had taken me in to teach me, and I walked out of the
center. And I had just my extra clothes and my house key and what I
was wearing, and bus fare that they gave me. My pockets were empty. I
had no money, no notebook, no Bible, no lucky silver watch, since I'd
given them up, and donated them, in thanks for my teaching. I felt a
pang about the watch. All of a sudden I thought of asking for it back. All
of a sudden it occurred to me—was I right to give up everything I had
of earthly value? Were the center teachers right to accept those things?
Maybe this place wasn't on the up and up! Maybe this so-called Tibetan
meditation center wasn't even accredited. Even as I walked the road I
could feel my anger and my indignation and regret coming to meet me.
Shame on you! I thought as I walked tearfully to the bus stop.

Riding in the bus, skimming over Pali Highway, I stopped my crying.
I stared out the window and I saw trees, and churches, and the con-
sulates of foreign countries. I saw the tall pagoda roofs of a temple that
stood in the great cemetery in the valley below. Among the cars on the
road, a convoy followed a hearse, and each car had a sign printed
FUNERAL. We drove into the city. In Waikiki the stores were filled with

shoppers, and between the hotels the ocean was shining blue and children were jumping in the tame little waves. The beach was shining and splashing and scented with tanning oil. The streets were jammed and materialistic and noisy. I felt stunned. I felt as though I'd just returned from another country, and in a way, I had.

WHEN I got to my house, it was shut up, and the paint peeling and blistering in the sun, exactly how I'd left it. I took my house key out of my backpack and stepped in. Wow, the place smelled bad. Like liquor and BO and vomit on the rug. Phew. The guys had probably had a party the night before, because there were bottles, and bits of food around, and paper cups, and on the walls were traces of their specialty cherry Jell-O that they used to make for parties, and which was spiked, and sometimes people used to throw at each other, causing Jell-O gobs and dribbles on the walls, which the ants enjoyed. The mess didn't faze me too much, because that was just who my housemates were, and in fact a lot of who I used to be, and now I had achieved some distance from that. I felt no rancor. But then I opened the door to my room. And there were two huge men sleeping there on my *buton,* snoring away in their underwear, dead drunk, fat as pigs, just two three-hundred-pound hairy swine lying there, and I took one look at them and I went ballistic. Because that was my *buton* that I had paid for, and that had been my space that I had lived in and prayed in and studied my Bible in and tried to keep clean and decorated with my Sojourner Truth poster, "Ain't I a Woman?" that Corinne had given me. I started yelling and screaming and tugging these oafs to wake up, and I think I kicked them a couple times until they retreated into the living room. Looking back, I was lucky they took it mildly and didn't haul off and kill me. They were actually nice guys, and fairly gentle, if not gentlemen.

I was so discomfited by the whole experience I had to go outside and just sit for a while on the lawn. The mondo grass was thick and overgrown, so pokey I couldn't meditate. I ended up sitting on top of my almost empty backpack and staring out at the street in front of me. I just sat until it got dark. Still, neither T-Bone nor Baron came home. They may have been working that night down in Waikiki. The sky darkened, and the mosquitoes came around as they always did at twi-

light, and then their hour passed, and they flew off to their little mos-
quito babies in puddles and stagnant pools in the suburbs. Night came,
and the night breezes that are warm on your arms, and damp on the
back of your neck and on your knees. I was so tired, but I didn't want to
go back inside and sleep in my old room. I couldn't go back in there to
that hospitable yet rotten little house.

Then who should I see strolling up the street? Marlon! My poor for-
saken black kitten, who was now a big scrawny cat. And he came
straight up to me! He recognized me right away and rubbed against me,
as if he were glad to see me, which he must have been, because even
though I'd left food and money for his care with T-Bone and Baron,
Marlon had clearly been living by his wits much of the time I'd been
gone. "Marlon!" I said. "What happened to you? What did you do to
yourself?"

He purred at me, and he looked up with his little furrowed brow.

I scratched him between the eyes. "Marlon," I said, "I can't believe I
left you for so long. I don't even know how long it's been. You probably
thought I was never coming back! Oh, Marlon, but you left me first,
you know. I started thinking you didn't want me around. I was thinking
you hardly even needed me." He rubbed himself against my legs. He
was like flea-bitten velvet. I caressed his tail, all slender and graceful until right before the end it bent. "Oh, Marlon, Marlon." I couldn't believe
it. Nobody in the world knew where I was right then, and Marlon had
come to me. There he was.

A Good Place

W<small>E</small> were very thin, Marlon and I. He probably had worms from catching mice and birds and things, and I knew he should go to the vet. But even if I'd had the money, I was too tired to take him. After all that meditation and fasting, I was wasted. I was so white my roommates called me shark bait. Then they felt bad. T-Bone got me oxtail soup and steamed dumplings from the King's Garden. And Baron even went to the Laundromat and washed my sheets for me—since he was guilty his friends had slept on them while I was gone. So I convalesced with Marlon on clean sheets. I opened up my Norton anthology that I'd left behind in the house. And I came to this poem by Thomas Hardy that was like a blue-note psalm. I started reading it aloud to Marlon.

He opened up one yellow eye.

I read the whole poem to Marlon a couple of times, until he started glaring at me—like Woman, now you go too far. I'll sleep on your bed, but Thomas Hardy is pushing it.

So I said, "Okay, okay, no more poems. Okay, I respect your silence." I got that now. You can't just invade the consciousness of other living be-

ings. They will be what they will be. They can never be what they are
not. And Marlon was no T. S. Eliot. He was not a literary cat.

But to myself I murmured the first stanza.

> Let me enjoy the earth no less
> Because the all-enacting Might
> That fashioned forth its loveliness
> Had other aims than my delight.

"The Buddha would have loved this," I said. Just the idea that the
universe is not designed for a person's entertainment. It was so true. You
can't just sit around waiting for the next revelation.

That very day I decided I was going to get off my duff. And a few
weeks later I actually did get off it. I networked with all my connections, and got a job at Crack Seed World, selling pickled plums, and a
weekend gig at a shop behind the Stop Light selling sex toys, and then
ultimately, I got a dream job, a very hard-to-find position serving at
The King's Bakery, which had as its major perk all you could eat for
the staff every night after eleven, and free day-old Portuguese sweet
bread, which even when they are a day old are just about the sweetest
loaves in the world and so soft and just a little bit glutinous so that you
can tear them apart with your bare hands and stuff enormous amounts
into your mouth, just like you're eating bread candy. So every day I ate
those loaves, and every night I got me a stack of dinner-plate-size but-
termilk pancakes, which I slathered with two miniscoops of whipped
butter. No syrup on top, just butter, smeared and dripping over the
sides.

I started putting some meat on my bones, and some of my energy
came back. I put our things in a couple of good brown paper grocery
bags with handles. I was all set to renew my life. So I got me and Marlon a new place, a room in this co-op that my old buddy Rich and his
girlfriend, Kathryn, had founded.

The co-op was near the Termite Palace, which was what people used
to call the old abandoned Honolulu Stadium, which stood for years being eaten out from under, before it was finally torn down. Our co-op
was a brown tongue-and-groove tract house with extra rooms slapped

on the back. From the outside it didn't look like it all fit together, but there was plenty of room for the five of us who lived there.

A singer-actor-dancer-doctor named Will had the front bedroom. He was tall and reedy and had blond hair and had come out from New Hampshire to Hawaii to do his fellowship in emergency medicine. Will worked a lot, but his passion was theater. He was a fair singer and an amazing actor. He had the title role in the Honolulu Players' production of *The Bourgeois Gentleman,* and he was in the chorus in several Gilbert and Sullivan productions at the Manoa Valley Theater, which was a tiny little stone church with a cemetery in the yard, so you walked up this short path, between the gravestones, into the sanctuary, which sat about thirty-five people, and you watched the shows on this pocket stage, the size of a large dining-room table, on which the actors barely fit, and the chorus was the bare minimum, three women and three men, who yet somehow conjured up all the shepherdesses you could wish, or all the fairies, or a whole navy if need be.

Also in the house was a preschool teacher named Tom. He was even taller than Will, and with skinny yet hairy legs and longish brown hair and a brown beard—not a real bushy beard—but sort of here and there on his face. Tom had originally come from Oregon and migrated out to Hawaii, and fallen into his teaching job as well as the co-op; he tended to fall into things. He played the hammer dulcimer, but not well— which was why he'd never made any money back in Portland when he was trying to be a street musician. He had a lot of feeling for the music, but he tended to hit the wrong strings, so when he took his dulcimer out of its case and played, you'd hear this beautiful angelic sound like quiet little bells ringing—along with some random extra little bells he hit by mistake. It was like Simple Gifts in a rain barrel.

And there was Rich, who looked just like he used to, except thirty pounds heavier, since he'd been sitting around so much writing his dissertation on those red-footed boobies we'd gone out and counted six years before. And then there was Kathryn, who was a featherweight woman with masses of auburn curls and blue eyes magnified by her glasses. She was my age, twenty-seven, but she always made me feel scruffy in that she had real clothes from stores, and she used moisturizer, and worked out at gyms. While my hair just sort of hung, and I'd gotten so skinny, my face looked gaunt and tired, and, I don't know, almost old. Kathryn was a one-woman revolutionary cell for Greenpeace in Hawaii—she'd come out from Santa Cruz to shake up the Honolulu offices, which was how she'd met Rich. She was also in a major domestic phase, which was one of the reasons the whole co-op got started.

We all shared the cooking and cleaning duties, and we were all dedicated to pure food and water, recycling, environmental activism, and the ideals of simplicity. We lived as a strict democracy, which meant you had to participate in house meetings every week, no matter how long they were. For example, the first meeting I ever went to was almost three hours. It was a meeting about how people felt about Marlon coming with me into the co-op, and whether or not litter boxes in the kitchen were okay, because some people were not cat people and they thought kitty litter in the same room as food preparation was gross.

"Plus, I'm allergic to cats," Kathryn said.

We were all sitting in the living room, and I was sweating it. I said, "Kathryn, to me, Marlon is not a cat."

"Well, he *is* a cat," Will said from the floor. "I personally have nothing against that, but it is true, Sharon. You have to admit that he *is* a cat."

"Biologically, he is a cat," I said, "but I feel like Kathryn is using the word as a pejorative term, and I have to object to that."

Tom spoke up. "I think the issue is not whether people are allergic, but how we feel about sharing our space with an animal."

"That's exactly what I was trying to say," said Kathryn. "Because we've never had an animal in the house before."

"But, but, I can't believe you guys," I said. "We're all animals. You're the first to say that. What're you—telling me an animal has no right to join the community? Kathryn, I can't believe you of all people would say something like that, considering your line of work, considering your whole green philosophy that you live by!"

"I don't want cat poop in the kitchen," Kathryn said.

"Oh, right, so you'll go on the *Rainbow Warrior* and defend the lives of marine mammals, but you won't let Marlon live with us?"

"Sharon, don't get worked up," Rich said.

"Well, I am worked up. I'm incredibly worked up, because I really want to live with you guys. I want to be a member of this community, but I feel like you are asking me to choose between you and Marlon, and I feel like that is a specious choice—because friends don't ask friends to choose between one species and another!"

Will got up and plopped onto the saggy green vinyl couch next to me. He gave me a big hug. He was the mad hugger of the group. He was such a peacemaker. Everybody loved this guy. He said, "Come on, we're all still friends here."

"I have an idea," Tom said. "If the kitchen is not okay for Marlon's litter box, could we put it in the bathroom?"

"Well . . ." I began.

"Which bathroom?" asked Rich.

"No!" said Kathryn. "I'm not stepping into kitty litter in my bare feet. . . ."

"How would you be stepping into kitty litter?" I asked her.

"In the mornings when I'm stepping out of the shower and I don't even have my glasses on yet, all I need is a cat box. . . ."

"Kathryn," I said, "you can't be serious. What's this really about? Do you not want me to live here? Is that what you're trying to do here? I mean, where is this hostility coming from?"

"Hey, it's not hostility," Kathryn said.

"Then what? Do you feel weird about me coming just because Rich and I slept together something like seven years ago?"

"Sharon!" she said.

"What?"

"That is so ad hominem."

"You guys, you guys," Will chided, "can we get back to the items for discussion. The agenda, remember?"

"I would be happy to get back to the agenda," I said, "I just want Kathryn to stop demonizing Marlon."

"Demonizing Marlon!"

"Yeah!"

On the first vote Marlon was not accepted into the co-op, and I was in tears, but with Will's amendment that we keep the kitty litter box in my room, Marlon had the majority of me, Will, and Tom. Rich voted with Kathryn, but I didn't hold that against him. I knew he had to. Then we had a third vote about what if we had a probationary period with the cat, to see how we all would adjust to him, and that was bingo! the magic consensus that according to the bylaws we had to achieve at our official meetings. We had a lot of bylaws. As I said, we were a strict democracy.

But the upshot was: Marlon was in! He was in like Flynn! I was hugging myself for about two days. And I moved us into the house, and we had a little back room with two windows with glass louvers and a white vinyl tile floor, and I put up my poster and I dragged in my *buton,* and purchased new laminate storage drawers for my clothes (I had no closet), and a spider plant and a Swedish ivy, and a ficus for oxygen.

You know how at times you can just love life? Not just as a necessary good, but in all the details—every little thing. I loved my life when I moved into the co-op. I loved cooking with the group and doing KP with Will, and bringing home the groceries on this rusty old bike we kept in the yard, just as a little runabout, since we were opposed to cars. I loved the smell of whole-wheat bread baking in the oven. I loved all my housemates—even Kathryn, although less so. Will and Tom and Rich were like brothers to me. Moneywise, I'd left the bakery and found a lucrative job in Ala Moana Shopping Center at Shirokiya, which was this incredible department store that sold games, and cosmetics, and perfumes, and suitcases, and shoes and gadgets and everything you could imagine, only they were all designed for life on a Japanese planet—so a lot of the shoes were little white tabbies, and the cosmetics were Japanese brands, and the kitchen gadgets were woks and rice cookers and deep fryers.

I worked in the luggage department, and my register was behind a glass counter that displayed items like voltage adapters and two-faced alarm clocks you could set to show the time in two different countries, and holster money wallets invisible under suit jackets. You strapped them over your shoulder so you could keep your money securely under your armpit. For ladies we had the bra stash, which was a white money pouch that snapped front and center onto your brassiere. So there I had a job, I had the house, I had Marlon, I was eating three meals a day. I felt like I was together enough to stop by Crawford Hall and see Brian.

HE was sitting in his office in his same old swivel chair with his dirty bare feet up on the desk, and his sandy beard, and his picture of Imo thumbtacked up to his bulletin board, and he was marking up a big floppy manuscript.

"Hey, Brian." I stood in the doorway.

He looked up, startled. I hadn't come by in over a year. Not since before my vision! "Sharon?" He sat up all of a sudden and skidded back his chair. His feet thumped onto the floor.

"Yeah."

"How are you?" he said. "I hear you're in the house with Rich and Kathryn and company."

"Yup, I am. I'm living the cooperative life. How's Imo?"

"She's great. She's here for two weeks. She's giving an invited talk at IWOMP."

"What is that? Wait . . . wait . . ." I was trying to puzzle it out. "Industry without . . . monetary operations?"

"International Workshop on Migratory Populations."

"That was my second guess. I was just about to say that. I was coming to see if you wanted to have lunch."

"Yeah, okay, I'll buy," he said graciously, and he ushered me out the door. "You look so thin. You look like a little waif!"

"Thanks a lot!"

"What have you been doing with yourself?"

"I've been good," I said. "I've been in a good place. I've been moving in all these new directions."

"New directions where?"

"Well, the house, and I'm working at Shirokiya, and also I've been studying, um, methods of seeking enlightenment."

"Huh?"

"Just doing a lot reading, and just thinking—you know, just taking a step back, because you can't just always be converting every day of the week!"

"Oh," Brian said. We'd arrived at the lunch wagon down by the parking lot, and he bought meat sticks, and manapua, and root beers, just like the time I first came to see him along with Gary. "I'm not sure I even want to know what that means."

We headed around to the side of Moore Hall and sat down to eat in the shade of a Bo tree.

"What about you? What've you been up to?" I asked Brian.

"Still working on my book."

I drank my root beer. I stared at the ants climbing over the sticky seedpods by our feet. "Look at those ants," I said. "Look at that whole civilization there. It's like to them, every crumb we drop is a meteor. Do you ever think about that?"

"No," Brian said.

I flicked ice at him with my straw. "And you're supposed to be the trained naturalistic observer! What a waste."

"Ants aren't my thing."

"That's because you're specialized up the wazoo."

"I think it's supposed to be up the yazoo."

"Whatever! The point is, specialization is your crutch! The point is— what's happened to being a generalist? What's happened to synthesizing all the parts of nature together? Nobody talks about synthesizing anymore, except in theology."

"So that's why you're studying enlightenment."

"Methods of enlightenment."

"Right." Brian was looking at the ground. Now I had him looking at the ants too. "How's Wayne?"

"I don't know," I said, surprised he had to ask. "We decided to go our separate ways a year ago."

"He hit you, didn't he?" Brian said.

"No," I shot back. I was offended he thought of me that way, as having so little self-respect I'd stay in a relationship with someone who beat me! Wayne hadn't ever really hit me. True, sometimes I'd been afraid he'd hit me, but that was different! "We just had different philosophies of living," I said. "It was like where I'm going he wouldn't follow."

"And you're going—where?"

"It's hard to explain to people like you."

"What kind of people is that?"

"Male rationalists," I said. "You wouldn't get it."

"Try me." He was partly laughing at me, yet still I felt this rush of pleasure. I could see myself through his eyes, and so I felt doubly his kindness toward me, and his friendship, and that he loved to look at me.

"I had a vision."

"And what were you on at the time?" he asked.

"See, that's just what I was talking about! You're immediately jumping to the rationalistic explanation! I said vision, not trip. I had this true, unadulterated vision of God! I saw something. I was out on a ship, and it was sunset. And the water actually turned transparent. And then a whale came, and she lifted up her tail; she opened up the whole ocean. And you could look and look all the way down. And I saw God's presence. In the deep."

"You're such a nut."

"See, I knew you'd say that."

"Well, it's true."

"If you knew God was out there, wouldn't you go seek Him?"

He looked at me like before his eyes I was turning into a toad. "What're you? . . . a born-again?"

"Oh, yeah, I did that."

"And now you're coming around to convert me."

"No, I'm not evangelizing or anything like that," I said. "I mean, I was born again, but it didn't take on me."

He grinned. "Only you, Sharon."

"It's just one path—it's like *The Varieties of Religious Experience.* They're just all different paths."

"Mm-hmm. Yeah." He gathered up his wrappers and headed for the trash can. I followed him.

"What? You think this is just my flakiness here? It has nothing to do with flakiness. Don't get me wrong. I grew up in a totally nondenominational family. My parents were the most irreligious people you ever saw. My dad was an economist, for Pete's sake. He worshiped the almighty dollar. My grandpa was a card-carrying atheist. I mean, this was not how I was raised! I never even gave the idea of God a second thought. I never asked to have visions. But now it turns out I am someone who is heading in the visionary direction. That's where my spirit is going. I can't even help it."

Brian turned to me. He put his hands on my shoulders. "Why do you always have to be going somewhere?" he asked.

I looked into his smart brown eyes. "Brian, you are such an agnostic," I told him. "You're like I used to be. You don't even get it. It's like love. If you fall in love with someone you just want to be with him. You want to see him and touch him all the time. It's like this searching all the time. It's like the song by Solomon: 'Have you seen him whom my soul loves?'"

"Who do you love these days, Sharon?" Brian asked me.

Somehow my metaphor of love and God escaped me. I said, "You."

We stood still a second and hushed. I was all tongue tied, but what I'd said was true.

"I mean, for example. You know, for instance: you. That's what I meant."

"I know, I know," Brian said. He let go my shoulders. He understood the whole thing. He saw I couldn't wait to get out of there.

I sprinted across campus and to the bus stop. And when I got to my stop by the Termite Palace, I ran the three blocks home, and I jammed my key in the lock and dashed for my room, where Marlon, who was essentially nocturnal, was sleeping on the *buton,* and I pushed him over to one side, since he liked to sleep right in the middle, and he snarled at me, but I didn't even care. I lay there and squeezed my eyes shut, just trying to calm down; trying to forget about the whole thing with Brian, yet playing back every word of our conversation.

I should never have confided in him. He, of all people—he was the last person in the world who'd sympathize with someone becoming visionary. And then how I felt about him, telling him to his face. "Oh, Marlon," I said. "It's so ironic, everybody used to think I was such a liar, but they didn't even know."

Admittedly, in middle school and even high school, I used to make things up—for example, that Mom was a photojournalist and that was why she was gone. She was riding jeeps all over Vietnam. Land mines were exploding all around her, but her camera shutter just kept clicking. There she was out in the battlefield documenting the slaughter. Or like the time I told my dad my friends and I had been abducted at gunpoint by a pair of car thieves running from police, which was how I'd ended up in Providence for several days.

But my far greater problem was always my compulsion to tell the truth. That was the thing I really got punished for. Run away for a while, and your father would try to get you into a probationary program for at-risk kids. But tell your father he was a fat-ass and his new wife was a gold digger, and he would beat the you-know-what out of you.

"Marlon," I said, "do you think I should call Brian up and sort of . . ." Sort of what? Apologize? Try to explain myself? Anything I said would just make it worse. Everyone always compared lies to spiderwebs, but no one ever talked about getting caught in a web of honesty. "Maybe I should write him a letter?" But Marlon was snoozing away. And as it turned out I was the one who got a letter that day. In one of those out-of-left-field situations a letter actually came for me.

We were all sitting down at dinner eating our zucchini-squash lasagna, and Rich said, "Oh, Sharon, guess what?"

"What?" I was still feeling down.

"This postcard showed up for you—from Israel!"

"No kidding. Who do I know in Israel?"

"It's from Gary," Rich said.

"No way. How did Gary know I lived here?"

"It came to the zoology department," Rich told me. "It was sitting there next to the mailboxes."

"That is so weird. I was just there!"

Rich handed me the postcard across the table. And the picture on the front was the ancient Western Wall in Jerusalem made out of blocks of stone and with little tufts of grass growing in the nooks and crannies. On the back, sure enough, there was my name, Sharon Spiegelman and c/o Department of Zoology, University of Hawaii, and some kind of message in Gary's wavy handwriting that you could hardly read, not just because it was tiny and illegible, but because it was so inconsistent. There was no pattern to it. "Dear Sharon," I read. "There has been this strangelement between us for too long. . . ."

"You came by the department today? I didn't see you," said Rich.

"I hate to say it, but we need to discuss the oven," Kathryn was saying.

"What's wrong with it?" asked Will.

"Jeez, you'd think he'd have the courtesy just to print," I burst out. I kept trying to read the card. I squinted up my eyes. I held it to the light. All I came up with was: "If I can be in our massage, markthing on a guest then only be thinking of you and histories we have slaved. You'll been such a fiend. Love, Gary."

I started passing the card around, and we all put our heads together to try to figure the damn thing out, but to no avail. Kathryn got a few words: "It's 'You've been such a *friend*,'" she said. "It's 'histories we have *shared.*'" But that was as much as she could do. "What's this return address?" Kathryn was sounding it out. "Torah-Or Yerusalami."

"It sounds like a deli," said Tom.

"You gonna write back?" Rich asked me.

I took the postcard from Kathryn. I started bending it in my fingers.

"Can't we hold off on the oven?" Will asked Kathryn.

"We've got Rich's party next week!" she said.

"Oh, yeah."

"Shit," said Tom.

There wasn't any way around that. We were having this huge blowout house party coming up, and there was no way to put it off. Rich had actually finished his thesis. A week from Friday—after eleven years—he was finally defending.

THE theme was Mexican. We were having vegetarian enchiladas and refried beans and rice and bag after bag of chips and salsa, not to mention a couple of kegs of beer. And we were having a home-baked chocolate-frosted yellow layer cake—so it was a good thing we'd got the oven fixed. After Rich defended, he was going to come home with his whole committee and then we'd party. Kathryn planned the whole thing like a military operation. The morning of the big day we had the whole house bedecked with streamers and balloons. At minus four hours the cake went into the oven. At minus three hours Marlon ran to the neighbors and hid in the crawl space under their back stairs.

Minus two hours, Tom was setting up folding chairs in all the common spaces. We'd actually moved the living-room furniture to the bedrooms. Will was at work. Kathryn was in the shower. That quiet-before-the-mob feeling came over the house. I started walking around the place. Just bopping a balloon here, tweaking a streamer there. What would I say to Brian when he showed up? I couldn't look him in the eye, let alone Imo! Maybe I should go away. Maybe I should just disappear for a while. I wondered if in the hubbub anyone would even notice.

I went into my room and shut the door. I sat down cross-legged on the pocked white tile floor. If I'd still had my guitar I could have played some. If I'd still had Grandpa's watch, I could have held it at least. What I ended up doing was taking out some notebook paper and writing back to Gary.

Dear Gary,

Thanks for the card and for mentioning histories we have shared and
still being friends. I might have been mad even after all these years, yet
I am not at that place any more. When I think back on you I see not
only the despicable jerk you were, but also the good times we had together. Perspective will do that to you.

It looks (i.e. the Western Wall) like you are travelling. I have been
too, but not in space so much as spirit. I see how human relationships
are dwarfed. The true thing is our relationship with God. That is the
one tie that lasts forever, so that is what I'm trying to get a handle on.

As far as the mundane goes: I am now currently single, but I am
living with my cat and some great people in a group house where we
all work together and support each other. Bird life, ecology, and peace
are some of the causes I am still espousing. How about you?

Sincerely,

Sharon

P.S. Next time could you please type?

I heard excited voices outside my door. People were cranking the
stereo up. So I folded my letter and stuffed it in an envelope and ad-
dressed it. Then I realized I had no stamps. I knew where Kathryn kept
the house roll, but somehow I couldn't leave my room. I sat and I sat. I
took my citronella candle and my punk coil that I kept there and I lit
them up, since my screens were ripped and I had mosquitoes. I watched
the punk slowly burn. The end turned white. Millimeter by millimeter
the coil was smoldering and crumbling. The party was growing louder
outside, yet still I stayed. I was starting to get that weirdly satisfying mellow melancholy feeling of being forgotten. Like there I was, citronella
Cinderella, having worked and slaved behind the scenes to get stuff
ready, and then I had to stay home from the ball. Except actually I
hadn't done anything for the party except chop vegetables. Kathryn was
the one who'd really put in the effort.

For around forty-five minutes I hid out, until Will came to find me.
Knock, knock, knock. "Sharon?"

"What?"

"Sharon?"

"*What?*"

He opened my door and stuck his head in. "Aren't you coming out?" he asked. He wore these little wire-rimmed aviator glasses. His face looked so gentle and mild yet surprised. "What's wrong?"

"I just don't feel like I'm in such a partying mood."

"How come?"

I shrugged.

"Oh, honey," said Will, and he hugged me.

His hug squeezed a few tears from my eyes.

"Are you feeling left out?"

I nodded and wiped my face with my hand. Then I smiled at him. "But I don't know why," I said.

So he took my hand and we moved on out into the huge mob of people that were filling the house. And he got me a couple of drinks and stood next to me until I was okay on my own.

Outside in the yard by the food, which was arrayed on a camp table, Rich was standing with Kathryn, and she was beaming. She was wearing a really small turquoise dress, and pumps on her feet without stockings. Rich had on a new aloha shirt, and he had a whole bunch of leis piled on his neck. His beard was trimmed and his hair cut. This patina of mellow handsomeness was covering Rich, which I guess is what monogamy and a degree at long last will bring. All around Rich and Kathryn was the zoology department drinking beer, and Kathryn's Greenpeace friends, and buddies from Kathryn's canoeing club. But I didn't see Brian at all. So I just went out and hugged Rich and hugged Kathryn and then bent over the casserole dish and loosened up a couple of enchiladas. As I straightened up I nearly bumped heads with Imo.

"Hey!" I said.

"Sharon!" She bestowed a smile. "How are you?"

"I'm good," I said loudly above the roar of the crowd.

Her tan was lighter than I remembered. I guess she'd been ashore more. She still had the short hair, and those sharp black eyes, but she was looking at me kindly.

All my blood rushed to my head. I smiled at her like crazy. I was backing away, and she was asking, "What have you been up to? How have you been?"

I just kept backing up with my plate wobbling in one hand and my beer in the other. We ended up standing inside, practically in the kitchen, with me telling her all about my life in the monastery, and various jobs like Crack Seed World. The great gig I had now at Shirokiya.

She knit her brow and leaned in toward me so she could hear. "You've done a lot of different kinds of things." She spoke so politely, like we had just met for the first time.

"Well, if it's one thing I've learned," I said, "it's that everything you do is connected. It's like this whole chain or circle—but that's how you learn, right?"

Imo said, "I thought the plan was for you to go back to school."

"Hey, school is just one form of education," I said.

"A useful one."

I looked through the louver window toward Rich, who was going to be starting his postdoc in the fall. His stack of leis was higher now that more guests had arrived. He was walking around chin deep in carnations, orchids of all colors. Wherever he went he left a scent of ginger flowers and gardenias. "Useful for what?" I asked.

Imo smiled.

"It's not like I don't respect Rich for all the work he did, but the kind of education I want to do is more on the inside. I mean, you can study to be a doctor or an accountant or even maybe some kinds of scientist, but I feel like what you're studying can only be the surface. It's like the tip of the iceberg! And the actual delving you need to do, and diving down below the surface—how can some degree give you that?"

"Well," Imo said, "isn't the idea to acquire tools? And to learn techniques? The point is to avoid reinventing the wheel."

"But you know, spiritwise every wheel is different," I retorted. My head was buzzing a little bit from drinking after being relatively abstemious for a long while. "And, see, being identical to some standard wheel—is that all you get from degrees?"

Brian had walked in. He was way off in the far corner of the living room, but I sensed him all the way over there. My heart was racing. I wanted to turn and run, but somehow now that I'd started talking I couldn't stop. I kept going, louder, faster. The words were pumping. "What about truth?" I brandished my fork at Imo. "And I don't mean window dressing—or just some academic game universities put on. I mean TRUTH. The whole enchilada. What about enlightenment? What about transcendence? What do you major in for that?"

Imo cocked her head.

"Mmm," she said. You could actually hear her voice crisping up, like the Imo of old—delicate and crunchy like colonialist toast.

Then all of a sudden she said one of the single most important things that up to that time anyone had ever said to me in my whole life. "Religion, of course," said Imo. "You would major in religion for that."

1 2

—

Magnetic Currencies

N my Father's house are many mansions; if it were not so, I would have told you: I go to prepare a place for you."

Jesus lifted his bare arms toward us there in Galilee. He was telling us not to be afraid, even though he knew he was going to die. All of a sudden I couldn't take notes anymore. I'd heard Professor Flanagan was good, but now I knew. Because he stood up there in his white robe with his long hair and no notes, and he spoke to us, and his voice was so tender, and the words so pure. Listening to him you forgot this was a class at all, and you couldn't see the books and the loose leafs and the rows of student desks. You couldn't think about lunch or getting to your job, or any of that. There was Professor Flanagan dressed in a simple white robe, and he made it true, what he said. "Now you are clean through the word which I have spoken unto you."

Since I worked, I could only take one class each semester, but Intro Religion was a doozy. You had to enter a lottery just to get in, because the course was so popular. And that wasn't just because instead of a final exam or research paper you submitted a journal of a personal religious investigation. It was because of the prof himself. Not for nothing did Flanagan have a joint appointment in the drama department. In Intro

Religion, Professor Flanagan came to each class dressed up in the style of the whatever prophet he was teaching, and actually took on that figure's voice and personality. So he gave all his lectures in the first person. He was Buddha, and Moses, and Jesus, and Mohammad—except my year was the last time he did Mohammad, because a sophomore who was an Omani prince started offering the Muslim Students' Association a large reward for bumping off Flanagan for blaspheming the Prophet.

"I will not leave you comfortless; I will come to you," Flanagan said. "Yet a little while, and the world will see me no more; but you will see me. And because I live, you shall live also."

I sat in the second row of the class. I was chewing on the top of my ballpoint, but I didn't even know. I only saw later that the plastic was all chewed up. That was Flanagan's charisma. It was as if he were inventing this stuff on the spot. It was as if he were standing there before you, coining the golden rule. And suddenly coming up with all the inspirational sayings, so that you listened to the Sermon on the Mount, and you felt like you were hearing it for the first time. And actually, in my case, I was.

When he ended, he stood in silence. For a long moment nobody breathed. Then applause rang out through the whole room. I stood on my feet, and the whole class was standing with me.

When we all drifted out into the sunshine we blinked our eyes. It was like coming out from a great movie. I pretty much floated to work. At Shirokiya I saw the customers come and go, and it was as if I was looking at them through glass—like they were great silent fish in an aquarium, and when they spoke the words escaped their mouths like bubbles. Until all of a sudden one big guy in a hurry cornered me. He demanded the price on a black Samsonite suitcase, and I was so shocked to be accosted like that I nearly turned my back on him before I remembered I was actually working in the luggage department.

This was the most studious period of my life. This was the time I became almost scholastic, because I was so infatuated with the idea of academic rigor. My housemates saw the difference in me now that I was back in school. I would hole up in my room and read the Koran. I would sit in the living room in our bowl-shaped papa-san chair and highlight Exodus in my Holy Bible—the King James edition. I copied quotes into my black composition book. Sometimes I quoted my quotes aloud—just to meditate on them. For example, I would be sitting in the papa-san cross-legged and I would say "I have told you, O man, what is good. Only to do justly and to love mercy and to walk humbly with thy God." And I would chant the verse, and I would rearrange it and shuffle it around—but with respect—just the way you would turn a jewel in the light. "I have told you, human, what is good. Only to do justly and to love mercy and to walk wholly with thy God. I have told you, woman, what is good. . . ."

Then Rich would walk by and say in a snide voice, "Om shanti shanti."

He always made fun of me. He kept joking I was trying to get religion because I wasn't getting anything else. He was so crude. One day I turned on him. I said, "Rich, it seems like you're really threatened by my growth."

Rich guffawed, "Yeah, I am. I'm afraid of what you're growing into."

"Very funny." I looked at his postgraduate beer belly. "Why don't you worry about how *you're* growing?"

The topic actually came up at our house meeting. Not Rich's weight, but my studies. We were all sitting around the table eating popcorn out of a punch bowl, and I said, "It's time for new business, right?"

"Yeah," said Tom.

"Well, under new business I'd like to say it really bothers me that people object to me studying in the living room."

"That's not new business," said Kathryn.

"What is it then?"

"That's an area of concern," she said.

"Okay, fine. Whatever you want to call it. When people walk by and make comments while I'm reading, then I don't feel like I'm welcome in the house."

"I never made a single comment about your reading," said Tom.

"I wasn't talking about *you*," I told him. "Om shanti shanti," I said. "That was harassment."

"It was a little joke," Rich said, getting on the defensive.

"To me, it wasn't a joke, okay? And I'm tired of being harassed just for studying religious texts."

"What, now you're getting into martyrdom?"

"You see what I mean," I appealed to everybody.

"I was being facetious. Give me a break."

"No, you give me a break," I snapped. "I never bothered you."

Rich glared at me. "How about demanding we all say grace before dinner?"

"Demanding? It was a suggestion. It was an idea. I said, I am floating this idea out to you that maybe we should consider discussing just possibly allowing some meaningful words to leave our mouths before we stuff our forks into them!"

"And we voted it down," Tom said.

"Three times!" Rich said. "Sharon, we all care about you . . . am I right?" he asked the others.

"We love you," Will said. "It's just that it seems at times . . ."

Rich jumped in. "Like we're living with this person who is slowly turning into some kind of humorless . . ."

Kathryn finished for him. "Fanatic."

"Fanatic? You guys!" I spread my hands. My fingers were shiny with popcorn butter. "How could you think that about me?"

"Sometimes I'm scared for you," Kathryn said.

"You are so hostile to me," I said.

"Stop!" said Will.

No one spoke for a minute.

"I guess we'll work harder on sensing people's boundaries," Will said.

"Amen," said Rich.

I shot him a glance.

He was staring down at the table with a poker face.

I began withdrawing somewhat from my life in the house. I spent long hours in my room with Marlon and the letters I received from Gary. Yeah, who would have thought? Gary and I were writing to each other all the time. He was sitting there in Jerusalem and I was in Hawaii, and we were writing to each other. I used to read his letters over and over to myself because they were so mysterious. They were so sadly beautiful. I'd never realized Gary could write in such a poetic style. (Now he was sending all his letters typed.) "Sharon," he wrote to me. "When I read your letter my hands trembled. All these years, and in the end, you, like me, are seeking God. I've traveled the whole world searching. Ten years I've traveled, and lost myself so many times on the way. Love, success, money, these were all mine. Yet all that time my heart was restless. Only now in Jerusalem I am coming to the beginning of myself. I am reading the ancient texts. I am living in the Old City of the angels and the prophets. I am finding the key."

It turned out that after traveling the Pacific with the German chick, Katrina, he had followed her back to Germany and lived with her for several years, after which she had unceremoniously dumped him for another guy. Gary had then taken off and wandered throughout Germany and Holland and worked for a while as a stringer for the Associated Press, during which time he visited Anne Frank's house. While he was there in the hidden rooms where Anne had lived, he saw the table where she had eaten and the bed where she had slept, and he began sobbing. All of a sudden he'd realized something. He was a Jew. Of course, he had been Jewish all his life, but it had never hit him before. That he was a Jew like Anne. He was Jew enough to be killed for it. As soon as he realized he was Jewish, Gary took off for Jerusalem. He didn't know the language, or anything, but he went straight from the airport to the Western Wall. There, two rabbis from the Torah Or Institute were waiting for him. They picked him right up and took him back to the institute to teach him Judaism, which was the key to himself that he had been missing all this time.

Of course, it took a lot of letters back and forth for me to get the whole picture. As I said, Gary had a very spiritual poetic way of writing. And yet it was the strangest thing corresponding with him. I understood so well what he had been dealing with in his wanderings. I knew exactly what it was like to have a heart that was restless. Reading his words was like reading my own. It was like meeting my own twin wanderer after years of separation. I thought: Could it be that in some karmic way, everything is coming around again? After all, he'd had no way of knowing I would still be in Hawaii when he'd written his postcard. As he explained, he'd only really written it for himself.

"Dear Gary," I wrote. "I believe in symmetries in the universe. Correspondences! I believe that people can fall into a certain pattern, even when that pattern is so complicated you cannot figure it out. Like you, I am into prophets. Like you, I am trying to reconnect. Here we are, on opposite sides of the world, yet magnetic currencies flow through us. We are both coming from the same place."

My letters to Gary were long. I used to write him page after page. It took me that long to express my thoughts. Plus, my handwriting was big.

I wrote to him all about my house and about school and Shirokiya and my vision and rebirth. I'd mail off my latest thoughts and then I'd wait and wait. But it took over a week just for my letter to reach him, and then sometimes ten, twelve more days for his answers to come back. Day after day I'd open our rusty old mailbox that Kathryn had spray-painted white. No cigar. Oftentimes all I'd find would be our house bills, along with the green chameleon who used to hide there in the back.

"Hi, little guy," I said one day, poking my face into the mailbox.

The chameleon looked at me calmly. He was about ten inches long, mostly tail, and he was bright green, like a leaf with the sun shining through it. He breathed in and out and spread his tiny little toes on the corrugated metal mailbox floor. He looked out at me. I looked in at him. We each contemplated the view.

"Can you change color?" I asked him.

He breathed in and he breathed out. He never forgot to breathe.

"I mean, it's okay if you can't," I said. "I have this friend. And it seems like he's changed so much and I've changed so much we've come full circle back together again. Do you think that could be?"

The folds in his neck puffed in and out. His eyes were like shiny black seeds.

"I'm thinking about dancing again," I said.

It was true. Ever since Gary and I had started corresponding, my whole body wanted to dance. My feet wanted to jump. My arms wanted to fly into the air. Gary and I were writing all the time about our memories. Admittedly, his were mostly of the Holocaust and of Our Sages, who he was learning about in Torah Or, while mine were mostly about the two of us spinning in the air. Mine were more about this dancing couple that was once us. Still, when I wrote about us dancing, Gary wrote back:

"Oh, yes. Oh, yes, I remember all of that. And now look how far we've come. We are still dancing on the same path! Sharon, I have learned this: *There are no coincidences.* This is truth. There are no coincidences. There are no random acts. Everything that happens in life happens for a reason. Even you and me, Sharon. Even us. We happened for a reason. You could call it karma. Or fate. They are just names. They don't matter. I am talking about God's will. I am speaking of *bashert.*"

I almost had to put Gary's letter down on my *buton* where I was reading. That was pretty heady stuff there. I mean, as I used to say to Kekui, this was not how I was raised—this was not my background—this whole providential view of the world, as if God were looking down at people and taking notes for later. Yet here was Gary writing and saying—could this be? That he still loved me? And it was intentional, at least on God's part? I looked at every typed word. The thin Torah Or letterhead crackled in my hands. A mysterious elation began to come over me. Mysterious, because my rational side just could not understand how all this might work. Elation because all of a sudden it was like the world turned inside out; the resurrection of everything I'd buried long ago. I could see my jerk ex-boyfriend transformed, and my old love reciprocated, and my dancing partner joined to me again. All of a sudden I had before me these tangible signs. And God's will and Providence were real to me.

WHAT happened to me that weekend clinched it. *Bashert* was here to stay.

I had been going for a few weeks to a discussion group that Professor Flanagan had recommended to me. The discussions were put on jointly by the Unitarian community and a Quaker fellowship that shared the space. The two groups were amicable partners that met on alternate Sundays three weeks out of the month, and on the fourth week held forums for learning where different people from the community would come and give talks about their beliefs or their work, or whatever turned them on. For example, a Catholic priest would come and talk to us about Catholicism, or an astronomer would come and show us slides of planets in the solar system and speak about his personal views of the origins of the universe.

The Unitarian church was just a lovely white house from the old days with porches and dark polished koa wood floors, and there was a scratchy sisal rug in the meeting room and folding chairs in a circle, and by the door a cork bulletin board where all the name tags for the combined membership of the Unitarian community and Quaker fellowship were pinned up. You reused your original name tag every time you came, and actually it was always a friendly feeling walking in and seeing everybody's name pinned up there. We used those name tags with the clear plastic sheaths.

Well, the Sunday right after Thanksgiving my bus rolled up on Old Pali Road and I walked over to the Unitarian church; and there, in front of the church, was this silver-gray Cadillac, and it had a placard in the front window that said CLERGY. Inside the meeting room stood a large man in a gray three-piece suit and tie and dress shoes, and also a tiepin. I hadn't seen anyone in so many clothes in years. He was a portly guy, but also on the tall side, and he had a little bit of gray hair on top and dark eyes, and he had reading glasses on, and he was leaning over and reading all of the name tags pinned up on the bulletin board. When I came up and took my name tag from the board and pinned it on, he extended his hand and introduced himself in this deep, rolling, yet melancholy voice. And he pressed my hand in his and said, "Rabbi Everett Siegel."

We were all there—all the regulars, in any case, which was about twenty people, and we sat in a circle, and that week's host, Dave, got up and said, "Let's all welcome Rabbi Siegel into our fellowship." And he gave Rabbi Siegel one of the leis we always gave visitors, a brown lei made out of seedpods and dry long grains. And people murmured, "Welcome."

It was an informal group. By which I mean T-shirts and shorts and the occasional muumuu, and when guests came they usually sat with us in the circle and did more of a round-table discussion, unless they had visual aids, like that astronomer and his slides. Rabbi Siegel, however, stood right up front in his suit, and he paced back and forth and he cleared his throat as if he was trying to figure out how to begin. He stood there and struggled for a few moments. Then he looked us in the eyes, and when he spoke his voice was low, not soft, but low. It was the strangest thing when he spoke. It was like he was calling us by name. He said, "Stan Lebowitz. Lucinda Stern. Henry Miesell." He said my name, Sharon. "Sharon Spiegelman." He just kept naming names. He named about half the people there at that day's fellowship. I thought at first he was doing some kind of getting-to-know-you game, but then I realized he was actually reading our names off our name tags. "Dave Aronson. Mitch Kahan." Siegel looked at all of us, and he said slowly, like he was telling the slowest saddest joke in the world, "Some of my best Jews are Friends."

I thought, what in the world? But Rabbi Siegel kept on talking.

He said, "We have questions. We have questions about God and about life, about religion and morality. We have questions today and we seek answers. And yet, and yet, I have a question for some of *you*. Why is it that those of us who are born Jews look for answers in every single religion but our own? Once our people were a light unto the nations. Once our sacred Torah, the First Testament, was called a tree of life to all who held fast to it. And yet, and yet, in this age of darkness—in our century which is blackened by the greatest evil known to any since the dawn of time, since the dawn of man's existence—our people are not a light unto the nations, but a flickering candle of indifference. Our tree of life is weakened with intermarriage, and ignorance. Our children and, in fact, we ourselves, do not know what it is to be a Jew."

At which point I raised my hand—but Siegel just sailed on without even acknowledging me. When other hands went up he didn't even look. Frankly, the guy was in love with the sound of his own purple prose! He was definitely not a Unitarian up there in his suit, with his Cadillac the size of a hearse. He went on and on. He said the Jewish people were God's chosen people. And the Jewish heritage was the one true thing to which all Jews should turn. This chosen people stuff, that just made you want to slouch down in your folding chair and disappear! But there was something about him. He reminded me of someone from a long time ago. It was something in his voice—this peculiar, deeply mournful sound like muted taxi horns, or deep dark cello music. As Siegel kept talking I would catch a memory and then it would be gone, I would catch it again for an instant, and then I would lose it. And then it came to me—that voice! You could hear Grandpa Irving in the rabbi's voice. All rueful, Brooklyn-Yiddish, dark, and smoky. You could hear him, my grandfather! Deep down underneath Siegel's poetic diction, if you listened hard enough, he was there: Grandpa Irving! And I sat up in my chair and I closed my eyes and I thought as hard as I could, Grandpa Irving, are you there? Are you channeling through this Siegel or what? Hey, I'm sorry I gave away your watch. Grandpa Irving? What are you saying to me? But hard as I tried, I just heard the tone of his voice, not any meaning—just this endless shushing, like when you hold a seashell to your ear.

Spellbound I sat for forty minutes while Siegel talked. Only when he was done and the questions and answers were over and people started to leave did the spell wear off. Then I stood up, and I stirred myself. And I was pissed! I walked right up to Rabbi Everett Siegel and I said, "Rabbi?"

"Hello, Sharon," he said. He was reading my name tag again, as if I were his waitress.

"I wanted to make a comment to you, being one of the Jews you mentioned who is a Friend."

"Yes," he said. His voice was growing lower and graver by the minute.

"I just wanted to say that personally I was a little bit offended when you spoke about people of Jewish backgrounds running way. Because I am not and I have *never been* a person who is running away from anything."

"I see," he said.

"I happen to be a comparative religion major at UH," I said. "I happen to be a person running *toward* spiritualism."

He looked at me with his melancholy eyes. "The question," he said, "is whether your spiritualism, as you call it, has anything to do with your religion."

"My what?"

"With Judaism."

"I never said Judaism was my religion."

"The irony is," Rabbi Siegel told me in his rolling tones, "we are a people who have survived by our memories. And now we are plagued with amnesia."

"I find it a little bit offensive that you keep accusing me of being an amnesiac when you don't even know me," I practically shouted. "For example, I've been an Israeli folk dancer for years. For example, I come from a Jewish home, and my stepmother was also Jewish. It's not like I could run away from Judaism if I tried!" And I was ready to go on, but at that moment the *bashert* happened! The Jewish fate Gary had referred to.

"You're a dancer?" the Rabbi said. "Then come to the temple and dance."

I wrote to Gary that night: "When he said that, I just stood there in awe of the fate that had in two seconds descended upon me! It's just like you said about coincidences. It is exactly what you were saying, that there are no random patterns in the universe. I've lived here ten years—going on eleven. I never knew there was folk dancing going on here. And now, today, I found out a group of women meet Thursday eves at Martin Buber Temple. They have music, but no instructor—since the one they had was deported back to Israel along with her sister—and they are looking to pay (top dollar!!) for a knowledgeable dancer to teach and lead them!"

I had never had a *portent* before. I had never felt fate come tap me on the shoulder. It was one of the spookiest yet most intoxicating feelings I had ever known.

The very next Thursday, at least an hour before class, I knocked on Rabbi Siegel's office door. "Come in," he boomed like the great big papa bear. And I entered his sanctum. I had never been in a rabbi's office before. It was quite a shrine! The wall behind the desk was covered with black-and-white photos of bigwigs embracing Siegel and shaking his hand. There were people in tuxedos, and people with ribbons and medals around their necks. This Siegel had obviously gotten around. One of the photos was of him and President Kennedy! The office had red plush upholstered chairs and two massive desks full of plaques and gold penholders, and commemorative crystal ashtrays, and about ten thousand books.

"You'll need this," the rabbi said, and he gave me a tape player. "And this." He gave me a carton of folk dancing cassettes. Then he gave me a really long official check, signed by the treasurer of Martin Buber Temple, for five hundred dollars, and said something about everyone in the group being so excited about meeting me, except I was staring so hard at the money I barely heard him.

I took the check, and the tape player and the tapes, and I set everything up in the social hall of Martin Buber Temple. No one was around, so I took off my sandals and stretched out. The floor was smooth terrazzo. Wood was better for your feet, but we'd deal with it. The space was big and airy. There was one of those accordion-pleat partitions between the social hall and the sanctuary, which was all done in earth tones, rust and ochre. As for the social hall, it was decorated with a wall mural of King Solomon in a great big crown and robes like a Freemason. The king was holding a sword over the head of a peculiar-looking baby, and on one side of him was a woman shrieking, and on the other side a woman sulking. In gold underneath was painted "The Wisdom of Solomon." I was contemplating this artwork when a couple of old ladies came in.

"Are you the instructor?" one of them inquired. She was very large and bosomy and wore a muumuu. Her friend had white hair and she wore a black leotard with a black-and-white check wraparound skirt over it. A couple more ladies came in behind them, and everybody kissed everybody else and called each other dear.

It took me a minute just to realize that these dames were actually my Israeli dancers!

"Are you Sharon Spiegelman?"

"Yeah, I'm Sharon," I said, reluctantly. The ladies all rushed around me to introduce themselves.

"I'm Ruth Katz," said the bosomy one.

A small plump blond lady also came up, and she had with her a taller woman with deep red hair and rouge and bloodred lipstick, and the blond lady said, "I'm Henny Pressman, and this is my sister Lillian."

"Betsy Sugarman," said the one in the black leotard and checked skirt.

"And my name is Estelle. Pleased to meet you," said the lady with white hair, and she held out her hand.

"Estelle—that's my mom's name," I heard myself say.

"Really? And where does she live, dear?"

I looked at Estelle blankly.

"On the Mainland?"

"Oh, she's dead," I said.

Estelle's face fell. "I'm sorry to hear that," she said.

"It's okay," I said. "I mean, I didn't even know her. She died in my infancy."

"Oh, that's terrible," said Ruth. They were all clucking.

"And your father?"

I looked down at my feet.

"Is he living?"

"He is, but he's not well," I said. "He's suffering from . . ." I hesitated just a fraction of a second. "Gout."

"Gout!" said Betsy Sugarman.

"In this day and age?" asked Estelle.

And I was standing there by the tape recorder, under the wall mural of King Solomon, and I was thinking, Why did I say gout?

"But there are medications for gout," said Betsy.

"He is one of the only people in the world who is just not susceptible to the medications," I said. "They just have no effect on him whatsoever."

"Really!" said Betsy. "I'll have to ask my husband about this! My husband is a doctor," she told me.

"Let's form a circle," I said.

We limped through *"Dodi Li"* as slowly as it was humanly possible to go. Yet still, when we did the turns, some of us turned one way, and some of us the other. I couldn't get everybody going in the same direction. The music was playing softly, and my feet wanted so much to follow the music. My feet remembered the steps even there, but I thought, Is this my comeback to the world of dance? Is this really part of the grand plan that Gary kept referring to? Because maybe all the pieces do come back together again in life. Maybe there is this pattern in the grand scheme of things. But what if the pattern turns out to be less of a gorgeous mandala and more of a sick parody?

I just ached to think of that. I wanted to stop right there. It was embarrassing to be out on the floor with those old ladies. The dancer I used to be was laughing at me now. Actually she didn't know whether to laugh or to cry. I wanted to turn off the music, but I gritted my teeth, at least to get through the first class. It wouldn't be right to quit on them—not then and there.

The one dance they could do was *"Hinach Yafa,"* this simple couples dance, which of course the ladies all had to dance with each other, since we had no guys. They all paired up, and I danced with Ruth. That was the one time we finally made some progress. I had the tape going, and we were all pretty much moving in the right direction, step right, one, two, three, brush, Yemenite, finger snap. Then all of a sudden Betsy Sugarman started in, "Sharon. Sharon?" And she stopped right in the middle with her partner, who was Henny, and everyone else looked up distracted, and Betsy said, "May I ask a question?"

Instantly, everybody looked over at me. All the ladies got distracted. The whole dance we'd patiently built up ground to a halt.

I let go of Ruth's hand and glared at Betsy. "What."

"Sharon, what does this mean?"

"What does what mean?"

"The song. What does the song mean? *'Hinach Yafa'*?"

"Beats me." In all my years of dancing I'd never worried about the actual lyrics. I mean, there were people I knew back in Boston who could translate the words, but dancing wasn't about *words*. Dancing wasn't for your mouth, it was for your feet! Dancing was springing up, and bouncing. Spinning. Snapping. It would take someone like Betsy, who had lousy rhythm, to start wondering about Hebrew words like that.

After the ladies left I packed up the tapes and took the tape recorder back to the rabbi's office. "Come in," he boomed once again. And I came inside holding the box in front of me.

"Sit down," the rabbi said.

So I plopped down, and when I did I realized I was exhausted.

"How did it go?" he asked.

I quit, I said deep inside myself. Still, I had that check folded inside my back pocket.

Slowly, I put the tapes and the tape player on his desk. I thought, Sharon, if you have any self-respect you'll give him the money back. "It went fine," I said, yet a few tears started in my eyes.

"It went fine?" the rabbi asked.

I nodded.

"Then . . ." He was too formal and polite to say, Then why are you crying? He said, "Then what, exactly, is the trouble?"

"Oh, just . . . the dancing, and the class, and the students."

"All of it?" he said.

"All of it."

He gave me a tissue.

I wiped my face. I pulled myself together. I said, "It isn't the way I thought it was going to be."

"What *did* you think?" he asked me.

"I don't know. I mean . . . I thought, um, they, the class, would, you know, be able to, like . . . dance."

"If they knew how to dance, they wouldn't need an instructor," he said.

He had me there for a moment. "I know, I know. That's true. But I thought they'd have at least some idea."

"Well," said the rabbi, "some idea will have to come from you."

"Okay," I said. "Okay, yeah, you're right." I stood up. "Listen," I said, "I have to catch my bus."

"Take the tapes with you," the rabbi urged. "Here, and the tape player."

"I can take them home?"

"Certainly," he said.

"Wow. Thanks!" I felt terrible complaining when I was taking all this money and the music too. I felt guilty hating those women in the class just for their lousy timing and their interruptions. Which reminded me. "Rabbi? What does *Hinach yafa* mean?"

"You are beautiful," the rabbi said. "Behold, you are fair."

"Whoa."

"Do you know where those words come from?"

"Hebrew," I said.

"Wait a minute." He was leafing through books on his desk. Then he swiveled around in his big leather swivel chair. He pulled a volume from his shelf and leafed some more. And then he said, "Ah."

And I said, "Ah?"

"Come back for just a moment." He sat down behind his desk in this hugely tall leather desk chair like a throne, and I sat back down, but just on the arm of my chair, just perched so any second I could go. And Siegel read from one of his volumes, *"Hinach yafa, raiti, hinach yafa, ay-nayich yonim. . . ."* And he translated the words into English for me in his rolling tones, "You are beautiful, my love, you are beautiful. Your eyes are like doves behind your veil. . . ."

And I said, "Wait, wait, I know this. This is the Song of Solomon."

"Or as we call it in our tradition, the Song of Songs."

"And it's about Christ making love to his Church," I said.

"It is *not* about Christ and his Church," the rabbi declared.

I was taken aback. "Well, I used to do Bible study, and that's what it said in the Bible."

"Not in our Bible," the rabbi said. He spoke very absolutely.

"You mean like that's not your interpretation."

"No," he said, "The Song of Songs is not about Christ and his Church. That is simply not true."

"Well," I said. "Well, you know, every religion has a different idea of truth."

He sat there and glared.

But I, being a religion major, said, "Every religion has its own metaphors of the unknown, you know. And just because those metaphors are different doesn't make them invalid."

Then Rabbi Siegel looked at me like if his conscience hadn't forbade it he would have taken one of the pointy pens sticking out of his gold penholders and stabbed me in the heart. And he looked at me, and he looked at me, and he said, "Sharon, I am a founding member of this state's ecumenical council of Christians, Buddhists, Taoists, and Jews. I have been a lifelong contributor to interfaith dialogue in this nation. And I will yield to no one in my conviction that all of our scriptures, whether prophetic or poetic, should be a bridge of understanding between the peoples of the world. These lines of poetry are measures of our commonality. . . ."

"Uh-huh," I said.

"But we had them FIRST!"

I nearly fell off the arm of the chair. I had to catch my breath. "Well, you know, that's not completely fair."

"It's a fact."

"Well . . ."

He leaned forward and stared at me with all his might, and he said, "Well, what?"

"Well, not really. . . ."

So then Siegel started in on me. "This may come as news to you. Nevertheless, there is such a thing as history. There are documents and texts that predate others, and traditions from which others have been spawned."

"I'm not trying to pick a fight here," I said. "I just asked one little question, since I didn't know the answer."

"Granted. Granted," the rabbi said, and he sighed again heavily. He was a man of sighs. Then he looked at me, and he said, "Don't stop."

"Don't stop what?"

"Don't stop teaching. Even if your students know nothing. Especially then. Even if they don't know the first thing. Then teach them that. You may be their only source," he said. "Then be that source. Be an oasis in the desert. Be like Augustine in Hippo. Even here," he said, "even on this piece of rock in the Pacific Ocean, there can be learning if you have the heart to teach."

I looked at him sitting there at the desk and a startling thought occurred to me. Rabbi Siegel was talking about himself! That was a profound moment for me. Not just because of what Siegel said—but because for a second I'd really heard him say it, and unlike talking, meditating, questioning, seeking, and screwing up, listening to other people was something I hardly ever did. Back at the monastery Michael was always harping about learning to listen, but I'd never really done it. I'd never listened to someone else before. Now it almost knocked me down, suddenly hearing the rabbi speak out like that. Suddenly feeling the strength of somebody else's heart. I looked at the rabbi, and that was when I realized: This man is reaching out to me, but not just because I'm a sinner, or a loser, or a returning student. This person is seeking me out because we are related. Because somehow, somewhere, we come from the same Jewish place—which is why Grandpa Irving was trying to warn me! This rabbi knows the code. He knows the Hebrew at the bottom of the Bible. He knows the text and the letters and the sound and the voice, and deep down he knows me, because I am his relative! He knew me *first*.

"Ah," I said.

Rabbi Siegel put his hands together and rested his chin ecclesiastically on his fingertips. He said, "You teach the dance. And I'll teach you the words."

13

Minotaur

COUNTING me, there were three of us who came to Rabbi Siegel's office each week for instruction, and we were a diverse group. There was a guy named Fred, and a girl named Alyssa. Now, Fred was about forty and quite tall but unbelievably skinny, and his face was always raw with sunburn. He did odd jobs, mainly fixing things in people's houses, which was how he had originally met the rabbi. For about ten years Fred had been addicted to drugs and blown a few gaskets, and lost some dear friends who had wound up dead of overdoses. Finding himself alive in Honolulu, he had decided to rededicate himself spiritually, but feeling that the Catholic religion he was brought up in was not the most comfortable for him, he had for several years been searching for a new religion he could relate to. So having worked for the temple on its retaining walls, and attended some services, he'd decided to start learning about Judaism. Alyssa, on the other hand, was this smart but somewhat disturbed thirteen-year-old who actually was from a Jewish family. Her dad was treasurer of the temple. She was in the awkward position of being on the verge of her bat mitzvah but at the same time having been expelled from Sunday school for inciting an insurrection in her class against its instructor, who was found

later locked in the art supply room. She was a fat freckled kid with
straight, shoulder-length brown hair and braces, sparkling brown eyes, a
foul mouth, and pockets full of candy and bubblegum, which she was
always offering to sell you. The rabbi was teaching her, as a favor to her
parents—as an alternative to Sunday school.

So we would sit in the rabbi's office, and we would be at all different
levels and at odds with each other. Alyssa would be sucking a jaw-
breaker and sometimes practicing the Hebrew chanting for her bat
mitzvah, and Fred would be studying some book like *To Be a Jew,* and in
between them I would be going over the Aleph Bet with the rabbi.
"Aleph," the rabbi would say, and he'd show me the large-print aleph in
the book, and he would say, "Aleph has horns like an ox." And actually it
was true, you could see the head of the ox and the two pointy horns up
top. "Bet. It looks like a *bayit,* or house." And bet did have a nice sheltering form, and even a dot in the middle, like a doorknob. "Dalet is like a
delet, or door." Okay, you could kind of see it, with that big long hinge
on the right, and the top of the door swinging out to the left. "Ayin is
like an eye." That one was fairly mystical to me, with its shape open on
top, but then cupped on the bottom and with a little tail. It could have
been an eye, or a well, or a fish standing with her tail up in the air. That
letter could have been the source of many things.

"Ayin. Ayin," I'd be trying to get it down.

And Alyssa would mutter under her breath, "It's only *been* a month."

And I'd say, "Look, kid, I happen to work. I happen to work and
go to school part time, and—I have three hundred pages a night of
reading to—"

"So. I go to school full time." Alyssa thought that was very witty.

And she sniggered, which was her specialty. When Alyssa giggled, she
would giggle *at* you, and that is pretty much the dictionary definition of
what sniggering means.

"Ladies. Ladies," Fred would say, and raise his rail-thin arms, and wave
his raw-boned hands. He was really a very sweet and gentle guy, but the
slightly spooky thing about him was his sweetness and all the rest of his
attributes had this residual feeling about them, like they were what was
left over after he'd had his big systemic cataclysm. He was sweet and
brittle like banana chips. He would say all the time, "Let's not lose our
concentration, now."

After a while, when it came to Alyssa, I really had to hold it in. I had to delve deep inside of myself and try to breathe. One time I came to class and I was almost the happiest I'd ever been. I'd written a letter to John Denver, just about his music and his vision of the environment, and what it meant to me to hear him express it so well. And I'd mailed the letter several months before, and then that week I got a large envelope in the mail, and it was, I swear, an eight-by-ten glossy black-and-white photo of John playing his guitar. "It was as big as that one." I pointed to the rabbi's large photo of himself and John F. Kennedy. "And he wrote on it," I told Fred and Alyssa and the rabbi.

"No!" Fred said, all impressed.

"He did. He wrote, *For Sharon. Peace, John.*"

"My goodness," said Fred.

"He didn't really write that, you know," Alyssa informed me. "He probably has a hundred people working for him to do stuff like that."

"Well," I began, "well . . . what do you know about *anything*?" I wished propriety in the rabbi's study hadn't forbidden me from adding, *you little shit.* I'd just never imagined it could be like that, with a hundred people in an office stuffing envelopes with photos. But when she put it that way—it sounded so mean, it must have been true. I blinked. I ducked my head down. My hair fell around my face.

After a minute Rabbi Siegel said, "I had a light lunch today. Would anyone care to join me for a bite to eat?" He got up and opened the door from his office to the vestry, which was this little passageway between the office and the sanctuary where his black robes hung. He went in there and he got his briefcase, and with great dignity in his three-piece suit he took his car keys and he drove the three of us out of the temple lot in his gray Cadillac, which had a license plate that said: SHALOHA. Fred and I were in the back, and Alyssa sat in front. He drove up to this little old local store just off Old Pali Road and he parked directly in front of the door, which he could do because he had his Clergy placard in the window, and because he was a regular customer. And Fred got a pack of pistachio nuts, and Alyssa got gummy bears and Sweet-Tarts, and the rabbi and I got those large homemade almond cookies that they always had in those local stores on the counter in a jar. And the rabbi paid for everything. It was his treat. He was actually a very compassionate man, Rabbi Siegel, and also, he told us that his wife,

Grete, had him on pretty much grapefruits and vegetables at home, because she'd put him on a diet. And he tended to get headaches in the afternoons.

We ended up going to the store a lot, and during those trips the rabbi
told us something of his life, and how he'd been raised in an Orthodox
home, very strict and scholarly, and how he had at one time wanted to
be a concert violinist, but the winding road of life had changed him and
his original ideals. He had found his calling in Reform Judaism, and not
in the dogmatism of Orthodoxy. When he drove us all in that Caddy, it
was just like sailing in a silvery gray ocean liner. He showed us the scenic
places out near the reservoir where he'd married people. He talked about
how this couple and that one wrote their own contracts and ceremonies.
We had some lovely times. We all relaxed to the point that we students
started getting along pretty well. The only thing was, we weren't really
learning all that much, or, if we were, it was at a snail's pace.

After around six weeks I had finally mastered the Hebrew alphabet,
and I was moving on to simple words in a primer about this little Israeli
kid named Uri. And then, guess what happened? A newly engaged guy,
Matthew, entered the class, and the rabbi had to turn his attention to
teaching the alphabet to him, leaving me to struggle mostly by myself.
So, of course, I didn't get very far—actually none of us did, because the
only serious learning happening there was the rabbi's descriptions of the
alphabet and his discussions of Judaism in general. I started getting frustrated, because I'd come in there with a very certain goal, which was to
learn the Hebrew words that went with the dances I was teaching. I was
still teaching the ladies every week, and a couple of them were actually
picking up some steps. But it seemed like the rabbi wasn't teaching me
any Hebrew words at all.

Finally, after class one Sunday I hung back until the others had gone,
and I brought my chair in close to the rabbi's desk, and I said, "Rabbi, I
hate to say this, but I feel like we're all wasting time in here."

Siegel looked at me over his suit and silk tie with its silver tiepin.
"Sharon," he said, "I'm sorry you feel that way."

"I thought I was supposed to be learning some Hebrew. Isn't that
what we're here for?"

"Sharon," he said, "I think you realize, that in the end, the words are
the least important aspect of what I'm trying to teach."

"Not to me!" I protested.

"Come in here," he said.

We walked through the vestry and into the sanctuary. He flicked on the lights, floodlighting the temple's vaulted ceiling and modernistic stained glass. We were standing on the dais looking down onto the rows of empty seats below us. And I saw the organ on the left with the seats for the choir all fenced off with a paneled wood fence, and I saw the marble altar, where there were two candlesticks with electric candles in them. The rabbi pushed a button and a pair of doors in the front wall opened, and you could see this open spotlit closet with four Torah scrolls inside, and they were covered with crimson velvet, and the covers embroidered in gold thread.

"Sharon," Rabbi Siegel said, "Judaism is more than a few simple phrases. It's a culture. One of music and art, poetry and light. It is the intimate and the sublime; it is the exalted and the humble. Think of the lyric music of the Psalms." He stood up there in the empty theater, and he gestured with his hands. You could see him turning all sermonic. "While the Egyptians were building tombs, we were singing of life and love. While the monuments of the ancients were crumbling to dust, we were treading over the ruins in a tradition that arched back over the millennia, and forward to the future. Our friends in class may never remember a word of Hebrew, but if they can sense something of the grandeur of our tradition—if they can only glimpse one part of the history of our chosen people. . . ."

"Excuse me?" I said. There he was, right back where he'd started with the chosen people. "I'm not talking about joining a people!" I told him. "Definitely not any people that thinks it's any better than any other people!"

So naturally Siegel heaved a big sigh. He folded his arms over his orotund bod. "Each people is dear to God in its own way," he told me. "I often make the analogy to the different states of the Union. . . ."

And I felt like it was my turn to sigh. He was actually a good human, Siegel, but when you asked him a question, it was like throwing a bottle in the ocean and watching it drift away over all his metaphors and comparisons, plus the incidents it reminded him of. And as far as where I was coming from with my folk background, he hadn't a clue, because he was into "high" art. He used to say, "When I say the Bor'chu—'Bless ye

the Lord'—I think how fitting a trumpet fanfare would be right there."
And I'd be thinking, trumpet fanfares? That was spiritual music for him?
If it turned him on—but to me God's music was this whole-world eth-
nic fusion that belonged to everyone! Bluegrass, bongos, recorder,
ukulele. Nose flute. Just a joyful noise, just folk. All the voices of the
planet raised in song and humming like one enormous family!

THAT night after my encounter with the rabbi I sat up late in the living
room writing to Gary. I was feeling so overwhelmed; I was so full of indignation. I scribbled page after page, just pouring out my heart. I felt
like he was the only one I could confide in. I was consumed with this
thirst, this huge desire to learn and to know, and to somehow draw near
the Creator! And the reality was I was teaching a bunch of senior citi-
zens to dance, and taking an adult ed course in Hebrew that had gone
way off track—not to mention my academic trouble. Yup, I was having
trouble at the university, but it wasn't what you might think. In Professor Flanagan's course I'd received a solid A. I was rock solid in that class.
My problem was the course had ended. Now it was spring semester, and
I had Professor Raymond Friedell.

"He is the antithesis of everything Flanagan stood for!" I wrote to Gary.

He is against personal expression; he is against independent work; he is
against *students*! He actually said as much. You'd think they would take
his license away! I'm serious. He said the first day he wasn't about to
stand in the front of the lecture hall and do a song and dance for us.
The material was dry, and it was meant to be dry, and we'd jolly better
learn it that way, from the texts, because he wasn't going to be putting
on any performances. He is against relevance of religion to modern
times. He said that! I wrote it down: 'This course is not about the relevance of religious ideas, and so you may as well get the notion of relevance out of your heads right now. It is a misplaced notion. These
texts are not about us; they are about themselves. They are not about
our time. They are about theirs.' Gary, this prof is anti-everything I
loved about school. He is anti-Flanagan. He is the anti-Christ! Oh
Gary. I dread tomorrow. I dread Mondays and coming to his class. I
don't understand his lectures at all. All I understand is this quality em-

anating from him of tremendous arbitrariness. Like he is drunk with power. He knows we would leave if we could. But his course is required for the major! I should quit Siegel's Hebrew class. That's what I should have done today, and quit teaching folk dancing too. Thursdays I should be studying. I've spread myself so thin. People at the house think I'm slacking off on chores. They're yelling where's our groceries! It's just I'm so tired. They don't understand all the stuff I'm doing. They have no idea. And that's the worst part—having no one to talk to—waiting so long to hear from you. Gary, I miss you so much. . . .

I was already at the bottom of the page, but I squeezed in the words right before I fell asleep.

RAYMOND Friedell had come out to UH from Oxford University, and he knew Latin and Greek and Sanskrit, and God knows what else, and he spoke in this forbidding English accent, cool as cucumber sandwiches, even there in Honolulu, even wearing polyester aloha shirts. Everybody said that in the past decade he had gone to seed somewhat, his hair having thinned, as had the rest of him from his dissipations, which were many. He had a certain fondness for his pipe and his bowl, if you know what I mean. So Friedell had this sallow complexion and straw-blond hair and slightly watery eyes, and this thin frame, and always gave the same course, "Themes of World Religions," which he packed with intimidating material and this unbelievable reading list with all these books he'd got down so well he could rattle them off in his sleep—and a lot of times did. He stalked up and down the stage like he was kicking a can in the ruins of his classical education. The rest of the time he hung in this deep, dank basement office, which was his lair. But by far the spookiest thing about Friedell was every single year at the end of the term, he'd give all his students terrible grades. Out of one hundred students he would give at most one to two A's. And he could get away with it, because he had these huge captive enrollments. Because his course was required—not just for religion, but for philosophy and history too. All the religion majors called him the Minotaur, because when he lectured it was like he was half man and half bull, and every fall he took a new classload of students to slaughter.

There must have been a hundred students in the class, and it was held in the art auditorium, which was designed for slide lectures, dark and deep. Friedell liked it that way. He was one of those professors like a jazz musician—bright rooms hurt his eyes. The floor raked up sharply, like a miniature theater, and he spoke down in the pit of the room and strode his little stage, although, as he'd warned that very first day, he did not impersonate anybody but himself, but spoke in his own tinder-dry English accent. It was as if he saw his role as making religion as inaccessible and obscure as possible; it was as if he were the last guardian of the relics of antiquity before we students got our slimy little hands on them and started watering them down!

The reading was so heavy that by the second week I was behind. It happened insidiously, like everything else in that class. I was just lagging a couple of chapters in the Confucius reader. Then I fell one section back in the Koran. But I made a mistake, which was instead of just moving on to the reading for the next lecture and staying current, I kept working on the stuff I was supposed to have read already. The result was the class was moving ahead, while I was stuck farther and farther back. I stayed up late and I got up early. And I read on the bus on the way to work, and during my breaks at Shirokiya. I carried my books with me all the time. I felt like I was doing everything right, but all of a sudden the midterm came up—and it was the next day. I flailed and I moaned and I waved my hands, and I tried to do a month's reading the night before. But it was all to no avail.

The morning of the test I was sitting there in the auditorium, staring three essay questions in the face.

1. *Compare and contrast the Confucian ideal of filial piety with that of the fifth commandment.*
2. *How did Mohammad attempt to synthesize the best of Judaism and Christianity? Why?*
3. *Explain Augustine's conception of illumination of the mind.*

Holy cow! I wasn't even up to Augustine yet. I must have stared at that third question for five minutes, just in total panic. I looked around the room and everyone else was writing away, hunched over those desks that swing up out of the arms of classroom chairs. Everyone was sitting there, one seat apart, the whole class evenly spaced, and Friedell was up front proctoring with his teaching assistants. My heart raced. My palms were sweating. I said to myself, Sharon, hold on. I said, focus your mind. Draw upon your inner knowledge. I started writing.

1. Confucius was similar because he got the concept of honoring your father and mother. Yet Confucius was different because he planned his society more in a building block formation rather than an authoritative legalistic do this or else kind of idea. Indeed Confucius was less hung up on authority than Moses and more into cooperation at all levels. Confucius had down the Eastern ideals of harmony and circularity, while Moses, being a founder of western civilization was more linear, and being, basically, a patriarch, more patriarchal, to the point where he tended most of the time to communicate by fiats or decrees rather than more open ended suggestions.

2. Mohammed had an idea that you could value other people's points of view by actually taking their ideas and using them in your own, and people like Jesus and Moses were not necessarily at odds with each other but onto some of the same important truths. Like when you boil it all down Judaism and Christianity could be summed up by the Golden Rule which is do unto others as you would have others do unto you, and just because people are different doesn't mean they're wrong. So he put that into the Koran and also wrote his own mythology of creation, etc.

So I felt like I was at least saying something for those questions. But when I got to the last one, I didn't know what to do. I hadn't read anything by Augustine. The *Confessions,* the *De Doctrina*—I was too far behind. And I felt like there was this hollow pit in my stomach. I felt like, Oh my gosh, am I going to get a zero? I was just frozen. Because I was not one of those people who could make up answers out of thin air. I looked at the words of that question, and I looked and looked, like they were tea leaves, or like they were tarot cards, or even the palms of someone's hands. The only thing was I didn't have the powers to uncover an answer.

There were only five minutes left to go, and Friedell and the teaching assistants were fanning up the aisles to pounce on all us students and collect our papers without giving us even one second of leeway.

"Just three minutes," Friedell announced over his microphone. My pen started moving. I started scribbling as fast as I could:

3. Illumination of the mind is when you have basically an aha moment and your mind is flooded with the light of understanding. Augustine had these very frequently being not only a great religious thinker but also a Saint. Illumination

Those proctors snatched my blue book out of my hands. They told me to put my pen down. *Down.* They made me feel like a criminal, or, actually, like someone in a penitentiary, with the big oculus on me. Friedell's teaching assistant actually pulled my blue book out from under my pen. It was like I was in some labor camp trying to scribble out my last words, and the guards snatched away my scrap of paper.

When that exam was over I wanted to go home and crawl into my bed and sleep. But I had to go straight to Ala Moana Center. At Shirokiya I had about one minute to dump my bag in my employee locker and put on my smiling customer-service face. You know how it is in retail. The show must go on. Yet I knew I hadn't done well. Not well at all.

The next week Friedell announced that all the midterms were graded. They were in a box outside his office door and we could pick them up at our leisure. But I, of course, had to go right from class to work. Also I dreaded picking up my test. It was Friday morning by the time I went down to Friedell's office to collect it.

I crept down the stairs of Webster Hall, my hands clammy on the bare metal railings. At the bottom of the stairs I crept past this boxy silver water fountain, and then I went back and leaned over to take a drink, but it was one of those water fountains that only trickles, so I just got a lick of water on my tongue. I crept past the vending machines, one for candy bars, and one for coffee, where you were supposed to hold your cup under the spout and specify dark or light. And then at the end of the hall I saw a battered old cardboard box that looked thoroughly abused and kicked around. And I saw Friedell's door, and it was open, and his light was on. I sidled over and looked into the box. There were just a few blue books left, maybe ten wilted ones at the bottom. And there was mine lying there. And right on the cover under my name was my score in red ink. Do you know what I got out of seventy-five possible points? I got a twelve. There it was, scrawled right by my name, like that was what kind of person I was. Twelve points.

And, I mean, what was that? A *twelve*! Did they give me credit for *anything* on that test? I opened up the blue book, and there it was: 5/25 for question one, 5/25 for question two, 2/25 for question three. My eyes were smarting. That whole dank basement hallway swam with tears. I just knelt down by that cardboard box like it was the gravestone of my academic future. "Why?" I started snuffling, "Why?"

"Yes?" the voice floated out from the open office door.

I froze.

"Come in," Friedell said, and his accent was so English it was like he was inviting me in for tea.

And that was it. That nonchalance, that breezier-than-thou. That was when I lost it. In one burst of indignation I marched into the office, and I slapped my blue book down atop the desk, and I said, "Did you grade this?"

"How do you do?" he said. "You must be one of my students."

"I'm Sharon." I said.

"Sharon. Won't you sit down?" And he drew up a chair for me right next to his desk.

And warily I sat down, and my bare knees, since I was wearing shorts, brushed Friedell's cool steel desk. And I said, "I want to know who graded my midterm."

"Why?" he asked.

"Did you?"

"Let me see." He picked up my blue book from his desk, and he opened it up and he looked inside. He read my work, and he kept a perfect poker face the whole time, except at the end he began to smile. But he stopped himself. He put down my exam. He said, "Well."

"Did you grade that?"

"No."

"Professor Friedell—" I couldn't get the words out.

He swiveled on his swivel chair, reached behind him, and produced a tissue box.

I took some. I wiped my face. "Professor Friedell, I can't believe this is happening to me. I mean, I have a 4.0 average."

That really made him sit up and take notice. That really got his attention. He leaned forward. "Really!"

"But I feel like in your course, at least at this point, I'm failing! It's not like I'm not working. It's not like I'm afraid of work. But you assign so much reading, I can't keep up. I feel like I can't read fast enough—I mean, I am not a speed reader. I mean, education is not a race, right? It's about delving deeper, not faster. And I can't delve at all at this pace we're going. I am a person who needs to focus on just a few things."

"There were only three questions on the test," Friedell pointed out. "Perhaps you might have focused your energies more on each one."

"Professor, you don't even know how hard it was for me to force myself just to write what I did. I was practically having panic attacks! Which made me get writer's block." I blew my nose. "I can't keep up because I'm thinking so much. I can't read so fast, because actually, I'm trying to learn this material to practice it in my life, because I want to grow as a spirit. And you know what? I'm looking at these great thinkers and trying to figure out which path is the right one. I mean, right for me. It's like I'm weighing their ideas in my mind—not just reading them superficially."

And I took my Augustine out of my backpack, the *Confessions* and *De Doctrina,* and I opened the books, and showed Friedell how by now I'd highlighted just about every word on every page. The pages were all bright psychedelic yellow, and the margins were all covered with my notes and questions and exclamation points.

Friedell said, "Oh, I see. Yes. I'm surprised you didn't have more to say about Augustine on the exam."

"Oh, I did have more to say. I did. I had too much to say!" Which admittedly was a slight exaggeration, since at the point when I took the test I hadn't read any of this stuff.

"Well," Friedell said, not unkindly, "perhaps you can take on Augustine for your research project." And he handed back my blue book to me, and he stood up. "May I walk you out? I'm afraid I've got to run to lunch."

I stood up. "Please—"

"What is it?"

"This test doesn't show what I can really do."

"I'm relieved to hear that," Friedell said.

ALL weekend I sulked over that conversation with Friedell. I sat by the pools and fountains at Ala Moana Shopping Center. Just slumped on the concrete benches and felt so sad. Hour after hour I watched the carp that lived there. Beautiful koi from Japan. They were white and orange. They were golden. Their eyes were bulgy on the sides of their heads, like blueberries. They looked so fat and happy as they swam in their shallow pools, their whiskers nosing a few pennies on the bottom.

They seemed a little bit dumb. Yet you had to give them this: They sowed not, neither did they spin. They were making the most of their God-given abilities; they were living their lives. Twelve points on a test would never faze them. Nothing did. They didn't rail or curse their fate, being mall fish.

Sharon, Sharon, I thought to myself, where is *your* detachment? How is it you're already after one semester caught up in this whole academic evaluation scam? That's not what education is all about. You know that. Do you need approbation from a guy like Raymond Friedell? No! You're learning for yourself. Just forget about Friedell already. Cut out the middleman.

I was not giving up on seeking knowledge. I was not going to let some prof stand in my way. Monday morning I strode into class with my notebook, and it was like I was coming back to the scenes of my nightmares, wide awake, in the middle of the day. I looked around, and I thought, Sharon, please. Is this what you were so intimidated by? The art auditorium, with indoor-outdoor carpet on the floor? Is this what you considered a temple of the gods of learning?

Friedell stood before us. He looked us over, and he started talking. He started walking and talking on the little stage down on the auditorium floor. And he said, "Some of you have been a little bit concerned about your performance on the midterm. And well you should be."

Despite my newfound freedom from caring about superficial things like Friedell's course and his opinions, I squirmed when he said that. I couldn't help it.

He went on, "Some of you have been feeling rather put upon, I gather, by the volume of reading in this course."

There were more than one hundred students in the class, but all of a sudden I felt like everyone was looking at me. I told myself, Sharon, remember the koi. Remember the koi. Do you think those carp could care less what this land mammal is carrying on about?

Friedell was saying, "Perhaps those of you with concerns would do well to remember that the drop date for the class is approaching. In the meantime before we move on I would like to touch briefly today on some misconceptions about Augustine."

Loosen your attachments, I thought. Let go of your anger toward this man. Let go of your resentment. He is neither an obstacle to you, nor a guide. He is nothing. He is neutral. He is . . .

"Augustine did not start out a saint, as some of you seem to believe. He was not even a Christian when he began his journey as a young man. It was much, much later in his life that he had what one of you so fittingly described as his aha moment leading . . ."

Aha moment! That was my essay Friedell was quoting up there. That was my exam he was exploiting in his lecture! There he was, plagiarizing my work, while at the same time flunking me for it! My eyes went wide. I clutched my notebook to my chest. I couldn't believe it. I couldn't believe what was going on in this class! All my calm went by the wayside. All those good thoughts the day before with the fish. Out the window. It's just that I was not a very calm person! It's just that he was getting off on my failed efforts. Appropriating them. Mocking them for his own personal entertainment! He was raping me in front of a hundred people.

"Augustine was a theologian," Friedell said, "He was a bishop. He was a writer. He was many many things. Augustine—"

"Fuck Augustine!" I screamed out into that dark theater of the lecture hall. I sprang up from my chair. I pushed past all the other students in my row. I was running up the aisle toward the red EXIT sign. The door slammed shut behind me.

14

Pilgrim

Prof. Friedell,

This is to apologize if I offended you in class—though I realize you probably forgot the whole thing by now. I was the one who said Fuck Augustine. It wasn't having anything against him—not at all. It was you lifting passages from my essay on him. And right after I came to see you and appealed to you on the harshness of the grading. It seemed like you were just using the occasion of my test to be making fun, which I realize now is probably one of your pedagogical tools. Nevertheless people's feelings are on the line there in your class, whether you realize it or not, and people's sparks of creativity, which you can either fan constructively or snuff out with irony and intimidation. Is that the way to go? Because actually teaching could be about tenderness and training up the little vines of people's imaginations onto strings, like they are bean plants, and then they would bear fruit, or rather, legumes. Teaching could be about inclusion, where you just let everybody come to the well and drink at their own levels, rather than about grading and public humiliation, where you hold up someone's exam for ridicule. That's all I was trying to say. Learning isn't really how many pages you can choke down. Learning isn't cramming Augustine down one's throat.

What I meant by my comment was I didn't take the class just to read about Augustine's hang-ups, I took it to learn about religion—God, prayer, ritual, Buddha, the Madonna mother-goddess figure, transmigration, forgiveness, miracles, sin, abortion, death, the big moral concepts. Because, obviously I am not eighteen and I work, so school is not an academic exercise for me, and not just me, as I'm sure you'd realize if you looked around the room one of these days and saw there are thirty and forty-year olds and some a lot older than you are in the class. The point is, when you've been through journeys and relationships, multiple careers plus unemployment—the whole gamut—and then you come back to school, you're ready for the real thing, and as far as I'm concerned Augustine's Conception of the Soul, or Illumination of the Mind, or whatever, is not it. What is "it"? you're asking—well, that's what I came to find out, so you tell me. Obviously what you are paid for is to deal with the big religious issues and you are not dealing with them, which again is what I was trying to point out when I made that remark in class.

My feelings still are that basically as a "mature student" I was supposed to feel grateful that the University of Hawaii let me in or gave me a second chance on life or whatever, like I am the lowly unwashed and I should come in the gates to be blessed by the big phallus. . . .

I was working on this letter to Raymond Friedell. Scribbling it down, and getting frustrated, and starting over. I just wanted to smoke him. I was so furious. I wanted him to see what he had done; how he had looked at me in his office and with that one look shrunk me into a little shriveling ball of snot. I wanted to tell him, because he, and teachers as a whole—they just don't get how they can affect students, for good or bad. They just don't get the power that they hold over us! They don't know!

Under the sausage trees by Moore Hall, the words were pouring out into my loose-leaf notebook. All around me the undergrads were walking by in their Bermuda shorts, and going to lunch without a thought in their heads. And I looked at them, and I thought—Who are these people? I looked around the campus, and I thought, what is this place? My notebook sat there in my lap, and my hand couldn't even keep up with what I wanted to say. Friedell thought I was just complaining about my grade, but that wasn't it at all. For some reason when I came "back" to "school" I'd believed in the *universe* part of *university*. That it was all about Life, and Time, and Freedom, but when I got to Friedell those things were just constructs. I'd thought religion was about God, but it turned out in Friedell's class it was just about the history of people's conceptions of God. And there couldn't be any saintliness in Augustine. He couldn't be a great believer, just a great bishop, writer, thinker, et cetera.

And that was when it hit me. I wanted to learn about religion—so what was I doing in academia? I wanted to understand—so why was I reading books? It was just like Rabbi Siegel said: words are the least important thing! Poetry and light, and the sublime. That's what mattered. The exalted. At the time I'd thought Siegel was such an elitist for mentioning the exalted. But wasn't that actually what religion was about? So here I was at the university, and where was the exaltation? I mean, I had seen a vision. I had in a boat, with my own eyes, seen the ocean folded back upon itself. I had received this precious gift, a vision. The sea had stood up upon its tail!

The fever was taking hold of me again—the heat to see and do and know. I raced home. I collected all my notes from Friedell's course that were lying on the floor of my room—I was thinking I would burn them! Except I had to sort out all the letters mixed in—the ones from Gary. Oh, Gary, why am I here while you're over there? I thought. Oh, man, how did we end up this way? And I uncreased all his letters and I smoothed them all down. I looked at Gary's letters on the Torah Or letterhead, and it was *bashert* again, dawning on me. Marlon was there with me, and Kathryn and Will were clattering pots in the kitchen, and Tom was practicing his dulcimer, like some clumsy angel, all thumbs and wings. I said to Marlon, "I'm going out there. I am. I am! I'm going out there to learn with Gary!"

My grumpy yet inwardly sweet cat looked at me with his yellow eyes. I said, "But don't worry, I would never leave you unless you were with really close friends." He went back to his food, nibbling from his dish. If I'd known then! Oh, my poor cat. My poor baby.

And I picked up the phone and I called Gary at Torah Or. All the way in Jerusalem.

There was a muffled voice on the other end of the line.

"Gary!" I said.

"Who?"

"Can I speak to Gary," I said loudly. "I need to talk to Gary. It's urgent. It's an emergency! Could you get him? Please. I have to speak to him."

The muffled voice got more muffled. It burst out something in Hebrew and then said, "Is something the matter?"

"I'm calling from the States. Tell him it's Sharon."

"Wait. Hold on the line, please."

I waited and I waited. At last someone croaked to me, "Hello?"

"It's me," I burst out. "It's Sharon! Are you sleeping?" I'd forgotten it was twelve hours later in Israel. It must have been early in the morning.

"Sharon?"

"Oh, Gary," I said. I was about ready to burst, there was so much I wanted to say. "Is that really you? Is that really your voice?"

"Sharon, where are you? Are you all right?"

"Yes!"

"Thank God. They said it was an emergency!"

"It is! It is! But not a bad kind. The good kind of emergency!"

"Sharon, Sharon, slow down—"

"Gary, I can't stay on the phone—this is probably costing like a hundred dollars a second! Gary, I'm coming out there."

"You're coming where?"

"To you," I said. "To Torah Or. Oh, Gary, I want to learn. I want to know. I want to reconnect."

"Baruch Hashem!" he said.

"What?"

"I said Praise God!" Gary's voice was breaking up. I couldn't tell whether it was him being so moved, or the connection.

"Just, you have to tell me what to do!" I shouted. "I mean, to get to the institute. Could you tell me? But talk fast, 'cause I can't even afford calling you—this is the most expensive phone call I've ever made!"

I don't even remember the flight. It was this long, hazy, yet euphoric trip. There I was, sailing through the air. There I was, leaving academia and Friedell and earth behind. Cleaning out my bank account, taking leave of my job. I wasn't sitting home reading, or teaching temple ladies left and right. There I was, with my three-week excursion ticket and my little photo of Marlon—and I was going to the source of this great religious debate! The root of all the questions in my mind, like who or what is God? And how do you get to know him/her? As in a pilgrimage. As in a quest. Like the great poet Yeats, when he picked up and traveled to Byzantium.

I was just so thrilled, having finally flown away. I was so tickled I'd up and done it after all those years. My ticket was for three weeks, but in my mind I was off to a whole new scene—maybe forever. I figured Gary and I would fly Marlon out to join us. We would send for him so we could all live together, since, in one of those huge miscalculations I excelled at, I was already convinced Gary and I were fated to get back together.

I was just floating when we finally landed; I was just levitating high up near the ceiling of Ben-Gurion International. Somewhere down below there was all this Hebrew, and all these guards, and a voice calling me, "Sharon!" I didn't even realize who it was there calling my name. "Sharon!"

It was him, Gary, with this emaciated white face, and a beard, and a big black yarmulke on his head, and a black suit jacket. He still had the same blinky eyes, like he was getting too much sun, but now he had glasses. He still had the same reedy voice. But standing there in those clothes—so thin, and with that pale skin—he looked like all the spiritual learning he'd undergone had scooped him out. Like, if once he'd been a pumpkin, now all the flesh and seeds and pulp were gone, so now he had this translucent candle glow, like a pale rabbinic jack-o'-lantern. Still, it was Gary. It was really him. My dancer. My letter writer. Long-distance confidant. I ran toward him and threw my arms around him.

He jumped back. "Oh, no, Sharon," he said. "No hugs." He looked so embarrassed, I let him go. And we just stood there, looking at each other. We both started to cry.

"You've changed," he said, which was the real shocker. *I'd* changed? I still had my hair the same way it was back in '74, straight to the hips like Crystal Gayle. I was even wearing an original Boston Folk Festival T-shirt.

We drove off in the Torah Or hatchback Hyundai, started ascending the hills leading up to the city, Jerusalem. All along the way were these tanks and rotted-out bunkers, monuments to the battles fought there in

that land for that city, for those hills. These chariots of war were corrod-
ing into the earth. I was dizzy. I felt like I was undergoing such an
Odyssey. I was so emotional and exhausted and jet-lagged and altogether strung out, I was at sea. The whole world was whirling around
me. I said, "I feel like this is the culmination of my whole life." I said,
"This is the ancient city of Jerusalem; I'm going to get some answers."
And the city rose up before us, made out of Jerusalem stone, naturally,
and with the olive trees and even flocks on the hillsides—I felt my
whole spiritual experience was coming together as in an epiphany. This
was The Land.

So, of course, I wanted to go right away to the Western Wall, but the
Torah Or school was in another place called Meah Shearim. We parked
the car, and walked—and we were in the middle of this funky neighborhood. I said to Gary, "Wow." I said, "This is unworldly." We were walking
through the tiny narrow streets and past vegetable stalls buzzing with
flies, and there were kids everywhere, these boys wearing black hats like
black Panama hats on one block and then round-brimmed hats on the
next block—these are like their school uniforms. There were shops selling silver candlesticks and olive-wood boxes. There were little stinky alleyways—these dark crevices between the buildings. And the alleys were
all strung and crisscrossed with clotheslines and clothes hung out to dry.
Gary was hurrying me along, and I was staring at all the white shirts
strung up: shirts, shirts, shirts, little shirts, little fringes, and then this satin
wedding gown hanging on the line. Everyone was rushing all around me,
and on the street corners kids were buying these beige twisted candles
and big feathers, like turkey feathers—which Gary said were meant for
the final cleaning up for Pesach, which was Passover.

"You light the candles to search out the last bit of hametz—any
crumbs of leavened food," Gary was telling me. "You sweep the crumbs
out with a feather and then you burn them. . . ." And I'm staring at this
guy, my former boyfriend, after all! Because, who would have known?
Once upon a time he'd cared about threatened indigenous species, and
now he was telling me all the details of Passover.

We got to this run-down old building, which was like a dormitory for
the students to sleep, and Gary was probably explaining to me the whole
schedule for the seminar program in exploring Judaism—but, as I said
before, I was just high as a hot-air balloon. I didn't hear a word he said.

* * *

THE first few days I just walked around glowing. Gary had to spend a lot of time in classes, so in the mornings I went out myself. I walked along the tops of the Old City walls. I walked on these incredible blocks of ancient stone. The light was so clear, the sun so bright. I peeked through the crenellations. And I saw the Arab villages in the hills outside the city; and I saw the gray ribbons of the modern roads. I saw the sky, and the old arthritic olive trees. Here I was, and every particle of me was screaming: Here I am! I am in Jerusalem, the place! Here I am. I am walking through the narrow little streets. I am passing the Armenian church! I am converging with my correspondent from the other side of the world. Let my feet step lightly. Let me step alertly on these stones. Let me worship the spirit of these rocks! I added several pages to my letter to Friedell—all about the ecstasy of breaking the bonds of academe.

The only problem was that during our separation, Gary had turned into a horrible worrywort! He looked at me, and I wanted to hug and kiss him and dance, but he said he couldn't touch me, and he pulled these long faces, and he said, "Sharon, Sharon. Please! Calm down."

"Why should I calm down? Why shouldn't I be excited?" I asked him the third day after I arrived. We were sitting in the reception room of Torah Or, which was a suite of rooms in a run-down three-story apartment building. The first-floor reception area was full of these American men and women coming in and out in their various degrees of religiosity and knowledge. Some guys were dressed like Gary with big black yarmulkes and beards, and some had jeans, and some had dreadlocks. All through the building flowed these streams of young kids and older religious wanderers—along with various disheveled people who muttered to themselves and smelled bad, which normally you would associate with homelessness, yet there at the institute you felt they very probably were prophets.

"Gary, couldn't we talk for a minute in private?"

"I'd rather talk here," he said.

So we stood there, and I whispered, "Gary, don't you still believe in the symmetries in our lives?"

He nodded.

I put my hand on his arm. "Don't you still think everything, including us, happened for a purpose?"

"Yes." He pulled his arm away. "But we can't read all the purposes of Hashem."

I said, "Gary, I don't think Hashem has a problem with people jumping up and down and being joyful because they've arrived in His or Her—"

"In His," Gary said.

"In His holy place. It's not like He doesn't know how to share! Gary, why are you always pulling away from me?"

"I can't touch you," he said.

"I don't get it. Was I so much better on paper?"

"I thought you came to Torah Or to learn."

"I did!" I told him. "But also to understand Jerusalem. And to reconnect? Remember? To reconnect with you."

He looked alarmed. "Oh, Sharon, there is so much learning; there is such a world of knowledge to uncover. You can go to class and learn every minute of the day, and all night, too, and you'll never ever come to the end of it."

"I know." I was just as serious as he was. "I know. I know."

That seemed to cheer him up tremendously. "Then it's time," he told me. "Sharon, it's time for you to begin!"

That very day Gary was going to speak to the dean of the women's division—since women and men learned separately. "Tell him I want to study the nature of God," I said. "And how He manifests Himself in the world, okay?"

But I should have known, after all those years, that Gary never listened to me. He got me into an intensive minicourse on Judaic law and history.

I'D come out figuring I'd be bunking with Gary, but the institute had separate dorms for men and women, so I got a bed in the women's wing, which was a maze of rooms in this really old, freezing-cold building, without any heat, next door. I had a little cot, and I slept in a room full of cots, and with these high vaulted ceilings and stone floors like ice. If Gary hadn't lent me a wool blanket and sweater, I would have come down with pneumonia the first week, just from the shock of that frigid Jerusalem spring.

That first morning as an official student I woke up and all my muscles hurt from tossing and turning in the cold. I could barely stand to get out of bed. Still, I stumbled downstairs for morning prayers in the synagogue/cafeteria. It was a small-scale school, so they had to double up. There were about twenty-five women students, something like twenty young ones on their junior year abroad from college, like Queens College, Brandeis, and a couple from Barnard. They were, I guess, in the advanced program. And then there were a few of us beginners in our thirties and forties. I was kind of in the middle, between the college girls and the mid-lifers, since I was twenty-nine. Well, I grabbed a Hebrew prayer book and joined everybody praying. The college girls just sped through the prayers and sat down for breakfast, while we older ones still stood there holding our books. Then eventually I saw the older women would start finishing up. Still, I wasn't done. Not that I was embarrassed, but I was the last one standing there, because the prayer book was all in Hebrew, except for a few English instructions. I was the last one standing there, because my Hebrew was so bad. I mean, obviously, all I knew was the alphabet! Yet I remembered what Gary said about a world of learning. I was determined to give these prayers my best shot.

It got to be a marathon session every morning. I would be spelling out the words there in the cafeteria. It took me around four hours to finish praying every morning. People finished eating. They went off to do their reading or their morning classes. These Yemenite cleaning women would come in, clear away breakfast, I was still there, praying. They'd fold up the folding chairs, I was still praying. They'd start hosing down the floor around my feet; they'd start squeegeeing the water—I'm still standing there like the rocks and the planets. There was one other woman who also took a long time. At first I was glad, since it was embarrassing standing there alone. Then I noticed she kept looking over at me to see what page I was on. She had a crew cut and severely plucked eyebrows, and boy was she competitive! She'd check my page, then turn back to her own book, bobbing up and down like a maniac. So after about a week I figured out this woman was into praying with feeling, which meant for each word you had to move your lips, knit your eyebrows, and shuffle around as much as you could. Obviously the slower you went, the more feeling you had, right? So she was envious of me, because I was going slower than everyone else, so I must've been the holiest one there, but she couldn't for the life of her figure out how to pray as slowly as I was. Every morning I drove her up a wall, since I never told her I knew hardly any Hebrew. She'd have to give up after about three hours. She'd stalk around glaring at me.

"Gary," I told him in the afternoon, outside—since he was afraid to be seen with me in private—"there's this kooky woman every morning, and it's like she thinks praying is some kind of competition or something. And she keeps giving me the stink-eye because I'm winning."

Gary gasped at me. He said, "Sharon!"

I threw up my hands. "What did I do now?"

"*Loshon hora* is a terrible sin."

"A sin of what?"

"Speaking ill of other people," he said.

"I wasn't speaking ill," I told him, "I was telling you the truth. You can come see. She tries to pray as slowly as she can, but she just can't cut it."

So Gary launched into this whole speech about how you had to guard your tongue, and never say a word about other people's flaws.

"Okay, okay, I'm sorry I mentioned it," I said. "Look at the sty in your own eye. I got the picture."

He looked puzzled when I mentioned that saying about the sty, and I was glad. Ha! I know something you don't know! Then he said to me, "Shouldn't you be at your class? Aren't you missing the afternoon session?"

"I was just taking a break."

"A break! You've been here less than a week!"

"A little fresh air." I leaned against the damp and grimy stone wall of the building. The whole neighborhood was stone. The streets were cobbled, the shops were little dark holes in the wall. We were right near the gates of Meah Shearim, which was such a religious enclave that there were big placards up everywhere in Hebrew and in English that you should not enter the area if you were wearing immodest dress, and you should not do anything to desecrate the Sabbath. All around us men in black suits and hats were scurrying by. It had been raining on and off all day, so they all wore clear plastic bags over their black hats to protect the felt. The air wasn't all that fresh, given the buses coughing up smoke, the crowds, the cooking smells, not to mention the occasional donkey.

"You came here to learn," Gary was chiding me.

"Yeah, but not from Morah Zipporah!" I said, referring to my prison warden, fanatical dictator, instructor. "Have you ever taken a class from her?"

"What's the problem?" Gary asked. Thoughtfully, he was pulling at his beard.

"She's a Nazi."

"Sh!"

"It's true! She starts every class announcing her agenda of converting us. Then she lectures about *kashrus*, *brachas*, *midos*—half the words I don't understand. And then, if you want to ask a question, she says no. If you say, excuse me, Morah Zipporah, I'd like to ask what the purpose of all this stuff is, and maybe have some dialogue here about our origin and our Creator, then she says, 'You are again sidetracking the class.'"

Gary kept telling me I should be more patient learning the details of the Jewish religion, because, essentially, God, or rather, Hashem, was in the details. He kept saying the point was to learn, not to get caught up in ego. "Sharon," he said to me, pulling at his beard, "it might seem hard, but I believe in you."

And I looked at him in his black suit jacket and his black velvet yarmulke and his face all pale, since he didn't seem to get outside unless I dragged him, and I watched him pull his beard, and I thought, Wow, he catches on fast—since all the Torah Or rabbis pulled their beards. Or maybe, since his was kind of thin and scruffy, he just pulled his beard to make it grow. And I looked at him, and I thought, Are you my old boyfriend? Are you the dancing, idealistic, environmental, horny guy I used to know?

He was the crow-black shadow of his former self. Thin, wispy, and ethereal. Yet it turned out, as he explained to me over the next few days, that a lot of his defensiveness against me came from my sudden arrival during his learning process. And naturally it had been quite a shock to him when I'd called and when I'd flown in so suddenly. He hadn't expected that. "I felt we were just beginning to reconnect in our correspondence," he said.

"You're right," I told him. "And then I barged in on you with my whole academic crisis. I'm sorry."

"I only wish I could be a better channel for you to Hashem." When Gary said that I could see that a lot of the sweetness and spirit of his letters was still with him.

We went for a walk together on the city walls. The sun was beating down, and Gary finally had to take off his suit jacket and make do with his long-sleeved white shirt. I took off the borrowed sweater I was wearing over my old tank dress. I was running my hands along the stone of the walls. I was saying, "My God. These walls are so thick. Oh, my God, they're so old." And you could see from the walls all the houses and apartment buildings of the new city of Jerusalem covering the outer hills of the city. But what left you in awe was those ancient stones, and those gates enclosing and cherishing old Jerusalem. The real Jerusalem. The city of David, the one you read about, the Bible place nestled together. The citadel.

"I can't believe we're standing here," I said.

And Gary said, "I know." Then all of a sudden Gary's worrying, and his prudishness, and his rabbinical mannerisms, seemed to melt away. Then it was as if finally he could speak freely. He told me about his ecstasy when he found his calling to be a Jew. "It was a moment of terror," he said. "It was a moment of sheer terror. That's the only way I can describe it. I was standing in Anne Frank's house, and I felt deep in the pit of my stomach that my identity was her identity. Her fate was my fate. We shared one blood. We were of one flesh and one spirit. I was a Jew! I felt like walls were closing in on me. I was gasping for air, and I was crying out. And the security guards came for me, but I couldn't stop screaming. I could see it all happening, but I couldn't stop. They began to drag me away, and . . ."

My eyes welled up just listening to Gary. I almost couldn't bear to listen.

"I felt what she felt being dragged down the stairs. I, a forty-three-year-old man, felt what she felt. A thirteen-year-old girl. They were dragging me away, and I was sobbing."

He couldn't go on. I put my arms around him, and he didn't pull away. He let me. The sun warmed us on the wall of Jerusalem. I hugged him for a long long time.

I didn't want the moment to end, yet I couldn't help it—this one small niggling comment escaped me: "But, Gary . . . I don't get it."

"Don't get what?" He tensed right up again. He drew right back, and put on his jacket for good measure.

"I mean, I'm sorry. But I mean, how could you have not realized before you were a Jew? You always knew you were a Jew. Your name is Gary Levine. How could you forget? You knew you were a Jew way back as long as I've known you. That's what I don't understand."

"Sharon," he started. He shook his head. "No, see, I knew I was a Jew, but I never knew I was a *Jew*."

"Oh," I said. "You didn't know you were a *Jew*." And I took that in, and I nodded, and I looked out to the distant hills with the white New City, and I lifted my eyes to the immediate hills—and what took my breath a moment—there was an actual shepherd walking there on the land, with his flock. There was a shepherd and he had a bunch of brown and black goats. "And you discovered you were a *Jew,*" I said again slowly. Then I turned to Gary again. I felt terrible doing it, yet I had to ask. "But isn't that a little bit like finding out you were speaking prose all the time?"

"No!" Gary burst out. "No, Sharon! Don't you see? Before, I had no history. I had no knowledge. I had no learning. And at that moment. In one split second in the Netherlands. My history came home to me. That was what happened."

"Oh, Gary," I whispered. Because now I saw what he meant. You could be a Jew in name, but not in spirit. Maybe that was me; I didn't even know. But mainly I was wishing we could go back to where we'd been before, in our embrace.

Too late. Gary had turned all testy and rabbinical again, and he was in a rush to get back to Torah Or to meet with his *havrusah*, which was his learning partner he studied with—and that couldn't be me, because I was a woman, and a beginner at that, so I might taint the atmosphere with ignorance and lust. Not that I minded that Gary had turned into such a model of piety, but he'd gotten so exclusionary about it. Dealing with him—not to mention the whole Torah Or program—was this experience of mounting frustrations.

And it wasn't like I didn't try. I went every day to class. Every day I sat there for as long as I possibly could. Yet Morah Zipporah's classes kept bringing me down. She was this small lady in a wig of short bristly black hair, and she had a chiseled little face, and her veins were purple in her pale-skinned hands as she thumped the table. She spoke with a thick German accent, yet she'd been born and raised in Alexandria before her family had emigrated to Palestine. She was about two hundred years old.

"Miss Spiegelman," she said. My first name didn't seem to ring a bell. "Miss Spiegelman, you have what to prepare today to do? And so."

And so was a complete derogatory sentence. It meant listen up, and get your ass in gear.

"We shall today discuss again kashrus. What we shall see. Laws of separation. *Milch*." She divided the air with one karate chop of her hands. *"Fleish."*

Everybody sat around the seminar table taking notes. Nine North American fellow travelers—including the dame who was jealous of my extended morning prayers—nine grown women totally cowed. And then there was me, raising my hand. The black sheep, and the troublemaker. The one who roused Morah Zipporah's ire. Everybody hated me. It was like third grade—I was making the teacher mad at the whole class. But I raised my hand in any case. "Morah?" I asked, with all the respect and politesse that I could muster. "Would it be possible, since we've been studying milk and meat for so long, and since some of us are actually vegetarian anyway, to maybe have some dialogue on other subjects as well?"

And Morah Zipporah, not being a product of the postwar American public school system, said, "No. Another subject will be another day."

Some support from other students would have been nice. Some class spirit! Yet we were all cows in that class. Milch cows. That seemed to be the real point of Morah Zipporah's instruction. That was what I took away from ten days of seminars. There was a realm that was dairy, and there was a realm of meat. There was cow and there was blood. There was Kitchen Woman and there was Rabbinic Man (being the one who'd invented the realms in the first place).

I sat there during Morah Zipporah's lectures, and I had my dog-eared photocopied text before me. Hebrew on one side, English on the other. All the fine print on milchig and fleishig pots and pans. I felt lightheaded. I felt confused. Because this was not what I had come for! I'd come looking for the truth. The truth about God, not cooking utensils.

I grabbed my backpack and I stood up in Morah Zipporah's class, and she said, "Miss Spiegelman."

And I said, "Sorry. Excuse me."

The other women stared at me. All my classmates: The lady who was jealous of my prayer capacity knit her brow under her razor-sharp crew cut. The lady who woke early to do her daily AA meditations. The widow from Passaic. The former English teacher from Oxnard. The gay divorcée. They all watched me walk out.

I started to run down the hall. I was looking for Gary. I was running up and down the decrepit staircases, poking my nose into classrooms, startling pairs of men from their learning, just barging in on them engrossed in text.

At last I found him. He was hunched over in an empty classroom fixing his glasses. Trying to pop the little screw back in the hinge.

"I give up," I said.

He looked up, startled. He held the tiny screw between his thumb and his forefinger.

"Sharon!" he exclaimed. "You've been here just two weeks! Sharon, how can I make you understand? Without learning you have no basis. You have no foundation."

"Learning! You call those classes learning? I came here to delve, Gary."

"To delve into what?"

"To delve! Just to delve, okay? I came here for truth. I came here for the truth about the Creator, not home ec!"

"Home ec?" He looked at me in disbelief. "You're talking about the *kashrut shiur*? Sharon, those halachos are the holiest—"

"I don't give a shit!"

So then he did his old passive-aggressive thing and he said he wouldn't listen to that kind of language, and he turned away.

I took a breath, then I rephrased my point. "Don't you think perhaps these seminar topics are just slightly narrow? Look, all I'm trying to say is I've been on the road of my personal journey for a long long time, and I've crossed some pretty serious thresholds—and not through studying, but *living*—being initiated into some pretty intense practices! And I probably don't know much. In terms of learning I'm probably way behind, but I have learned one thing, and that is—I am seeking God. And to me that is not about silverware, okay? To me that is a matter of life or death!"

Then Gary said in this quiet voice, "Sharon, you don't even know who you are."

"Yes, I do."

"No," he said, his voice even quieter, "you really really don't."

For a moment I felt the truth in that. I was taken aback. Then I shook myself. I said, "No. No, see, that's backwards—because I know who I am, obviously. I'm right here! I'm here all the time. It's God that's the enigma to me. It's like He's this mystery and I can glimpse Him for just a moment, and then He's gone. And not that I'm a great visionary or something, but I know Him when I see Him. I do! Or at least I know when I'm getting warmer. And when I'm cold. And in that women's class I'm ice. Antarctic!"

He shook his head at me. It almost broke my heart seeing him without his glasses. Those brown eyes were still the same in that bearded face.

I checked we were alone. I whispered, "Gary, let's get out of here."

"What do you mean, get out of here?"

"Let's go. Let's go hiking! Let's hike Mount Sinai! Let's leave this place. Gary, it's just a little tiny school filled with little tiny questions. The big ones, they're all outside. How can you sit here and read—"

"You don't understand," he told me. "I'm learning how to live a Jewish life."

"So we're Jews, and we're living. What's the problem? Can't we go? Can't we just get out?"

He didn't answer.

"Gary, I feel like you're slipping away. I feel like the person who wrote me letters, that person whose history I've shared, all that is somehow disappearing by the minute! I feel like you're in the clutches of some kind of—some kind of cult!"

"How dare you." His face flushed. "I thought I could help you."

I gasped. "Oh, 'cause you felt sorry for me? Oh, right. Well, which part were you feeling sorry about? Leaving me? Or leading me on, pretending you wanted to get whatever we had back?" And I grabbed his glasses he'd been trying to fix and I smashed them to the floor. And I said, "You can let go the screw now, Gary," since he still had that tiny hinge screw in his fingers. "You won't need the goddamn screw."

And I ran down the stairs, and I could hardly see—it wasn't even so much the tears, as my anger. And I ran down to the reception room, and started pushing out the door.

Then the Israeli office lady suddenly called my name.

"What?" I snuffled.

"Telegram has arrived."

So then I thought, On top of everything. I thought, Oh, God, now what. And there before me was this white telegram from my former life. And it was from Will, and it said:

Marlon very ill. Feline AIDS.

I took the piece of paper outside and I walked and walked with my backpack slung over my shoulder. I didn't think about my feet touching the ancient stones or any of that crap. I thought about poor Marlon, home sick. Probably dying there alone. And I thought about his little cat body, and his paws all limp. And I thought how I'd let him down again, and I remembered his face when I got so excited about coming to Torah Or, his little wrinkled seen-it-all face; his baleful yellow eyes. He was so knowing. He saw right through me. Every time. He just never, due to the ancient eco-socio injustices of man, had the power to change my mind.

I had no idea where I was going. I just kept walking on. And I walked all the way up the road, up the hill, and I got to this park with a building that was the Jerusalem Nature Conservation Office. And I sank down, too tired to walk anymore. I sat on a bench. Well, I thought. Now you're all alone. Now your boats are burned in all directions.

I shivered, I was so chilly. My bench was actually a huge stone from an olive press, a huge round stone lying on its side. It looked like stone money from Yap. I didn't have a sweater. I just had my backpack at my feet, all full of notebook paper and doodlings from class.

This thing I had about looking for truth. The truth about what? About God? About the universe? Who did I think I was kidding? Truth probably wasn't meant for humans—not in such large quantities. Dosing on truth. That would be a dangerous game. That would be like breathing pure oxygen, and you would explode. Or sipping absinthe. You could become addicted to the true. You could become one of those lost souls in the boulevards and the cafés. The absinthe drinkers.

The sky was starting to fade. The round olive press stone was so cold. I thought: Marlon knew the truth. I thought: You dilettante. It was actually cleansing to think so ill of myself. It was actually some relief.

I opened up my backpack. I pulled out my loose-leaf papers and, in there with them, my hothead letter to Friedell. "The big phallus," I'd called him. "Classical shit," I'd called his course. Yeah, that would show him. Yeah, right. I looked at my letter and I saw all that anger. I saw

exactly the kind of person Friedell thought I was—another shrill femi-
nist anti-the-educational-system ranting about her ideas and her emotions.

All around me the sky was turning lavender. The evening was coming
on from far away. I turned over my letter, the cheap typing paper all
scribbled over with indignations. And I took out my scratchy ballpoint,
and I wrote:

That stuff before. That place I was before—please excuse my language
(or spelling if there was any). Let me clarify what I was talking about:

I know you don't take this, coming from me, seriously, but I am serious, Professor Friedell—a lot of times I feel like I could explode
(which I did unfortunately at the time of your St. Augustine lecture).
I hear and I see and I read, but I don't understand. It's like with Hebrew—I can sound it out but I don't know the meanings. That's the
metaphor of how I feel.

You think I am not a committed student. You think I am not trying. But I am too committed. That is my whole problem! That is why
your comments got me so upset. It was because I care so much about
learning. To me Augustine is not just about his time; he is about my
time too. To me the journey is not a trope. I came all the way out here
to Jerusalem. That is how committed I am. Yet I am almost in despair.
Even though I am in Jerusalem I don't feel gathered up. I don't feel
healed. And I mean I came from far; Honolulu has to be one of the 4
corners of the earth. But where is the canopy spread over me—forget
of peace.

The light is white lavender gray blue and there are two stars and
the moon. They say the stars up there aren't even the stars; they're just
the ones that used to be there, and it takes so long for the light to get
down here the real ones have died already. So is it just dead bodies up
there? Are they messages from the past that we don't understand? Just
words floating down, but no one can read them? Two stars are shining
here. They're burning holes in the clouds. They aren't dead, they're
definitely alive. I believe they are alive. Ha. I believe. What does that
mean? Do you want to know the truth? I believe in God without any
reasons. That's the part that drives me crazy—I know He exists but
I'm not sure how I figured it out. Maybe you're born with it. Who

knows? Maybe it's just basically because I've had a good life. I mean, not always lucky or smart, but I've seen stars, more in a night than some people get to see in their whole lives. I've been to places hardly anyone else has been, and some places, on the inside, where no one has been. I've had a good life—maybe more like Coyote than Road Runner and with those crackly bloodshot eyeballs once in a while and flattened like a cat under a truck once in a while and mad as Hell most of the time about these completely meaningless things like, no offense, your lecture that time, but inside me somewhere there's this person naive and ready to do something totally different—then boom, you get a telegram, and it's your best friend, it's Marlon, and he's dying—and you just wonder all over again if it makes any sense. I guess I'm basically an optimist with nagging metaphysical questions. Why else would I clean out checking and savings and come to Jerusalem?

I came all this way. I got here and I drove up, and I saw the flocks and the ancient walls, and the thing that hurts most is that Jerusalem is just a place. It's just a place. I thought it was going to be so much more. I thought it was going to transcend, and it was going to transform, and that people here within the walls would revert to their true selves. They would go back to their former states, the personalities and the spirits that they had once been, or at least should have been! So I came here flying so high. I went up to Jerusalem, and it is just a city, and there is traffic, and laundry on clotheslines. And you come here, and everybody is carrying his own burden, and still traveling his own little individual (selfish) road.

I have stood on the walls of the Old City. I have walked through the gates, and I'm no better than I was. (Maybe worse.) Which has got to be me, right? I know it's what you bring—I realize that. It makes me cry, because I don't have it in me. I thought seeing this place would make more sense, but it doesn't, it doesn't at all. There is this whole spiritual existence out there and I can't get there. What do you need to do? How many books? How many journeys? What are the words and what kind of food? macro? micro? do roots feed the soul? carrots, turnips, potatoes? or the ancient songs? I lift up my voice in the wilderness, eyes to the hills, my timbrel and lyre to the mouth of the sea whence cometh my aid and dance on the sand a song of praise

with words I don't understand. What can you do with just an alphabet, when you don't know the constellations, just that ayin is an eye
or a well, and what's down the well? You live in this thin layer on the
crust and you can never delve down to the underground rivers or get
onto the other planets and get any perspective. And they say you
should climb to the top of the hill and cry God is in this place! and
lift up your voice along with your eyes whence cometh your help, but
what if you do that and afterwards it wears off and you're just sitting
there on the hill back where you started?

If the hills would start teaching. If the mountains would come
down to my level! If Jerusalem had arms to embrace me, and lips to
speak. Then I would be getting somewhere. If philosophy were a
dance. My spirit has dancing feet. I have to keep moving. I am a
kinesthetic learner! That's how I understand.

My point is I am different from what you thought. My point is I
am not a critical negative person, as in "everyone's a critic." I am not
interested in negativity. Dwell on the stars, not the negative. That is
my whole tenet!

So I'll be back in Honolulu on May 1—or before that, if I can
change my ticket—to be there for Marlon, and I was wondering if
you could possibly take this as my final paper for the course, since it
basically summarizes some of my current views and independent research into religion. I realize it only touches Augustine briefly, but
since he was sort of the starting point of the research it was justified. I
could type it up if you want—but the main thing is if you would give
me full credit for it, because, obviously, your course is required.

                                        Thanks,
                                        Sharon

15

A Table Before Me

I stood in the hallway outside Friedell's door, and I looked at the grade lists taped up to the wall. There were lots of other letters posted up, typed in black. Lots of Cs, millions of them—and getting a C was what I'd once been so afraid of! And there were WDs for withdrawn, which I could have done if I hadn't been out of the country, too far away to do it! Then, there was my ID number, and like a drum roll the dotted line across the page: .... and a great big letter F.

"Sharon Spiegelman," said Professor Friedell, opening his office door. He recognized me right away.

I couldn't even speak at first. "Did you get my letter?" I blurted out finally.

"Won't you come in?" he said. In his office he started ruffling through the piles of stuff on his desk. Then he plucked my letter out.

"Did you read it?" I asked him.

"I did."

"Then why, why . . ." My voice started to tremble. "Why did you do that to me?"

"Sharon!" He sounded surprised. "I didn't do anything to you." He was so maddening.

"You gave me an F!"

He neatened up my fourteen pages, and they rustled like tissue paper. "Well, you've missed the final and skipped the research paper."

"But, but—" I spluttered.

"This is not a research paper," he said.

"Maybe not a conventional one. Maybe not the formal definition of one," I said, "but you can't say there's no research in there. You can't say I didn't put my time in there. I put my whole *life* into that paper." I came up close. I leaned over his desk. I almost shouted, "Don't you understand? You are negating not just my paper, but my whole experience! Don't you see? You are canceling out not just my words, but the thoughts and feelings in my head!" I said, "You just see the tip of the iceberg, and that's all you want to see. I've been through hell. It took me six days just to get a reduced fare back here, and then I was flying for twenty-four hours, and the minute I touched the ground, I had to find out about the death of possibly my closest friend left on this island. And I didn't even make it back in time to say good-bye."

"I'm terribly sorry, Sharon," he said. "But this is still not a research paper."

"What, because it has no footnotes?"

"It has no thesis statement. It has no argument. It has no outside sources. Do you want me to go on?"

I picked up my letter from the desk. I picked up all the crinkly translucent pages of it, and the curves and lines of my words were like veins scribed in the paper. They were like living veins of blue ballpoint! And I said, "You don't get it. You just don't get it at all what I was trying to do here. This is a critique of the whole educational system here! You think this is just all about me. But it's about you, and all the people like you. This is about the failure of higher education to teach me."

"Now, that may be true," he said.

My ears pricked up. "And I could type this up. I could put a lot more time into this. If you could just give me an incomplete, I could do this as an independent project over the summer. Because you know what, I'm the kind of person that when she gets interested in an idea never gives up, I'm the kind of person who is not afraid of hard work. . . ."

Yet Friedell kept murmuring over and over like a spell, "But, Sharon.

Sharon, this is not a research paper. This is simply. Not. A research paper."

I never took a class at the university again.

You know how fields have to rest sometimes? You know how the earth has to lie fallow before it gets planted again? The next five years I was lying fallow that way. And I didn't know if anything would ever sprout in me again. A lot of times I was thinking this was it. This, meaning living in the house with Tom and Will and a postdoc here and there, since Kathryn and Rich had moved away and bought their shack on the North Shore and had their kid. The co-op sort of ran down without Kathryn to ride everyone. We stopped having our communal dinners, and it was more like everyone for him- or herself in the kitchen. A lot of times it would be just you alone there in the night facing the odd rice cake.

Having no educational goals, boyfriends, or visions—I just eddied. I got no exercise, apart from teaching the ladies at the temple, and I guess that didn't count, since in class I never broke a sweat. Rabbi Siegel's class petered out. Matthew converted, and Alyssa had her bat mitzvah, so they stopped coming. Fred was working a lot, and as for me—I didn't have any great excuse. It was just that after all those years looking for inspiration and education everywhere, I didn't have the heart anymore for Hebrew lessons, not to mention Siegel's rabbinic wisdom. I was turning into something of a lump. And not just my soul, the rest of me too. I ate a lot of take-out food, especially from Patty's Chinese Kitchen. I ended up gaining weight—at least twenty pounds. It was ridiculous—I'd grown so hippy. I tried not to care. I kept my head down, worked my job at Shirokiya. Paid my taxes to the IRS aka Ronald Reagan, despite the situation in Central America. I stayed sober, stayed clean, ran into Brian once in a while at the Manoa Safeway, and told myself I didn't even care. I flattered myself how much I'd mellowed when it came to guys. I barely slept with a single individual, except for Will, and that was such a calm and stable relationship, we didn't even break up, we just mellowed away—which might have been a hopeful sign of my evolution in dealing with the other sex—except that back then I wasn't yet that knowledgeable about the evolution of other people, so it hadn't been foremost in my consciousness that Will was in the process of evolving to be gay.

Well, what are men? I thought after our relationship had ended. They are like eating sweets. And you get older, and it could be your whole appetite starts to change. It could be after you stop eating sweets, then you will feel no desire anymore to try sweet things. You'd rather eat kumquats, skin and all. What is dialoguing with a kindred spirit? Way overrated. A lot more entrancing the first few nights than subsequently. I practically swore off relationships after Will, just like I'd sworn off classes and religious seminars and meditation workshops. My main activity was music, which I pursued in the used record and tape bins at Froggy's. My happiest event was buying myself a new guitar. Yet strangely once I had the instrument I didn't play it all that much. When I did take my guitar out, I played strictly for myself. I never imagined performing my compositions anymore. That's what happens when you get to be twelve years older than you were—it turns out your audience, or at least, that great public you imagined once, has shrunk.

Every once in a while the question would arise in me: What's happening to you, Sharon? I'd sit up and say: Woman, don't you have any kind of plan? But mostly not.

Then along about 1988, in the spring, the ladies of Martin Buber Temple did come up with a plan—not for me, but for themselves. They were going to perform *"Kora Bushka"* at the Israel Independence Day Fair in Kapiolani Park. I think it was Henny Pressman's idea. She was the one who designed the costumes and bought the material. The ladies sewed up the outfits—one for me too—since at that point there were five of them and they needed me to round out the group. So I got to be their coach and their pinch hitter too. I was fairly grumpy about the whole thing; I was actually fairly nervous. I didn't want to get up in front of several hundred people with these old dames. Mostly I was a believer in humility and that one person shouldn't think she was any better than anyone else, but when it came to dancing, a little bit of pride still stuck in my throat.

We had our dress rehearsal in the temple social hall. Our costumes were royal blue, and hung either straight or funny on you depending on who had sewed yours. We had long-sleeved white blouses and then these blue jumper things over us. There weren't buttons or zippers or anything, so you pulled them over your head, and on mine the neck hole and the armholes were just a little bit too small, so I could barely get the jumper on, and I couldn't really raise my arms. And they were trimmed with purple rickrack around the hem and neck, and we wore matching kerchiefs over our hair out of the same royal-blue material, so we looked like, I don't know what, maybe royal flying nurses, or a bunch of older novices at a funky convent.

So we were all set for *"Kora Bushka,"* which was probably the simplest, most repetitive dance in the repertoire. I turned on the music, and immediately Henny Pressman started turning the wrong way. She started doing everything mirror-image backwards. We were all dancing and clapping and stamping and making with our hands in these retarded costumes, and Henny was completely, totally, one hundred percent of the time, on the wrong foot. I mean, after something like six years practicing this dance! I mean, why?

I shouted above the music, "What the hell do you think you're doing?" I ran to the tape player and stabbed the off button with my finger. Everyone was looking around. I said, "Henny! I'm talking to *you!*"

"I'm sorry," Henny said. She was a bit flushed. She wasn't used to being yelled at. "I got a little excited."

"Well, get unexcited. This is not exciting. What we're doing here is not exciting." I was so furious, I felt so ridiculous, tears were starting in my eyes. Then I thought, What are *you* doing, Sharon? What kind of teacher are you being, yelling at this poor woman? I thought, Are you forgetting everything Siegel told you about the vocation of teaching? Are you turning into some kind of Friedell snooting at all the world's amateurs? And I stopped myself. In a quiet voice I said, "Let's try again. Henny, let's see it. Start on the left."

She lifted her right foot.

And that was when I hit rock bottom. I'd been sinking down pretty low. I'd been sedimenting down for years, and yet at that moment I felt lower about myself and about my life than I'd ever felt before. I felt at that moment the whole truth of my situation, which was that I'd gotten to a point where I wasn't a rebel or an experimenter or a seeker after God, or even a drifter in exotic places. I was a thirty-three-year-old permanent resident of Honolulu, and purely for the cash I was rehearsing a bunch of sixty-year-olds in a dance that some of them still didn't get.

"No," I told Henny, "your other left."

In Kapiolani Park Sunday there was a bandstand and a white-and-blue plastic banner that read ISRAEL INDEPENDENCE DAY. All around under the ironwood trees people were standing with their kids and buying food from the food booths. Not just hot dogs, but falafel in pitas, and "shave ice," and bagels. Hawaiian Bagel had a booth of its own and was serving its genuine Mainland-style bagels, the boiled kind, which were a great exotic delicacy at that time. And there were a couple of booths set up by the Israeli consulate from San Francisco and the Jewish Federation, and there was the floating random crafts fair that always materialized at big community happenings, with ceramic planters and polished wood bowls and miniature Hawaiian sculptures and tables in the back displaying burnished glossy hardwood dildoes. There were blue-and-white balloons, and the mayor spoke, and Rabbi Siegel said the benediction. The Air Force band played the Israeli national anthem, and a medley from *Fiddler on the Roof.* People sat on the park benches, and on tatami mats on the ground in front of the stage, and the kids ran around on the grass. Toward the end, after a lot of speeches, and a kiddie choir, we went up onstage. I looked out over the crowd and saw about four hundred people, actually quite a lot. And I made myself say into the mike, "Please welcome the women of Martin Buber Temple."

Our music cranked up over the loudspeakers, and we took our partners for *"Kora Bushka,"* and we started to move more or less in the right direction. Henny was doing all right this time; Betsy Sugarman was rushing. But mainly we were correct and in the proper places, thumping the stage, turning heavily in each other's arms. I tried to keep up my smiling face. I tried to keep my body light, but my feet were so glum they clomped like wet clay on the ground. By the time it was over, and applause came up from here and there, and we bowed, my shoulders just sagged.

When you're young you get to be, in your own mind, at least, the star and ingénue. But then there is that moment when all of a sudden you're too old for the part. And you know, because of the way people treat you. The way they look, or rather, don't look at you. You aren't in the center anymore; you're off to the side. You aren't the dancer. You're the teacher. Because you have to be a character actor now! And you just aren't prepared for that. It's just a shock. You never needed any character before. I was relieved to be done, it's true, but just so humbled by the experience, not only from dancing with seven sacks of potatoes, but from connecting so intensely with the sack of potatoes inside of me, with just my out-of-shapeness and my age, not being twenty anymore, not being spun by young men, not being anymore even in the same vicinity as those people who could leap in the air.

Afterwards I ripped off my costume—literally—since it hurt squeezing my head out through that neck hole. I changed into my shorts and T-shirt and put on my rubber thongs. I couldn't even see straight. All I wanted was to go home.

On the way to the bus stop I ran into this couple in costume, dressed like Hasids from Jerusalem. The guy had on a black hat and a beard and a white shirt and black trousers and black dress shoes, and, to top it off, one of those long frock coats with the black silk-fringed sash around the waist. The girl had on a long-sleeved dress and white stockings and pumps. The works. "Cool," I said, because having been to Jerusalem I could appreciate their authenticity.

"Shalom aleichem," the guy said.

"Aleichem shalom," I said back, which was the reply I'd learned from Torah Or.

The two of them lit up. "You see?" the guy said to the girl, as if to say, I told you she would understand.

Then I saw, all of a sudden, they weren't just a couple of kids dressed up, they were the real thing, a Hasidic couple in Honolulu.

"My name is Dovidl," the guy told me. "This is my wife, Ruchel."

I looked out at them from the middle of my deep blue funk. His wife? How old was this character? Seventeen? "Are you visiting from Israel?"

"No, no," Ruchel said, "We live here. We've been here six months."

"We came from Crown Heights. We're Bialystokers," Dovidl explained.

"You're from what, Bialystok?"

"We are not personally from Bialystok. That was the seat of our rebbes. Now we are here to start a CHAI house in Honolulu."

"A CHAI house?"

He nodded at me. "So we could bring Yiddeishkeit to Honolulu."

His brown beard was curly, like a spaniel's ear. And she had bobbed hair, which must have been a wig, and sunglasses pushed back on top of her head. They stood there together all covered up in black and navy blue, in these throngs of T-shirts and shorts and midriffs and bare legs. And they were telling me all about how they were sent out from their rebbe (whose seat was now in Brooklyn) to set up house here in the islands, as emissaries of religious Judaism, and they'd just arrived, and they were renting a home in Manoa Valley near the university. "I've been here before," Dovidl said. "When I was single I came to help with the shul for Yom Kippur services. That was how I got the idea."

"The idea to live here?" I said.

He gestured at the trees and the mynah birds squawking and picking at the crumbs on the ground. The blue sky was shining down on us, and a fresh breeze was blowing. It was just the same kind of day that had so amazed me when I first came to Hawaii. "This is like Gan Eden!" Dovidl said. "The Garden of Eden!"

"You'll come by us for Shabbes?" Ruchel asked.

So I guess then a new seed was planted in me, but I didn't know it. I hardly believed in seeds anymore. If I did see one I thought the worst of it. Whereas before when I was so naive I assumed just about any stray idea could possibly turn into a gorgeous flowering shrub, now I'd think—Well, you never know. It could just as well be a haole koa—a weed that starts out as small as a dandelion and then grows and grows, and its stem hardens and the thing puts down taproots deep into the soil, tunneling into swimming pools or any underground pipes it can find, and sprouts ugly branches and turns into a tree which you then have to pay serious money to get removed.

But a few weeks later, when I was at The Good Earth grocery shopping, I ran into my old friend Fred from Rabbi Siegel's class, and Fred told me that he had actually been going to the CHAI class, to their services and all, and they served these unbelievable lunches afterwards. Like five-course meals of unbelievable food. And they did have classes there every week, which Dovidl taught, since he was a rabbi, but they were completely free and open to the public and were on Jewish thought—

not just the rules of Judaism but on the mysticism of the religion, and at the classes there was more food. He said, "You should go, Sharon."

"Nah."

"I thought mysticism was your cup of tea."

"Nah, I've sworn off all that stuff."

"How come?"

"Just some really bad rides, Fred."

"You can really learn a lot about the divine presence in the world."

"Yeah, well," I muttered, "I'm just feeling like I'm a little too old for all that shit."

Fred looked confused. "I'm surprised at you, Sharon."

"Why?"

"Because you seem so bitter. I never had you pegged that way."

"I'm not bitter!" I protested. "I'm not bitter at all. I'm just settled within myself."

"Oh." Fred was really a very sweet guy. "Well, that's a good way to be." And he headed off to the bulk grains.

"Fred. By the way. How old are they?"

"You mean the rabbi and the rebbetzin?"

"Yeah, I wondered, but I didn't want to ask."

"They're twenty," he said. "Can you believe it? And they've already been married a year."

"Geez."

"I know!" Fred said. "When I was twenty I barely knew what planet I was on!"

Something stirred in me when he said that. Nostalgia mixed up with regret. Not that I regretted where I'd been when I was all young and twenty, but that I couldn't be twenty anymore. And maybe I *was* bitter now that I was older. I'd just turned thirty-four. Maybe I was getting kind of set in my tracks—so afraid of sticking my neck out to try anything I was turning into some kind of hermit woman. Some kind of cat lady, without even any cat. So I felt Fred's question. I mean, had I become that conservative? Had I changed so much that I clung to even the most tepid boring equilibrium? All that day and the next my imagination kept piping up, all curious and spurious. "Whatsa matter, scared? What's wrong with you?"

"No, I am not scared. It's not about being scared!"

"Yeah, yeah."

"I'm at a place right now—"

"You're *no* place right now!"

"Shut up!"

"No, you!"

"You!"

"YOU!"

So then I would be quiet and my imagination would be quiet for a moment, too, until a little later in the day I'd hear, "How come you never go anywhere anymore? How come you never want to do anything anymore? How come mysticism isn't your cup of tea? I want some tea."

"You just want to poke your head inside every door you can. . . ."

"Yeah! I wanna go see! I wanna get some free stuff! Free food! Free food!" And this would go on and on, that little voice inside of me, that little imp, even at this late date not completely cured from that idea I could get rich (spiritually speaking) quick. Almost just to shut myself up, I went to the CHAI house for the first time.

DOVIDL and Ruchel lived in a rented tract house with a lot of white walls and a bare parquet floor. There were just a few sticks of furniture, a couch and armchair, and against the wall, a few tall bookcases full of Hebrew books. When I came Saturday morning, they had the living room set up with around twenty folding chairs and a tall screen down the middle to separate the men from the women. They had prayer books with Hebrew and with English, but they were different from the ones I was used to from Torah Or. They were big and fat and full of prayers I'd never seen before. Dovidl started up chanting the preliminary songs, but it took a long time for the service to get rolling, because although we had ten people if you counted me and Ruchel, they were waiting for a ninth and tenth *man*. So that was a little bit offensive, but I kept quiet, since I'd come purely to observe. Eventually Fred showed up, and then, lo and behold, Betsy Sugarman appeared along with her husband, Dr. Sugarman. With Fred and the doctor, Dovidl had his ten males, so he started steaming ahead. Since, of course, he knew Hebrew, and the service was all in Hebrew, Dovidl did the whole thing, the singing, the chanting, the reading from the Torah. Everyone followed along, while Dovidl announced the page numbers as he went—but he directed his voice toward the men's side of the room. I sat on the other side with Ruchel and Mrs. Sugarman, who had a look of resignation on her face, a look of He-Made-Me-Come-Here, My Husband. She had a round lace doily pinned onto her hair.

The service was around three hours long, and for me it would have been even longer if during the silent parts I'd stood and sounded out every single Hebrew word to myself as I used to at Torah Or; but I didn't bother. I just sat and daydreamed. My eyes wandered around the room, and I kept staring at the two pictures Dovidl and Ruchel had up on the wall. One was a big photo of an old rabbi with a white beard, and a smile on his face, and underneath it, pasted right up on the wall, was a shiny copper penny. The other picture was an even bigger photographic portrait, maybe three feet tall, and it was in a fancy gilt frame, and was an almost life-size wedding picture of Dovidl and Ruchel, he in his black frock coat and with his silky beard, and she in a white high-collared wedding gown all covered with lace, and her brown eyes glassy like a doll's.

When Dovidl finally wrapped everything up, we all folded the chairs and the screen as well, and Fred and some of the other guys brought in two long tables from the other room, and we all helped out setting them with white tablecloths and real china, cloth napkins, wineglasses, and silverware. Dovidl raised his silver wine goblet and sang the blessing over the wine, and we all had some. We washed our hands in the kitchen with a two-handled silver cup, pouring the water over one hand at a time, and we filed back to the table, and Dovidl said the blessing over two loaves of challah, and we all had pieces. And then we had chicken soup with real pieces of chicken floating in it, and pieces of carrot and celery and matzo balls. And Ruchel, who all of a sudden I noticed looked quite pregnant, brought out two platters, one with roasted chicken with stuffing, and yams on the side, and the other with brisket of beef, sliced on a bed of onions and stewed tomatoes. It was rib-sticking Mainland food in Manoa in the summer, but you couldn't stop yourself from taking more. It was like Thanksgiving. Just about when you thought you were completely stuffed, along came these desserts, which were bundt cakes with vanilla and chocolate swirled, and a lemon glaze. I didn't mean to be a pig, but now here was this table spread before me, and the food was so good, I couldn't help it. My mouth and stomach opened wide. My hunger was huge! I downed a couple of pieces of cake, before I even realized that Dovidl was telling a story. He was standing up at the head of the table and talking, and as he talked, he was swinging one end of the black silk sash he wore around his black frock coat, so the black silk fringe was swishing around. And he was telling this story in that slight Yiddishy accent he had.

"Once upon a time there was a town that had no watchmaker. Watches and clocks of all kinds the people had. Yet their watchmaker had long ago passed away. There was no watchmaker, and also there was no one in the town to fix the watches when they broke. The people of the town had to wait for the traveling watch repairman to come to them to take care of matters like these. Well, usually the repairman came every year. Every year he came to see the watches. But all of a sudden one year he didn't come. So all right, he's busy—next year he'll be here. But the next year he didn't come either. The next, and the next. What should the people do? They had no one to help them with their watches or their clocks. Some showed this time, some showed that. Matters were growing more and more confusing! The proper time was already a thing of the past! At last, after ten long years, the watch repairman arrived. 'What took you so long?' the people asked. 'What was keeping you?'

"He said, *'Nu,* all right, show me your watches.'

"The people lined up, one hundred in line, to bring him all the watches and the clocks and every timepiece they had. The repairman put his jeweler's glass up to his eye. He got to work. What do you think happened? Some of the watches he fixed right away. A little of this and a little of that. A few turns here, a few screws there. Done. Those watches belonged to people in the town who wound them up every day, and polished them every night. When they had a little problem, the owners fixed it as best they could. So, at the end of ten years, a little alignment, a little tune-up, was all they needed! But some of the other watches in that town. They were another story. The repairman opened them up. He looked at them. "*Oy vey!* They were going to need major surgery." Those watches belonged to people in the town who did not wind them every day, and did not polish them every night. When those watches had a little problem, the owners said, forget about it. This is too hard for me to fix. Let it sit in a drawer, let it wait for the repairman to come. And the watches sat in a drawer and they grew rustier day by day, and they grew slower, and then finally they stopped!

"Now imagine that the people in the town are you and me, and their watches are their *Yiddishe neshamas,* their Jewish souls. And imagine that the repairman is the Moshiach, the Messiah we are waiting for and expecting to arrive any minute! The question for us is—should we be those people who give up and say let my *neshama* sit in a drawer, let my soul wait until the Moshiach arrives? Or should we be those people who keep after it and polish and wind every day? That is the question we should be asking. . . ."

Ruchel was passing around more cake, and tea with lemon, and booklets with songs printed in Hebrew and English. But you know what I was doing? I was crying. It wasn't just that the food moved me, although it did. Or the songs—which I didn't know. It was the story suddenly hitting me all at once. Because it reminded me of my watch, the silver one I used to have, that I'd inherited from Grandpa Irving, and that had been like my lucky charm, and that I'd brought with me all the way out to the forest on Molokai, and Tonic, and on *Gaia* and everything, and it had been my only thing from back home on the Mainland, and the only thing from my family, and I'd actually not kept up winding it, but I had been careful of it all the way up to the monastery, and then I'd just given it away. So what did that say about me and my soul? After all those years I didn't even have a broken run-down watch to show for myself. I'd thought I had to give it up. It was like a sacrifice. I donated it to the monastery to prove I didn't care about material things. And now I didn't have my watch at all. I had nothing.

People at the table noticed that I was crying, but then pretended not to, except for Betsy Sugarman, who was sitting next to me. She said, "Would you like a tissue, dear?" and gave me a whole wad of peach-colored tissues from her purse. So that attracted attention, and then Ruchel came over, and she asked if she could do anything.

I snuffled up my tears. I said, "It's just been a hard week."

"Would you like the last piece of cake?" Ruchel asked me.

"God, no." I clutched my stomach, and pretended to laugh.

"I'll eat it," Fred volunteered. So he did, and then he took me home in his rusted-out pickup truck. That was a relief, because Fred was the kind of guy who was perfectly happy not to have a big long conversation.

I got home and everything was quiet, and I lay down on top of my bed, and my sadness welled up inside of me about my *neshama,* and my silver watch. Except just like it always happens, now that I was all alone and I felt like I could cry as much as I wanted, I couldn't do it anymore. All my sadness was still there, all my pitifulness, like an underground lake, but the tears wouldn't come.

So then Tom knocked on my door.

"I'm sleeping," I called out.

"Sharon, do you have the toothpaste?"

I opened the door. "Tom, I have my fucking own toothpaste. It is not the house toothpaste. If you want toothpaste go to Longs and *buy* it!"

He was hurt. He looked down at me from his mellow heights. "I was just wondering."

"Not everybody has jobs where they get to take naps as part of their day," I snapped, it being a well known perk of Tom's profession (early childhood education) that he had naptime every day after lunch.

"Hey, sorry I woke you up," he said, ambling off.

I don't know, I don't know, I thought, back inside my room. I don't know how much more I can stand. I don't know if I can even take co-operative living anymore. I felt like my whole outer skin was peeled back. I just felt like I could hardly bear to deal with people. What did that say about me? Seven and a half years in the house, and my cooperative powers were all used up.

That weekend I almost skipped Will's opening night in *South Pacific,* I was feeling so down. I actually had to remind myself that Will was one of my best friends, and supporting him was my duty, and if I was in *South Pacific* (which I would never be—not being a Rogers and Hammerstein fan to say the least—but if I was) he would be down in front to support me. So I got up and washed my hair and put on a dress, which was a patchwork dress I owned back then, and I went along with Tom to the Kennedy Theater at the university. I sat there with Tom and the curtain went up, and everybody clapped, since it was such a great beach scene with the waves and the sky and tons of sand everywhere, and there went the sailors, running on the beach, and there went Will running by in his white shorts, and Tom and I started beaming. It really was a fine production. By intermission that feeling of relaxation came over you where you weren't worrying about the performers at all. So I went out into the lobby, and I milled with all the other people, and I'd calmed so far down I nearly had a heart attack when I ran into my ex, Wayne.

"Sharon?" he said.

He'd gained weight in the past couple of years. His hair must have been at least a quarter of an inch long. I realized he was out of the military.

"How have you been?" he asked me. He was so warm and friendly, as though we barely knew each other. "Whatchyou been up to?"

"I'm just here watching my friend," I said.

"It's a great show, isn't it?" Then he said, "Mom, Dad, this is Sharon."

Wayne introduced me to his mother, Rosemary, who was about five feet tall and wearing a blue-and-white muumuu with a white cardigan sweater, and to his dad, George, who took my hand in his iron grip. He was about six foot six in an aloha shirt and jeans, and exquisite hand-tooled leather boots. They'd come out from Colorado to visit Wayne, who was now through with his tour of duty, during which he'd lived in Germany for a year and a half, and had come back to settle down, as he put it, and gone into the construction business and had his own place in Aina Haina, which he had fixed up himself.

It was so weird. It was like an out-of-body experience. Me saying to Rosemary and George, "Is this the first time you've been in the is-lands?"

"Oh, yes. Yes, it is," said Rosemary.

Me saying, "It's lovely, isn't it?"

"Just about the prettiest place I've ever seen," said George. "Sharon, where are you from?"

"I'm from Boston," I said.

"And have you lived here long?"

"Just about fourteen years," I said. All of a sudden my voice was sounding like theirs. It was just like talking to somebody from England and starting to talk British. It was awful, but I couldn't stop. "Sure beats Boston," I told them. "How long are you staying?"

"Just a week," said Rosemary.

"My folks came out for a week too," I said. "They came out for their golden anniversary last year. Mom said it was the best anniversary present she ever had."

"You bet," said George.

"Now, did they come on a package?" Rosemary asked.

IT was the boots I kept thinking about during the second half. George's gorgeous cordovan leather boots with their long, pointy toes. So that was where Wayne was from, I kept thinking. The Mainland, where there was such a thing as dress boots.

I told Tom we had to hit the road as soon as the show was over. I told him I was going to have to make a break for it. But somehow, while Tom was off congratulating Will, and I was running away, there they were, Wayne and his folks, smiling at me, and there I was, coming up to them and getting all folksy myself. It was one of those compulsions I had—liking strangers, and somehow wanting to please them. I'd thought I was over that kind of thing, but I guess not.

We just stood out in the lobby of the theater and visited together. We just stood there and had such a pleasant time we all spontaneously decided to go back to the Tahitian Lanai and have a nightcap.

So we drove to Waikiki, and we went into the bar, and sat around at a table, a respectful distance from the paintings on black velvet, and we talked about life at high altitudes. And Rosemary and I had little drinks and Wayne and George had big ones, until Rosemary said it was really past her bedtime, and I said it was past mine too. And George and Rosemary kissed Wayne good-night and went to their room, and Wayne was going to take me home. And it was amazing. We just strolled down Ena Road to get the car, and Wayne didn't invade my space, or rehash our breakup, or talk about our past at all. He was so relaxed and calm I couldn't get over it.

A full moon was shining over the hotels. People were streaming out of the late movies, and we walked out to the marina on the sidewalk ribbon between the traffic and the beach. Streetlights on one side and on the other the gentle night, the white waves coming in small and soft onto the sand. "Wayne," I said, "you're different."

"I've been working a lot on myself," he told me.

Then it was my turn to look at him funny. He'd never talked that way before. "You're a lot different from the Wayne I used to know," I said.

"Thanks," he said, looking at me with his clear blue eyes. "I appreciate that."

"Can I just ask you something?"

"What?"

"Are you into est?"

"What's est?" he said.

"Never mind."

"Sharon," he said, "I have one real regret."

"Just one?" I teased him.

"Let me rephrase that," he said. "I have one major regret."

"Which is?"

"I didn't treat you with respect."

I thought about that a minute. Then I said, "Actually, I didn't treat you with that much respect either."

"I didn't listen to you."

"I know."

"And you were saying important things," Wayne said. "I didn't get that. When you were talking about seeing God and all. I never considered maybe you were really after something."

"Yeah, maybe. I thought I was. I didn't get very far, though."

"No?" He sounded surprised.

"Not really. I think I went about it wrong. I mean up on my high horse. Why're you looking so surprised?"

"Sharon," Wayne said, "if anybody could go far, you could."

Now we'd reached Wayne's beat-up Jeep. "That's the nicest thing you've ever said to me," I told him.

He came around and opened my door for me. "Can you forgive me?" he asked.

I told him the truth. "I forgave you a long time ago."

16

—

Candlelight

How can I put it? I went back to Wayne. And actually we did fairly well together. We went camping. We drove around in Wayne's new black truck. We made dinner at the co-op. All of that. We hardly fought, except a few times. I was very rarely scared of him, because I warned him straight off that if he started looking at me funny, I was out of there. To be perfectly honest he didn't lift a hand against me all that time. Just about the only thing he did was break one of the co-op chairs, which did frighten me. But it was just that once. And I'd never even liked that chair.

So one fine Saturday all full of cheer I ran up the stairs to Brian's office, since I was so tired of waiting to bump into him to tell him my news. I knew he would be there. He was trying to catch up on his work on the weekends, given that his magnum opus on the Pacific birds was still unfinished, due to writer's block, and also due to the fact Imo was in New Zealand for the semester. She had tenure now in Auckland, but she hadn't been able to parlay that into any kind of real job at the University of Hawaii. So Brian and Imo were still dealing with a commuter relationship, which made him pretty miserable.

But I came bounding in, and I shoved over some papers and plopped myself on his desk and said, "Hey, Brian, what's up, man?"

"Sharon," Brian said, "What's up with *you*?"

"Nothing! Life is good!" I jumped up and pulled on the cord of his miniblinds and they swooped up in a cloud of dust. "Don't they ever wash the windows?"

"You've converted to something, haven't you?" he said.

"I have not. You are so cynical. I am at a totally stable place right now. I am in a state of rest. Wayne and I are talking about moving in together."

"You're kidding me. Wayne!"

"I kid you not." I was so peppy.

"Wayne is back in the picture."

"He's back in my life. No, really, the thing is, he's a different human being. He's been through a lot. He's thought a lot."

"Uh-huh."

"He's the gentlest guy now. He owns his own business. He has his own house; he's helping out his brother, who he's really close to. Brian, you don't even know, he is so good to me. Before it was like we were reading different books. Now it's like we're reading the same page."

"Are you out of your mind?" Brian said. "This is the guy who would not for one second leave you alone. This is the guy that had his hands on you at all times."

"He was threatened by me," I said.

"Oh, he was threatened by *you*!"

"Back then he didn't get it that I was an individual. He didn't understand about me having my own spirit. Now, you should see, he just wants to learn from me and explore with me. Now he's the one encouraging me to . . ."

"To what?"

"To seek."

Brian scooted back in his swivel chair and took me in. "Wayne. You're moving in with Wayne."

"People change, you know," I told him. "He is a person who has profoundly changed. You just remember how he was. You just remember how he always tore me down, but now, he just gifts me."

"He gifts you. Is that even a verb?"

"Yes it's a verb!"

It was true, Wayne gifted me. And not just with material things. He actually wrote me cards. He wrote me messages about our relationship. He wrote about how he felt that we were closer now than we had ever been back when we'd gone out before. And we *were* closer. We were both older. We'd both been through stuff. Good and bad. Wayne had actually been married and divorced by a woman on the Mainland he'd thought he loved, but she was only interested in money and clothes and fancy things they couldn't afford. She had been a clinical shopaholic, maxing out her credit cards every single day. It was a sickness for her. It was like compulsive gambling. She'd gotten them so debt ridden George and Rosemary had to step in and help Wayne out. Then, during the divorce, this woman had demanded more than half of everything Wayne owned! After which, Wayne had started rethinking some of his prejudices toward my desire to lead a more spiritual life, and his disrespect of the idea of visions coming to people. "Your vision that you had was of God, and her vision was strictly name brand every time," he told me. "I didn't know when you went through your vision how lucky I was!" Being so distraught Wayne entered therapy, which was probably the best thing he'd ever done. He began to think about what actually did matter in life, and what one's priorities might possibly be.

Our new relationship was on such a completely different plane from what we'd had. For example, before Wayne had never listened to me when I said how I'd love someday to get a tattoo, because he'd insisted that tattoos were out of place on women, and they were just a guy thing. But now, when I spoke of it, he heard me. He was attuned to my thoughts about how it would be so beautiful to have an artwork engraved on your own body, and he took me down to Waikiki, to his own guy, who generally only did enlisted men, and he held my hand while I had it done: a tattoo the size of a silver dollar right under my belly button. A tattoo of the earth. He stood by me the whole time while the earth was inked into my skin. Tears slid from my eyes, and not just because of the pain. He gifted me.

"See." I rolled down the waistband of my shorts to show Brian.

"Sharon!"

He was so embarrassed and appalled and all, I had to laugh.

"What did you do to yourself?"

"Why do you have to be so negative all the time? You're supposed to be happy for me."

"I'm not happy for you," he said.

"Brian, what is wrong with you?"

He didn't answer. He looked at me with stranger's eyes.

"Look, it's not like I came here to ask your blessing to move in with the guy," I said. "It's not like I came here for you to lecture me on how you never liked the guy. It's not like I said to myself, Well, I'd better make sure I know what Brian thinks of all this."

"I think you're a fool," he said.

"Thanks a lot!"

"I think you talk so much about your seeking and your spiritual growth you don't actually ever manage to do any. I think you're so focused on yourself you're blind to what's actually happening to you."

Slowly, I backed away. It was as if he'd reached out and slapped my face. My eyes stung. I said, "What'd I do to you, Brian? What'd I ever do to you to make you talk that way?" I said again, "I thought you were my friend."

"I am your friend," he said.

But I didn't see what he meant. I walked out of there so defensive and so hurt I didn't see anything anymore. I just wandered through the campus about to cry. If I'd bumped into anyone I knew I'm sure I would have, I was so full of tears. Brian, of all people, had turned against me! I'd just thought we could hang out for a while and then have lunch together and we could talk about me moving into Wayne's place. I'd actually come in thinking Brian might help me move some of my stuff!

So now I had a whole Saturday ahead of me, and Wayne was at work. I went out to University Avenue and I got on a bus, and I thought—I'll go and see Leilani. But halfway out to Sea Life Park I changed my mind. What was I going for? Another lecture, only this time in dolphin language? Instead, I got off at Wailupe and trundled over to Dovidl and Ruchel's new and bigger CHAI house, where they'd moved since they needed more space, and where I hadn't even set foot in months.

Everyone was eating lunch at two long tables, and the place smelled like beef stew, and there was Fred chowing down, and the Sugarmans, and various other people, and a couple of kids. Dovidl jumped up as soon as I came through the door. "Sharon!" Dovidl cried as if I were his own long-lost sister.

"Sharon, come, sit!" Ruchel said, and I saw she wasn't pregnant anymore. She'd had her baby. She was busy making a place for me while she held her baby girl.

Everybody was so happy to see me. They said blessings and gave me wine and challah bread and stew, which was called cholent. We sat, and ate, and ate, and sang songs in Hebrew from little books, where the texts were transliterated and translated so you could follow along.

"We missed you," Dovidl said.

Sheepishly, I smiled. As I said, I hadn't been around the CHAI house much. I wasn't crazy about the CHAI services with the segregation they had going between men and women, not to mention them being so long and all in Hebrew. Yet it was comforting, after Brian, to be welcomed like that. It was such a relief after my so-called friend who just criticized and picked away at me every chance he got. *He* never took me in with open arms.

The food was so good, I actually started to get drowsy eating lunch. Everybody did. Dr. Sugarman started telling all of us how the services and the food reminded him of his childhood, and Betsy started pursing her lips like she always did when he went on like that, since apparently the doctor had grown up Reform in Ohio, not the Old Country. Betsy thought the doctor had some kind of nostalgia delusion going on. But I said to her, "No, Betsy, see, I understand what he means. Cholent makes me nostalgic too."

And she said, "How can you be nostalgic for something that never was?"

She didn't understand that's the strongest nostalgia there is, when you're missing and reminiscing about what you never had. I would have pointed to Fred, except I didn't want to put him on the spot. He was the perfect example. He practically got tears in his eyes from Ruchel's kugel, and he'd grown up Irish Catholic.

I was feeling a lot better by the end of lunch, but then as everybody started to leave, Dovidl twisted my arm to stay for his beginning Judaism class—which at that point had a somewhat low enrollment, of one: just Fred.

A little voice inside me said, You really should stay, since you just ate all this food. But I looked at Dovidl and I sighed and said, "I wish I could."

"Aw, come on, Sharon," said Fred. "I can give you a ride home."

"I don't know," I said. "Dovidl, I'll be honest with you, Judaism classes aren't really my thing."

"Why not?" He smiled at me encouragingly.

"It's the details. I took a whole intensive course in Jerusalem."

"Oh, you've been to Yerushalayim," Dovidl said, impressed.

How to put it. "I just don't relate well to some of the details of the religion."

Dovidl looked at me sagely, or as sagely as he could, given he was now twenty-one. It was great, here he was a bearded rabbi, while in another life he could have been a college sophomore. He said to me, "I have a sense you're looking for something."

Fred smiled and looked down at his hands. He must have heard the line before.

But I nodded.

Dovidl said, "What is it?"

For a long moment I couldn't speak. After all my classes, and my wild goose chases, part of me didn't even want to have this conversation. Yet inside of me still there was such curiosity. There was such desire to ask about God. All my repressed curiosity was pulling against the caution I'd learned. And there was Fred, and Dovidl standing next to him waiting. They were waiting and waiting. I was getting squirmy in front of them.

Squirmy. Squirmier. And then my caution snapped. "Well, I'm looking for spirituality," I said. "I'm looking for magic, and miracles. I'm looking for God—not being some abstract concept but appearing in the world. I'm looking for the Creator—not just slam bam, thank you, ma'am—but in a feminine way, too, all the time interacting with the heavens and earth and the light and dark and all the animals and people and the plants. I'm looking for God to reappear in my life. That's what I've been seeking in religions for a lot of years—but I've never got there—all the way. It's like I get to a certain plateau and then I get stuck, and I can never get to the next level, so actually, even though I want them to, religions just tend not to take on me."

Dovidl didn't even blink an eye. He just nodded, like what I was saying made all the sense in the world. He said, "That was because of your

Yiddishe neshama—your Jewish soul! You have a *Yiddishe neshama* inside of you, so naturally, no matter how hard you tried, no other religions in the world were going to stick to you. That's the way it is with us. Once you're born a Jew, a Jew you will be, no matter what things you do or religions you try. Your parents are Jewish, therefore so are you. As simple as that."

So that stopped me short a second. But then I said, "You know, you can't just be born a certain way, you have to believe. Something's gotta click"—I thumped my heart—"in here! See, Dovidl," I said, "what I'm looking for is to be inspired, and reborn, and transformed, and for miracles happening nowadays, and to me, not just back then and to the children of Israel. Is there some kind of Judaism like that? Is there some kind of Tantric Judaism like that?"

And Dovidl said, "Yes! Yes, there is. Hasidus is Judaism like that!" And he went and got me a book and Fred a book all about Hasidus, which was the Hasidic flavor of Judaism. And the book was called *Tashma*. It had been written by the grandmaster Hasids back in Europe, and it was printed up in English and Hebrew, and it was the most amazing thing. There wasn't a line about cooking utensils in it. It was all about spirituality and magic. It was actually a kabalistic environmental creed.

We started discussing the *Tashma* right then. We began with the first chapter, and Fred and I were just looking at each other in shock. This was really one of the most mind-blowing things we'd ever seen. The book was an explanation of how everything was connected, every soul and every heart, every element and every tree. In the *Tashma* your soul is like a spark flying up to heaven, and also a root, just one of six hundred thousand tiny roots delving down into the earth. Your mind is like water, and your heart is like fire. Your body is a plant, and when your soul is clothed in holy prayers your plant-body feeds your divine spirit. In the *Tashma* each person is a world, and each world is an organism. And there are worlds and worlds and worlds, layered on top of one another, and a higher and a lower of nearly everything, depending on what level your soul ascends up to, and it's like everyone is climbing staircases trying to move up to the higher realms from the lower, but the angels get to run up and down the staircases between them. And it turned out God did have a feminine side! There was a feminine and a masculine side to God, and they wove together the whole fabric of creation, just like warp and woof; they meshed together in this one sexy cosmic loom.

I took the book home, and I began reading it every night. And you know what the most amazing thing about the *Tashma* was? You could close your eyes and picture the whole thing, just this whole planetary system of elements and roots and wings, and these stairways. My imagination was having a field day romping around. I really dug the Garden of Eden, both lower and upper, and I could totally get how the aspiration of one single drop of semen could be a whole universe right there. Probably some of the theological concepts were escaping me, but I was latching on to this stuff at my own level, which was the whole point of what you were supposed to do, because the *Tashma* was *about* levels. That was the point of the whole thing.

So if fire was the element for hearts, I guess at that point I was stoked. The day I moved into Wayne's house in Aina Haina and he carried me over the threshold, I uttered a line: "A good thought joined to God is like wings." And Wayne set me down and he said, "That's beautiful." And we stood there with my boxes and various plants around us in the vinyl tiled living room of his tiny and hot ranch house—where he was in the process of installing ceiling fans, but hadn't had time to finish—and I said, "Fear of God is one wing and love of God is another."

Wayne closed his eyes a little bit. He was so supportive of my studies he used to close his eyes while I would tell him things.

"There's this whole concept," I explained. "If you just have fear of God you only get half the experience, and if you just have love, you only get half. But if you put fear and love together, you get the whole bird."

"And what is the bird?" Wayne asked.

I plunked down onto our nubby yellow couch. "It's a metaphor," I said. "The whole bird is a soul that can fly."

Wayne sat next to me. He said, "This stuff is like poetry."

"It is poetry," I said. "That's what kills me. Dovidl doesn't even realize it. Half this stuff actually comes from the poetry of William Blake."

"No kidding." Wayne was stroking my hair.

I had the feeling he didn't really know who William Blake was. Yet explaining would have ruined the moment. I just put my head down on Wayne's shoulder. I just whispered to myself, "Brian was so wrong about you."

"What about Brian?" Wayne asked.

"Nothing."

"The guy was always jealous," Wayne said.

"Jealous!" I was really surprised.

"Yeah, when we were together before. He had such a crush on you, I could tell." Wayne was laughing softly.

Actually I knew better. The opposite was true. But it was just like with William Blake. You were sitting there with your live-in boyfriend who you loved in this little starter house like married people, and you didn't want to go off explaining things.

I would have brought Wayne to those Saturday classes, if he hadn't been on the job. A lot of times when I told Wayne about the singing and the stories, he said he wished that he could go. But since Saturdays were a workday in construction, it was just me and Fred learning together with Dovidl. And I said to Dovidl, "When I'm reading, I feel like I'm learning stuff I knew all along. I feel like when I see these metaphors I'm seeing these things for the second time!" Because, hadn't I seen those birds flying upward into the upper worlds? Hadn't I seen whole islands of birds? And hadn't I seen the Infinite Light, pouring out of the depths of the sea? I said to Dovidl, "These classes are the best I've ever taken!" I would stay up every night reading in the *Tashma*, in the English. And without any help, or even the slightest medication, I could imagine myself inside those word pictures on the page. I had these unbelievable all-natural dream visions. I'd be on the runway with my wings outstretched ready to leap into the next dimension, and I'd run faster and faster, and then off I'd zoom up into the air, and I'd fly upward to the Upper Garden of Eden past the moon and the sun, and I'd camp there in Eden, and farm there and live there all alone, and none of the insects would bite me, because they would all be praying.

The next three years I was probably the happiest I'd ever been outside of Tonic or Molokai. No more frustrations with the ladies at the temple. With Wayne's business going so well I stopped teaching. I didn't need the money anymore. No more cooperative living. No more pressure-cooker academia. I had my job at Shirokiya; I had my home with Wayne, and hardly ever even thought of torturing myself wanting what I couldn't have. In fact whenever Brian and I ran into each other, for example, at Longs Drug Store, he'd say, "What's up?" and I would just reply, "Not much," and smile, rather than tell him everything like I always used to. And I think, to tell the truth, he was a little bit hurt the way I breezed on by. Yet how long can you open up your heart to someone like that with nothing (except maybe disapproval) in return? Now I had Wayne, and I was studying this mystic Judaism. My soul was like a cat in the sun catching those mystic rays.

Everything was great. The only problem was, at times it seemed like my personal and my spiritual trajectories were heading in two different directions. By which I mean, Wayne and I were living this comfy American life, and my religious classes were preparing me for something else entirely—which I didn't realize at first, since I was so busy drinking up mystic truths, but after a while it started to dawn on me: the whole point and moral of kabbalist religious teaching was that you were supposed to become a religious Jew! Before you could get to all the higher realms enumerated, you had to become religious here on earth according to sixty volumes of Jewish law, and follow every jot and tittle of the 613 commandments. So that was a fairly heavy asterisk attached to all these goodies. That was a fairly big hook to swallow. Yet Dovidl and the *Tashma* kept that hook coming; they kept dangling the laws of Moses, from kashrus, which was keeping kosher, and Shabbes, which was the Sabbath, to marrying a Jewish man. There were all the holidays, there were big and little fasts, there were a thousand rules you had to live by, not to mention praying, morning, noon, and night. And whereas the religion was so beautiful in its visions, to practice it was like digesting the entire telephone book!

I felt like saying, Give it a rest! I felt like saying, Let me have my desserts. Leave me with the cosmos and the spheres of angels. I'm of the holistic persuasion, man, I don't take prescriptions. But yet the classes always came back to what you gotta do to earn your place on the stairs to paradise. And what was weird was, when I was reading alone, the whole universe and the fires and sparks floated free, and the spirits and the angels just flew by, but then in class, it would turn out to be this slow progression, this slow crawl up sheer mountain walls. At home I'd see all humans were like monarch butterflies poised to migrate upward these incredible distances, ready to storm at least the nearest heaven with the beating of our countless wings. And then in class it would turn out we were all just brown ants creeping upward, and we had to carry all the fine print in our mandibles.

Still, I couldn't give up learning—even though I wasn't prepared to go through with some kind of total switch to Jewish observance, and accept the Hasidic way of life, if you'll excuse the expression, whole hog. I guess I'd been around enough to be a little bit careful with my own enthusiasms, and also to realize that Dovidl and Ruchel weren't just a cute young couple or great Old Country chefs, but missionaries out to cleanse my mind and save my soul. Dovidl and Ruchel had a whole agenda all planned out for me. First, they'd have me give up *man-apua* with pork inside. Next thing I knew they'd try to break up me and Wayne. I had moments when I left CHAI house and I thought, Run! Run for your life! Run as fast as you can! They're coming after you! They're coming with the prayers and candlesticks! Even while part of me thought, Wait. Wait, let me just finish this chapter.

I felt like I couldn't discuss all this with Dovidl, this feeling that I was a fish and being angled for, being lured by these gorgeous hand-tied feather lures. But in the end I did come clean to Ruchel. I picked a day right after Passover, when Betsy Sugarman and the doctor were out of town, and I stayed after lunch. She'd just had her second baby, Hershele, so I did all the dishes. She held the newborn, and I scrubbed up at the sink, and I said, "Ruchel, I have to tell you something."

She looked over at me from the dish rack.

I said, "There's a lot of things about Judaism that I love, but a lot that really turn me off. I mean, I love the poetry and the songs and stories and all of that. And a lot of the traditions are really beautiful to me, like Shabbes lunch. But a lot of it I find just rigid and disturbing, like the hi-erarchies of the religion, with the priesthood and all that, and the separa-tion of the people of Israel from other nations, like we're better, and the separation of the men from the women, like *they're* better. And, I mean, I don't want to offend you, but I feel like I shouldn't be leading you on to think I can embrace all that in my life—I'm offending you, aren't I?"

"No!" Ruchel said. "Are you kidding? No, not at all!"

"I just felt like I had to be honest with you."

"That's right. Absolutely!" she said. "What you're doing is getting to a new stage in your learning."

"But, I mean, what I'm trying to say is, I like the stage where I'm at now, and I don't think I'm going to be progressing any . . ."

"You need to be around other women," Ruchel said. "Learning with women. These are women's issues you're talking about—"

"Well, not just women's issues—more like existential issues—"

"I think," Ruchel said, "I think I know a program you would *love*."

"Well, I don't want to do a new program, I mean . . ."

"The Bais Sarah program in Bellevue," she said.

"In Bellevue? What? Are you talking about a hospital?"

"Bellevue, Washington."

"Look," I said, "the thing is, I feel I have to set myself some limits here, because limit setting has been one of my weaknesses in the past. Because I have a very eager spirit. . . ."

"You have a *goldene neshama*," Ruchel said.

"But, see . . . Golden? Is that what you said?" And I stopped, because those words so touched me. Just the idea that she and Dovidl might look at me like that: a golden soul. My spirit could be golden and not just silver; it could be golden and impossible to rust or tarnish. I was just so moved by that idea.

"This program," Ruchel told me, "it's all for women and girls who want to learn together—and they live in one big house and the most intensive learning goes on every day. An unbelievable rabbi runs the classes, Rabbi Shimon Simkovich, along with his wife and daughters, and only the best young women teachers come to live with the women and counsel them."

"No, no, Ruchel," I said. "See, first of all, I'm in a serious relationship. Wayne and I have been together again four years! We have a home. I doubt—"

"Every student there has doubts," Ruchel told me. "Having doubts is exactly what they're looking for. Their specialty is doubts!"

"Okay," I said. "Great, but I'm thirty-eight years old. I'm practically engaged. I'm not going to leave my home and go to boarding school in Bellevue, Washington. Even if I had the money—"

"For some cases, for the most qualified, it's all free!" Ruchel said. "It's all on scholarship, even the plane tickets."

I said, "Ruchel, I am not going to turn into a religious Jewish lady."

Her bright brown eyes peeked out from under her bouffant wig. "*Im yirtzeh Hashem*, God willing, we can only wait and see what happens!" She said she and Dovidl were going to write to the director of the program about me and my learning and my need. They were going to do a whole recommendation for me.

I kept saying, "Please, that's not what I'm interested in doing with the next part of my life."

But she kept saying they could just send the letter and see what happened. Why not wait for a reply from the program before deciding what to do? If I didn't want to go, then fine, that would be the end of it, but you shouldn't say no before you even had an invitation.

All that talk made me slightly nervous—even though rationally I knew Dovidl and Ruchel had no power over me. They couldn't exactly kidnap me or steal Wayne away. Yet deep down, something frightened me when I heard Ruchel speak about Bellevue. I was afraid of the idea of going off and learning Jewish mysticism. It was too tantalizing. I knew myself well enough by now—to me a new creed was like liquor, and I was a person just a few years into recovery! I knew the life I wanted was the one I had, with Wayne in Aina Haina. I knew the place I lived was this middle-class, middle-of-the-road neighborhood, no enchanted island anymore. Yet still, deep down, I was parched for the holy spirit. I thirsted for the smoothness on my tongue, and the sweetness and the burn.

The ironic thing was that Wayne, being now supportive of me, was egging me on to bring some Jewish practices to our home. He was the one who wanted to learn about lighting candles on Friday nights. I said I wasn't ready, but Wayne was so encouraging to me and loving about the whole thing that right before Memorial Day weekend I ended up taking home a box of stocky white candles from Ruchel, and I picked up a pair of brass candleholders that looked like flowers from the India Imports store. And that Friday night in the kitchen Wayne and I turned off the light and set up the candles on a tray on top of our avocado laminate counter. It wasn't all that dark, because the sun was just starting to set. Yet when I struck the match, the tiny little flame flashed at us. And Wayne bowed his head, and I lit each of the candlewicks, and I opened up my prayer book and sounded out the blessing with an eastern European accent, which was how I'd heard Ruchel do it: *"Baruch atoh adonoi eloheynu melech haolam, asher kidishonu, bimiszvosov vitzivonu, lihadlik ner, shel Shabbos."* And then I read the translation aloud: "Blessed art thou,

Lord our God, king of the universe, who hast sanctified us with thy commandments, and commanded us to kindle the Sabbath lights."

Wayne and I stood together and looked at the two candles shining in this huge pool of twilight.

"What do you see?" Wayne asked me.

"I don't see anything," I said.

"You were looking at those flames like you saw something in there," he said.

"No, I was just thinking they're so small."

"Oh," he said.

"And I was thinking, maybe lighting candles is like sending up a flare. Maybe there really are a lot of other worlds out there. Maybe we're just part of an archipelago stringing out into space, and maybe all our acts are truly connected with the infinite."

"I feel that way too," he said. "I feel like there's something out there too."

And we stood there hushed, and we watched those white candles melting down.

The next morning, after services at Ruchel and Dovidl's house I told Ruchel, "I have good news!"

She was sitting with the baby in her lap and holding a bottle, and also trying to close up her little prayer book, but she looked up at me right away and she practically shrieked, *"You lit?"*

"I lit candles," I said, and I grinned.

"Yaashar koach!" she burst out. Congratulations! And then she said, "I have good news also!"

My heart fainted, as it says in the Psalms. I wished I hadn't told her. I mean, I was a grown woman here, yet there was something about all this, Ruchel's reaction, it was like she was my troop leader and I was collecting Girl Scout badges, like one with a little pair of candles on it, and one with challahs, and one with a prayer book, and on and on, and when you got the whole set, then—then what? Then you would make full Yiddish Scout?

She said, "You've been accepted to Bellevue. To the program, with full scholarship!"

I said, "Ruchel, I already told you, that's impossible for me. It's impossible for me to go there."

"They said you were at the top of their list," she told me.

"Yeah, right." I laughed.

"You don't believe me? That's what they told me," she said.

"Listen, I really appreciate all the trouble you went to, but . . ."

"Rabbi Simkovich said you were the perfect candidate for the program," she said.

"Oy, oy, oy!" I threw up my hands. "I'm telling you. No can do."

"So it's okay, it's all right. Maybe they can hold your place," Ruchel said. "So go when it's more convenient."

"No, don't ask them to hold my place," I said. "I don't want them to do that."

"It's okay. Rabbi Simkovich would do that for you, because he thinks you are a perfect candidate."

"No, I don't want him going to all that trouble," I said.

"It's no trouble," Ruchel insisted, and she shook up the last of the formula in the baby's bottle. "So he'll hold the place at least a little while. I'll tell him he should just wait. It won't be a problem. He is very impressed with your desire for learning. And also he's my brother-in-law."

On Memorial Day, Kathryn and Rich were having their traditional barbecue blowout. The tradition really belonged to our old co-op house, but like a lot of other things, including most of the pots and pans, Kathryn had taken the tradition with her. Still, she and Rich invited the former housemates and all their friends, which amounted to at least forty people. And since no one else ever took the initiative to have a Memorial Day party, everybody always came.

Wayne and I drove out to the North Shore in his truck, and I was saying we didn't have to stay long. Actually I had to twist his arm to come at all, since Wayne was still convinced all my academic friends looked down on him. But we drove out there, through silvery green cane fields, and we stopped and Wayne cut down a few stalks with his pocket knife, and we sucked them as we drove. And we got there to this expensive shack Rich and Kathryn had on the beach, and we hopped out and Wayne surprised himself. He actually had a great time, and nobody looked down on him once. Wayne was the star when we played volleyball on the sand. There was swimming, and coolers of cold beer,

and Kathryn manning the grill serving up hamburgers and chicken
breasts, and her great marinated vegetarian kabobs. Kathryn was a great
cook, and an incredible hostess—I appreciated that now. I really had a
lot of respect for Kathryn, now that I didn't live with her. She had all
this energy and these organizational skills. She was such a doer. Who
else would think of stringing up little Christmas lights to the volleyball
net when it got dark? Who else would clear out every stick of furniture
in her living room to create a dance floor? She had a boom box, and
music, which was tapes of everything from the Beatles to Talking Heads,
and Tom was appointed DJ. Will, and Kathryn, and Rich, and Kathryn's
girlfriends from work, and Kathryn's kid, and me and Wayne, we all began to dance. We danced until everybody was just about exhausted, except me. Wayne went out to get another beer. But Tom had just put on
the soundtrack tape of *Dirty Dancing*. "Hey, Wayne," I called. Terrible
timing. "Ba-by, my sweet ba-by, my sweet ba-by, You're the one. . . ."
Here they were finally playing all the really danceable songs! My fingers
were snapping, my whole body was twirling. I looked out through the
open doorway, and there I saw Brian smoking his pipe pensively.

So naturally I danced right over to him, and I took his pipe.

"Stop that! Sharon!"

And I tapped it out.

"Sharon. What are you doing? I'm not dancing."

"Yes, you are."

"I'm not going in there," he said. But he was laughing. I had both his
hands. Everybody was crowding around after us.

I danced him inside where the music was pounding.

"I don't want to!" he said.

"Will you shut up!"

"All right, Sharon!" Will called out to me.

"Go, Sharon!" yelled Kathryn.

"Sharon, no." He was like a drowning man.

"Follow me!"

And I put my hand on his shoulder, and I put his hand on my waist,
and I led, and he followed, and by God, Brian was doing the box step.
"Stop laughing, and stand up straight!" I ordered him. And I counted
out the beats, and everybody circled us, and the music encompassed us.
"Follow!" I said. "*Follow* me."

I can't even tell you how everyone was cracking up to hear me ordering Brian around like that.

But I didn't notice, because by then a huge revelation had come over me, which was that Brian knew how to dance just fine, because he was leading, and all of a sudden he was improvising, and he was spinning me out.

"Whoo, all right!" yelled Rich.

People were clapping.

"Liar!" I said. But Brian had never lied to me. It had been my mistake all along, assuming he was a klutzy naturalist, thinking it would be some kind of joke bringing him out onto the dance floor. I guess deep down I still thought real dancers looked like Gary. Brian was stocky, but he was light on his feet. And then I realized something. He hadn't been dancing because Imo wasn't there. It was loneliness, not two left feet. The house was throbbing with "I Had the Time of My Life." Who would have thought? The guy could swing.

He twirled me and I twirled him; he brought me in close and I followed. He curled me into him and he spun me out. Everyone was clapping. And we looked into each other's eyes, and we forgot ourselves. We forgot about Wayne and Imo. We were buddies again. We moved together and all our differences just blew away.

We danced out wilder and wilder, until this time I was nearly out of breath. I almost collapsed, but still I yelled to Brian, "Let's do hips!" and he mirrored me and we wiggled our hips. And I beckoned to him and I leaned back and he leaned over me, and I would have fallen all the way over I was laughing so hard, except he caught me. And that was when the music ended and everyone burst out clapping. Brian and I were drenched with sweat, and we were going to stagger out for drinks except Wayne got to me first. I thought he was coming to bring me water, but he grabbed my hand and hustled me outside.

"What?" I said. "Wayne!"

"We're going home," he told me, and he led me to the truck.

"Why?"

He looked at me with such a hurt expression I almost forgot for a moment he was being a total jerk.

Then I remembered. I said, "Wayne! What is your problem? You're mad because I danced with someone else?"

"Get in. We're going home."

"It's not even midnight!"

"Get in."

"No!"

Then he grabbed my arm.

"Wayne! Don't you think you're being a tiny bit unreasonable?"

He got in the truck, and he started the engine. He was waiting for me to climb in.

"No! I'm not coming!"

He slammed the door and drove off.

"Geez," I said. Actually I was pretty upset.

I went back around to the yard and got a drink. Brian was standing out there cooling off. "Where'd you learn that?" I asked him.

"What?"

"To dance."

"I had lessons," he told me. "When I was a kid."

"You had *lessons?*"

"Where's Wayne?"

"He went home."

"He was annoyed with you," Brian said.

"He has to get up early for work," I said, which was true.

"You're a flirt," Brian said.

I guess I looked kind of aghast when he said that. It just really surprised me to be accused of that. I'd never thought of myself that way. "You know I'm not."

He snorted.

"You looked so lonely without Imo," I said.

He didn't answer.

"Why'd you let her go to Auckland?"

"Well," he said, "it'd be pretty unreasonable to have her give up her job."

"There's such a thing as being too reasonable," I said.

"Do you want a ride home?"

"Why?"

"It's late."

"No, it's not."

"Well, if you want a ride, I'm going," he said.

So we said good-bye to Kathryn and Rich and the thinning hordes still dancing, and we hiked up the beach road to where Brian had parked his rusted-out Datsun. And we got there and we stood for a minute by the car and looked at the black waves and the black sky. "There aren't as many stars as on Tonic," I said.

"Well, there are. . . ."

"Yeah, yeah, I know," I said. "There's just as many, only you can't see them all here. You're so predictable." And I guess that was when I kissed him. I admit it, I kissed him on the lips.

He stood there completely still. For about a minute neither of us could even move. Then he put his hands on my shoulders and he kissed me back. And my kiss had been fast and shy, but his was slow. I couldn't even breathe for a second there. I was sure it was a dream, because I had dreamed it so many times. His hands spread over me; they stroked my hair all down my back. They were wide gentle hands; they hesitated at my waist. Don't stop, I thought. Don't stop. Don't stop. He was too polite. He was too good. Any second he would pull away. But he didn't stop. My shirt was old and loose, and I wasn't wearing anything under it. Slowly his hands drifted up my bare back; his touch was so light and so warm I felt drowsy with him. A sleepy heat spread through me like the sunshine trapped in sand. He touched my breasts and I bent my head down. I couldn't look at him, my heart was beating so hard.

Yet we did get in the car, and I think we still intended to take me home to Aina Haina, but somehow the car didn't go that way. We never said anything. It's just that we ended up driving to Manoa. Windows open, nobody else out on the road. The car drifted on the freeway. In silvery phantom freeway light we drove to Brian's place. We glided up to his apartment. We took no stairs or elevators; we had no keys that I remember. We just levitated through the door. We never turned on the lights, just floated into the bedroom. It was all dark and shadows, except the pale sheets tangled up on the bed. We might have been a pair of ghosts the way our clothes slipped off of us. My shirt and shorts—they'd grown and grown until they slipped off, too big for me. Brian took one step back. He took one breath. But that was all. We were transparent. I reached out to him; he stepped inside of me.

∗   ∗   ∗

WHEN I opened my eyes it was morning, and the first thing I saw was Imo staring at me, her face framed in a photograph right by the bed. There she was, examining me with her dark eyes. So I turned the picture facedown. And I saw a stack of dog-eared page proofs from *Atoll Research Bulletin* and clean laundry piled in a plastic basket, and brown curtains pulled back, and, covering most of the wall behind the bed, a Rand McNally map of the Pacific Ocean. An enormous rectangle of sky-blue, flyspecked with islands. "Brian?" I called out.

"I'm in here," he said from the living room.

So I padded out there where he was sitting with a mug of coffee. "Could you get dressed?" he snapped.

"Why?" I said.

He was all dressed and tense and sitting on the couch reading the newspaper, every single word.

So I left him alone and took a shower and found my clothes and all, and I came out again brushing my hair.

He didn't look any happier. "Sharon . . ."

"Do you have anything to eat here?" I asked.

"Sharon!"

"I'm sorry," I said in a small voice. "I'm hungry."

"Listen," he started again.

"I know," I said.

"This was a really big mistake."

"Well," I said, cautiously, "it wasn't a mistake at the time."

"Yes!" he said. "It was a mistake at the time!" And he rattled his paper, and he shook his head. He was horribly upset. "What were we thinking?"

I came up to him, as near as I could, which was about three feet away. The distance between us was growing again, but I came up to the edge, and I said, "Brian, I know what I was thinking."

"What?"

"Just that I wanted to be with you."

"And that was wrong," he said. "Given the circumstances. Given each of us is committed to someone else."

"Well, I guess for a while we forgot. You know, people forget."

"Oh, Sharon," he said. "God, what a mess."

And I saw what he meant. I could see the mess in front of me, or at least I was beginning to see. What had I done? What had I destroyed by spending the night with him? It was like sleeping with your own conscience. I was still so fuzzy from the night that Wayne barely even crossed my mind. "We won't tell anyone," I said. "It won't happen again."

"Damn right," he said, but more to himself than to me.

"I'll go," I said, but I didn't leave.

He wouldn't even look at me.

"Brian," I whispered.

Finally he relented and got up and opened the door for me. "Sharon, I'm sorry."

"I'm not," I said.

He touched my face, but still he shook his head at me.

I went home—where else would I go? I figured the less I thought about the whole thing the better. And I got there, and Wayne's large glossy truck was still parked in front of our small scruffy house. I let myself in, and he was sitting on the couch. He looked terrible. He was still wearing his clothes from the night before. He hadn't shaved. It looked like he hadn't slept at all.

So I figured I'd go into the kitchen and get myself some cereal. I really was hungry. I got a bowl and spoon and poured myself some Wheaties.

"Where were you?" Wayne said. He was standing in the doorway.

I poured the milk in. "At the party."

"All night?"

"Look," I said, "it took me a while to get home."

"A while? It's eleven o'clock in the morning!"

"You were the one who took the truck," I said.

"Where were you really?" he said.

"At the party."

"You're lying," he said. "You were with Brian."

I decided to keep eating.

"You were with him."

"I don't think you really want to have this conversation right now," I said.

"Oh, yes, I do."

"Well, it's not happening. I'm not talking now."

"Tell me the truth," he said. And he grabbed my bowl and he hurled it to the floor, milk splattering, soggy bits of cereal flying. But the bowl didn't break. I was staring at it, fixated by the bowl wobbling there on the white tiles. "Look at me." He put his hands on my head, and he forced me to look him in the eye. He kept at it, asking and asking, "You were with him, weren't you? Weren't you?"

"Stop it!" I screamed.

But he kept on saying, "Tell me the truth! Tell me the truth."

No. No, I thought. I won't talk. I refuse to talk. "I'm not telling you anything until you calm down!" I finally said.

He backed off of me. He went back in the living room and started walking around. When he came back he'd calmed way down. He said, "Sharon, I can't have lies between us."

"I know." All of a sudden I felt tearful. Suddenly I was starting to feel remorse.

"I can't live in a relationship without honesty."

"You're right," I said. "We can't live that way."

"All I'm asking—what I need to know is—were you with him last night?"

"Yes," I said.

He hit me right there with the flat of his hand. I could taste the blood in my mouth. I could hear my ears ringing. He hit me again. My whole head was growing on my shoulders, my eyes were swimming, tiny particles were coming before my eyes. My whole mind was being shaken up, and I saw stars—the tiniest solar system with pea-size planets orbiting around. I saw a whole constellation of stars; they were leaping and jumping like a flea circus. The room was going dark, but this whole microcosmos was coming down in little flecks of light. And there I was, falling. I guess actually I was blacking out. I was falling into this minute universe; this small blackness that was inside my head. And Wayne's voice was getting blurry, and blurrier. "But I loved you! I loved you!"

I found myself some time later on the kitchen floor. There was one of our old termite-eaten cane chairs lying beside me, and there was blood, and there was milk, and the white cereal bowl still unbroken. The vinyl tiles were caked with dried-up cereal. I didn't see the spoon. One of my eyes wasn't opening, so my view was skewed. Gradually I lifted up my head, but the room was going around. I thought, Is this what it's like to have a concussion? Then I remembered Wayne. I was afraid he was still in the house. I put my head down and listened. The house was very still. I listened harder. I could hear the mynah birds outside, and little white-eye birds—the ones who'd driven out the native Hawaiian honey-creepers—the white-eyes were in the bushes singing to each other. I heard no cars on the street, only far away a motorcycle, like the buzzing of a fly. Slowly I lifted up my head again. I sat up, but I couldn't put any pressure on my wrist. I must have sprained it. I crept along the floor into the living room, all the way to the louver windows in front, where I had to stand to see out over the bushes that his truck was gone.

Then I went to the bedroom and took my guitar. I stuffed a canvas beach bag with some clothes. There was a necklace Wayne had given me, and there were other pretty things, but I didn't take them, just the extra clothes to wear, and my toothbrush, and my old book, my falling-apart Norton anthology—I thought of that.

All that week and some of the next I stayed at Corinne's house, and she and Rae doctored and nursed me and alternately begged and scolded me to go to the police and swear out a complaint against Wayne, but I wouldn't do it. And they said they couldn't believe me, and they told me I had to stop acting like I was at fault—they didn't understand how I, the victim, could be blaming myself for what had happened. I kept telling them I felt so guilty, but they didn't see why, since I never told them straight out I'd slept with Brian or anything.

Corinne said to me that I was a battered woman, even though Wayne had never battered me before. She said I was in denial, but I owed certain things to myself like safety. She told me that above all I must stop blaming myself for what went wrong. She said that I must have a plan. I did have a plan, which was to go back to the way my life had been before, i.e., back to the co-op house, and to my friends, and to my job at Shirokiya, but Corinne and Rae were worried about my safety. They were convinced Wayne would come after me and kill me. They were talking me into going to a safe house for a while; going underground for shelter. And when

we talked I tended to agree with them. Yet, when I was alone and thinking, when they were at work and I was home with the cat, Jane, I rebelled
against the whole idea. Why should I hide? Why should I live under
house arrest? Hiding was not in my personality, not at all. "Jane," I said,
"I'm not going to hide. I am not going down into some little hole."

I fluffed up Jane's black-and-white fur. I fluffed her up and down.

She lay on her back and purred at me.

I said, "I'm not afraid of Wayne. Well, even if I am, how can I live that
way? In fear?" I said, "The truth is I'm more afraid of me."

She wrinkled up her pink nose. "I'm the one," I said. "I'm the one who
all of a sudden upends the apple cart. I don't even know why. Whatever happened to the person I used to be, who used to meditate?"

Jane just squinched her eyes shut as I rubbed her front, since cats do
not tend to empathize much with guilt and self-loathing. I was wishing
myself back in time so I could change what I had done—except I could
never decide how far back I'd go. I just felt like now I'd really burnt my
bridges. All of them. Wayne hated me. Corinne pitied me. And Brian—
how could I ever face him again? Well, how could we face each other?
I wanted to call him. I was dying to go see him—to apologize, or say
good-bye, or tell him he'd been right about Wayne—he did hit me. It
almost didn't matter what I'd say, if I could talk to Brian one more time.
Maybe just to confirm the whole thing with him had been real, and not
just my dream. But I knew better than to seek him out. He'd hate me
for dwelling on that night, and I couldn't stand the thought of that.

I felt like a latch-key child waiting in Corinne's house alone. Every
day and every hour I decided to devise a new plan, and then I couldn't
think of any. Go see Leilani? She'd see through that in an instant. Me
coming over to feel sorry for myself—as if she weren't the one imprisoned in a saltwater tank! Take the bus up to the temple? Break down and
cry all over Rabbi Siegel's desk? "Sharon," he would say, "what is it after
all that you are searching for? You have searched and searched. Even in
the uttermost parts of the world. And yet, what is it that you really
need?"

I sat and watched through the window as the mail truck drove halt-
ingly up the winding street. Squeak, squeak. The brakes squeaked at
every stop as it crept along each day. It was like something from one of

Dovidl's stories, the broken-down mail truck needing maintenance, but the Postal Service never fixing it. It was like one of those allegories for your soul.

I picked up the phone. Ruchel was the one I called. "Hello?" My voice wobbled.

"Who is this?" she asked.

"Sharon."

"Excuse me? Who is this? Oh, Sharon! Sharon! We missed you on Shabbes! How are you?"

"I've been away," I said. "But I'm back now. I've been in Britain," I blurted out.

"In Britain! That must have been a short trip."

"It was," I said, "but it didn't feel short. It was very full," I said.

"You went to see family?"

"Oh, yes," I said. "I was seeing them. . . ."

"I didn't know you had family in Britain. I have cousins in Golder's—"

"I was also thinking; I was thinking a lot," I told her. "I had this powerful experience, Ruchel. I had this cataclysmic experience."

"*Has v'shalom!* Are you all right?" she asked.

I couldn't answer. For some reason, now of all times, I was starting to cry.

"Sharon, you're all right? You're crying?"

"I have a frog in my throat. Excuse me." I coughed. I caught my breath. Still, it was hard to get the words out. Every word I spoke I started to cry harder. "Ruchel, I have to change everything. The place I am right now. I can't stay in this place any longer. The place I am, it's not working. It's untenable. The person I am right now—it's no good. I have to try to learn to . . . I need to learn how to . . ."

But it seemed like I didn't need to say any more. To her ears what I was telling her was as clear as clear. "You want to learn!" she exclaimed. "You need to learn!"

17

White Cloud

Ruchel and Dovidl drove me to the airport in their little putt-putt Honda. The day was hot and muggy, and the vinyl uphol-stery sticky against my skin. I leaned out the open window, since the back seat was so cramped with the babies. Dovidl wasn't wearing his frock coat, just his black suit pants and white shirt. Instead of his black hat he was wearing a big black velvet yarmulke that covered his whole head. Ruchel was wearing designer sunglasses, and a long-sleeved navy striped blouse, and a cotton duck skirt, yacht style. I realized, They're Hawaiian Hasids now. They've gone tropical!

I, in the meantime, also had new clothes. I was wearing a long-sleeved T-shirt and a skirt instead of shorts. I had white ankle socks, and pure white athletic shoes instead of sandals. I was actually going to the Bais Sarah women's program in Bellevue.

From Shirokiya, with my employee discount, I'd bought a good down sleeping bag, and a couple of towels. One of those state-of-the-art rolling flight bags, and a red rain poncho that folded up into its own pocket. I could have bought a travel iron for really cheap, but since I never ironed it didn't seem worth it. I did buy a bra stash, though! You couldn't tell from looking at me, but I had something like two hundred bucks in cash squirreled away between my boobs. Two hundred in twenties, as my mad money, in case I got to Bais Sarah and it turned out to be a heavy-duty brainwashing facility and I had to sneak out to the road and hitch a ride to Seattle and buy tickets on a Greyhound bus that would be leaving for someplace no one would ever find me.

Curbside at the airport, Ruchel gave me a hug, and Dovidl gave me a laminated card printed with a special prayer for safe journeys that I should read right before takeoff. The babies were fussing and people were milling around. It was a confusing scene, and I was rushing rushing to get away before I started to cry. I remember actually feeling relieved when I said my last good-bye, and trundled inside to agricultural inspection. The inspectors looked inside my suitcase and inspected my guitar. They slit open the cardboard box that I had so carefully packed with my five hundred or so records and tapes. Then they slapped some Agricultural Inspection tape of their own over the box and I finally checked my bags and went on my way. There were no paper cups of pineapple juice anymore. Free juice had been discontinued.

When my plane lifted off into the blue sky I looked out from my window seat, and I could see Oahu under me, the whole island and the ocean surrounding it, all in perspective. All the houses were receding, and the cliffs and the beaches, and then the other islands close by and just as green, strung out in the ocean. There were Molokai, and Maui, and the Big Island. There they were, smaller and smaller, like lazy turtles lying in the sun. Then the clouds wisped over the view.

I leaned back in my chair and stuck out my feet just to feel my backpack down there. My guitar was in the overhead compartment, and all my other earthly possessions were in the belly of the plane. I felt this calm desolation, as though I had died.

WHEN we got to Sea-Tac Airport, though, my stomach was in knots, just realizing that here I was on the Mainland ready to enroll in some kind of hostel or halfway house or boarding school, depending on how you looked at it. Dovidl and Ruchel had told me I was going to be met at the airport, but I almost hoped, walking down the aisle of the plane with my stuff, that no one was going to be there after all, and that the whole thing had been a mix-up. Part of me almost wished I would ar-

rive in Seattle, anonymous and alone, and have to go exploring and find
a job, like maybe in one of the famous Seattle coffeehouses, and maybe
hanging there I'd find out about the folk-dancing scene and hook up
with the folk community. But when I came out into the airport with
the other passengers filing off the plane, I saw right in front of me, impossible to miss, a tall, burly, bearded man in a black frock coat and hat,
who I realized was Rabbi Simkovich. He had three or four children
swarming around him, and he was carrying a placard like from a rabbinic limo service: SHARON SPIEGELMAN.

So I took a good look at him with the kids, and I walked right on
past. I took my backpack and guitar, and hurried all the way out to the
concession stands, and bought myself a bag of trail mix, which despite
my stomachache I opened up and started eating. And I looked way
down to the escalators and to the glass doors of the baggage claim,
where my suitcase and my sleeping bag and my cardboard box would
soon be circling round and round. The thought definitely crossed my
mind, the thought of leaving. But there I was with the stubs of a free
ticket all the way from Honolulu to Seattle. I knew running off wasn't
right. I headed back to the gate.

The people there were thinning out, but the rabbi and his kids were
still standing there expectantly. I hung back out of sight for maybe five
minutes and I watched them waiting, looking all around for me. Then I
put down my backpack and I watched them a little more, and as I
watched, I nibbled on my trail mix. I was willing myself to come up to
them, but I was nervous as a squirrel, nibbling, nibbling. Ready to run.

Finally I went up to the rabbi and admitted who I was.

"Sharon! *Baruch habah!*" Welcome! he exclaimed, and he took my
backpack, and the kids swarmed around me. They were all about four
years old. We went down to the baggage claim, and piled into the club
wagon, and the rabbi drove us out to Bellevue.

The roads were big, and they were long—and they weren't circular
like the ones in Hawaii; you knew they were connected up to big free-
ways and highways, by which you could drive clear across the country.
All around us were verdant Mainland trees, deciduous ones, and ever-
greens. And there were mountains, also green, and huge enormous shopping plazas. Everything was large scale and bright and new, and then
downtown Bellevue came up, and it had two office towers of tinted

mirror glass, one bronze, and one blue. We kept driving out along this pretty green lake, which I thought was Lake Washington, but later I found out was Lake Sammamish. I saw boats in the lake, and kids fishing, and ducks. I had my eyes glued to the windows of the van; I was trying to get my bearings and check out the surroundings, but at the same time this music was pounding through the van's sound system. It was that Bialystoker pop song about the Messiah who they called Moshiach, and it was very cheery and up tempo and loud, "Mo-Mo-Mo-Moshiach! Mo-Mo-Mo-Moshiach! Mo-Mo-Mo-Moshiach! Moshiach, come to-day! Hey!" The kids were busy offering me candy and also eyeing my bag of trail mix to the point where I started looking at it myself. Peanuts, raisins, dried papaya and pineapple chunks, banana chips, dried coconut flakes. Was this stuff somehow not kosher? So there I was checking out Washington State from the inside of a Moshiach mobile.

We started driving through some real old-growth suburbs with Tudor houses set back and plush green lawns, and oak trees. I thought, Well, this is nice, but where are we really going? Where's Bais Sarah going to fall out? And then we started up a sweeping drive, and there on the hill I see a great big mama house, all red brick and turrets, a Victorian castle with a slate roof and bay windows and the biggest front lawn of all the houses we'd seen yet. And it turned out *that* was the Bellevue Bais Sarah Insti-tute. Whoa! From the outside the place looked just magnificent.

When the rabbi opened the door, we came into a vast entrance hall with curving stairs, and everywhere was marble and carved wood, ex-cept the walls were peeling and stained yellow. The mansion was seri-ously run-down, but no one seemed too worried. Up in the stairwell hung a grand portrait of the Bialystoker rebbe in a niche in the wall that looked like it had been designed for an even bigger painting.

"The house was left to us," the rabbi said. "Alice Rosensweig, *oleva-sholom,* left it to us in her will five years ago."

"You mean, she didn't have kids?" I asked.

"She did have kids," the rabbi said. "But she left the estate to CHAI of Bellevue." And he put up his hand, like nothing more should be said. So, of course, I said nothing more.

Then the rebbetzin came down the stairs, with all these women, the ones who studied there in the institute, and they milled around me, and they started asking questions, about the flight, and about Hawaii, and the rebbetzin, whose name was Chaya, was asking all about her sister, back in Hawaii, and about Ruchel and Dovidl's kids. Chaya Simkovich was very plain and skinny, despite having so many kids. She had a somewhat long, horsy face, no resemblance to Ruchel, and this sardonic way of talking that made me think she was a real New Yorker.

I was pretty much mobbed. There were fifteen women already studying there for the summer, and there were maybe five girls who were called *madrichot*, who were teenaged counselors who had come from back east in Crown Heights to help guide the students and give them one-on-one tutoring, and then there were more little kids, I wasn't even sure at that point how many, but later I found out there were eight, and the kids were all the rabbi's and his wife's.

My arrival was a big event in the house. Everyone was so excited I'd come all the way from out in the Pacific Ocean, and they couldn't do enough for me, carrying all my stuff up to the second floor, showing me my bed, which they'd pushed up near the window. I was going to be bunking with three other women in a grand old bedroom with flaking paint, and a pocked and pitted hardwood floor, and a fireplace with a mantel carved out of marble veined green like Stilton cheese. Above the fireplace there was the rebbe again, like Chairman Mao, watching from his picture frame. My bed had just a bare mattress with black-and-white ticking. Everybody slept in sleeping bags like at camp. A little black prayer book lay where my pillow would have been. There were two dressers in the room, and I got the top half of one. There was a washstand right in the center of the room, for ritual washing right when you rolled out of bed. For regular washing there was this mildewy powder room with rusty old sconces and a claw-foot tub and a shower rigged up with a voluminous plastic shower curtain that you pulled around you.

Everyone was fussing over me, and talking at once, and then suddenly Chaya said, "Girls, look at the time! It's time for afternoon *shiur*!" meaning, afternoon class. And she said to her own children, "Kids, go downstairs now. Give Sharon time to rest." And they all left me alone so I could unpack and settle in and take a shower. They all stampeded back down the dark wood stairs.

I was tired, but too jazzed to lie down. I unrolled my sleeping bag onto the bed. Then gently I laid my guitar on top. I started unpacking everything into my drawers. All my new T-shirts, nightgowns, and skirts, brand new from GEM in Honolulu. I undressed and stuffed my bra stash in with my socks.

Stepping into the claw-foot tub, at first I couldn't figure out how to make the handheld shower come on, and then I ended up spraying myself in the face with cold water. I washed my hair really quick and got out shivering. I got dressed in a white T-shirt and a long, pretty much ankle-length blue skirt, and my white socks and my blinding white athletic shoes. And I combed out my hair, all down to my waist, and started walking around the bedroom nervously with that extra bouncy step you get when you're wearing brand-new running shoes. My hair was squeaky clean down my back, and my clothes were new and fresh, and I was wearing a slip. I just felt so peculiar, and expectant, and clean, and yet strung out. There I was, dressed up like Alice in Wonderland. There I was, thirty-eight years old. The newest girl at the orphanage.

WE were all called girls at Bais Sarah. I wasn't even the oldest one there. One of my roommates, Ruth Ann, was fifty-two. Another one, Linda, was forty. And then the third, Nicole, was just seventeen. We were all called girls, because we were in school, and because we weren't married. Some of us had been married, but weren't anymore. Some of us had even been homeless, or addicts, or turned tricks on the street, but at the program none of that mattered. Everyone was back in fresh clean skirts, like we were starting over, like we actually could be girls again. So, in an old house in Bellevue all covered with vines, lived sixteen big girls in two straight lines. We woke each day at seven A.M. We said hi to the rebbe in his frame. At seven-twenty we broke our bread. At seven-forty grace was said. We prayed in small groups from eight to nine. The beginner's group was, you guessed it, mine.

Every morning we sat in a circle in those school-type chairs with built-in desks, except that Rabbi Simkovich had an armless chair, because he was too big to fit comfortably in a desk chair, and also when he got inspired he hopped up and walked around as he talked. Every day he would take some little tiny passage from the *Tashma* and we'd all turn to it and read it, him in Hebrew, and most of us in English on the facing page, and then he'd explicate it, and extrapolate from it, and basically develop out of that one passage this entire lecture about the Jewish philosophy of life. He'd take just a few short phrases, and he'd be off for hours on this whole improvisational mystic odyssey. For example, he would say, "Turn please to page four hundred eighty-five." He'd start reading in Hebrew in this singsong voice, and then he'd look up and say, "What does this mean? There are two types of love. And we're speaking here about love for our God, Hashem. The first type is *'ahavah be-ta'anugim,'* which is love with delight! Ecstatic love for Hashem! Can everyone feel this way?" He looked around the room.

I was thinking, Yeah! because I had felt that kind of charge before. Sometimes in confused circumstances, but yeah.

"No," Simkovich said. "Not everyone can attain this kind of love for Hashem. This love is born into the very few, only to the tzaddikim, the greatest of saints. This is the love of tzaddikim dancing from their own goodness, and rejoicing from their delight in Hashem."

Whoa, I could be a saint, I thought in my little desk-chair.

"But the second kind of love is for all of us to attain, and what is this? A love which we feel as yearning and desire. This is the desire of our spirits to come closer to Hashem, through our prayers and our mitzvos. Every Jew can follow this type of love. Not only that, every Jew, no matter what he or she has done in the past, has this yearning love and desire in her heart. No matter what wrongdoing she has done, that yearning is still inside of her! Now, since this yearning is inside of us, right here!"—he tapped his chest—"then what prevents us from taking advantage of it? What's stopping us?"

Everyone looked at him, but nobody said a word.

"The so-called modern world is stopping us, that's what. And the culture we have been taught in the schools and in the neighborhoods of that modern world. What is that culture about? It's about technology and money and materialism. It's about capitalism, and do you know what capitalism boils down to? Advertising. Now, advertising is so prevalent in our world that we don't even notice it! And yet do you know who the greatest consumers of advertising are? What is the market that all advertisers are trying to reach?"

I raised my hand.

Simkovich hadn't really expected someone to answer the question, but he nodded to me.

"They want to reach women," I said.

"That's right!!!" he thundered. "That is one hundred percent right! They want to reach women. Because women do the shopping in this world, and so they want to sell them all their products. But also, women are the pillars of the families of this world, and so they want to sell them all their lifestyles too. And, now, what is the major lifestyle that has for twenty years been marketed to women, in magazines, movies, television, in everything under the sun? That lifestyle is mobility, and the so-called women's liberation. These are the two big *metziyas* being offered to women, they should have the chance to go wherever they want, and do whatever they want!

"But the question is, once you buy this lifestyle, liberation, what do you get in the long term? To have every option open and to drift this way and that? Is this liberty? To keep every option open to you and never have to commit to anything? Wonderful. Women and men can move from one shallow relationship to another, and from one fly-by-night occupation to the next. You are sitting here today, because you have decided maybe to take a closer look at those choices you are making. You have decided, maybe, to look more critically at how you spend your time.

"It's a very simple question. Where do you want to invest your life? In the cheap fly-by-night? Or in Hashem? In material things, or in the holy law, halacha? Do you want to take your time and spend it on quick pleasures? Or do you want to move that time from checking into savings? And invest it all in Torah? So you may think, Later there is time for that; in the future; when I'm older there will be time. Or you may think, Someone else will study Torah, someone else will live a Torah life, not me. Well, let me tell you something. What the great Rav Hillel once said. He said, 'If not me, who? If not now, when?' "

And Simkovich would go on. He would go on and on, and we all sat there in that circle, and we were galvanized by what he said. He was really one of the only speakers I've ever heard who could compare to my old pastor—I mean, Pastor McClaren at Greater Love. Listening to Simkovich, I would forget the time. Sometimes when I left that room, I was shaking, just from the power of everything the rabbi said. Because it seemed like every thread he picked out of the *Tashma* he could connect to something about me. He could read this mystical text, and it would become a horoscope, so every quotation he made was relevant to your own situation! I mean, I'd been through relationships, and classes, and jobs, and I'd had all the choices in the world, but what had they left me with?

The rabbi wasn't embarrassed to say, Hey, the old days *were* better, and sisterhood was powerful for women. Separation from the guys actually gave us more freedom to be ourselves. Nowadays, women were trying so hard to be equal to men that in fact they were forgetting they were better than men—we had powers of purity and spirituality that no men could match. And so, in fact, women all around were giving up their specialness that they had been born with, their pure white mantles were getting all stained, their own mitzvos were being forgotten, and their modesty violated because they weren't taught to protect it.

Man, when I heard him talk sometimes, and I sat there all covered up in my skirt, I thought more about sex than I had in a long while, because the rabbi kept bringing up those kinds of behavior I'd enjoyed so much when I was younger. And now in class, I was almost embarrassed to think about the guys that I'd been with, and how I'd wanted them, and how I'd enjoyed myself. In the rabbi's class it seemed like even my memories were X rated. And that was when I realized I wanted to be a Jew. Not just a Jew in name, but a Jew in deed. A praying Jew. A baking Jew. A Jew in a dress. A Jew like maybe my great-great-grandmother might have been. A *frume leibe*. A religious heart. A pure, strict heart.

I felt such nostalgia for that better, purer life from way back, I wanted to go there. I wanted to time-travel and grow my sleeves out long, and let my skirts blossom around me and take up counted cross-stitch and write epistles. Listening to the rabbi speak, I wanted to head back to pre-Revolutionary days, or at least before the sexual revolution. I felt this compelling urge to be a virgin again, and the crazy thing was how sexy the idea seemed to me. I felt so heated up about it, all throbbing to reform. I'd be thinking, Oh, oh, oh, if I could undo those things I'd done. If I could close my legs again. If I could go back a ways and sleep alone in my own bed. Or be like Madeline—not just the little girl in the old house in Paris, who naturally slept in a twin bed—but Madeline in *The Eve of St. Agnes*, in her wakeful swoon, all innocent in her magic castle, "Blinded alike from sunshine and from rain, / As though a rose should shut, and be a bud again." That's what I wanted—all my experiences and my desires folded back into themselves, all my petals folded up into this intense bud of chastity. It almost made me blush thinking about it; I'd always thought that poem was so hot. That was where on Molokai I'd ripped the page in my old anthology, which was a book that never could shut up tight again.

I'd come out of Rabbi Simkovich's class determined to dedicate my every waking hour to *snius,* which was modesty, and to *tefillah,* which was prayer, and to *limudei kodesh,* which was holy learning, and to *midos,* which were virtues. I'd come out planning to buy long-sleeved T-shirts, so my elbows would not be exposed, and tights, so my legs would not be bare under my skirt. I'd come out planning to throw away all my records and my tapes, which were music from the other side, the so-called modern world, and probably advertisements of its seductions. And I'd be thinking of my past delusions and tisking my tongue at myself, and I'd be fired up thinking about cleansing my heart and soul and all the passages to them. I'd throttle any stray man—even any stray thought of a man— that might try to trespass me again. And that was all before lunch.

Even better than Simkovich's class was Torah study. We worked in small groups with our *madricha.* And we would study a chapter of the Torah, which the *madricha* would read to us in Hebrew and then translate and explain in English. And what I dug was we spent a lot of time focusing on our foremothers, Sarah, Rebecca, Rachel, and Leah, who were role models for us to emulate, since they were totally dedicated to Torah, and family. My *madricha* was a young girl, Estie, who was seventeen years old, and counseling was her summer job before she went home to Brooklyn to get married. She looked like Snow White with her long dark hair, and fair skin with a few tiny moles, and dark brown eyes. She knew a million midrashes, which were stories for every phrase in the Torah that we read. She was a girl genius, I was sure. It seemed to me she knew every legend of the Hasidic masters, not to mention all the vast traditions of Judaism. I was in awe of her learning. I looked upon her teenage face, and I saw the wisdom of a thousand Bialystoker rebbes.

I said to her, "I feel like all the rabbis are speaking through your lips."

That seemed to make her nervous. "No, no," she said. I guess she didn't like to think of herself as supernatural. "I learned midrash in school. See?" She took out a bunch of spiral-bound notebooks and she showed me pages filled with big round handwriting. "These are my notes." She was trying to make it look like she'd studied the wisdom of the Hasidic masters just like spelling or geometry. But I didn't buy that.

I held Estie in reverence, the way monks worship the child incarnation of the Karmapa Lama.

Estie also taught our small group's halacha class, which was a very practical class on Jewish law, and, to be perfectly frank, the one I dreaded, since I'd had such bad experiences with Jewish kitchen laws in Jerusalem. Yet in the environment of Bais Sarah, my prejudices against religious rituals started to melt a little bit. By week three of the program I could get excited even about this stuff. Because every rule and ritual was actually one step closer to Hashem!

"I feel so aware here," I said to my roommate Nicole. "This place is just like my old monastery, except with food."

Nicole looked at me like I was crazy. "It's like a prison here!"

The two of us were walking around the neighborhood in the afternoon, and all around us were these Victorian houses and stupendous trees. And I protested, "How can you say it's like prison? How can you say that? This is one of the most gorgeous areas I've ever seen."

She lit a cigarette. Smoking wasn't allowed inside Bais Sarah, so Nicole smoked away in the glorious suburban countryside. Her straight blond hair looked like damp straw against her raggedy black dress. She wore borrowed clothes, because her own stuff had been deemed inappropriate for the program. She had the look of a little match girl. "I have to get out of here," she said.

I just shook my head. I really couldn't imagine what her problem was. "You're in a place where all you have to do is learn, and breathe and imbibe Judaism! How can you call that a prison?"

"You're here of your own free will," she reminded me. "My parents sent me."

Which was true. I had to give her that. I'd forgotten that Nicole was only seventeen. She was the same age as our *madricha,* Estie, only a far different seventeen, having been locked up at various times by her parents and sent to a military-style alternative boarding school for troubled teens, where your shoes were confiscated for insubordination. When she was sixteen she'd run away from home and lived on the streets, where she'd supported herself by selling her body, until now her parents were doing a last-ditch heroic religious intervention, except as usual they hadn't asked Nicole's permission first. "My mother hates me," she said. "She wishes I was dead."

"She's just pissed off."

Nicole drew herself up. There were tears in her blue eyes. Her eyes were actually a stunning aqua, like the blue sky shining into swimming pools. She was offended at me for belittling how much her mother hated her. "Do you even know her? Do you even have a right to say anything?"

"Look, all I'm trying to say is this place is a gift here. This place is actually a gift and you don't even know it."

"I'm going to kill myself," Nicole told me, really seriously.

"God forbid!"

"Cut the crap," she said.

"If you would just open up your eyes," I said. "Look. The mountain is out today." There it was, above our heads, and far away. Mount Rainier. Small and white, like the moon in daytime. "Don't you see," I said, "it's a sign." I looked at the mountain and it seemed to me like God's chop mark on the landscape. It seemed to me Mount Rainier was living proof. God had touched the sky in this place. He had left His mark on Bellevue and Bais Sarah and Washington State! Even apart from all the trees, and the beauty of the lakes, He had placed His finger on the horizon, and left His fingerprint, that snowy mountain that would never melt, a permanent white cloud.

But Nicole barely glanced at the mountain, she was so miserable. The wings of her soul were bent out of shape from having to give up her freedom, or, as Rabbi Simkovich put it, her so-called, illusory freedom. Her mind was closed shut from her parents' spying and harassment. And there was more that she had been through. I knew that from my own experience, coming from a not entirely perfect family myself. So I didn't ask. I just kept on peppering her with how great things might be if she actually opened up her eyes and ears to Torah. I just kept regaling her until she didn't trust me anymore.

I was becoming known among the other girls as somewhat hard core. Compared to a lot of them my background was pretty sheltered, never having been in a mental institution or imprisoned, for example, but in the Bais Sarah environment a lot of the girls were actually afraid of me, because I guess I just seemed so intensely happy. My roommates Nicole, and Linda—who was clinically paranoid anyway—and Ruth Ann—they all looked at me at times like they were afraid of what I might do. Apparently I used to pray and sing in my sleep, and I'd wake up my roomies in the dead of night raving and demanding the Moshiach to come down into the world.

Yet it wasn't like I was trying to evangelize anybody in my sleep. It wasn't like I was cracking up or anything. It was just that Bellevue swept me off my feet. I was in a whole other zone. It was like going under the waves until you think you're going to faint or drown, and then suddenly discovering you can breathe the water. I barely thought about what day or year it was. I was surrounded by these tides of poetry and these great kelp forests of prayers and halacha. I was swimming way down among the tuna with their bulging, learned foreheads, and the silver sardine schools, and the leviathans, great rabbinic whales of the deep.

IT was a full moon in August, and we were sitting in the music room. The moon was floating up through the window, so big and near you could see all the craters pocking the silver. And I looked out at the moon, and I felt a sudden wistfulness for Grandpa Irving's silver watch. I wished I could touch it and rub my fingers over its round silver case with the pawn marks stamped inside its back. I felt regretful when I saw the moon.

Yet when I turned back to listen to what was going on inside, the feeling left me, because Rabbi Simkovich was standing up in front of our whole group, and he was pacing back and forth and in thought, and then he started telling tales of great rebbes—what they'd done and what they'd believed, and the miracles they'd caused to happen in their holiness and their delight in Hashem. He was telling the tale of Rabbi Moshe of Samdor, who worked as a peddler trading with peasants when he was a kid. Whenever he got home from work and said his prayers, he felt this *light* kindling his body! And he asked his older brother, Rabbi Zevi Hirsh, why am I all lit up like this after just walking around working all day? And Rabbi Zevi Hirsh answered, "Because whether you're walking or working or what have you, if you are following in the ways of Hashem, then wherever you go all the little holy particles throughout the world will catch on you like burrs on your clothes. All the holiness of the trees and the road and the rocks and the bushes will spark onto you, and that's how that light is kindled in you!"

"Yes! Yes!" I exclaimed. "*Amen v'amen!* Bravo!"

Nicole looked up at me from under her gold hair that she'd been busy picking through for loose ends.

Linda's eyes widened with alarm, but a lot of the other girls started echoing what I was saying. The majority of us girls loved the stories of the rebbes best of all. How the first Bialystoker rebbe transformed sticks into bread. How the fourth Bialystoker turned into a bird for three days and three nights, so great was his feeling as he prayed. His soul became so light he flew right off the ground. The majority of us related to everything that happened to the rebbes, and wished we could apply the rebbes' lessons to our own lives. That's what I argued to my roommates as we got ready for bed that night. We four clothed in our modest long-sleeved nightgowns, so you couldn't see the odd tattoo or self-inflicted wound.

I said, "Light is what it's all about. Don't you get that? Judaism is all light and kindling and flames! That's what's incredible. Your soul can be walking along, and all of a sudden it can ignite!"

"Could you just give it a rest?" Nicole said, and she got into her sleeping bag and zipped herself up.

But Ruth Ann was nodding her head. She had been a housewife and a mom who had led a really idyllic life in Redmond with no troubles at all, except gaining a couple hundred pounds, and then all of a sudden one day her three children were grown, and her husband left her, and she realized that there she was with her house and her cars, and her furniture, and her money, which, having pretty much the best lawyer in the state, she'd got from the divorce, and she had many things, but they were just like a memorial of the person she had been. They had no meaning, which was when she began returning to her own faith, Judaism. So now she said, "I know exactly what you mean. Our *neshamas* are like little candles. . . ."

"And they're just waiting to be lit," I said.

Linda sat on her mattress. "Now, I'm not sure I would want to be lit up like that—like a firecracker," she said slowly.

"What do you mean you don't want to be lit?" I tossed my hair over my head to brush it out.

"I don't want to go up in smoke," Linda said. She was rather cautious, due to some of her past experiences—forgetting who she was and becoming homeless for a time.

"No, see, it's not like a firecracker," I said. "It's not like soaking yourself in kerosene and lighting a match. It's like the eternal flame. It's burning forever. That's what we're talking about."

"But I don't like the feeling of burning up," Linda said.

"It's burning up in spirit," I insisted.

"Go to sleep," Nicole intoned from inside her sleeping bag.

"Or look at it this way. It's like being magnetized," I said. "It's like having all your little iron filings suddenly aligned in this new direction. And the direction is upward, toward enlightenment. Or like phototropism—"

"Shut the fuck up," Nicole groaned.

"You could be like a green plant," I said, "and you could be growing in one direction, but then all of a sudden you notice the sun is over there, and you push all your cells toward the light, and you're growing somewhere totally different."

"I'm tired. I'm tired. I'm tired," Nicole said.

"Okay, okay." I got into bed.

Linda climbed into her sleeping bag and curled up on her side, and Ruth Ann turned off the light and carefully lay down on top of her sleeping bag, which she slept on unzipped like it was a duvet. We all lay quiet in the dark. Then suddenly Linda began to cry.

So then Ruth Ann and I had to get up out of bed and comfort her, because Linda was afraid she was going to have nightmares, having been spooked by all the talk about fires and burning, which she was afraid of. "Oh, honey," Ruth Ann said, "it's just metaphors. It's just a way to describe how your soul can feel."

"I don't want to burn," she said.

"It's just poetry," I said. "Look, I'll prove it to you." And I got out my puffed-out anthology and I said, "Listen to this. Energy is Eternal Delight. That's William Blake. That is probably the source Rabbi Simkovich's story came from!" I said, "Listen to this one:

> The Human Dress is forged Iron,
> The Human Form, a fiery Forge,
> The Human Face, a Furnace seal'd,
> The Human Heart, its hungry Gorge.

But that only made Linda cry more. And she said, "I can't take this. It's too hard. It's too hard! I don't want to be thrown into a forge."

"But it could be good!" I said. "Being forged could be a good thing. See, I never was forged, and that was why my sparks never lit. That's what I honestly believe. I never got hammered and molded like I should have when I was younger. That's why I was running around all the time. I was molten."

Ruth Ann put her hand on my arm. "Sh."

"It's too hard," Linda cried. Her cheeks were wet with tears. "Now I can't sleep. Now I'll be up all night."

"Make her stop!" Nicole's blond head popped out of her sleeping bag. Nicole was almost in tears herself by this time, being so exhausted and strung out.

"I can't, I can't," Linda sobbed.

"Hush, little baby, don't say a word, Mamma's gonna buy you a mockingbird," Ruth Ann sang. She was rubbing Linda's back. "And if that mockingbird don't sing, Mamma's gonna buy you a diamond ring. . . ."

I shuffled back to my own bed, and I lay down. Instantly my arms and legs went limp, I was so tired. My eyes shut; my words escaped me. All you could hear in the room was Ruth Ann singing on and on, making up rhymes whenever she had to, just to keep going. "And if that cart and bull get broke, Mamma's gonna buy you an artichoke. . . ."

I don't know how long I slept. A noise woke me—a sharp crack, then a crunching sound. I jumped out of bed and I stood there in the dark. Then I saw the light coming up through the window from below. I ran to the window and there was a yellow taxi easing around the circular drive. Nicole! That was the first thing I thought of. Her bed was empty.

In my nightgown I sprinted down the stairs. In my bare feet I ran into the marble entry hall outside where Nicole stood with her bags.

"What are you doing?"

"I'm leaving," she said.

"You can't."

"I am." She started dragging her stuff outside.

"But where will you go? You can't run away. You can't!" I ran after her.

She just walked calmly toward the cab.

I leapt for her in the driveway. I probably scared her to death, jumping on her like that.

"Let me go!"

"No, wait," I begged. "Nicole . . ."

"Let me go!" She clawed at me. She scratched me, but she was smaller than I was.

"No, wait. No, listen. Please!"

"You're hurting me!"

"You don't understand! You can't go back out there." The lights of the taxi shone on us. "You can't go out there again." I was holding her with all my strength. "You don't understand! This is a matter of life and death. Nicole, Nicole, how will you live?" I demanded, since I hadn't realized yet that she had stolen all my cash from me. "You'll go out there and you'll be killed. They'll fuck with you and they'll kill you. . . ."

"No, you're fucking with me!" She bit my arm. She actually bit me.

The driver was poking his head out the window. "Hey! Which of you ladies wants a ride?"

"Don't you see . . ." I was pleading with Nicole.

She wrenched away. She ran around and opened the taxi door and flung herself and her stuff into the back seat. The taxi took off in a shower of tiny rocks.

"You have this chance," I screamed after her. "You have this chance to change your whole life. . . ." But the car was halfway down the street. "You're only seventeen!"

Rabbi Simkovich and Rebbetzin Chaya must have had heard the noise. They came running out of the house.

I could barely tell them what had happened, I was so upset. "Can't you call the police?" I kept asking them. "Why can't you call the police? Why can't you get her back?"

Yet, apparently, Bais Sarah not being a prison, the Simkoviches had no way to force Nicole to stay. They could call the police, and they could call her parents, but when it came to transforming her into a religious girl, there wasn't any more they could do. Chaya helped me back inside. The other girls, who had heard the commotion, came running downstairs, and I was wailing, "But she'll die out there!"

"God forbid," Chaya said.

"She doesn't understand. She doesn't even know what'll happen to her out on the street, and without Hashem."

"Sh!" Chaya said sharply, as if to say not in front of the children. She was hustling all the girls back to bed.

Chaya took me to the kitchen and gave me a mug of tea. The house was quiet again. When Rabbi Simkovich came to check on me I was starting to calm down.

"But, see," I said to him, "the Torah is the tree of life. It's the life raft, right? It's the one thing that can hold you up. Then how can you let go? How can you just leave this place and let go?"

"Torah is not so small you can't also hold on to it in other places," Rabbi Simkovich said.

That was when a terrible realization came over me. The chill and fright came right back again, only now I was starting to fear for my own self. Because just then it hit me: this Bais Sarah business wouldn't last forever. The summer was coming to an end. We were all going to be set loose again and scatter. We were all getting pushed from the holy nest into the valueless abyss! In my case they'd be returning me to Hawaii, which mean Wayne, and Brian, and Imo. As if I hadn't hurt them all enough already. Later, much later, I heard from Rich that Brian had finally wangled a job at Imo's university, and he and Imo had settled down in Auckland, and they had a house, and they had a boat. While Wayne, according to Will, had been spotted with what looked like a wife in the new Costco that had opened up, and they were buying big flats of strawberries. And so, years later, it turned out they were all fine—but at the time, in Bellevue, I could only picture them as the mortally wounded victims of my sins. And coming back to Hawaii, I'd have to face them all again—not to mention all the religions I had flunked, whether in school, or on my own in real life.

So naturally I was terrified by the idea of going back to Honolulu. I just wanted to erase everything I'd ever done. I just wanted to forget the person I had once been. Don't look back, I screamed inside myself. Don't even turn around and look. I was sure I'd turn into a pillar of salt. It wasn't just that Hasidic Judaism promised me a new life and new identity. The Bialystokers promised me a new world as well. They were holding out to me a new earth and diet and language. They were providing an entire protective bubble—more protection than I'd ever found anywhere else. So now I was panicking! Because how could they pull the plug on my snow globe? How could they send me out from my brand-new sparkling little cosmos into the immodest Hawaiian sun?

"I can't go back out there!" I burst out. "I can't go back to the islands."

"What's the matter?" the rabbi asked.

"There's no Yiddishkeit there!" I told him how for the first time I felt like I was onto something. I said at Bais Sarah I had finally started my real life, and tapped into what at the bottom I truly was: a Hasidic Jew. I could not slip back now. I would fall. I could see it now. I would go back and I would fall away.

Rabbi Simkovich stroked his beard and he nodded to me, and he said he would think about this, and he would discuss it with Chaya. Perhaps they would find a solution. *Im yirtzeh Hashem*, God willing, we would find a way for me to continue learning.

"*Im yirtzeh Hashem*," I echoed. "I need to take my Judaism to the next level," I said. "I have such a need. Because I want to go up those staircases, I want to, *so* much. I want to find my way up to the higher realms, because I feel like that's my calling. Like it's *bashert*. I just need a little bit of help along the way."

"Of course," the rabbi said. "Of course, a little bit of help. I understand."

Which I took to mean that I could stay at Bais Sarah forever. What a relief!

The sun was rising, tinting the kitchen pink. Pretty soon everybody had to get up and pray. Yet I got to rest in bed after my ordeal. I got to curl up inside my sleeping bag with the shades down. And there I dreamed about my future life. I would be a Jewish nun, forever dedicated to prayer and raising bees and traveling on pilgrimage each year to the Holy Land, and maybe even founding a winery for the vinting of the most exquisite kosher wines (since currently at Bais Sarah all we had was the purple Manishewitz type), and then I would find Nicole and bring her back, along with the infant daughter she would have by that time, and she and Ruth Ann and Linda and I would live together, and the little child, Estie, would lead us. We would live together in one transcendent Jewish-feminist commune: the Holy Order of Felicity.

18

—

Discovered

THAT afternoon I was still so groggy, I thought that when Rabbi Simkovich came up to me at lunch, he was going to chastise me for nodding off during his talk at dinner. But right away I saw that wasn't it. The rabbi seemed so pleased. He was beaming.

"*Baruch Hashem,*" he said. "I have been talking to Chaya, and we think we may have found a solution for you. Estie Karinsky's mother has offered you an invitation to come to Crown Heights."

"Estie's mother? How . . ."

"She has heard about you, and she and Estie, Dr. Karinsky, the whole family, has heard, and hope to see you, and for you to come to Estie's wedding. They would like for you to come and visit them in Crown Heights."

Crown Heights! I thought. Wait, but I'm planning to stay here. What happened to staying here forever? What about my women's community?

The rabbi didn't seem to be reading my mind, however. He was talking about the Karinsky family and going on about the Bialystok community in Crown Heights, and the very special neighborhood they had there that he himself had come from, which was in fact the home and headquarters of the Bialystoker rebbe, who lived in a grand house that was an exact replica of the original rabbinical palace of his ancestors in

Bialystok. The community had built the home for him in the middle of Crown Heights. Number six-thirteen, it was called, and not by coincidence, since there were six hundred thirteen commandments.

Crown Heights, I kept thinking—but how can I leave Bellevue? Yet the very name Crown Heights sounded so regal. The way Rabbi Simkovich spoke about the place, you could tell immediately this was the center of the whole Bialystoker community. And to live near the rebbe of Bialystok—that was like ascending those holy staircases three steps at a time! How would it be to live right near the home of the Bialystoker himself? You might bump into his retinue on the street! You might touch the shadow of his robe!

I couldn't help confessing to the rabbi that I had been hoping to stay put, yet the more he talked about Crown Heights, the more in awe I was. No other woman in the whole program had an offer like this one. Not a single one; I had been chosen, and singled out for Estie Karinsky's invitation. I had been selected personally by the rabbi, and when I'd least expected it! All of a sudden I realized something important was happening to me. All of a sudden I realized what I was being given. I walked around the rest of the afternoon in a daze. It was essentially like being discovered—but on the highest spiritual level. Like if goodness had a Broadway; like if there were an angelic Nashville! For several days I couldn't even say whether I would accept Estie's invitation. I couldn't even figure out if I was worthy. Yet I felt myself drawing nearer and nearer to saying yes. I dreamed of Crown Heights as this illuminated citadel. I dreamed of all the crowns of silver tinkling with little silver bells. I dreamed of black ink crowns adorning the Hebrew letters of the Torah, the tiny prongs leaping upward. And I said, Yes, yes, I'll go. Yes, I'll rise up to the heights. Yes, I will enter the Heart of Light!

I'D forgotten the grime back east. There we were at the end of August in Estie's cousin's car driving to Brooklyn, and the sky was gray, and the streets were gray, and the buildings were covered with *schmutz*. Estie and I were in the backseat, and she was so excited to be coming home, and I was excited, too, don't get me wrong, but I was also thinking, Where are the crowns? Where are the heights? All those years in the Pacific, I'd forgotten how the other half live—with old brick, and cracked-up sidewalks, and snivelly malnourished excuses for trees. Brooklyn was the most built-up place I'd ever been. Where there were yards, they were maybe the size of a small car, and a lot of times that car would be parked on them.

In Estie's neighborhood some of the houses were brick, and some were two-family buildings with siding or fake fieldstone divided right down the middle in different colors. When you looked in the windows, you could see little shoe-box rooms with crystal chandeliers hanging down like stalactites in a cave. It was like Jerusalem, in that so many men, and also little boys, wore black suits and black hats, and the women were covered up in skirts and white stockings—just like me sitting there in my CHAI clothes. Estie's cousin Shmuley was driving, and he wore the hat and the coat and the pants, the works. I said to Estie, "How come your fiancé didn't meet you at the airport?" She and Shmuley both burst out laughing.

Estie's house was freestanding, with brick front steps and a couple of bushes in the front. There was a loose gravel driveway on the side, and there was even an old garage that the Karinskys used for storage. Wobbly from the plane and the new scenery, I hadn't even stepped out of the car when Estie's nine brothers and sisters surrounded us, squealing and shrieking and shouting, climbing on the car, picking up our stuff for us and carrying it inside. The munchkins were all talking to me at once. They told me all their names, which I forgot instantly. I was just too tired to take it all in.

The Karinskys' place was packed. On the first floor there was a living room and dining room and a kitchen. On the second floor there were just four bedrooms for all those people. Mendy Karinsky, Estie's father, was a pediatrician, and had his office in the basement. He, it turned out, had not been born a Bialystoker, but came from a non-Hasidic community and had married in when he was finishing his medical training. He was big and barrel chested like an operatic tenor. He used to throw back his head and laugh. Nothing seemed to faze him. He had a lot of joy inside—and never did anything around the house. With the children he was always the good cop, while Feige Karinsky was the enforcer. Dr. Karinsky used to come running up the stairs from his office and open the door to the kitchen and roar like a lion and the kids would come squealing, and he'd toss them around and tickle them into hysterics while Mrs. Karinsky worked around him, trying to get dinner on the table.

Mrs. Karinsky spent all her days trying to keep the rest of the house under control. At any given time someone was crying or screaming or praying. The decor was formal, with wallpaper and fake Oriental rugs, and a chandelier in the dining room, but the place was so overrun with kids and trucks and tricycles and decapitated dolls you didn't really see the decorations or the furniture. The stairs creaked; the window-unit air conditioners were straining; the whole place was buckling under the weight of the family. Estie kept saying how she was so excited for me to be there, and I was excited, too, only, seeing how full the house was, I was amazed I'd been invited. The bedrooms were packed with bunks and trundles and cribs and toys and prayer books; there were no garden views or anything like in Bellevue; there were no empty spaces. Still, somehow Mrs. Karinsky made room for me. She gave me guest towels and special nonfoaming toothpaste to use on Shabbes. She was a big lady, really big, almost like Mrs. Eldridge had been, and she wore this great big housedress and breathed heavily when she climbed up the creaky stairs. She might have been pregnant, but she was too heavy to tell for sure. You could hardly believe she was Estie's mother, Estie was such a slip of a thing.

So a lot surprised me, but you know, I was there to learn, and to be forged in the crucible of Judaism. I was there to lie down every night and wake up every day Jewish. To pray every prayer and observe every fast; to celebrate every new month according to the phases of the moon. I was there to forget everything else I'd ever been, or rather, to remember everything I truly was.

The next day was Friday, and I helped in the kitchen cooking, while the kids were fighting in the living room. The children fought all the time: scratching, biting, hair pulling. You name it. I was kind of shocked—partly because the Simkovich kids had been pretty quiet, and partly because I guess I'd thought that coming from such a religious family, the children would be little angels, but they were just as mean and vicious as regular kids, and to tell the truth, it seemed like they were worse than normal, because there were so many of them, and they were so close in age.

I'd also assumed that Mrs. Karinsky would be an incredible kosher gourmet cook. But it turned out she actually hated cooking, and the food she made was really bad. Her chicken would be greasy, and her brisket would be all dried out, and her hot dogs were boiled so they went boing! if you dropped them on the floor. All the kids made fun of her cooking—even Estie. They'd dangle stuff from their forks and ask in Yiddish, *"Mama, vas is dos?"*—What is this? She pretended she didn't care. She let the little ones eat as much candy as they wanted. She told me, "I don't have the kind of kids who'll come up and say, 'Can I have a *pulke?*' "—which was a chicken leg. "What do my kids eat? They eat junk."

Mrs. Karinsky also hated cleaning, so the dishes were chipped, and there were lollipops sticking in the carpet and stuff like that. She didn't seem all that happy about the situation, but in a Zen-like way she accepted it. She said, "So people come in the house and they see a mess. So what? I'm not in the business of caring what people think."

Still, Friday night was special. I laid the table for a feast under the dusty chandelier, and so what if the food was barely edible? There was a lot of it, and it was all steaming by the time Dr. Karinsky and the boys got home from shul. The Shabbes candles were aflame, more than a dozen. They stood in their candlesticks on foil like a shining altar on the sideboard. And we all stood around the table and everyone was singing nigguns, which were these wordless tunes sung at the Shabbes table. After all the blessings we sat down to eat, and Dr. Karinsky welcomed me and said I could stay as long as I wanted, and he told everyone I was from Hawaii, and all the kids looked at me, impressed. Later, after dinner, the boys got out a book they had that was a yearbook of all the Bialystoker emissary families in all the CHAI houses all over the world, Anchorage to Zaire, and they looked for me under Hawaii, but, of course, I wasn't in the book, not being officially part of any Bialystoker embassy.

Two days went by, and even though they hadn't seen each other all summer, there still wasn't any sign of Estie's fiancé. The September wedding date was set; the hall was rented, Mrs. Karinsky was flustered with the preparations. Still, Estie was mellow. She had her white wedding gown hanging wrapped in plastic in the coat closet in the downstairs entrance hall, because the bedrooms were so short on closet space. During the week she just went to her usual job, which was watching kids at this little corner preschool. I tagged along and earned a little bit of cash as a teacher's aide. I used to lead the singing. I had everyone singing "Mo-Mo-Mo-Moshiach!" which was a big hit. All the kids were clapping their little hands. They were about two years old, the ones Estie taught, and they came just a few hours in the mornings. The girls wore tights and little dresses, and the boys still had long hair pinned back with barrettes, and they looked like girls, because in the Bialystoker community you didn't cut little boys' hair until they were three—which might have struck me as a weird custom at some earlier stage of my life, but seemed to me, living there in Brooklyn, only weird in a good way, not crazy at all, but wild and fairylike, and just magical. It was all magic to me.

And at the school at naptime I used to hum those nigguns to the kids when they lay down on their mats. Sometimes I almost went into a trance singing. I used to close my eyes, and the children would lie there perfectly still. One by one they would drop off to sleep.

Estie was the one who said I should bring my guitar to school. I hadn't played in months. When I took it out at naptime my fingers were stiff. Creakily they found the chords. They just played from their own finger-memory, but gradually a song took shape. Softly my voice was humming. Gardens and islands began to fill up my eyes, and green plants, and mists—they all came to me in this joyful dream. Slowly words came to me, and I began to sing. "Puff the magic dragon, lived by the sea. . . ." And I sang and sang the verses, all of them, until finally I came to the end and my eyes opened, and all of a sudden there I was in the classroom again. The pale dark-eyed children were lying on their mats; their soft soft hair was spread around them and their little limp arms; they were all asleep. And Estie and her senior teacher were staring at me.

I was a stranger there, no matter how welcome a guest. And most of the time it didn't bother me at all, because I was so dedicated to my future. After all, I was essentially entering the Hasidic novitiate! And my host family tried so hard with me—despite the fact that they could barely keep their kids from killing each other. Mrs. Karinsky had so many dishes to clear every night, that during the week she used paper plates and plasticware. One time I'd actually said to her, "Don't you think that's bad for the environment?" She looked at me aghast. She looked like she'd been slapped. But she was too polite to say, Who do you think you are? Fuck off and die. So she said nothing, and I felt terrible. I looked down at the floor, ashamed of myself, that I had brought the subject up. How tactless. There were the Karinskys feeding and sheltering and teaching me by their example. There they were, springing me from all my predicaments, and all they wanted was my soul. What a small price to pay. What a simple thing to give, if only you knew how to do it. If only you could extricate yourself from the person that you were before.

I hated thinking of the past, but then the future frightened me even

more. Estie's wedding was imminent. The house was filled with relatives, and every bed and couch and inflatable mattress was full, and there
were even a couple of kids sleeping under the dining room table. I was
beginning to feel so anxious. I was afraid I was going to lose my own
cot to some cousin from out of town. Every day I thought Mrs. Karinsky was going to move me out into the hall or to a friend's, and then I
didn't know what I was going to do. I was in a fragile state—I was terrified somehow of being separated from the family, not to mention Estie
herself and her example. What would happen to me when she wasn't
around for me to shadow through the day? What would happen when
she was married off, and my whole excuse for being in Crown Heights
had moved away?

ESTIE'S wedding was in the evening, and it was a hot Indian-summer
city night. Everyone gathered in the courtyard of the rebbe's palace,
which was wooden, and gated and turreted, with peaked shingled roofs.
Six-thirteen was actually a cluster of three-story buildings surrounding
an open courtyard. One building was the synagogue, and one was the
library and center for advanced study of the Bialystoker texts, where the
best and brightest of the young men learned all day and night. The third
building was a great hall used as a social center, with various rooms for
parties, and offices for the rebbe and his assistant rabbis. All the buildings
were painted in dark reds and greens and chocolate-brown, and on the
inside they were decorated with carvings and plasterwork in the shape
of flowers and vines and pomegranates. The whole complex looked as
exotic and antique as could be, except for the fire escapes, and the air
conditioning compressors. The rebbe himself had decided on central air.

The ceremony was getting started in the courtyard. There was a
chuppah, which was a canopy; dark blue velvet cloth fringed and embroidered in gold, set up on four poles. It was dark out, the idea being
that Estie and her fiancé, Yitzy, would get hitched under the stars, except
you couldn't see any stars, since the night was hazy and the city lights so
bright. There were rabbis and witnesses and siblings crowded around.
There were something like three hundred people all standing in the
open air, men in their black suits, women in lace and silk and embroidery and pearls and diamond pavé brooches. From the back I watched

the kids running around in party dresses and patent leather shoes, and the boys in these tiny white dress shirts and black trousers and jackets askew. It was so humid everyone was sweating. The relatives up by the chuppah held candles, but I wasn't a relative, of course, so I stood in the back, tangentially—me and my feeling of increasing dread. Around and around Estie walked. She was circling around Yitzy seven times, with her mother and Yitzy's mother leading her. As she walked, the skirts of her long gown trailed behind her, and almost wrapped up Yitzy as she went, so, from where I stood, the two of them, the bride and groom, looked like a mystic caterpillar turning and turning, wrapping itself in white silk, winding up into a cocoon.

She's gone, I thought. She's gone; she's gone. There were blessings being said, there was wine sipped, but all I could think was, My teacher and my counselor is gone. There she goes, abandoning me.

Crash! Yitzy stamped on the glass. Everyone burst out singing and swarming around the families crying, Mazel tov! Mazel tov! And dancing and whooping right there outside, the men in one mob and the women in another. I was lost in the crowd, smashed between old ladies.

When I came up for air, the newlyweds had disappeared. The bride and groom were supposed to go off and be alone for a while after the ceremony, and then they had to do family pictures, so, in the meantime, everyone else went inside the hall and started partying without them.

There were two parties in two separate ballrooms, with two separate bands. One party was for men only, and the other was for the women, so that, without the men around, we sisters could let loose and really dance. There were circle dances and line dances and polkas, and even jitterbugging, women partnering each other under twinkling crystal chandeliers. There were maybe a hundred women bopping around that room. I thought, Sharon, how can you just stand and watch? Sharon, how can you be so melancholy? Mrs. Karinsky was holding out her arms to me, the bride's own mom was reaching for me with a smile on her lips. I shook myself; I reached out into the center of the mob and plunged in. This trio was pounding out the music; and I have to say, the band wore frock coats, but these guys could swing. The drummer pounded out the beat, and the guy on sax was belting out Hasidic nigguns and show tunes. Sometimes his solos sounded like a cross between the two. He wailed "Old Man River" as if the song encompassed all the sorrows of the Jewish people. But then the third guy would break in on keyboard and bring everything back up to speed. He was the most amazing one of all. His hair and beard were bright flaming red; his fingers were so lightning fast he'd have run away with every song if the other two had let him. He had no music, not even a cheat book, but just played while he looked out at the dancers. Any chance he got, he'd be improvising and hot-dogging on the keys, until his colleagues would start glaring at him.

So there were some tensions in the trio, yet everyone was dancing too hard to care. As long as the music kept coming, as long as those rhythms kept pouring on, we danced. And I held hands with the other ladies; I locked arms with Estie's cousins. I had several different drinks from the bar, where there was also a whole smorgasbord set up with crudités and chopped liver sculptures in the shapes of swans, and miniature rye breads, and whitefish salad, and turnips carved like roses. I was wearing a borrowed dress from one of Estie's cousins, which was an old bridesmaid dress, a lace-covered apricot satin concoction with great big muttonchop sleeves, which was not exactly my style. Yet who knew what my style was at that point? I had the shoes that came with the outfit, the kind dyed to match, so they were apricot, too, but scuffed in back and big on me, so my feet and my toes kept feeling their way inside these hollows and little caves that Estie's cousin's feet had previously established. I must have looked ridiculous, but I danced and danced. I kicked off the shoes into a corner of the room. I sweated up the satin of the dress. My face was hot.

The band stopped. There was a playful drum roll, and everyone burst out clapping. There stood Estie, alone in the doorway, like Princess Aurora, perfect and smiling, not a wrinkle in her white satin gown. She had a crinoline underneath, so her skirts poofed out and swished as she walked, and her dress was covered with frothy white tulle. Yitzy was off with the men. It was as if Estie had ditched him at the door. There wasn't going to be any of that first dance as a married couple, or feeding each other bites of wedding cake. None of that. Estie smiled upon us, and her face was lit up with joy, but also confidence, as if to say, I'm back! She danced with her mother, and her grandmother, and, like the song says, her sisters and her cousins and her aunts, and as she danced, her dress flew up across the floor, and you could see the white slippers she was wearing underneath. Her lacy double veil came loose, and people had to help her pin it back onto her hair, and she had to stop and wait patiently, and she was so beautiful, I have to say—not just her face and her fair skin and slenderness, but the hope in her eyes, and, I want to say, her youth, but it wasn't just that, it was the way she carried off being young, the way she was at peace with her seventeen years, so joyful in her family's expectations. Gorgeous in her conformity.

Inspired by the sight of her, I ran up to the band. "Could I request a niggun?"

They couldn't hear me at all, what with their earplugs and their massive speakers.

"Could I make a request!" I screamed.

The sax player knit his brow at me, as if I were disturbing him during a sacred act. The drummer ignored me altogether and just kept pounding on. So I went over to the guy on keyboard and I started humming to him. He looked at me and grinned, and immediately started picking up the tune. He began to play and then the drummer followed. When the sax looked peeved, my keyboard player started making exhortations in Russian, and after some back-and-forth the sax finally picked up his instrument and began to play, or rather, belt, the tune.

Then I ran over to Estie and said, "I want to teach you guys a dance!"

I got everyone into lines. Then I put on my teacher's voice. "Okay, ladies, this is a traditional dance from the seventies. Let's go now: forward, walk, walk, walk, back, walk, walk, walk." I taught everyone the Hustle.

The party went on long into the night. The children were crashed out near the dessert table, so when people started leaving and collecting their kids, they had to pick through the sleeping bodies on the floor. The band was packing up, the caterers stripping and collapsing the tables, revealing them to be particle board. Some ladies collected all the centerpieces, which were silk flowers rented from the ladies' charity group. Estie took off with her new husband and a bunch of other relatives. You had to wonder when the bride and groom got a chance to be alone for real.

As for me, I wandered down the hall to the ladies' room, and then padded back in my stocking feet, slipping and sliding on the tile floor. The women's ballroom was deserted. No one had thought to collect me and bring me home. Not being a child, no one had thought to include me in the head count of cousins or carry me back to the house. Everything hurt. Maybe I'd had a little bit too much to drink. Nausea was starting to overtake me. Real life was coming crashing down. I leaned against the wall in the hallway. In my shiny apricot dress I slid down to the floor and sat.

"These are yours?" I looked up to see the red-haired Russian-speaking keyboard dude coming over and holding up my satin shoes.

"Not really," I said. Still, I rustled to my feet and took them.

"You are related to the bride or to the groom?" he asked.

"Neither one," I told him. In my current state, wondering if I was still even going to have a home at the Karinskys', I felt offended at him asking. I felt as if he were asking a really personal question. I shot back, "Are you?"

"No! No, I am a musician," he said.

"What do you have, a pickup group, or a regular band?"

Now it was his turn to look offended. "They are a regular band," he said. "I came to try them out."

"Oh, it was a tryout," I said.

He lowered his voice. "I do not like their tempos."

"Yeah, I noticed."

The other two musicians were coming out now, wheeling the equipment. As they walked, I felt a ripple of contempt sweep past.

"Their style is not mine," Mr. Keyboard was telling me. "In fact I am a classically trained pianist! I have been a student at Berklee College of Music!"

"No kidding," I said. "That's a good school. Do you live in Boston?"

"Yes, in Brighton."

"That's bizarre! I used to live right there. I lived in Allston!"

"Oh, yes?"

"Years ago. I'm from Boston—originally. Probably from a somewhat different background than yours," I added, taking into account his black frock coat, and his black tasseled sash, and in general his whole Bialystoker outfit, which I knew by that time was the exact garb of the gentry of Bialystok in the eighteenth century. "My background is somewhat secular," I said. "I am in the process of learning the Hasidic lifestyle."

He beamed. Everyone was always beaming when I mentioned my learning. "I am also in the process!" he said.

"You! You look like a rabbi already."

"I have been learning three years."

"Well, I've just been learning something like—I don't know, three months," I confessed. "I'm just scratching the surface. Estie was my teacher. That's the main reason I'm here."

"No. No, Hashem brought you here," he said solemnly. And he looked right into my eyes. He was freckled, and still sweaty from playing. His face, and beard, and his whole body, were long; his brown eyes were so bright and intense he looked like someone from an El Greco painting—he had such a beautiful yet unrealistic look about him.

"And, what brought you to . . ."

"When I was twenty-two years old I received a Jewish visa to leave Leningrad. I came to this country in 1980."

"I was going to say what brought you to Hasidism."

"My divorce," he said promptly. "During which my wife was leaving me for another man, and I grew mad."

"Mad angry, or mad insane?" I asked.

"Without a mind. I returned to life through Rabbi Nachum Jarosiewicz—you have heard of him?"

I shook my head.

"He came to me, and together learned with me until once again I remembered who I was, and so I lived with him a time until once again I returned to the apartment of my aunt, who has kept my piano. To which I returned for my studies and my learning together."

"What are you studying for now?" I asked. He looked to be in his thirties at least.

"I am to be a concert pianist," he said.

"What, classical?"

"Everything," he declared. "Classical, romance, jazz, rock."

"Rock."

"Rock, ragtime, pop. Also harpsichord."

I must have been looking skeptical, because he said, "I would show you now if they had not taken my equipment."

"They took your stuff?" I looked down the hall to where the other two musicians had disappeared.

"The stuff was belonging to them," he admitted. "However, they do not understand musicianship."

"Do you do a lot of weddings?"

He reddened. "This is my first wedding." He was starting to get that offended look on his face again. I don't know what the rest of the band had told him, but it was probably something like You'll never play in this town again. He said, "My wish is only to be a Bialystoker Hasid living as a concert pianist."

For a moment I pictured the guy up onstage in white tie and frock coat. Then I tisked my tongue. I said, "It's hard with Shabbes." Meaning, it's hard to play all those concert dates and travel internationally while still observing the Sabbath and the Jewish holidays. "You could always work in the studio like Glenn Gould," I said.

"You know a studio?"

"Listen," I said, "let me tell you something. Music is all about connections. Believe me, I know. These big stars work in a world of their own. They have whole staffs of people just to answer their mail. Music is just an industry like everything else—it's just part of the human machine. But Hashem!" I said. "He is forever!"

"Baruch Hashem!" he declared.

"Hashem is the ultimate reality, and the rest—all the things of this world—they're just illusions—that's the one thing I know," I said. "And all of us—all we can do is try to ascend nearer to His presence."

Then he smiled at me such a quick smile, it was like a flash of light across his face. "In the past I feel that I have known you before."

"I doubt it," I said.

"It could be possibly we knew each other before we were born."

I hesitated a second. I wasn't sure whether that statement was part of Hasidic Judaism or a mystic pickup line. "What's your name?" I asked.

"Mikhail."

"I'm Sharon."

He was looking at me intently. "I think yes I knew you before."

"Seriously, do you think people's spirits could float around like that? Do you think they're like birds, and then they're born into human bodies, but still they try to fly, and they ride prayers like updrafts . . . ?"

"Of course!" he said.

I stood there with my mouth open, I was so surprised. I whispered,

"Do you think a soul could be like a molten fire, and you have to throw it in the furnace to be forged?"

"Oh, yes. Yes," Mikhail said. "In mitzvos, and halachos." In good deeds and Jewish laws.

Oh, my God, I thought to myself. Oh, Hashem, what is happening? He knows everything in my heart. He understands. He can see all the things no one else can see. "Do you like Blake?" I blurted out.

"What is Blake?" he asked.

Oh, well, I thought.

The two of us walked outside into the hot city night. The two of us walked along the dark streets where all the stores had their metal grilles pulled down and the shadowed houses were surrounded by herds of cars parked in alleyways. It wasn't far to the Karinskys', which was a good thing, since the neighborhood was not the safest. But we weren't thinking about that. We were discussing the stars we could not see, and the way lights could be illusory or they could be true, and only God could help you tell the difference.

Since Mikhail didn't really work, apart from teaching piano lessons, he stayed on in Crown Heights for three days with friends of his Brighton rebbe, so we could pursue more dialogues on theosophy. We talked about knowledge, and how you had all of yours before you were born and then you lost it at birth. And we spoke of music and how it came straight from Hashem, and how the rhythms and the melodies could carry you straight upward to the angels, and how the angels themselves were singing Holy! Holy! Holy! for everyone to hear, if only you would listen. If only you opened up your ears to their delight. And we talked of instruments, and my long-lost guitar, and Mikhail's piano that had been something of a sticking point with his ex-wife, since he had found the money for the down payment by selling their car. His wife just didn't get that. She called Mikhail selfish. As if a piano weren't just as much a vehicle as any car could be—and more, given pianos can take you across time and states of consciousness, and cars only drive on the ground!

We talked music. We talked about my songs that I had once composed. We discussed the folk movement in America, and how there were these divisions between so-called high culture and low and middle, just to keep some people out. And we talked about how even democracies can be so exclusionary and voices can be silenced and people's self-expression

unheard, because they might not have the right connections or the
money or education—or their vision might be just different! But most of
all we talked about Hashem and how he had taken hold of each of us and
how when that happens you just want to dance and sing. And how we
were both impatiently expecting any day for the Messiah to come—how
we expected his arrival even right that second, even at that very moment,
which is what we as Bialystokers devoutly believed. And I said how I
imagined it would be when he came—how the night would turn to day,
and the dirt swept away. How the stars would dance and every plant and
animal and insect and human and spark of fire and particle of dust would
rise and proclaim, "The Lord God is King! His majesty rules forever!" And
Mikhail said people would play the music of the angels, and angels would
play human music! Because there would be no gaps anymore between the
two. The people would play music they had never heard. But the angels
would play Stravinsky's *Symphony of Psalms*.

"Why that piece?" I asked.

"I personally should not predict," he said, philosophically. "I myself
couldn't say. But if I have to mention one candidate for them to play,
Symphony of Psalms would be the one."

"I've never even heard it," I said.

"You will," he said.

We were sitting outside on the Karinskys' brick steps, and the sun
was setting. The sky was growing pale, and above the buildings the sun
was even shinier than an apricot satin dress. For a second there the two
of us could barely breathe. For a second there we could almost imagine
the Messiah actually coming forth out of that sunset, illuminating the
brick and fake fieldstone and corrugated metal storefronts. We heard a
roaring like the depths of the ocean! Yet then we saw the roaring was
just a delivery truck breathing down the street, and a bus fwishing its
hydraulic brakes. Which was kind of prosaic, yet did not ruin our mood
at all, which I attribute now to the fact that the two of us had found
each other. When you think about it, isn't that practically as miraculous
as the Messianic age? The two of us were both in thrall of music and of
angels, and the miracles performed by the rebbes of Bialystok. We were
full of lore and piety, yet still, somehow, even then, when I looked at
Mikhail, I didn't just see another Bialystoker. I saw someone who was
questing and seeking and searching and yearning. I saw someone on a

pilgrimage, and with the kind of soul that asks a lot of questions, and the kind of imagination that loves God to pieces. Except his imagination was calmer than mine, so when I was with him I felt like I was just gliding into cool pools. As opposed to splashing around all the time.

We walked into the Karinskys' air-conditioned living room, where the last of the relatives were sitting among suitcases, and poring over photos, and sipping iced tea, and Mikhail and I sat there with them. We ate bialys with soft shredded onions at the center. We ate a whole bagful that we'd bought at the bakery, and we licked our fingers. And still we talked and talked. The main thing we discussed was why does the Messiah tarry? What is he waiting for?

"He waits for all Jews to celebrate Shabbes," Mikhail said. "If every Jew would rest and worship on the Sabbath, then he will come."

"I don't buy that," I said. "Because he cares about the whole world, not just the Jews. I think he's holding out for world peace."

"Stop that," Mrs. Karinsky said in passing as her little four-year-old boy knocked his one-year-old brother down.

He let go, yet the baby was crying.

"The baby's crying," I called to Mrs. Karinsky in the kitchen.

"*Nu,* pick him up," she called back.

Gingerly I picked him up. He was sticky, not to mention loud.

"He waits," said Mikhail, "for the solution of the divisions within man's mind and heart. The question therefore is not why he is waiting but why we delay to receive him. Why are we not ready?"

"But I am ready!" I exclaimed. "Oh, my God, I am so ready." At which point the baby started screaming like he was about to die, and I ran into the kitchen, where Mrs. Karinsky was already making a bottle. Her brow was beaded all over with sweat, and the sleeves of her housedress were pushed up from doing dishes, her forearms soapy. And more kids were running around, and all the counters were piled with boxes and bags of paper plates and plasticware, and a soup was simmering in a giant stockpot. And I'd been intending to hand over the baby but I just meekly took the bottle and turned back to the living room.

Thursday, Mikhail figured he should go home, so his piano students wouldn't forget about him completely. He had dinner at the Karinskys', and then afterward we stood on the brick steps in front of their house, and he gave me his address and he said he would write me a letter, and he invited me to come visit him and his aunt Lena in Brighton. I could stay with nieces of his rebbe. We stood there some more, even though he had to go or else miss his ride to the bus station with his rebbe's friend, and I wished I could just give him a hug, and I think he wished he could do the same to me, yet in the Bialystoker community that was not done. Instead, I said to him, "I feel as if we are standing on the exact same step of the same staircase. . . ."

"It is *bashert*," Mikhail said. "We are on one plane." It was such a serious moment; I was half afraid the guy would get down on his knees and propose to me! Yet he said, "I will wait for you to come to Brighton, and I will play for you. Do you know Scott Joplin? I will play him for you by heart."

And then something inside of me woke up. Some resonance began to sound inside of me. All my instincts were telling me: Go with this guy. Go to Brighton with him. Don't go back inside the house. Go now. There is nothing for you back inside. There are only air-conditioning units. There are only large numbers of children. Go with Mikhail. All my instincts were telling me this, and I would have gone. I really would have taken off right then, except for one thing, which was that my instincts in the past had proved to be so unerringly terrible!

So Mikhail went off to catch his bus back to Boston, and I went back inside the house and helped Mrs. Karinsky reorganize the refrigerator and freeze the mini-knishes from the reception. A deep melancholy began to envelop me, along with a headache, and I thought to myself, Well, now I've lost Estie and Mikhail both.

Well, I thought, for once in my life I've actually held back. For once I've learned from my behavior in my past relationships, i.e., following Gary, and running off with Kekui, and hooking up with Wayne (twice!), and loving Brian so much I could never believe he was married. Now I have reached a point where I am in control of my feelings and I don't actually do the first thing that comes into my heart. Self-control. That was my thing now. I'd stood there on the steps and I had actually experienced self-restraint, and it tasted so strange. Like anise.

But what was my reward? Two entire weeks went by and Mikhail never once wrote to me! Every day I'd check the mail, and no letter had arrived. Every day I'd wake up and pray in the bedroom so full of beds there was hardly any floor space, and I'd help the little kids get dressed,

and do a couple of loads of laundry, or at least try to clear the toys from
the stairs, and then I'd sit like a lady from olden times wondering
silently—how much longer till I hear from him? If I'd carried a hand-
kerchief I would have twisted it up in my hands, just helplessly waiting
for the mail.

Mrs. Karinsky, however, was acting quite cheerful. She seemed to
think all my prospects lay before me. In her mind my path was clear.
She said to me at Friday-night dinner, "We will talk to our family in
Brighton. We will mention Mikhail's name and discuss him. God willing
we may make a match."

A match! I thought at the other end of the table. I don't even like
him anymore!

Yet Mrs. Karinsky brushed all this aside. She and the doctor, her husband, were delighted, because my *bashert* had come to play at Estie's
wedding. Dr. Karinsky sat at the table and tucked into his brisket, and
tickled any of his kids that came within arm's reach, and he said to me
enthusiastically, "There are maybe possibilities."

"Hee, hee, hee!" squealed one of the toddlers, whose name was
Moshele.

"I'm not even touching you! Look at this!" We all looked. Dr. Karinsky wiggled his fingers in Moshele's direction, and the kid went into
hysterics, even though his dad was just waggling his fingers in the air.
The kid was on the floor. He was going to lose his dinner. Along with
eating everything put in front of him, that was one of the doctor's specialties: phantom tickling. You had to admire his prowess.

As soon as Shabbes was over, Dr. Karinsky got on the horn to his
brother and his brother's cousin, who was related to Mikhail's rebbe.
Within days the Karinskys were full of glowing things to say about
Mikhail's learning and his character, and his strivings, and the parallels
between us in our spiritual journeys and our growth toward Hashem.

Isn't this a little quick? I kept thinking. Aren't you all a little bit eager?
Particularly when the man in question, my supposed match made in
heaven, has not once picked up a pen to write me a letter. Even after he
promised he would! I was disillusioned with my fine musical friend, to
say the least. Out of sight, out of mind, was what he had turned out to
be. Deeply philosophical on the spur of the moment, yet thoughtless
and fickle in the long haul. I trudged over to the preschool every

morning, and I was feeling somewhat hurt that everybody wanted to match me up so fast to such a fly-by-night. In my white stockings and my dirndl skirts and long-sleeved blouses, I sang the children to sleep. I watched them on their rest mats in the shadowy blue light of the classroom's blue curtains. To the Karinskys, every little act was going to bring on the Messiah. One by one you took all the jumbled-up pieces and people of the world—then you snapped them together to complete the picture. And that was what I believed, too, or so I'd thought. It's just that I'd never considered that I was just a puzzle piece myself to slide in place. Just a little bit of foliage. A piece of sky. Nobody wants to be part of the twig on the third tree on the left. You want to be Eve, or the tree of life, or an angel in the picture. It's true: just as Harrison and Margo said all those years ago at their workshop: you want to be a whole.

THEN that Wednesday a letter did come for me, and it was from Mikhail.

My Dearest Sharon,
Many times I have thought to write a letter to you, yet three difficulties prevented me: 1. I have little time from learning 2. In your person I prefer to speak to you 3. I do not know what to say.

Patiently I have been waiting for God's will to show himself: whether we are to be intended for each other. Each day I asked of him this question, yet he did not speak to me about this subject until today he spoke into my ear. This is how it came about: I was sitting at my table, and in front of me my holy books I was reading. All at once a musical tune began to play inside my ear. Twice I tried to ignore it, yet each time the tune returned. When a third time it came back, I went to the piano and played the melody.

The tune was nothing I had before heard, nor my aunt. Yet I could not stop it singing in my ear. Therefore I asked my Rebbe to come to the apartment. I played for him the music. One moment my Rebbe listened. He then exclaimed, "Mikhail, but this is the third Bialystoker's wedding niggun! This is the wedding tune composed by that Tzadik of Bialystok in the years of the eighteenth century! Yet very rarely now is it sung—only on a few occasions." My Rebbe said, "Mikhail, you have never before heard this tune?"

"Never, indeed," I told him, "until today I heard the music humming in my ear!"

"This is astonishing!" exclaimed my Rebbe.

"This is surely a sign or miracle," I said.

"There is no doubt," said he.

For it was a sign from *Hashem* I should be married. Two times I tried not to listen, yet the third, I have realized what the divine One through the Rebbe's own melody is telling me. Namely that I make a proposal to you for a marriage. Therefore this is what I propose. Will you answer me?

Well, I looked at the letter, and I looked at it, and I thought, Oh, my God; I thought, Sweet Jesus (if you'll excuse the expression), what is happening here? I felt such a rush and a confusion of emotions. Awe, and wonderment, and joy, but also, I'm ashamed to admit—a tiny bit of jealousy that Mikhail had been the one to hear the music. That Hashem, through the spirit of the third Bialystoker, had chosen to whisper in Mikhail's ear. It was so petty of me, so small minded, yet I couldn't help feeling—what about my ears? What about me? Yet I squashed down that feeling. I forced back down the jealousy that I was just the object, and not the instrument, of divine revelation. Grow up, I told myself. You can't traipse through life hogging all the epiphanies. And I went to the kitchen and ate maybe half a pound of assorted cookies, just turning and turning in my mind everything Mikhail was asking me. A proposal of marriage! That was wild enough. But a proposal at the behest of Hashem himself! One inspired and directed by the Lord God. At that point I just had to go upstairs to my bed and lie down.

There I was lying on my mattress in the girls' bedroom, and it must have been a couple of hours before anyone discovered me. Mrs. Karinsky happened to be coming up the stairs in the process of dragging her daughter Chaneleh up to her room after she had injured one of her siblings.

"Sharon, what's wrong? You're sick?"

"No," I said, and I gave her the letter.

She read it quickly, then knit her brow, and read it again. "I never heard of such a thing!" she said.

"Is that good or bad?" I asked.

"You are going to answer him?"

"I don't even know!" I said. "On the one hand, this miracle has happened. On the other hand, I don't know."

Meanwhile, Chaneleh was trying to escape down the stairs again, and Mrs. Karinsky had to run after her and haul her back. "So it's all right, you don't have to make up your mind in one day," she shouted over the kid's screams. "So take your time to think about it!"

"No! No! No!" shrieked Chaneleh.

"This story!" Mrs. Karinsky exclaimed. "I have to tell Mendy!"

Everyone was so impressed by Mikhail's tale. The family, the whole neighborhood, couldn't stop talking about it. The story of the niggun that had come to Mikhail almost overshadowed his marriage proposal. Everybody seemed to forget for a moment that I was supposed to write him back—or if they remembered they assumed that I already had, and naturally that I had already accepted. But the truth was, I had not written back. I had not accepted. There I was, alone in all the flurry, a lonely celebrity. I had no idea what to do. As a Bialystoker there was no question: I had spoken to the man, we had exchanged our deepest thoughts; I'd researched him through the Karinskys' friends and relatives. His references were great, and he had received a miraculous sign from God. No question: the answer was yes. As myself, however, as my own woman, which I used to be—all I could think was: who did I think I was kidding? And—where did Mikhail get off writing now after all this time? Did he really believe I was going to jump to marry him after just one letter? A relationship of a week, plus a revelation on his part alone. He might be a psychopathic criminal! I didn't want to prejudge him; I didn't want to go by stereotypes; but by his own admission Mikhail had gone nuts at least once, when his wife left him. If the divine wedding niggun had come to me, that would be one thing—but I hummed and hummed, and all that came to me was Peter, Paul and Mary. Sometimes The Mamas and the Papas. Trust was the key—that I knew. But I didn't even trust myself. I had no reason to trust myself. None at all.

Everybody was so eager for me. Everybody was so pleased. Estie said she would give me her wedding gown to wear. Mrs. Karinsky said we could have the wedding right there in the house, in the living room. But the happier they all were for me, the more miserable I became. What Dr. Karinsky kept emphasizing was how Mikhail and I were on the same level—how the wonderful thing was the way we matched up in our learning, and our desire for holiness. He was probably right. But was that a good thing? It sounded dangerous, marrying somebody on my level. It sounded like a recipe for disaster. Was there even room for someone else on the same little parapet I was hanging on? And there was something else too. There was something I feared even more, which was that marrying would be the ultimate commitment to Bialystok Hasidism! To marry: that would be to make my final vows to the community. To pray for keeps.

Mikhail began calling the house. In the evenings he would call me on the phone. Yet somehow I could not speak to him. I just could not pick up the telephone and discuss matters. I told the Karinskys I couldn't talk to him while I was in my decision-making process. No way, I told them, could I get on the line. I was so riven. I was so torn up with doubts. Some days I was sure the answer would be yes. And other days I would hear the voice of my inmost spirit calling me inside: Sharon! Sharon! NO! Deep inside me my old self lay dormant. Deep inside, all my memories and deeds pressed against each other. All my years in Hawaii; all my time out in the ocean. The mistakes I'd made; the loves I'd had. I was still filled with the person I had been.

Late at night, scrubbing out pots piled in the kitchen sink, I began crying.

"Sharon? Sharon? What?" Mrs. Karinsky turned off the faucet.

"I can't," I cried. "I can't."

She put her arms around me and held me there in the kitchen. "It's all right. It's okay." She was warm, and she was damp. She was always sweating, what with her weight and the physical labor of her job—by which I mean, cleaning, cooking, and child rearing—and I thought, all of a sudden, She probably already has high blood pressure, or at least a heart condition, and I thought, What have I done coming here and adding to her burden when most likely she's sick and never takes care of herself, and she could one day all of a sudden have a stroke because of me?

"I'm just a sham," I sobbed. "I have no potential. I get no signs. I've been waiting and waiting. I don't hear any voices. I have no path," I said.

"I have no way!" I couldn't even go on. I just put my head on her shoulder and cried and cried. I soaked through the fabric of her housedress. And I wanted to say, Please let me go. It's too late for me; I'm too old for even you to mother. Please just throw me back into the world again. Scared as I am to go there, it would be better to give up than to go on like this, standing on the brink of commitment, stranded on the threshold of the divine kingdom, and afraid to enter. I wanted to say, I'm taking off now—I can't impose on you any longer. I wanted to say, I don't have any peace of mind. My spirit is willing, but my faith is weak. Don't you see, I'm easy? I wanted to say all that, but I was crying too hard to speak.

At last Mrs. Karinsky sat me down, and she got me tissues, and she finished the dishes, because it seemed like nothing she could say would comfort me. But as she scrubbed the pots, Mrs. Karinsky was thinking, because when she finished she dried her hands with a determined look. And she pulled down her sleeves and she said to me, "Come to the rebbe's spiel," which was one of these speeches the Bialystoker rebbe gave after services. "Ask him what to do."

"He'd have an answer?"

Mrs. Karinsky whirled around. "Of course!" she exclaimed, as if to say, What kind of question is that?

A shiver went through me. In all my time now in the community I had not met the rebbe. I had seen him in the distance, surrounded by his aides and junior rabbis. I had seen him far off, dressed in black, but never met him face to face! I almost forgot my troubles just contemplating the idea of meeting him. I wanted to pick up the phone to call Mikhail and tell him what for the first time I was about to do—he would be stunned; he would be speechless that I was going to have this opportunity. I felt such an overwhelming desire to tell Mikhail that all at once I ran into the dark deserted living room and I did pick up the phone and call him.

Bring . . . bringgg . . . bringgggg. A deep old woman's voice answered as if from at the bottom of a well, "Helloooooo?"

"Hello, this is Sharon," I said.

"This is who?"

"Sharon," I said.

"Pardon me, you are?"

"Sharon," I repeated, loudly.

"Yes?" she said. "I am Lena."

"Oh, Aunt Lena, I've heard about you," I said.

"And I also." Then she waited.

"Is Mikhail there?"

She didn't answer at first.

"Is Mikhail there?" I asked again.

"Inside he is a good man," Lena said, judiciously, as if she had just come up with a verdict. "To me Mikhail is like a son. I have no children of my own. My sister gave him to me for me to watch over. She said to me before she died—I give you my son. Practically he has a zero, but his heart is one hundred percent." She paused thoughtfully. "And this is true."

I was nervous about running up the Karinskys' phone bill. "Could you tell him that I called?"

"You wish to speak to him?"

"Is he there?"

"Of course," Lena said.

So then she put Mikhail on the line, and he burst out, "Sharon, so long I've been waiting to hear you."

"Well, I was waiting to hear from you too," I said, a little testily, but then I said, "Forget about that for now. I have to tell you something. I am going to see the rebbe."

"The rebbe!"

"Yes!"

"When?"

"After his spiel!"

"*Baruch Hashem!*"

"I know!" The two of us were all of a sudden like a couple of teenagers swooning over some celebrity.

"What will you say?"

"I'm going to ask him about us."

"Oh, yes! Good! Wonderful!" he cried out.

"I'm going to ask him whether I should marry you."

"Of course! Yes, of course. Sharon, ask him for a *bracha*," he said, meaning ask him for his blessing.

"I will."

"Sharon, this is good fortune. This, too, is a sign."

"Well, I'm going to see," I hedged.

"Since our meeting I am overwhelmed with signs," Mikhail said. "I see more closely patterns every day. I see now it is not we but fate moving us in the same direction."

"The thing is," I whispered, "sometimes I believe that too. But sometimes I have doubts. That's why I haven't answered your letter. That's why I've been torturing myself day and night."

"Dearest Sharon!" he exclaimed. "Don't torture."

"I can't help it," I said. "I have this fear I can't tell anymore what is delusions and what is true."

"But Hashem will tell you," he said.

"That's the thing—he's not talking to me."

"He will," said Mikhail. He spoke with such solemnity and calm.

"I'm jealous of you," I confessed.

"Why?"

"Because you have it, and I don't."

"What is it I have?" he asked.

"Grace," I said. "You've really really got it—and I don't. I try, but I don't. If I had it, I wouldn't be jealous in the first place."

"The rebbe will tell you what to do," he said.

"I hope so."

"I have read that with one word or gesture the Bialystoker can mend everything that is ripped or torn. I have read that with his eyes he can penetrate inside every people. He can lift up the wounded and raise the ones who lick the dust."

"Im yirtzeh Hashem"—with the help of God—"it will happen to me," I said fervently.

"How could it not happen to you?" Mikhail asked. "You are most miserable and wretched."

"Thanks a lot!"

"Therefore you are the perfect candidate to be redeemed, and become as graceful inside as you are out."

"I was talking about grace, not gracefulness."

"With God's help there is no difference between them!" he said.

"You're right!" I whispered. "I never thought about it that way before!"

*   *   *

THERE were about a thousand people crammed together in the Bialy-stoker synagogue. The men down below, in this bobbing sea of black, the women up above in the balcony, all weighted down with babies. When we stood and prayed together the whole building seemed to crack, and the words poured out in torrents. When we sat down together the building seemed to sigh. The service was short, since it was a weeknight, and afterward everyone was waiting expectantly. Everyone hushed. It wasn't a gradual hush, where people keep on shushing one another. It was as if someone had turned off the sound.

Then the rebbe rose, short and old, yet spry, in his black coat and black hat. He sat at a table down in front, and there was a microphone before him like at a press conference, and a satellite hookup from that table. Everyone hung on his every word. And I hung, too, except I didn't understand a thing because the whole talk was in Yiddish. Yet I felt from the audience how powerful his message was. I took in the feeling of it, the way I guess deaf people sometimes feel music in the vibrations, in their feet. The rebbe never once looked down to read from notes. He just talked, and kept his eyes fixed on the audience. And they watched him, and you could see in their faces this total trust in his words. Everyone knew that they were sacred. There was a tension in the hall, like there better not be any interruptions. There better not be any babies crying. All the babies had bottles stuffed in their mouths. All the kids were sucking candy. I had this fear I was going to cough. I was going to break the spell. But I didn't cough. Nobody did. The silence was magical. All the people there were learning at the rebbe's black-trousered knees.

Fortunately I didn't clap when it was over. That wasn't done. The women were all getting up around me, murmuring to each other and filing down the stairs. I followed Mrs. Karinsky and Estie in her new married woman's wig.

There were lines in the bottom of the sanctuary. Long lines snaked before the rebbe's desk, and slowly, one by one, people were filing in front of him, pausing a moment, and moving on. I got on line, and Mrs. Karinsky stood with me. My stomach was tight. I tried to formulate in my mind everything I wanted to say—all I felt, all the dilemmas of my human experience! There I was, coming before this totally saintly man. The line was inching forward. It was like moving toward this ultimate weighing station of my soul. There were ten people in front of me.

There were two. I bent my head down. My head was bare. Next to all the married ladies, I felt naked showing all my long straight hair.

The rebbe looked up at me. He had the most amazing blue eyes, that pale pale ice blue you only get when you are something like ninety years old. And they twinkled. That was what surprised me. His eyes were full of fun. He had the white beard and the black hat, and the wrinkled face, but his eyes looked like he was joshing you. So he twinkled at me, and I started talking, fast as I could, since people were waiting. "Rabbi, my name is Sharon—I hope you don't mind me talking in English, but I heard you know most languages. I had to ask you. There's this guy, and he's a religious man, on the same level I am, and a musician, and he's had a sign that he should marry me. He's had a sign from God, but yet, I have doubts, since I barely know him, for one thing, which is customary in the community, I understand, but where I come from you tend to take more time getting to know people of the other sex. To me the whole relationship seems like it's moving way too fast. I'm just not sure I'm—I mean— philosophically we seem to be very close—but I have a fear we might be too similar—I have this foreboding—but I don't know if it's justified. I can't tell anymore whether my doubts are real—or if they're just leftover prejudices from my past life. . . ."

The rebbe lifted his hand. He nodded, like, Say no more. I was shivering. It was as if he could read me without even hearing my whole story. It was as if he could read the writing on my soul! He picked up a roll of pennies from a big pile of penny rolls on the table. He broke the penny roll in half and gave me the freshest, shiniest penny I'd ever seen. The copper shone like autumn.

"Should I marry him?" I blurted out.

In the gentlest voice he said something to me—he answered me, but in Yiddish! The line moved. Mrs. Karinsky took my arm.

"What did he say?" I asked her, as we left the building. I held the penny tight. I was supposed to pass on the coin to charity, but I couldn't ever let that penny go. "What did he say?" I asked Mrs. Karinsky.

"Nu, freg dina eltermen," she told me.

"What does that mean?" I pleaded.

She translated for me, *"Nu,* you should ask your parents."

19

My Hand in Marriage

My parents! The idea had never once occurred to me. Go to them? Ask *them*! The concept was so radical it shook me to my toes. Yet it was so wild, it was right. It was totally, cosmically right. I was in awe, because in one moment this unbelievable man had seen inside of me. In one instant the rebbe had put all these pieces of me together. Because of course! You had to go back and face down your dad. It was like in Tibetan Buddhist practice. On your journey you had to cross one final river. Or, like in Western culture, you had to venture to the underworld, whatever your personal underworld might be. You had to visit the ghosts of the suburban dead.

As soon as Shabbes ended I packed my backpack—but I left my suitcase and my guitar in Crown Heights for safekeeping. The next morning Estie's cousins Shmuley and Itchel drove me to the bus terminal. I waved good-bye, and they waved back earnestly from the car, their faces all young under their black hats, their beards still scraggly. I hopped aboard a Greyhound bus, and sat right in front, pointing myself toward Boston.

.   .   .

As the great poet Yeats once said, the trees were in their autumn beauty. They were flaming out against the sky. Maybe it was the scarlet leaves and raving gold—Brookline was prettier than I remembered it. The elms were tall and stately. They must have grown while I'd been gone. Some of the houses were stucco, and some were brick, and they were all old and solid and had lawns, and they were spaced apart with hedges. A lot of the roofs were slate, and the garages looked like carriage houses, and—this, I had remembered—everything was pretentious, built in a Style, like French Provincial, or American Colonial, or half-timbered ersatz Elizabethan. My dad's house was mock Tudor. I stood a long time on the sidewalk taking it in. The garden was landscaped, unlike when I'd lived there. The lawn was lush and green, and there were ornamental shrubs and flower beds. There was a little sign planted on the edge of the lawn, a "This Property Is Protected by . . ." sign. That was new.

I felt funny, looking at the place. Actually it was a good-looking house, but then you can never tell anything from the outside. It had never been a home to me—home had been Mom's split level, which she got from the divorce. It was when I was thirteen and Mom took off that I'd come to this fake Tudor place, because I didn't have a home anymore. I came to live with Dad and his wife, Joanne, which had been Very Hard on Them. I'd been all squared away, back with Dad's old wife (my mom), in the old house, with the old car, and then it turned out all of a sudden that I and my raging hormones had to move in with Dad, which impinged on his lifestyle, since, during those teen years, I tended to light little fires in the school rest rooms and occasionally hang my head upside down between my knees and make myself pass out—in addition to the regular teenage stuff like getting stoned and sneaking off places at night and having sex all the time like a little squirrel. I guess even in middle school just my presence had frayed my father's nerves, he being a professor and all—and so into his academic dignity.

A woman answered the door. I didn't recognize her at first, but then I saw it was my stepmother. I said, "Joanne! Wow, you look great!" She must have had some kind of surgery. Her whole face looked thinner and tighter, and her nose was delicately pinched. Gone was that original eagle beak. And she was blond now, and probably twenty pounds thinner.

She said, "I'm not Joanne; I'm Cathy."

That threw me for a second. I said, "Is this the home of Professor Milton Spiegelman?"

She said, "Yes." She looked at me funny. She said, "May I help you?"

I said, "I'm his daughter, Sharon."

She looked a little bit afraid.

"I've been out of touch for a while. Are you his wife?"

She nodded. She looked like she really wanted to close the door.

"Huh," I said. "What happened to Joanne?"

But she wasn't inclined to answer that question.

I said, "Is my dad home?"

"He's in back," she told me.

"Oh," I said. "Could I see him? Don't worry. Please. Don't be alarmed. I'm not here to stay with you guys or anything. There's just a question I want to ask."

She took me around the side of the house. She wasn't going to let me in, so I couldn't see whether Dad had redecorated in addition to remarrying, or if he still had his pipe collection in the den. He used to have all these polished wooden pipes on little wooden stands, and little boxes of loose tobacco, all organized in rows. My friends always thought it was a waste, the way Dad had those pipes standing there so pristine—he barely ever used them. So then we did. I wondered if he still had satin sheets on his bed—we thought they were wasted on him too. Sheets so smooth were wasted on the old. A couple of times my erstwhile high school boyfriend and I screwed around on them. And Dad never knew, except I got no pleasure from it. I never told anyone, but I was afraid of his bedroom, and of the pictures he had there of my brother, Andrew. In one of the pictures Andrew wore overalls. He must have been about one year old. I didn't remember him then because I hadn't been born. In the picture he wore pinstriped overalls and a matching engineer's cap, and he was smiling, and he had huge dark eyes. You felt a little sick looking at him. You could practically get an ice cream headache.

So now we turned the corner, and there was my dad raking leaves in the backyard. His hair was almost gone, and he'd lost so much weight I thought for a moment my eyes were fooling me again, and it wasn't really he, but some newer model like Cathy. Yet looking closer I could see it was Dad, all right. Same slightly round-shouldered frame; same paunch, although so much smaller. Behind his glasses his eyes were brown and weak, molelike, which was deceptive, they appeared so gentle in that mild-mannered professorial way. I said, "Hey, Dad, how've you been?"

His hand sort of drifted up, involuntarily. His fingers drifted to the base of his throat.

"The place looks great," I said. There was a new Japanese maple, with drifting wine-colored leaves. There was the swimming pool, with its aqua pool cover on it, and new flagstones on the border.

"Sharon." He looked at me warily. I realized he was checking out my clothes. My denim skirt and long-sleeved blouse. On me my outfit must have looked like a nun's habit. He said, "What brings you out to Brookline?"

I said, "Look, I'm not here to ask you for anything. Don't worry. I'm not here to get anything from you. Honestly." I felt like I had to reassure him like that, since we'd had so many misunderstandings. After my little drug-dealing incident in college, after my letter to him from Hawaii all those years ago. Now, God, I was so different, and he was so much older. The whole world was a different place.

I said, "Dad, I'm not even going to mention the past, because, you know what? The past *is* past." I said, "Dad, I just had to come here to ask you this vital question about the future. Dad, I am a *frum* Jew. *Baruch Hashem*, I'm Orthodox! I've grown and evolved, and come to a place where I believe Hashem is the one who controls my destiny. And my life is not about grudges or conflicts or getting things from you, or getting away from you—and it hasn't been for a long time. It's about Torah. Torah is my life now; my guide and my blueprint. Torah is my map of the whole universe, and the rebbe, he is the one who saw inside me all the way to where he said I should bring my question—I mean the question of my future—to you.

"And it's not about what you should have been as a father, and what you did to me—because, you know what? I don't define myself as a victim—even if I was one. I would rather define myself as a *frum,* joyful, ascending spirit. So whatever abuse and trauma I underwent, that's all in the past, which is not where I'm living; I'm not dwelling on that. And right now, this visit is about where I'm heading, and who I should marry, because I have a proposal right now being offered to me, and I'm figuring out what I should do."

So my dad was pretty stunned by that speech, somewhat agape, almost fearful—like who was this woman claiming to be his daughter? And what new kind of weirdo had she become? At his side Cathy looked even more baffled, since, naturally, she had never met me before, but she was bravely dragging over lawn chairs, and bringing out iced tea. So we sat down together, and I chugged on. I explained my whole situation; how I was in the process of becoming a Bialystoker Hasid and learning my tradition, entering, so to speak, the novitiate of Jewish life, and how the crowning glory of the Jewish woman's experience was marriage and creating a Torah-true household, and how this was what I wanted, too, I was pretty sure, and I had a chance to do this, and a suitor, but since I barely knew the guy, I was struggling with the decision whether to say yes to his offer, which was why the rebbe—who was my spiritual leader and the prime candidate to being the Messiah as soon as the world had prepared itself—had advised me to return to my origins, or rather, my parental roots, and do my father and mother and myself the honor of asking their advice. And that was all I wanted from him as my dad. Just his opinion.

After all this my dad looked at me, and he said, "You're asking me whether you should marry this Russian Orthodox . . . ?"

"Jewish Orthodox Russian," I corrected.

My dad said, "I have no opinion at all."

It was funny, I thought I'd gotten to a point where he couldn't wound me anymore. Still tears came to my eyes; my voice broke. "But you're my father," I said. "Can't you see how different I've become?"

"Sharon, I can see you're different. I'm happy for you. But you can't expect to come here to me after, what, twenty years? and pick up—"

"Nineteen years," I said. "But, see, that's not the point. I don't want to pick up the shreds of our relationship! I want to start over!"

"Well . . . Sharon . . ." He told me ours was a relationship severely damaged. Ours was a relationship where his trust in me had been utterly destroyed. And even after he had got me admission to BU—gone out on a limb for me, given me that chance—which had been probably his biggest mistake—then, what with my drug use, and my partying, during which, he reminded me, I'd trespassed on his property while he'd been away, and trashed his house; what with me and my so-called friends being arrested for dealing, and my breaking every rule he'd established . . .

"Dad! You're still talking about freshman year! Dad! Give it a rest! This is my whole point, I'm talking about letting go."

He told me that as usual I was interrupting him. He told me it had always been about control. He said I had no idea what he and Joanne had put themselves through with me. He said, in fact, I had contributed to the stresses in their marriage.

"What *you* put yourselves through with *me*?"

He told me to stop interrupting. He reminded me that they had tried everything. That they had tried counseling. That they had thought about sending me to a residential home. That they had tried tough love.

"No," I said, "you never tried any kind of love."

He stiffened.

Cathy said, "Milt, please."

Deliberately my dad said, "I guess the thing that I couldn't take anymore was being lied to. Over and over and over again. The lying."

"I only lied because I had to," I burst out. "I only lied when it was absolutely necessary." I felt myself drawn in, somehow, sucked in closer to his heat. Still, I tried to stave the feeling off. "I'm here to tell you I'm past all that; I've been past it for a long while, that whole sick power struggle we had going. That's not who I am anymore, and I hope that's not you. Because, see, I forgive you, Dad. I want you to know that. I forgive you."

But he looked at me, like How dare you say that, he being in such denial he couldn't even see what I would forgive him for. "I'm sorry, Dad," I said, "I'm sorry you've held on to all that anger. But could we get back to my question, I mean, about the future?"

"Sharon," he told me again, "I have nothing to say about your question."

"Oh, Daddy." I knelt in front of his lawn chair. "Daddy, Hashem can heal anything. The Moshiach is going to transform the world. All the dead will rise, all the wrongs will be righted. If I get married, I want you and Mom to walk me down the aisle, one on each side. I'm not that kid you remember anymore. I've worked so hard on myself, you don't even know. Actually, it turns out I have a *goldene neshama*. I have a twenty-four-karat golden soul! I don't want to cause you pain anymore. I want to cause you joy. I've been clean for years, and I've been climbing upward even longer. The only thing I'm interested in now is goodness, and your blessing."

He didn't push me away. Actually, he held me there a moment. He told me he wished me well. He said, look, he wished me luck. He hoped I really was getting my life together.

"Thank you," I said, and we stood up. I told him I would go now; I wasn't going to intrude on his life. I smiled through my tears. I hugged him good-bye. Then I said, "Oh, and just one more thing? Could I have a thousand bucks?"

He froze.

"Just kidding!" I let him go. "Cathy," I said, "it was great meeting you."

I could feel their enormous relief as I headed back around the side of the house to the street. They ushered me along. I said, "Dad, by the way, where's Mom?"

He hesitated a moment. "I think she's still up in Provincetown."

To get out to the Cape I went to Rent-a-Wreck and got a car and drove. I'd kept up my driver's license all those years, but I'd hardly ever driven a car, since of course, I'd never been able to afford one of my own. So now there I was behind the wheel again, which at first was a little frightening. I had a couple of near misses in the burbs, not remembering some of the niceties of driving, like yielding before left turns and things like that. But it all came back to me pretty quick. Pretty soon I was blasting rock 'n' roll, just speeding along the open road.

There wasn't much traffic so I skimmed right on over the Sagamore Bridge, high above the boats and barges, the canal underneath. And I drove up the snaky two-lane highway, up the Cape past Hyannis and Chatham and Wellfleet. Past a large Polynesian-themed motel with fake Hawaiian sculptures out front, pairs of imitation war gods. Past restaurants decked out with nets and lobster traps draped over the roofs. Past pottery showrooms and strip malls, all the way up to P-Town.

The bright afternoon was turning cold. After parking my wreck I dug a sweatshirt out of my backpack and started walking up and down Commercial Street, looking for Shambala Books, where Dad thought my mother was now working. I could have asked for directions, but instead I walked along looking in the windows of the stores. Everything there was so expensive. There was a store that sold these miniature Japanese fountains where water bubbled over smooth black river stones; they cost about a million bucks. I mean, what price tranquility? There were a few stores selling S & M tchotchkes: chains, collars, whips, and leather. There were bars, and ice cream parlors, and several bookstores, including one for kids. There were little huts down by the wharf that sold crafts, like stained-glass suncatchers, and leatherwork. There was one that sold seashells, all different kinds, that you could pick out from bins.

After asking around, I found out Shambala no longer existed, but the old owner had opened up a new place a couple blocks down, a store called Gamalan that sold crystals, games, and books. By this time it was almost five o'clock, and I was worried everything was going to close, so I ran over to Gamalan, which was a place I can only describe as tinkly, it was so cluttered with crystals, and miniature wind chimes, as well as games of chance and strategy, like Go.

The saleslady said, "May I help you?"

And I said tentatively, "Yeah, I'm looking for Estelle."

The saleslady said, "I'm sorry, we don't have an Estelle."

"Oh," I said. "Was there ever one? Estelle Spiegelman?"

And the saleslady said, "Not that I can think of."

I turned to go, but out from the back came this other saleslady, rather fragile looking, with bright blue eyes, and long straight hair, white and brown mixed.

"Mom!"

"Sharon!" She recognized me right away. "Hi, sweetie!" She opened up her arms and hugged me. We were both talking at once.

"Did you change your name?"

"Oh, let me look at you. Sweetie! Baby! Yeah, years ago."

"So what's your name now, Mom?"

"I go by Stella, and that's it. No last name." And right there with the other saleslady behind the cash register, and the occasional customer coming in and going out, Mom hugged me, and I cried. I loved it.

Mom never stinted in showing her affection when she was in the mood. Even though she was, like me, in general a bony, thin person, her spirit could be fat and soft and bosomy. She was wonderful at lying on couches. When it came to motherhood, it was more the outdoor stuff she hadn't kept up with—like buying food and taking trash out, and re-membering to register me for school. Kids thought I was cool in sixth grade or so, because at my mom's house there were no rules. They knew that being a poet, Mom didn't work outside the home, but unlike their mothers, my mom was laissez-faire. She never picked me up, or expected me home or anything, so she was a legend in my middle school. She was this invisible supernatural anarchist homemaker. Of course, even when I was ten, I knew that actually it was her alcoholism, not her altruism, that kept Mom so thoroughly off my case. I just didn't let on— I just burnished up that myth people had of her and me. Then Mom took off and left me sleeping alone in the empty house. She blew her legend status, and no one envied me anymore.

Still, I stood there in that New Age store on the Cape, and I said, "Mom, I want you to know, I haven't come here to dwell on the past. I'm not here just to go over and over again all the damage that was done. I just came to find out how you are and—"

"I'm good," she said, "I'm doing pretty well. This place is real good for me. It's a sanctuary for me." And she told me about the store, and how she'd worked there the last five years, and lived in an old house with her cat, Sappho, and she was affiliated with a Wellfleet-based coven of witches, with whom she practiced magic and womyn's rituals. She had just had her croning ceremony.

"Oh, Mom," I said, hushed. What would my community think of this? "Oh, Mom. You're pagan."

"Yes, I am," she told me. "And sober."

"Mazel tov!" I said. *"Baruch Hashem,"* and I meant it, but the words were a little bit painful coming out. I wondered if she was remembering the same things I remembered. The times she'd been sober before.

"Three and a half years," she said. "I wrote you a letter."

"Oh," I said.

"I didn't have your address, so I couldn't mail it. Do you want me to find it for you? How long are you in town? I could find it for you and give it to you."

"No, that's okay, Mom."

"It's about the steps I've taken in my sobriety."

I really didn't want to talk about her sobriety, since it made her so serious, since the whole subject was so important and so painful and about the past, and I kept promising myself we didn't have to go back into the past. That was not what my visit was about! The past was just

not a happy place for me. Growing up in my family had not been altogether hunky dory, which was maybe why later on I'd had to go
through growing up again extra times.

"There's a big thank-you to you in it," she said, referring to the letter.

"Really? For what?"

"For being my daughter," Mom said. "I wanted to thank you in the
letter, since I realized I'd never thanked you for that before."

"I don't get it," I said.

"What?"

"Why did you need to thank me? I couldn't help being your daughter, could I?"

She looked hurt. "I just wanted to thank you for supporting me. You
know, when you were a little girl, you were a great support to me," she
said.

What choice did I have? I thought, but I kept my mouth shut.

"You always tried to cheer me up," she said. "And you did. Did you
know that? You did cheer me up. Do you remember when you used to
make those puppets for me?"

"No, I don't remember," I said.

"You don't remember Madeline and Pepito? And you tried to make
the horse, but you couldn't get the mane to stick to the sock."

"No." I shook my head, even though of course I did remember. It
was second grade. The yarn wouldn't stick, because I didn't have fabric
glue, so the horse looked somewhat bald, but the show went on anyway.
I didn't really think it was fair for her to bring it up. It seemed self-
serving of her to remind me of when I was her little girl.

I said, "Mom, that's not important. That's done. That's gone."

"It wasn't all bad," she said.

"I know! Did you think I came out here to accuse you or something? Because I didn't. Not at all! That's the farthest thing from the
truth! The thing is—"

"You were a big help," she said. "That's what I was thanking you for
in the letter."

"Hey, I'm glad," I told her. "Here's the thing, though. I'm a Bialystoker Hasid now."

"What's that?"

"It's sort of like a transcendentalist Jew."

"Oh, Sharon!" She turned a little pink.

"It's just who I am right now," I said.

"If it's you," she said, "it's you."

"But the thing is, I need to know about the future. That's why I'm here. I've come to ask your advice."

"My advice?" She sounded surprised. I guess, despite being a crone now, people didn't often seek her out as a person with a lot of wise advice to give.

I told her about my whole predicament. The way I'd changed my life, and how I was involved with Mikhail, but when it came to marriage I didn't know what to do.

So she cocked her head to one side. "Well, I have to say . . . I have to say, and I think you know this about me, when it came to deciding who to marry, I wasn't too terribly successful."

And I said, "I know, but my rebbe said to ask you. . . ."

She wavered a moment. She said, "Well, do you love him?"

"Yes," I admitted.

"Well, that's your answer right there. Isn't it?" she said.

"You loved Dad, right?"

"Well, you know he was an asshole," she said matter-of-factly.

"I know. I know. But originally, at the beginning. You loved him, right?"

"Very much."

Then we both just stood there quietly. Since it was a fact Mom and Dad had loved each other so much once, and then look what happened to them, i.e., my mother the fragile wreck, my dad the pathological provider, et cetera. So I couldn't help thinking, No, *that's* my answer, right there.

LATER, I walked alone down by the wharves, by the whale-watching boats lying high in the water, the *Portuguese Princess, Dolphin Fleet I,* and *Dolphin Fleet II.* It was gray and misty out, and the horns of incoming fishing boats sounded mournfully in the water. Mom had offered to put me up for the night and have my palms read and my cards done, and introduce me to a terrific fortune-teller, but I'd turned her down on all counts. Being a religious Jew, I figured I couldn't make my decisions based on tarot cards, and as for spending the night, remembering the holes Mom had dwelled in before, the newspapers piled up to the ceiling, the rotting fruit, the paths between her piles of bric-a-brac, I was a little bit afraid to accept her hospitality.

It was misty, and my hair hung down damp around my shoulders. I rested on a park bench near the arts-and-crafts huts by the water. A golden retriever was sitting there, too, leash tied to the bench leg, just waiting patiently for his human. He sniffed my backpack, which was full of kosher food from New York.

"I'd give you some, but it's not good for you," I told the dog, whose name, according to his collar, was Sam. "Oh, don't look at me like that." I ruffled the fur on his neck. We were both so down in that misty sea-weather. We were both sitting there so clammy.

He started snuffing me. He licked my hand.

"Hey, you," I said, "don't you think it's always lonelier at the edge of land?"

Lick. Lick.

"Yeah, I'm just really tired. I just came from really far away. I'm far from home. Do you know what I mean?"

Sniff, sniff.

"Well, I guess food is part of home. But also shelter. Also your bed. You know—just that one place you can curl up, and you can chew it up and shed all you want to—that's what I'm talking about."

Sniff.

"Hey, if you were mine, I'd give you the sandwich. I would." I reached over to Sam and put my arms around him. "I wish you were mine."

Not wanting to be rude eating in front of him, I walked all the way down the pier before I ate the lunch Mrs. Karinsky had packed for me: roast beef sandwiches on challah rolls, and plastic containers of what her kids called rubber kugel cut in squares. Mrs. Karinsky packed my lunch, I thought. Yet your mom and dad—they're indelibly in your genes. You couldn't deny that, even if you tried.

The water was gray and deep. The whales out there were all probably just starting to unwind after all those fleets of whale-watching boats. They were all probably just stretching out in the water together enjoy-

ing their quiet time. The whales out there, they understood about family; they lived in pods. The whales, they knew. You could tell from the
bones in their flippers. You could see from those spreading bones like
fingers, they had once been animals on land; they'd looked like wolves
and run in packs. And even when they took to the seas, even when they
were buoyed by the waters and changed their shapes and grew humon-
gously, they swam together, and they sang together, and they were kin.
They lived a communal life. They played and swam and nursed their babies in their big extended aquatic families. They called to each other
through the waters, all the way across the oceans, they recognized each
others' voices. They knew whose voice belonged to whom.

After feeling sorry for myself a good long while, and realizing I
would never be a whale, I went back to the car. What I really need is
just a nice cheap clean motel room, I thought. What I really need is a
shower. What I really need is a good night's sleep. But all I wanted was
Mikhail.

A day later I stood in Brighton in front of a tall dilapidated brick building, and I checked the number with the envelope I was carrying, and I
went inside. The foyer was scuffed-up white and black tile, and the inner door by the mailboxes was propped open with somebody's old
shoe, so I just let myself in and slipped inside the elevator, which was
slow and saggy. Over the years the cables must have lost some of their
bounce. But I made it up to the fourth floor and knocked on number
404, which was Aunt Lena's apartment.

A tiny yet beautiful lady came to the door, and behind her a flood of
light. I saw this big cluttered sunny room and the shining back of
Mikhail's baby grand piano, a swish of light satiny wood.

"Hello," said Aunt Lena.

She was not at all the way I'd imagined her! I'd thought from her
voice that she was about a hundred, and with white hair and rosy
granny cheeks. But actually Aunt Lena was a firecracker, no more than
seventy, and had wavy black hair and makeup, and a plum-colored dress
with gold buttons.

"Hi," I said, "I'm Sharon."

"Yes? You are Sharon!" Lena exclaimed. "Come in, come in. He is teaching. I will get you tea. If you will wait . . . if you will come into the kitchen."

Mikhail looked over the top of the piano, naturally surprised to see me there since I'd never warned him I was coming. He called something to me. Yearningly, he stretched his neck and his whole body toward me, except his arms were down, because he and the little girl next to him were playing "Lightly Row" and what looked like the girl's mother was sitting on the couch waiting. So I went with Lena to the kitchen, which was one of those oblong rooms you get in old brick apartment buildings. It was filled with plants, and tea tins and hanging wire baskets full of onions and potatoes, and apples, and nearly black bananas, and I sat at the table, which was piled with loose-leaf paper, carefully written over in Russian, page after page in heavy black ink, which Lena told me were her memoirs she was working on, and all about how she had come from Russia to New York right after the Second World War and left everything that she had once known and gone into the fashion industry. In a low voice, something of a stage whisper, she told me all about her three husbands, one worse than the next, and what they'd done to her during the marriages, during which she had no children, and how she came to Boston years ago, pursued by a certain gentleman, whom she refused, but who had secured for her this apartment in this rent-controlled building, after which she went into the communications field, working as a translator for Russian patients at the Brigham and Women's Hospital, from which, only two years ago, she had retired.

"To me Mikhail is my adopted son," Lena said. "To me he is my son altogether. His mother wrote to me before she died. She asked me that I sponsor him, and of course this was what I must do. It has not been easy for him," she confided in me.

"Why?"

Her eyes widened in surprise. "Because he is a genius!"

I leaned over to see Mikhail at the piano with the little girl. He was counting as she played. "One, two, three, four. One, two, three, four." On the couch the kid's mother was also somewhat anxiously counting the beats, mouthing, "One, two, three, four. One, two, three, four."

"He has piano students," Aunt Lena said. "It is not a living. Yet there is no support for music in this country. His wife said, no, she will no longer support. Income. Salary. Money. Car, plus insurance. Furniture. What she cared for was earning a living, not for him. She left him—for what?"

"Shallow material things?" I said.

"A timpanist!" Lena spat out the word. She started telling me about this timpanist who had once supposedly been Mikhail's friend, and how he played so-called New Music that had no rhyme or reason, and was the darling of the music department at Harvard, and had a concerto being written just for him—while Mikhail sent tapes yet never succeeded at the competitions, because you see there were so many pianists. Yet there were few timpanists, and he, this so-called friend of Mikhail, took advantage of the fact, and of Mikhail's trust. Mikhail never dreamed anything was going on between his wife, Elise, and John, this so-called musician. But then, just when Elise and John were about to run off together—the piano lesson ended.

MIKHAIL was seeing the little girl and her mother to the door; he was ushering them rather hastily out of the apartment. When they were gone he rushed over to me. "Sharon. *Baruch Hashem,* you're here. You spoke to the rebbe?"

So I told about my audience with the rebbe while Mikhail paced back and forth in the living room with his hands clasped behind his back. And I told him about going to ask my parents for their advice— and their answers being so noncommittal. And detached, I wanted to say. Distant! But somehow I couldn't speak so freely with Aunt Lena in the room. It felt strange trying to tell him all this with his aunt standing there—despite the fact that she'd told me the story of her life, and had started on Mikhail's history too. I said, "I couldn't tell, from what they said, exactly what their answer would be."

"Did you explain to them that this was what the rebbe advised—that you should go to them?" Mikhail asked me.

"But they don't know the rebbe," I said. "They don't really"—my voice dropped lower—"they don't really *care* what he says."

Mikhail looked somewhat offended, standing there in his black trousers and his white shirt with the sleeves rolled up and his black velvet yarmulke on his head.

"It's awful," I confessed. "They don't get how holy the rebbe is. They don't understand the value of his words."

Mikhail put up his hands. "It's enough. It's all right. I understand. What can we say? We can only try. I before did not know from the rebbe either! Time only will tell them who he is."

"Maybe," I said doubtfully.

"Im yirtzeh Hashem," God willing, "in time they will learn and they will know."

"Im yirtzeh Hashem," I said. "But what about—in the meanwhile . . . ?"

"In the meanwhile I will play," he said, and he pulled a chair for me right up to the piano, and he seated me, just as if he were seating me at a grand table for a formal dinner party. He adjusted the bench with the knobs on each side, because he was so much taller than his little piano student. And gently he laid his fingers on the keys. Without music he played one piece after another of Scott Joplin. He played all those Joplin rags, and I'd never heard them played that way before. I'd always heard them tinny and quick and kachinking along like old-time ice-cream-parlor music, but Mikhail played them like so slowly I nearly fell off my chair. He was so sure, and he bent the rhythms in such a way—I'd never realized the "Maple Leaf Rag" could be so sexy. He was beyond good. He was a natural. All over again I felt that mix of joyfulness and awe and jealousy. I was envious of him, so at home in his instrument. But it was just a twist of envy like a twist of lime. When I looked at Mikhail I saw a person who was deep down much more subtle and humorous than I had ever thought. I saw there was magic inside of him. It wasn't grace; it was a smaller magic of Mikhail's own. It was his own self that shone in his eyes; it was his own energy that emanated through his fingertips.

Then he played Debussy for me. He played *Suite Bergamasque* like jazz. The room was starting to fill up, as if vines and plants were opening leaf after leaf. The room was starting to fill as if a twilight lavender had come inside. And I thought, This is better than words; this is better than anything I have ever said, or anyone has ever said to me. But then he stopped.

"Go on."

"Listen."

He played for me the niggun that had come to him. The Sign he had actually received from the third rebbe of Bialystok—which was just a

melody he played out with his right hand. Just a pretty yet plain melody
that sounded to me like all the other nigguns that we Bialystokers
hummed and sang around the Shabbes table. And Mikhail put his hands
down and he hummed. He hummed the niggun just as he said he had
heard it in his ear.

"What do you think?" he asked me.

I looked down at the keyboard. I stared at the silent white and black
keys. "How do you know," I said, "that the niggun was really a sign
from God we had to get married—and not just . . . you know, wishful
thinking?"

Mikhail grinned at me. "I did wish it," he said. "And that is why the
niggun came."

For one long moment I stared at him. I just had to take that in. I had
to catch my breath while all the facts I'd delicately been balancing, like
for example, that although he played like an angel, this guy was living
with his aunt, and had gone nuts at least once in the not-too-distant
past—all those facts came crashing to the ground. Because all at once
Mikhail had told me the one thing I really wanted to know. That he
wanted me underneath everything else—beneath all the signs and miracles, and even the most wonderful Messianic portents—which of
course I absolutely believed, but still. He wanted me in the old way,
older than the old religion. And then the getting-married thing didn't
matter anymore, and the amount of time we'd spent together, and all
the matchmaking. None of it got in the way at all. I thought, He loves
me. He does. And I also thought, Aunt Lena is eavesdropping on us. I
was sure of that. But I didn't really care. Instead I whispered to him, in
such a low voice he had to lean closer to hear. "Okay, but there's just
one thing."

"What is it?"

"I'm sorry for asking. It's just a prejudice I still have. It's just a ves-
tige—do you know what I mean? Left over from my former life. I
know people don't do it in the community. I know it isn't done. Don't
be shocked, okay? Please? I have to kiss you first."

For a second he did look shocked. Then his mouth crinkled up. "You
want to know if I taste like a frog or a prince."

I burst out laughing, just hearing him put it that way.

He leaned closer just a quarter of an inch more, and he kissed me. He put his two hands on my face and he kissed my lips. He kissed me like he played, deliberately, gently, not too fast.

And there wasn't anything between us anymore. Our religious costumes that we wore, our pious language that we spoke, the things that we believed, the innocence that we put on—none of that stood between us. We were just two people, equal seekers, and we understood each other. We really were on the same plane.

So that was how we got engaged. Aunt Lena brought out a bottle of slivovitz, and we each made toasts, and we each drank shots, and Lena said again how Mikhail was a son to her and how she wished him this time everything that he deserved and that we should live a long and happy life and never want for anything, and Mikhail should one day, despite that there was no support for art in this country, achieve recognition for his gifts. She didn't mention my gifts, but I didn't take offense, since I realized naturally, given her age, Lena was going to be thinking more about the man's career, and also she'd just met me. And I said we must drink to the coming of the Moshiach when truth and justice and liberation would all triumph, and Mikhail said, and also when peace would cover the earth. And then Aunt Lena said again, how she had hoped so long for Mikhail to find happiness. And she said, "Sharon, I have burned many many candles for this."

"Really? What do you mean?" I asked.

Mikhail said, "She burns candles for what she hopes from God."

"Wow," I said to Lena, "that's unusual for a Jewish person."

"She is not Jewish," Mikhail said.

My drink went down the wrong way. I started coughing and gagging, and the liquor burned my throat. Mikhail had to thump me on the back. Aunt Lena sat me down and got me water. "Oh," I said. Cough. Cough. Splutter. Cough. "She's not?"

"She is not," Mikhail said.

Aunt Lena shook her head.

I composed myself. I got my breath. "But, wait . . ." I began.

Then Mikhail told me. He began telling me the whole history and explanation of his family, which had some Christian—very pious Christian—people in it. Despite the fact that he and his parents, of blessed memory, were of course Jewish.

"When my sister married Mikhail's father she of course became Jewish," Aunt Lena said. "When she died she gave Mikhail to me, and she said, Lena, he must be raised a Jewish man."

I guess I looked somewhat taken aback. I shook my head at the two of them.

Mikhail said, "Please, I beg you. Do not think worse of me!"

But being over my initial surprise, I said, "Why would I?" I said, "Isn't there room in God's heart for all the religions, whatever people's personal beliefs might be? Isn't believing in itself the most important thing?" I said, "I've learned that, if I've learned anything!"

Mikhail looked so relieved, since to a lot of people—even to his own rebbe, to whom otherwise he would tell everything—he had actually been afraid to mention his aunt's background, because he had the fear that, given their stormy history and theological differences with a lot of Russian Christians, somehow the Bialystokers might not accept him into the bosom of their community if he brought up the subject of his aunt's religious faith.

"That is so sad," I said. "That is so awful to think that we would be prejudiced like that in America," I said. "When any minute the Moshiach will arrive, and anytime now there will be such harmony from all the voices in the world rising up together. Let's drink to that!" I said. Aunt Lena was already pouring another round, and so we raised our glasses, and we did.

And we made more toasts and Mikhail played wedding songs, sacred and secular. He played Hasidishe tunes, and he played Mendelssohn, and a Hawaiian wedding song I hummed for him and he harmonized on the fly, and I wished I'd brought my guitar so I could play along. And then we had lunch, which was omelets that Aunt Lena cooked, and since I had to go return my car and catch my bus, we called the Karinskys and we made plans. First I would go to Brooklyn and get ready, and then Mikhail and Aunt Lena would rent a car and follow, and then a week from Sunday we would be married.

I tell you, when I got back to Brooklyn I was changed. Whereas before I had hemmed and I had hawed, and I had sat up nights ambivalent and melancholy, now this enormous happiness came over me. And I said to myself, Now I am ascending! I am marrying, and I am joining myself to another soul, and completing my arc, and fulfilling my Hasidishe destiny. I thought, here I am rising, I could literally feel myself rising upward, my soul was so light and springy, lifting up like rising bread. Every once in a while I did wonder what Mikhail and I were going to live on, and how we'd all fit in Aunt Lena's apartment, but mostly I thought of his spirit, and how together we would live as Bialystokers in such joy. And I thought of his music, just the way Mikhail played, just the chance to live with someone who had a gift like that (even if the concert world had not yet discovered him). I felt like I'd never have to listen to the radio again. I would never need any other sound.

As far as the wedding went, there weren't any fancy preparations to be made. We were going to have both the ceremony and the reception in the Karinskys' house. There weren't really any invitations to send out, which was good because the wedding was at such short notice. Mainly it was going to be the Karinskys with all the kids and one of their rabbi friends. I kept meaning to invite my parents, but somehow whenever I tried to pick up a phone to call my father, I couldn't think what I would tell him. I rehearsed a thousand conversations in my mind, but in the end I couldn't think what I would say. The words just wouldn't come. As for Mom, I felt guilty being prejudiced, but I didn't feel right having a witch at the ceremony. Witchcraft ran counter to this whole Jewish life I was embarking on. In general, Mom ran counter to everything the Karinskys believed. I figured she would offend them in some way, or make them uncomfortable. I guess I was afraid she would embarrass me. Mrs. Karinsky kept asking about my parents, and telling me she hoped that they would come, and I kept telling her that I was definitely inviting them. In fact I already had invited them, except their health was poor. Except they didn't like to travel. Mrs. Karinsky looked puzzled. I could see she wanted to ask more, but she didn't, which was a relief. I was trying to cut down on my lying, since I was in the process of ascending upward. To be honest, I'd never thought about cutting back on lying before. In all my previous phases, rebirths, et cetera, it had never once occurred to me that lying might be bringing me down. Yet now, being engaged—not only in an altered state but in an altered state along with someone else—lying felt different. It wasn't anonymous anymore. To me lying had always been like an anesthetic, or a little pill you took for privacy, and comfort, and forgetfulness, when it came to talking about your parents. But now I had Mikhail, and he knew me on the inside—as someone dedicated to truth, and love, and the Messianic age. Now I could see myself through Mikhail's eyes, and lying looked like a disgusting habit—just so petty and destructive, just polluting the reality around you. Therefore I was planning to quit, or at least wean myself, as in smoking. As in, just occasional fibs outside.

IN the meantime, Estie came over, and she brought her white wedding gown for me to try on, which cheered me even more. How silly I'd been to think that marriage would dissipate Estie's powers. There she was, as wise as ever, in her married woman's wig, which had bangs that hung down in her eyes. In the girls' bedroom, Estie's old room, I stepped into all that shining white satin of the wedding dress. But the bodice wouldn't button in back. "Whoops!" I said. "It doesn't fit. I hope that's not a bad omen."

"God forbid!" Estie exclaimed. "*Im yirtzeh Hashem* we'll find you another one. There's a whole wedding-dress library, did you know that? My aunt keeps dresses in her basement. Fancy gowns—gorgeous—that brides donate. She lends them to whoever needs. And she has every size."

With the wedding gown gaping in back I sat down on the bed next to Estie. I said, "Estie, I don't really care about a wedding dress. That doesn't matter to me."

"You have to wear a gown!" she exclaimed.

"It's not important," I said.

"But you're a bride!"

"I think, maybe it might be a little bit different for me," I said. "I mean, I'm a lot older."

"It doesn't matter what age," she said. "You need a gown."

"I don't know."

"Why?"

"Maybe it's just not me. I think maybe I'd feel ridiculous," I said, looking down at the swishy tulle surrounding me. "All this white stuff makes me nervous."

"Don't be nervous," Estie said.

"I'm not nervous about the marrying part. It's just the wedding stuff. It's just, you know, the formalities, taking the plunge."

Estie said, "You shouldn't worry, Sharon. It's not that bad. He'll be gentle with you. You'll see."

Then I realized what she was getting at. "No, no, it's not what you're thinking. Not that at all! Estie, I don't want to offend you or anything, but I'm no virgin here."

"Sh!" said Estie, and she put her hand on my arm. Then we looked at each other, and we both began to laugh. We went into complete hysterics. I flopped back on the bed, helpless. Estie kept trying to stop, but then the giggles would rise up in her again. "I don't know what's so funny," she kept protesting, wiping tears from her eyes. We laughed and laughed.

I didn't want to go, but Estie insisted. She took me to the wedding-dress library in her aunt's basement, which was dark, with naked light-bulbs hanging, but fairly dry. Not too dungeonlike. There were several old washing machines and dryers, and utility shelves and cartons pushed to the side. But mainly there were gowns. They were all hanging up in clear plastic dry-cleaning bags, just forests of them on industrial-strength garment racks. And there was a full-length mirror leaning against the wall so you could look at yourself.

So since there weren't any guys around, I just stood there in my slip and bra pulling wedding dresses over my head. Estie's aunt Malka, who was old and spoke Yiddish to Estie, kept pointing me toward these incredibly elaborate dresses all covered with white beads and rosettes and seed pearls on the sleeves and giant bows in back, so when you turned around you looked like a pincushion. I said, "Do you have anything a little more on the simple side?"

"Simple? Simple?" Aunt Malka tisked. "Once only you get married. Once in your life! Here. A gorgeous dress. Gorgeous."

My head was swimming with satin and satin-covered buttons, and crystal beads. I pulled on more and more gowns—one fancier than the next. Until at last, when I was worn out to the point that I could protest no longer, I tried on a monster that didn't just have beads and seed pearls, it had whole seedpods on it. The bodice and the sleeves were stiff—in fact the whole thing was so encrusted with gewgaws, the dress probably could have stood up by itself. And it came with a headpiece so puffed up on top, Cher might have worn it at one time. "This!" Aunt Malka declared. "This fits!"

She looked at Estie, and Estie agreed.

There I was in the mirror like some strange mannequin. Actually, like some very covered-up, very modest showgirl. No cleavage, no legs, no wrists, just solid glitz.

"This is one hundred percent!" said Aunt Malka. "*This* is a bride!"

I said, "Okay. Fine."

Aunt Malka turned on me. "If it is not one hundred percent, I would not say. This is my rule. Not only it should fit. Also it should look one hundred percent. Now I see. Now you are a bride. Out, out," she said, meaning I should step out of the gown. Estie was unbuttoning me in back. "Now we wrap." She put the dress on a padded hanger. She fluffed it up and stuck tissue paper in the sleeves and bodice and then she zipped it and the headpiece into a long plastic garment bag, and she said, "Mazel tov. Wear it in good health. Bring back after the wedding." She kissed me on both cheeks.

THE night before the wedding Estie and I went to the women's mikveh, which was a plain little brick building with pools of fresh water housed inside. There was a changing room with a shower, and Estie waited outside on a bench. I took off my clothes, and I felt for a minute like, where's my swimsuit? But the mikveh pool wasn't exactly like your local Y. You went into the water completely nude, and instead of laps in the pool you plunged down deep and submerged yourself, every bit of you, so you could get spiritually cleansed.

I showered, cut my nails, shaved my legs. I combed my hair straight down my back, and when I was done I had to stand in front of a lady named Mrs. Burstein, who was the mikveh lady, and she checked I wasn't wearing jewelry or anything on my body at all. She looked me up and down. She started back when she saw my tattoo, the earth on my belly. I guess that was not what she was expecting. Still, she didn't say anything.

Mrs. Burstein held a towel around me for privacy when I got into the pool room. But also—and this cracked me up—she put a washcloth on top of my head—like I should be modest somehow, and cover my hair, even while I was stark naked!

I started down the steps into the mikveh. My body was pale from wearing clothes, a far cry from those days when I was all tan, top to bottom, those years in Molokai when I was brown all over. I looked down at myself and I saw my stomach spread wide and round. I had hefty thighs. Just as well my bikini days were done.

I moved out into the center of the chest-high water, and I stood in the center of the tepid pool. Then, when Mrs. Burstein gave me the signal, I went under for the first time. I dunked down all the way in the water without touching the sides or bottom of the pool. I kept my eyes open, and my nose open, and my legs open, and the water entered into me, every orifice and every pore, and I prayed. I wished and wished. Oh, God, please come into me like this water. God, please cleanse me. Heal me. Change me from the inside out. God, just like once you made me beautiful—now could you make me good?

When I got out, my mikveh lady looked really alarmed. She started tisking me and draping towels all over me, and telling me, "I was worrying about you! I was afraid of calling nine-one-one about you!"

"Why? What did I do wrong?" I asked her.

"So long! So long you were underwater!"

I told Mrs. Burstein the truth. "I wished I could have stayed forever."

"What? Under there?"

I saw she might be taking what I said the wrong way. "Listen," I told her, "don't worry about me." I kept trying to reassure that mikveh lady: "One thing I can do. I can swim."

THE day of the wedding it poured. Mikhail and Lena were supposed to arrive in the morning, but they must have got stuck on the interstate in the storm. Rain streamed down the windows and drummed the roof. The water washed the streets and pooled up in the potholes. It was nasty out, but I didn't mind. In fact, I thought, This is good, all this water coming down. This is cleansing. I thought, Let this rain wash away the bad. Let this rain dissolve all the past. I sat near the window in the living room and watched the rain streaming, and I felt happy because I was still rising up, and my being was growing. Meanwhile, Mrs. Karinsky had one of the kids pick up a big sheet cake from the bakery. No second or third tiers or anything like that, just lots of white goopy frosting. We stuck it up on top of the fridge, because the kids kept putting their fingers in it. I vacuumed, and we pushed all the living room furniture off to the side of the room. A neighbor friend who was also a rabbi came over from across the street with the ketubah, which was the marriage contract, but since Mikhail wasn't there yet we couldn't get started, so he went back to his house in his raincoat and his rubber overshoes. Just like the men in Jerusalem, he had clear plastic wrapping his black felt hat.

The afternoon wore on. And then finally Mikhail called, and he told me they were having car trouble. They had borrowed a car from Aunt Lena's friend, but it was an older car and Aunt Lena's friend was older as well, so it turned out she hadn't driven it for a couple of years. Now Mikhail had got the car running, but they couldn't stop for fear the thing wouldn't start again. Mikhail was calling from a pay phone in Connecticut while Aunt Lena sat in the car with the engine running. So they'd be a few more hours. "I'm sorry, Sharon," he said.

"Don't sweat it," I told him. "I'll still be here." I was feeling so cheerful.

It was starting to get dark, and Mrs. Karinsky was starting to look a little bit unhappy, because I think the kids were getting on her nerves, all on top of each other in the house, and it was more than a few hours and Mikhail still hadn't shown, yet he didn't call again. Mrs. Karinsky said something in Yiddish to the doctor and it sounded like "Where the hell is he?" but I couldn't tell for sure, since I didn't know the language.

"Feige, Feige," the doctor said, meaning don't be such a worrier.

I myself wasn't worried at all. I knew Mikhail would come eventually. I didn't bother getting into the wedding dress. I figured I'd leave it till the last minute, because it was so uncomfortable. Instead I built block towers for the kids and they knocked them down. And I talked to Estie when she walked over the second time. I sat with her at the kitchen table while Mrs. Karinsky was putting up dinner, and we talked about *bashert*, your intended. And I said, "Even if you have a feeling the other person might be your *bashert*, I still think it makes sense to find out some more about him."

"Of course," Estie said. "I agree."

"That's why I had to go to Brighton," I said. "I had to see where he lived; I had to understand where he was coming from, you know? It's because I wasn't born a Bialystoker. See, you're used to it," I said, "being fixed up for life. I mean, marrying a guy you don't even know."

"Yitzy and I knew each other since we were three years old," Estie said.

"Seriously?" I was shocked.

"His sister made the match," she said. "His sister Leah—because she's my best friend."

Almost for explanation I looked over at Mrs. Karinsky at the counter, but she didn't turn around; she just kept grappling with her half-frozen chickens. I was so surprised by this. It was just so different from what I had thought. "You mean you—sort of—*liked* him? From before?"

Estie giggled nervously.

"Wow," I said. "I thought it was just me; I thought it was just my old culture—wanting to know him better before I got engaged. But the thing is, now I do know. I know about his music. He's a genius! I had no idea before. I could hear it as soon as he started playing; he's going to make it. He's got the stuff. And I know the details of how his wife actually drove him nuts, and I know all about his family on both sides—the Christians and the Jews. . . ."

Then Mrs. Karinsky did turn around.

"The Christians!" Estie shrieked. Her eyes widened.

For a moment I couldn't even speak. It was as if accidentally I'd dropped a hand grenade right there on the kitchen table. Catastrophe!

"What do you mean?" Mrs. Karinsky asked in a dreadful voice.

"A few members of his family back in Russia were—Christians," I said.

"A few members? Who?" Mrs. Karinsky exclaimed, and she stood there with the cold plastic bag of chicken giblets in her hand. "Who?"

"Well, like his aunt."

"His aunt? Oh, my God," she cried. She tossed the giblet bag onto the counter. She went running to get the doctor. I heard her banging down the stairs into the basement office. I heard her calling, "Mendy! Mendy!"

"But his parents were Jewish," I said to Estie.

She looked at me with terrified eyes. "This is a horrible mistake! Sharon, what's happening?"

Breathing hard, Mrs. Karinsky came in from the hall, and Dr. Karinsky behind her.

"Sharon, what did he say about his family?" Dr. Karinsky asked me.

His jovial manner was gone. He was sad and gentle and cautious. He had the look of a doctor about to tell bad news.

"Which side of the family is this aunt?" Mrs. Karinsky asked at the same time. She was practically wringing her hands. Her whole face was full of woe.

So I started telling them, all about his aunt and how she'd practically adopted Mikhail when her sister died.

"Her sister!" Mrs. Karinsky turned away like she was going to be sick. "Her sister was Mikhail's mother!"

"I guess so," I said.

"But no one knew," she said to the doctor. "He said nothing of this, or God forbid, he lied."

"Let Sharon tell," Dr. Karinsky said.

"*Veyismere,*" she groaned.

And I was trying to tell everything I remembered about Mikhail's family, but the whole time Mrs. Karinsky was sighing, and Estie was shaking her head like she couldn't believe her ears, and whenever I tried to comfort them and tell them that to me this wasn't such a big deal, I'd set off a new flood of moans and groans—and any kid who tried to come into the kitchen was screamed at so harshly he ran away as fast as he could—which is why we didn't even realize Mikhail and Lena had finally arrived. None of the children got a chance to tell us.

It was such a scene when Mikhail peeked in the kitchen door. Mrs. Karinsky was carrying on, and the doctor acted as though there were a death in the family. It was such a scene of tragedy, you never would have guessed we were about to have a wedding.

"I'm sorry," Mikhail said, first thing, when he saw everyone's faces.

"They're not happy," I said.

"We should have rented," he said.

"No, it's not that. It's not the car." All of a sudden I felt like crying myself. The Karinskys were so beside themselves, they were starting to get to me. I looked at Mikhail and I wanted to run to him and bury my head in his black frock coat, but I was trapped in the kitchen, with Estie at the table and her mom and dad practically blocking the open doorway.

"We must talk to you, Mikhail," said Dr. Karinsky sorrowfully.

"All right," Mikhail said. He still did not know what was the matter.

So he followed the doctor down the stairs to the office. I wished I could fling myself down the stairs after them, but I was left with Estie and a hysterical Mrs. Karinsky, and poor Aunt Lena, who was sitting all dressed up on the living room sofa, and not exactly receiving much of a welcome after her car trip! So I got Aunt Lena some ice coffee and I admired her crimson suit, and all the while Dr. Karinsky was giving Mikhail what for. So after about fifteen minutes I couldn't stand it any longer. I said, "I'm going down there. This is ridiculous!"

I went down to the office, which was where Dr. Karinsky did the books for his practice and kept his files with colored tabs on shelves. And there on the wall was a bulletin board with school pictures tacked up of his children in all their years of school. A row of pictures for each of his ten children showing the progression from nursery on up. And there on one side of his desk was a bookcase with his thick medical books in red and royal-blue bindings, and on the other side a bookcase with his holy books bound in black with gold letters on the spines. All over the office were humorous paperweights and coffee mugs, yet the atmosphere when I walked in was not exactly jovial. Mikhail was standing in front of Dr. Karinsky's desk looking red, you couldn't tell from embarrassment or just from being angry, and the doctor's lips were pursed, and he also looked quite huffy.

I said, "Dr. Karinsky, please, please, don't take this the wrong way. We know what we're doing, and I promise you that we are Jewish people. It's not like we're some kind of sheltie dogs at the kennel club. His parents were Jewish, so what more do you want?"

And Dr. Karinsky said, "Sharon, now he says his mother converted."

"So what?" I said.

"So how she converted is a very serious matter. What kind of conversion and where and when are very important to find out. And not to know anything about this until now ..." He looked at Mikhail. "That is something I do not understand."

"It is my fault," Mikhail said. "I take responsibility. Yet my mother died many years ago, and I may tell you that I love Judaism."

"Isn't that the key?" I appealed to Dr. Karinsky. "Isn't it what you feel in your heart that ultimately really matters?"

"Please, Sharon. Let us—Feige and I—speak to you alone," Dr. Karinsky told me.

So Mikhail was banished upstairs now, and Mrs. Karinsky came down—all so I could be harangued. Mrs. Karinsky was begging me to wait and stay, and unpack my things, and Dr. Karinsky was telling me about the vital importance of conversions, and they had to be the right kind. And Mrs. Karinsky was saying, "It is the mother, it is only through the mother, a child may become a Jew!"

"This disease, this intermarriage, is infecting, it is diminishing, the Jewish people," Dr. Karinsky told me.

"But Mikhail and I aren't intermarrying," I said. "We're two Jewish people. We are. We're just marrying each other. The rest is just technicalities," I said.

"Technicalities!" Mrs. Karinsky exclaimed.

"Sharon," said Dr. Karinsky, "if his mother did not have a proper conversion, then she was not Jewish. And if she was not Jewish, then Mikhail is not either."

"God willing we will find proof," Mrs. Karinsky said fervently. "Then there will be no problem."

I looked at the two of them. "You want me to wait for some kind of document search?" I asked them.

"Yes," Dr. Karinsky said.

"Isn't there any other way?" my voice wobbled.

"Of course, Mikhail can convert." Mrs. Karinsky brightened a little.

"Convert? To his own religion?"

"He could go before the *bais din*," Dr. Karinsky said, meaning the rabbinical court.

"And how long will that take?"

"Maybe only six months!"

"Oh, no. No! We're not going to wait that long! See, this is the thing. I know I'm going to marry him. We can't help it. Because it turns out he's my *bashert*. We were destined to find each other; that isn't even our choice. And this paperwork, and conversions—I'm sorry. I just don't see it. I just can't see God being so literal minded. All I can see is Mikhail's Jewish, no matter who his mother was. He loves being a Jew. He has a *Yiddishe neshama*."

"But it is not a question of how he perhaps feels," Dr. Karinsky exclaimed. "It is a question of the future. The generations to come. It is a question of whether every year and every day through marriages like

this we weaken and dilute our Jewish people, little by little diluting until there is nothing left!"

"Why is marrying Mikhail a dilution?" I pleaded with him. "Why is
dilution bad, anyway?" I burst out. "Haven't you ever heard of homeop-
athy? The point is, he is my *bashert*."

"We must find out about the conversion," Dr. Karinsky said.

"To me it doesn't make a difference," I told him.

"Without knowing, there is no ketubah," Dr. Karinsky said, meaning
the marriage contract. "Without the ketubah there is no wedding." His
voice was one of laying down the law. He asked me how could any
wedding happen in these circumstances. He asked me how could this
be accomplished if Mikhail's mother had truly been a Christian. Or if,
God forbid, Mikhail under false pretenses had pretended he was someone he was not, then, then . . . Dr. Karinsky couldn't even say what.

Quietly, I walked upstairs. I no longer felt my *Yiddishe neshama* rising
upward. I was just flummoxed. If I had been one of the Karinskys'
daughters, no question I would go upstairs and do as I was told. Of
course, if I had been one of their daughters I never would have been in
such a pickle. They were, to continue that deli metaphor, a whole different kettle of fish. Yet I knew I could not do as I was told. That was the
amazing thing. I had lived in this house for all these weeks, and studied
in Bellevue, and strived so hard, and yet inside of me I was myself. I
didn't really have that strict *frum* heart I admired so much. My regular
old wild heart was still beating inside of me. I was still, after all these
years, and my mistakes, and seeming to know better, going to do what I
wanted. Quietly I went up to Mikhail. I shook my head and said, "It's
no use. Arguing about it just isn't going to be constructive anymore.
Come on," I said. "It's time to go."

Aunt Lena's friend's Buick stood moored in the driveway like an ark
in the rain, and when Lena and Mikhail and I dashed out there with my
stuff we all got soaked. Aunt Lena got into the backseat and she was
telling us that she might have some letters at home from her sister that
would explain all the mysteries, and that we might read them, and also
her own recollections and impressions of her sister that she had written
in her memoir. And Mikhail and I went back to the house and stood
dripping in the entryway and apologized many times for breaking
everyone's heart and for falling in love before we got married, and go-

ing perhaps more by the spirit than the letter of the law when it came to Judaism. And Estie was crying and blaming herself for everything— for bringing me to New York in the first place.

And then all of a sudden I looked at Estie, my teacher, and guru, and child-goddess, and I said, "Estie, you're a good kid. You didn't do anything wrong." I'd realized that, all of a sudden. Estie was just a kid. It wasn't a feeling of disillusionment. It wasn't one of those moments of triumphant debunkment like pulling the curtain open and finding the great and terrible Oz is just a little old man. It was just me finally calming down. It was just me feeling all my Hasidic excitations melting away. My imagination that had been so fevered and dervishy was finally taking a little break, and it was so quiet inside of me. So peaceful.

Hello, I heard.

Who's that?

Just me, I heard. It is I.

Is that me? Hey, it's good to hear your voice.

Yet while I was getting in touch with my inner pronouns, Mrs. Karinsky was shaking her head, her lips twisting in anguish.

"Aren't these things all fictions?" I said to her. "These rules that humans make up to regulate themselves?"

"When the Moshiach comes such artificial distinctions will have no place," said Mikhail.

"You'll see. All the wrinkles will be ironed out!" I said.

Dr. Karinsky was aghast. That unmarried, I would even think of going away with someone. I almost couldn't look at him, because of his sorrow. I knew what the Karinskys were thinking. Haven't you learned anything? Is this how you thank us? Is this how you act, after all our teaching? I could see it in their eyes. Such betrayal. Yet, ultimately, Mendy and Feige blamed themselves. I was taking off to Boston with this guy of murky provenance. So they thought they had failed. And maybe, looking back, that was the greatest difference between us. To the Karinskys breaking away and leaving was a tragedy, but to me it was just the opposite. Not that I liked to say good-bye, not that I didn't miss people, but to me, deep down, leaving had always been a happy thing.

20

—

Flight

AFTER we eloped, we went into a flurry getting Aunt Lena's friend's car towed most of the way back to Boston, organizing our blood tests and marriage license, me getting a job, us all settling into the apartment, and dealing with our general euphoria. What I remember is Mikhail's narrow room and his narrower bed, and sometimes rolling off, except there was always laundry on the floor to break the fall, so a lot of times you didn't wake up. Softly we made love. Softly, we fell off the bed. Since we'd been such religious Hasids, we didn't even dream of using birth control, yet we were flabbergasted at how fast I got pregnant. We felt so lucky, we could hardly believe it. I'd assumed when you were almost forty, babies were something you had to work on. I'd figured by this time all my eggs were getting kind of old. Yet there we were, expecting a child in September. I'd wake up in the morning so glad, and not even knowing why—and then it would all come back to me! There was Mikhail squished next to me in bed, and there was that baby inside me bouncing around where you couldn't see.

I went off every day to work at Fresh Squeezed on Com Ave, where I was a juice technician preparing power protein shakes and smoothies with fresh wheat grass that we grew right there in the store—we had our own little patch. I went off every morning and opened up the place, which included me having my own blueberry banana drink with zinc, and then serving our customers (with guidance from my boss, who was a licensed herbalist), which could mean anything from a quick shake to diagnostic queries about their physical and spiritual states, so that every night when I came home I pretty much had to lie down, I was so tired from being pregnant, and working so hard and learning so much, and I'd come up the stairs and be aching to lie horizontal on the couch, except Mikhail would have a student in the living room, and Aunt Lena would be in the kitchen talking on the phone in Russian to her friends, so I'd have to lie on our bed and listen to scales until finally the piano student would leave and the next one, too, and Aunt Lena would get off the phone and maybe even go out, and then Mikhail would come.

"Sharon!" he would say, so happily. And he'd rub my bare feet with his hands. He would knead the balls of my feet, and roll his knuckles over my arches until I just sighed, it felt so good after standing up all day, and then he'd take off my clothes and rub the rest of me and I'd lie still, not even whispering, because Mikhail's ears ached from teaching piano all afternoon. We'd lie there on the narrow bed, nursing my feet and his ears, rubbing our bodies up and down, just throbbing. Our days would disappear. We couldn't even say anymore who we had seen or what we had done, because we could not remember.

It was that newly wedded time when there are so many plans and schemes in your head, and you are so full of the future that at night, even when you are done with each other, you can barely sleep. Because we were busy cooking and trying to figure out what teensy unborn babies liked to eat. And I was studying my books of herbal remedies. Mikhail was entering more competitions. He was taping his recital programs in studios and sending out the tapes to all the piano competitions so that he would be discovered. We were filling out the forms in black ink, and mailing the packages and entrance fees. That was already heady stuff, sending away to be discovered like that. And then there was me, getting started on a career in herbalism under the mentorship of my boss, who was a young kid named Telemachus Cohen, whose parents were a pair of famous herbalists well known in the community and who were funding the Fresh Squeezed venture. Telemachus Cohen was planning to franchise his company nationwide, and I was going to own and

operate one of the pilot stores once we branched out. This dude
Telemachus was about twenty-five and had long pre-Raphaelite hair
that he tied back in a ponytail. We both tied back our hair to keep it out
of the drinks. He was something of what I would call a natural philoso-
pher. He took everything in stride. It was as if whatever life dealt him
he would accept with total calm—and, since life had never dealt him
anything bad so far, he went about his business with perfect serenity. He
had tanned skin, and dark brown eyes, almost black. He was a walker
and a hiker and biker, and he had thick thick calves, the thickest I'd ever
seen. I wondered sometimes if I could even half span them with my
hands, but I never did. That was being married.

Being married was such a solemn happy state. I'd never thought those
two words went together, but with marriage they did. When you were
married you thought about the present moment, but you also thought
about the future—so that was happiness and solemnity together. When
you were married you just did not act on every idea or desire that came
over you. You tended to come home to your husband and act out your
desires on him. He would play Debussy like jazz. Then the two of you
would pray together standing in the narrow shoe-box bedroom facing
east. You would say all the evening prayers together in Hebrew. *"Baruch
atah, adonoi, elohenu melach haolam, asher bidvaro maariv, aravim."* Blessed
art thou, Lord our God, King of the universe, who at thy word bringest
on the evenings." You said all the words by heart, and you thought, God,
give us more days just like this one. Whereas before you might pray for
someone or something new to come along, now you were praying for
everything to stay just the same.

Only slowly, like water slowly seeping, the outside world slipped in. It
was winter, and we had no place of our own to go. Not that we didn't
love Aunt Lena, but we wished we could get away from her for a while.
We were living like a couple of teenagers in her apartment, waiting all
the time for her to leave. We were always waiting for her to go see some
friends or go to church or to the store. If the weather had been warmer
we might at least have gone for walks outside, and sat on park benches
and talked, but now already the snow was coming down, and the freezing rain. I have to say the weather was a nasty shock. It was my first
winter in twenty years. I'd forgotten how much time you had to spend
indoors. And if you wanted to go out, you couldn't go anywhere for

free. You had to go for coffee or ice cream, or at least for tea. And we didn't have the money to go out all the time like that. We had no money at all, since all our earnings were going toward taping Mikhail's recital program for those piano competitions he was entering. The best we could do was go to Brookline Booksmith and stand around and browse the parenting books in the aisles. Mikhail felt bad because he loved books and we could not afford to buy them. If we saw a great new book we got on a waiting list to take it out from the library. Still, we were hopeful that when the competitions came through our lives would change for the better. We used to say that to each other all the time, when the piano store would call and pester about late payments on the baby grand piano.

"Hey, I got you, babe," I would tell Mikhail, and he'd give me a blank look—since, coming from Russia, the Sonny and Cher reference escaped him.

Our only real sorrow was Mikhail's rebbe. This great and gentle rabbinical man, who had been Mikhail's spiritual guide for over two years, had really cooled toward Mikhail since he'd found out Mikhail's Jewish heritage was a little bit murkier than Mikhail had originally let on. Mikhail's rebbe just could not get over the fact that Mikhail's mother had converted to Judaism, and that Mikhail had never mentioned this, or provided all the documents to prove the conversion's authenticity. We would come to the Bialystoker services, and Mikhail's rebbe, who was called the Boston Bialystoker, and had once been so kind and outreaching to Mikhail—he would just look right past the two of us as if we didn't exist. The Boston Bialystoker was portly, and middle aged, with a salt-and-pepper beard in the same style as the rebbe's beard in New York, but his black eyes never twinkled. Or at least they never twinkled at me. The one time Mikhail tried to introduce me to his former teacher, the rebbe only knit his brow and turned away. Of course no one in the congregation warmed to us as a couple, either, given that their spiritual leader would barely look at us. They'd tolerate us in their midst at services, but that was all.

Every time he went to pray at the Bialystoker *shtiebel,* which was their house of worship, Mikhail would emerge more and more depressed. The corners of his mouth would droop. His whole body would sag; he would actually grow shorter by the time services were over. One day as we trudged home with the slush coming in at the seams of our shoes, I turned to Mikhail and I saw him with his head ducked down inside his hood and his face tight against the cold and his whole body hunched over like he was in pain. "Mikhail!" I said. "You're shrinking! Your whole being is shrinking from all this. I can't let you go to the *shtiebel* anymore. This is not working for you."

"I must go, Sharon," he said.

"No! You go in happy and you come out sad. You go in tall and you come out short. Is that what praying is all about? Praying is about joy! It's about love! It's about expansion! If it doesn't come as naturally as leaves on a tree, then you shouldn't go at all!" I said, paraphrasing the great poet John Keats.

We got to the vestibule of our old brick building. I swung the outer glass door open. We rushed inside and shut the door behind us. We were out of the cold. We could unsnap our hoods. "You hear me?"

He sighed. "Where else can I go?"

"Somewhere else!" I said. "We'll go together somewhere else!" But even I wasn't sure where that would be.

We trudged up the stairs to the apartment, and Aunt Lena was in the living room playing cards with her best friend, Natalya, and there were newspapers piled up in stacks on the living room floor. Aunt Lena had probably a year's worth just of *The Boston Globe.* They made me nervous, because to me they looked like a fire hazard. I wanted to take them downstairs to the recycling bins, but she wouldn't let me. Aunt Lena just liked having a lot of newspapers around. So there she was with her friend playing cards, and we came in and she tisked us for tracking slush into the apartment, and we meekly wiped our shoes on the mat, and Mikhail went into the kitchen and saw the mail there piled on the table, along with Aunt Lena's various writings—her correspondence and memoirs and literary papers. "Sharon!" he said. There it was—a letter from the Polish Chopin competition that he had entered. I recognized it right away, since it was my handwriting on the envelope. It was one of those self-addressed jobbies with a foreign postal order for a stamp. Of course it occurred to me, Hmm, that letter looks thin, but I held the thought in. I didn't want anything negative to escape me. I didn't even want to breathe the wrong way on the envelope.

Mikhail opened it up and read it and then put it down on the table. He looked not so much disappointed, as bewildered. The folks at the Chopin competition didn't want him to come out to Kraków. They didn't want to hear him play. It was such a strange incomprehensible thing. It was one of those senseless tragedies. It was like choking to death on a fish bone. People didn't want to hear Mikhail play Chopin. Mikhail couldn't understand it. I couldn't understand it. Aunt Lena was dumbfounded. When Natalya left, we discussed the letter over and over together, the three of us. All that night we talked about it, Aunt Lena and I on the couch. Mikhail pacing up and down. Why, oh, why did they refuse to hear Mikhail play? Why did they shy away from the chance to hear him? It was like having an opportunity to drink the elixir of life—the little crystal vial held out to your lips—and then saying, thanks, but no thanks.

Finally Aunt Lena had to conclude it was anti-Semitism, plain and simple. "Your name," she told Mikhail. "They saw your name, Mikhail Abramovich. They saw that you were Jewish."

"But why would the judges care if he was Jewish?" I asked her.

"It's the *Polish* Chopin competition," she said. "What do you think?" She turned to Mikhail and she said, "You need a name."

"I have a name," he said.

"A stage name," she told him. "All performers have a name for the stage. You are American. You need an American name. *Michael*. Not Mikhail. Abramo*witz*. Not Abramovich."

"Michael Abramowitz?" I asked.

"That is an American name," Aunt Lena said.

"Abramowitz?"

"It has to be with a -witz," she insisted. "Berkowitz, Kantowitz, Horo-witz . . ."

"I will not change my name," Mikhail said.

"Then you will never win," Aunt Lena said.

All of a sudden Mikhail got angry. "Did Yehudi Menuhin change his name? Did Jascha Heifetz?"

"Heifetz!" Aunt Lena shrieked, as if to say QED! "With an –itz!"

"Did Arthur Rubinstein?" Mikhail demanded. "Did Gil and Orly Shaham? Did Yo-Yo Ma? Does Yo-Yo Ma call himself Joe-Joe Moskowitz?"

"He doesn't have to change his name," Aunt Lena said.

"And why not?"

"Because," she said, "he is Yo-Yo Ma."

She was a little bit of a conspiracy theorist. She had a touch of paranoia in her makeup. She believed that Mikhail was doomed to obscurity because he was Jewish and because he did not have the right politics to become a concert pianist. We refused to believe her. We refused to let her get us down. Yet now more and more of our self-addressed stamped envelopes were returning to us. One after another the competitions were sending back letters, and not a single one wanted Mikhail. Not a single panel of judges wanted to hear him in person. He couldn't even come and play in the first round. Hour after hour I would listen to Mikhail play. I was trying to find some answer or some clue. To me Mikhail sounded exactly like the angels must play piano up in heaven. And I had never been a huge fan of classical music before. I had never sat transfixed listening to Debussy and Satie and Joplin and Chopin before. But maybe that was the answer. Mikhail didn't play like a classical musician. Whatever he played, he made it swing. Whatever waltz or rag or gymnopaedia he took on, he bent the rhythm a little bit and lushed out the phrases. He made it bloom up around your ears in an unbelievably sexy way. And I didn't figure this out at the time. But now I realize what was really happening with his tapes when those piano judges listened to them in their dark judging room. They put on Mikhail and all of a sudden from the first notes they sensed this sensuality about him. They sat up straight in their chairs, five white males, and they said, but, no, no, this cannot be. They said to one another, "We cannot accept this one. I sense in his performance a whiff—good heavens—a whiff of the *popular*." That's what they said. What was actually happening was that Mikhail's playing turned those judges on, and they couldn't stand it. I see that now—although at the time I could not imagine what was happening.

It was the end of January and we'd spent all our money on the competitions. One hundred twenty dollars an hour just for the studio time, and then fifty dollars per hour for the cameraperson—since Mikhail had to be videotaped, so the judges could see that he was actually the one playing the music. And that was a special rate Mikhail got for the videotaping—since the cameraperson was an old friend of his! We couldn't make our contributions to the rent, or buy food, or clothes, or anything, so we had to depend more than ever on Aunt Lena, which most of the time she took pretty well, but in the long term was not so great for our relationship with her. She tended to snap at us about all kinds of little things, and we'd have no recourse but to go to our room and sulk like kids. It was terrible how quickly we were disenfranchised. All of a sudden we were trying to figure out some way to buy just a little bit of dignity back. I sold all my old tapes and records at a used music store on Harvard Street. I took my precious collection I'd brought with me from Hawaii, and I sold them off. Mikhail tried to talk me out of it, but I said, "It's okay, I don't need them anymore."

Then he sent his black frock coat and his good black felt hat, and all his black slacks, to a Hasidic consignment store in Brooklyn. He had to wear jeans and T-shirts after that. He wore an oatmeal-colored sweater with raggedy cuffs and a green embroidered Bokharan cap I'd got him for his birthday. I wore jeans, too, that relaxed-fit style, since I'd started expanding at the waist. We didn't look like Hasids anymore, but, oh, well. We didn't go to the Bialystoker *shtiebel* anymore either.

"Your energy is way down," Telemachus told me at work.

"Down!" I said. "I'm running on empty. You don't even know, Telemachus." When I first started working for him, I'd found it strange using that whole Homeric name all the time, yet now I hardly noticed. You just yelled, "Hey, Telemachus!" and you didn't think anything of it.

"What's going on?" he said.

"We're broke, Mikhail can't even get a toe in the door, and our rebbe has completely turned his back on us," I said. We were standing there in the roar of the juicers, and our customers were straggling in with their rotten winter colds. It was a miserable gray day and every time the door opened you flinched from the bitter draft. All our customers were coming up and asking for citrus with extra C, and hacking all over the counter, and blowing their noses into soggy tissues. "I'm sure I'm going to catch a cold," I said bitterly.

"Hey," said Telemachus, "if you say you're going to catch one, then you are. It's up to you to decide. If you're broke, I can't do anything, since I don't have the revenues to pay you any more than I already do. And I'm sorry about Mikhail's toe. But if your rebbe has abandoned you, why don't you come to our Brighton Havurah?"

THE second Shabbat in February we made our way to Telemachus's apartment, where the Havurah was meeting. The Havurah was a group that came together every other week at different people's homes to hold potluck

Shabbat services. Potluck, Telemachus told me, didn't just mean everyone brought a different vegetarian dish to share for lunch, but also that everyone should bring some spiritual contribution to share with the group as well. So this was a matter of some confusion for Mikhail, since he'd only really been exposed to the Hasidic branch of Judaism, where you concentrated on the liturgy that was already there in the prayer book and you didn't add new material to the regular service. Mikhail wasn't even sure he wanted to go to a service that wasn't based on a fixed text. I was kind of dragging him up the stairs. I had him in one hand, and our side dish in the other. A great big plastic bowl of wild rice salad with dried cranberries that I'd thrown together from what I remembered of Kathryn's recipe. I'd had to whip up our prayer by myself as well—which I kind of minded, but I didn't grumble to Mikhail, because he was feeling so low.

We got to Telemachus's apartment, which was in a much newer, cleaner building than ours, and he ushered us into his living room, which had beautiful soft sand-colored wall-to-wall carpet. Telemachus's girlfriend, Chris, was there greeting everyone really politely and graciously. She was not at all what I'd imagined his girlfriend would look like. She was so small and scrubbed, and she had blond hair tousled just so. She probably even shaved her legs. I guess I'd expected the woman Telemachus had lived with for three years to be more au naturel. But she introduced us to everybody, and put our wild rice salad on the table with all the other foil-covered bowls and platters. And then we sat on the carpet in a circle.

"Shalom," Telemachus said in his perfectly Zen-like way. He had a real gift. He had such peace inside of him. Then he reached behind him and he pulled out a guitar.

That was a shock. When we were Bialystokers Mikhail and I never went to services with instrumental music. It just wasn't done, because all Jews were in mourning for the loss of the Temple. We could only pray with our voices, and no musical accompaniment. Guitars were absolutely verboten. So there was that initial prickle in our stomachs when we saw Telemachus's guitar. Mikhail and I looked at each other for an instant in fear. Yet we didn't get up to leave. Softly Telemachus started playing. Softly everyone began to sing.

> Hinei mah tov umanayim
> Shevet achim gam yachad.

And the English version:

> *Nothing on earth could be better*
> *Than brothers and sisters together.*

Then an older gray-haired lady took half the circle, and Telemachus took the other half, and we sang a round. Then Chris took a quarter of the circle, and the old lady took a quarter of the circle, and Telemachus took a quarter, and a bosomy girl in a low-cut T-shirt took the last quarter, and we did a four-part round. And softly, softly, we sang until the last notes died away—or rather, the last stragglers in the round finally made it to the end. And there was silence, and we all sat still. There was a beautiful gentle stillness.

Telemachus was about to speak when another humming could be heard, and it came from Mikhail! He was rocking gently back and forth and humming out a strange melody, intricate and in a minor key. It was in the style of a Bialystoker niggun, but just when I thought I had it pegged it changed. Everyone sat rapt listening to Mikhail. He closed his eyes. Back and forth, gently, gently, he was rocking. A new niggun was coming to him. He was actually right there before us receiving the transmission of a new niggun! Gradually the tune began to coalesce. Gradually the wordless syllables came together in a pattern. *Ay die Ay die aaayyy aayyy, daydie daydie Daaaay Dayyy.* The other people in the circle began to follow. Other people started closing eyes. Then Telemachus picked up the notes on his guitar. Everyone was humming together; everyone was adding and embellishing. Telemachus and Chris were humming the niggun in descant. And I have to say the rest of the service had its ups and downs. When it came to dialogue, some of the people in that group were incredibly long-winded—not to mention positive that only they had the key to Biblical exegesis, so only their opinions were right! But at that moment in that wordless song, I could feel something I hadn't felt in a long long time. I could feel the presence of the divine. God was there in that niggun, pulsing through the room. God was arising and manifesting in this sudden harmonic grace.

So that afternoon, when the Havurah was done and we left with our empty plastic bowl, I said to Mikhail, "See."

"What do you see?" he asked.

"See," I said. "You're taller."

And he was. After the music he'd created, and the divine inspiration, and the uproar he'd caused, with everybody wanting to learn more Hasidic melodies from him, Mikhail was at least an inch taller than he'd been when he came to the services. And as we walked back home on that February day even the weather seemed to have taken a turn for the better, and the dirty snow that had been piled up against the curbs for weeks was melting around the edges. "Everything is changing over," I told Mikhail. "Everything is turning. There's going to be a whole new year, and the baby, and everything is going to be different. Look, new people are moving in," I said when we got back to our building. Right in front was a huge moving truck, and it said ALLSTON PIANO MOVERS on it. "And it's a pianist," I said.

We poked around the truck and the back entrance to the building to see where the piano was going, but no one was around, so we ran up the stairs to Aunt Lena's apartment. Her door was standing wide open to the hall.

"This is strange," said Mikhail.

I followed him inside, and that was when we saw that the piano movers were actually in our own apartment. And they hadn't come to deliver a piano. They had come to take ours away. Aunt Lena was standing right in front of the baby grand and screaming at two of the piano movers and trying to beat them off the instrument. They stood there in their Allston Piano Movers jumpsuits listening to her sympathetically, and in the meantime two other men were actually unscrewing the top of the piano from its legs!

"Stop!" I screamed. "What are you doing?"

"We're removing the piano, ma'am," said what turned out to be the senior piano mover. He was an African-American gentleman with gray hair. His name, Richard, was embroidered in script on his uniform. He handed me a clipboard which he said had paperwork and was full of forms in legalese, and copies of contracts, that supposedly Mikhail had previously signed back when he'd bought the piano from the Bosendorfer store, about how he'd make monthly payments on the instrument and if he didn't, then said instrument would be repossessed.

"This"—Mikhail put his hands on the piano's satiny wood—"this is my livelihood!"

"Mm-hmm," the head piano mover said sadly, with his eyes on the top of the baby grand.

"This is my art," Mikhail said.

"Mmm-hmm. I know," the head piano mover said.

The men just flipped the top of the piano on its side and onto a dolly. There they were, wheeling the piano out the door. There they were carrying out four dismembered piano legs. It was like watching someone being drawn and quartered.

"What can I do to stop this?" I begged Richard.

"You're eleven months behind," he said.

Eleven months! I thought. I guess Mikhail had sort of forgotten about making payments. "My husband has a gift," I told Richard. "My husband has a magical gift. He just hasn't yet been recognized. Don't you see?"

Richard opened up the piano bench and took out all Mikhail's music. Chopin waltzes, and preludes. Old dog-eared Satie. He started giving all the music to us—to me and to Aunt Lena and Mikhail.

"Why are you giving us all this?" I asked miserably.

"Because the music belongs to you," Richard said.

"What's the point of giving him his music, if you're taking away the thing to play it on?"

"The music is your property," Richard said. "But unfortunately how it works is the piano has to be paid up."

"No, you aren't listening!" I was starting to feel breathless. I could barely get the words out. I was panting for air.

"I know. I know," Richard said, almost tenderly.

One of the guys was coming back now for the piano bench.

WHERE the piano had been was now a huge hole. It was like a crater in the living room. There was the dust that had gathered under the piano, and there were the newspapers that Aunt Lena had piled there. And there was just this empty space; this great silent void. You could only walk around it.

All the rest of that day Mikhail sat on an old folding chair in our room. We usually threw clothes on top of that chair, but he'd shoved the clothes onto the floor, and now he just sat and sat. His mouth was set in a hard line. His face was flushed, his fingers eerily still. I think that was what frightened me the most. The way he didn't even fidget. He had been such a fidgety person, always keeping time with all his fingers and his toes. Now he'd had all his fidgets stamped out. I wanted to talk to him. I wanted to rant and rail with him, because it hurt so bad. It was as if somebody had taken away my hope, and my career, and stabbed me in the heart. It was as if somebody had repossessed *my* art, even though when it came to pianos I couldn't play a note. And I was in crisis, and I was in turmoil, because Mikhail was. And I was grieving, because he was. And I doubted the whole world, because he did. And I just wanted to put my arms around him and cry, but I didn't, because I thought maybe that would make him feel worse. So I kept away, and I let Aunt Lena go on about how Mikhail never opened any mail, and how I should have known that about him, that he just threw it away. Also Mikhail didn't know how to run a business. He didn't charge enough for lessons, and he allowed his students' parents to become late with payments. Thus they took advantage of him, which I should have known. While meanwhile he himself kept spending, including money for competitions. Mikhail did not understand money, and Aunt Lena blamed me, which wasn't really fair, but I let her, because she did it out of love for Mikhail— and it got her off his back.

Mikhail went to bed early. Then Aunt Lena went to bed. But I stayed up. I sat on the sofa in the living room and I stared at the piano crater on the floor. The newspapers and dust. A million practicalities buzzed in my mind. Like how would we tell all of Mikhail's piano students? He had no instrument to teach them on. How would we tell them? He couldn't call up all their parents. I would have to do it. I would have to tell them Mikhail was now making house calls. He would come teach in their own houses and apartments! Except we had no car. How would he manage to get to all of them? I thought, we've got to find some money. I thought, it's up to me. I've got to find us some money to get that piano back. I have to beg, borrow, or steal some. Which brought to mind my father, of course, except as usual I didn't know quite how to ask, given the awkward situation. All my situations were awkward situations. Given that I had used those options up before. The begging, borrowing, and stealing. And with Dad just plain helping never was a possibility. I stared ahead of me at the empty void, and I thought, how? How? How? But I could not see a way to get the piano back.

Then, for the first time, I saw how crazy we were to be having a baby in September. We couldn't even take care of a piano. How could we support a child? And where would we even put a baby in Aunt Lena's apartment?

I thought and I thought until, even with all my worrying, I could barely keep my eyes open. I thought until I practically had to dive for bed. But when I lay down to sleep, I had a terrible dream. Mikhail and I were birds. We were huge white birds flying. We were albatrosses, but we were too big. Our wings were so heavy we could barely lift them up. Our wings stretched out, so we had to wait for the wind to help us fly. When the wind came, only then, we lifted off the ground. Then we pumped and pumped with all our might, and we stretched and reached until we felt as though all the fibers of our bodies were close to break-ing. There above us was the sky, and it was cool and smooth and serene, and we gasped for air and opened up our beaks and we pumped our ungainly wings, and the wind lifted us like two gliders and we pumped some more and with all our effort we rose into that blue—it was such a color, not even blue, more purple. It was like blueberries and muscat grapes. We were so close we could taste it. Then all at once we crashed. We'd hit the ceiling. Glass sprayed down and cut our faces, and chicken wire tangled up our flight feathers, and we fell back again, and we were wounded, both of us. We were bleeding. But all the time I heard a voice, and it was calling, "Sharon! Sharon!" And I tried to raise up my wings again, but they didn't work anymore. They were broken.

I opened my eyes. I was thrashing around on the bed. I was bathed in sweat, but Mikhail was holding me, calling, "Sharon, what is the matter?"

"What do you mean, what's the matter?" I cried out. "You know what's the matter."

"I thought you were hurt," he said.

"I am hurt," I told him.

"Oh, Sharon," he whispered to me. "I'm sorry I have made such a mess. It was my fault."

"Your fault!" I said. "They didn't even give you the benefit of the doubt. They just took the piano away!"

"It was my fault," he said again.

"I'm afraid," I told him.

"Don't be afraid," he said. "Please do not fear. We will start paying bills!"

"I don't know. I don't know," I wailed.

"We will."

"I had a terrible dream," I told Mikhail.

"What did you dream?"

"It was . . . I was . . ." Even as I began describing it, the whole scene was melting away. I was already starting to forget the whole thing. But I told him, "We were birds, and we were trying to fly, but we couldn't get up there to the sky. It was like we were land animals, but we thought we could fly. And whenever we got close we got tangled in nets, and we broke our wings. But all the time a voice was calling to me."

"A voice?" Mikhail asked intently. "What did it say?"

"Just my name. Over and over. Sharon. Sharon. And now I can't sleep. And I'm afraid to go back to sleep," I said.

"But this dream is from God!" Mikhail said.

I looked at him. He sat bolt upright in bed. "This dream is from God. It must be for us to instruct us what to do!"

I propped up my head on my hand.

"This is a vision," Mikhail said.

"It didn't feel like one," I told him.

"At the time, no. You were asleep," Mikhail pointed out.

"True," I said.

"In the dream you were flying."

"And you were too."

"We were flying. We were moving. We were traveling. We must move!" he said.

"But how?" I asked.

"Then a voice was calling Sharon . . . Sharon . . . And saying what?"

"That was it," I said. "Just my name."

Mikhail got up. We both got up. We padded out into the living room. I was still wearing my shirt from the day before, but no pants. Mikhail was wearing his underwear. He started pacing around the apartment. He paced and paced, trying to come up with the meaning of my dream. He turned on one reading lamp by the couch so he wouldn't trip. He began leafing through the last few days' papers on the end table. He was looking for words. He was looking for any words of inspiration. "Real Estate," he said to me. "Relocation. Houses. Sales. Rentals."

"No," I said, slowly.

"Allston, Belmont, Brookline, Cambridge . . ." He was skimming the names of the towns. "Medford, Newton, Peabody, Quincy, Randolph, Revere, Saugus . . . Sharon!" he exclaimed.

"What?" I said.

"Sharon, Mass. Apartments, sales, rentals. This is the meaning," he told me. "Flying upward. Calling Sharon. This is what it means: go upward to Sharon."

"You mean the town? The town of Sharon? But Sharon is south," I said.

"Figuratively upward," he told me.

"Oh," I said.

"Arise," he said. "To Sharon."

Gosh, I'd probably been to Sharon twice in my life. Who went out there? It was an hour's drive! The only thing I could think was, well, it's cheap in Sharon. You have to give it that.

"To Sharon!" Mikhail said, and spoke with such joy. I felt myself rising even then. There we were, the two of us, looking at my vision. There we were, and we had no piano, we had actually nothing, except for the most important thing anyone could possibly want. Instructions that had come from God.

So of course, there were those worrisome economic issues, like we had no money and no car, no credit rating, a baby on the way, et cetera. But at that moment there was no question in our minds that there we were dealing with a commandment, and a categorical imperative, and a bolt from the blue. This was about miracles and mystic faith, in which case you had to put aside the practicalities. You had to abandon your initial prejudices and assumptions, i.e., us move to Sharon? That suburban wasteland? And you just had to concentrate on the crux of the matter, which was that I—actually we—had together been called out of our chaos by God. Just like the Israelites. Just like the pioneers. Just like the first settlers of this country. Like the pilgrims themselves when they were called to the wilderness to dedicate themselves and to find in their own personal American desert a new Sharon, and a new Canaan. And when you looked at it that way, when you considered my dream that way, then how could it not come to pass? A dream of such flight and divine provenance. You sat by the light of one lamp with newspapers scattered all around you and you just wondered. You were just in awe. And there I was with my husband. And there I was with my vision. Who would have thought? It had been so painful inside while it was happening, yet once told—who could have guessed?—like rocks that polish up to gems, my dream interpreted so resplendently.

2 1

——

The Refusniks

ONCE we had the word from God, we knew exactly what we had to do. Get out of debt, save up, and work and work to meet the income requirements for a Sharon apartment building. I worked extra hours at Fresh Squeezed, and since he couldn't teach, Mikhail started driving a taxi for the Red Cab Company. Sometimes Mikhail drove all night. Sometimes both of us worked straight through the weekend. Even on Shabbat. Yet we never had any misgivings. When you have such a precious gift—a divine message—when you receive your destiny like that you don't look back. We worked so much we barely noticed anymore that we had a space problem living with Aunt Lena; we barely noticed the lack of privacy, because we were hardly in the apartment. Those space troubles seemed like a thing of the past. In fact all our troubles seemed now to be merely temporary.

We were full of sleepless energy. Sometimes it felt as though the two of us were outrunning winter, we worked so hard; the days went so fast. And all the time I was growing. There was no getting around it. My stomach was expanding. My skin was stretching out like a balloon, and underneath there was a baby, and that baby kicked and squirmed. But the strangest thing was, my earth tattoo, which had only been about the size of a silver dollar, began to expand as well. It stretched out bigger and bigger, and the lines grew thinner and thinner, but the earth was expanding on my belly. The earth just grew and grew.

I thought, This is what it's like to have a baby. To stretch out taut like the head of a drum. To be the tip of a tree. To live on the edge. Late at night I would take baths. I would pile my clothes next to the damp stacks of Aunt Lena's *New Yorker* magazines, and ease myself into the tubful of hot soapy water. My knees were two small islands, and my belly one big round one in the water. There I was, three floating islands. There I was, two knees and one planet earth. I'd learned from the Talmud that if you save a life it's as if you are saving the whole world. There I was bringing forth a life, and I could see on my own flesh, on the ink traces of my tattoo, that this was also true: When you birth a child, it's as if you're saving the earth from smallness. I could see it happening, the baby transforming that flat ink-and-needle drawing on my belly into a wondrous globe.

There was such joy, even though we worked day and night. It was because we could see the future ahead of us, and we were racing toward it. Running all the time, and so fast, we almost made ourselves sick, but the difference was, we knew we were running in the right direction. Doubts and worries, Hasidic aspirations, desires for Mikhail's pianistic glory—they'd all gone by the wayside—and it was tremendous to have thrown them off. It was like throwing off all our extra weight and ballast. We were light, we were free, we were crazy busy. That was when we started our band.

WE didn't plan on a regular band, just a pickup group to play for a couple of Havurah friends, Josh and Beth, who were having a shoestring wedding. We got together once at Josh and Beth's half a house in Belmont just to look over the music. Josh and Beth had been engaged for several years, so they were very particular about their wedding. Josh looked like the man who ate no fat, and he worked as a lab technician at MIT. Beth looked like the gal who ate no lean, and she was a technical writer for the company BB & N. Josh had dark eyes, and Beth had wide watery blue ones. Their house was a two-family that they'd bought together, and they rented out the other half to another couple.

They'd bought their furniture at estate sales. That was the kind of people they were: fiscally sound. They'd moved to Belmont for the schools.

It was going to be Mikhail on keyboard, me on vocals and guitar, and then, from our Havurah, our friend Philip on drums, and his friend Deb on clarinet. We all gathered in the living room, and Beth's little terrier dogs were running around and barking, and had to be locked out on the screened porch, because they were jumping and nipping and worrying the music. Deb took out her clarinet and got right down to business. She was originally from Jersey, but was now a famous street musician in Harvard Square, and she had the most expressive face, with the kind of nose that in books they always call aquiline, which you have to guess must be a euphemism for big. Philip was unpacking his drum set. He was an unpublished novelist around six and a half feet tall, and he had a very small neat head up there on his shoulders, and he wore little round glasses, and khakis, and was afraid of microbes. He was so introverted and straightlaced, you would never imagine him in a band. Yet there he was fussing with a set of drums that must have cost ten thousand dollars, fiddling with the little metal stands. We all said, "Geez!" He was like someone coming to a friendly bowling get-together with his own professional bowling ball in its custom vinyl zipper case. My hands stroked the varnish sides of my beloved, yet admittedly plain vanilla guitar. Mikhail, who really was a pro, made no bones about anything, and just stood behind Beth's electronic keyboard.

"I want you to play 'Dodi Li,'" Beth said. "For the processional."

"Do you have the words?" I asked.

"No," she said, passing out the music.

"I need the words if I'm going to sing," I pointed out.

"That's okay, you don't have to sing," said Beth.

"Oh," I said. I'd been kind of looking forward to singing. I was a little bit disappointed. But fortunately at the bottom of the page there were words in Hebrew, and they were the lyrics. Philip set the tempo, and we plunged in. And I, who could read the words, given the hours I'd put in praying when I was a Hasid, actually did begin to sing.

"*Dodi li, va-ani lo, ha-roeh, ba-shoshanim. . . .*" I am my beloved's, and my beloved is mine. . . .

"Too fast! Too fast!" said Beth. "We want to *walk* down the aisle!"

Rehearsal with Beth around proved to be impossible, since she had an opinion about everything, and not a great understanding of the creative process. Josh was perfectly happy to let us do our thing, but Beth could not stop interrupting. After about twenty minutes of "Too fast! . . . Oh, no, now it's too slow! . . . Are you going to play it that softly at the ceremony?" I could sense that the energy in the room was not positive at all. I could sense a lot of resentment from my fellow musicians. She'd interrupt, and they'd raise their eyes to the ceiling. They'd mutter to themselves. They'd sigh. Still none of them spoke up.

Finally, I had to say, "Hey, Beth?"

"What?"

"Could you cool it?"

She looked at me with those big pale blue teary eyes. All of a sudden I remembered a girl from seventh grade named Lisa Frank, except we called her Lisa Frankenstein. She'd had blue eyes just like Beth's—the kind always threatening to cry. Frankenstein always had those tears ready. It was one of her main assets. It was like having a high water table.

"Beth," I said, "I know it's your wedding and all, but we need some space. This is only the first time we've ever played together!"

"But the wedding is Sunday!"

"But we're a pickup band. Of your friends. Remember?"

In the end we just had to put her out, like the dogs. We just had to get Josh to take her away all afternoon on errands so we could do our job.

"Thanks, Sharon," Philip said to me, when we'd got rid of the audience.

"Alone at last!" I said. "Let's play ball!"

And so we played. Mikhail began, and Philip took the beat, and Deb lifted up her clarinet and just whomped and wailed. We played klezmer, and Israeli folk, and corny renditions of *"Hava Nagila."* And we played loud, and we played fast—except I gave Mikhail a dirty look when he tried to run away from the rest of us. I reined him in with one wifely glance. And we played the songs of Naomi Shemer, during which, of course, I took the lead, fronting the band. I sang *"Machar"*—Tomorrow—and *"Yerushalayim Shel Zahav"*—Jerusalem of Gold. We played all the music Beth had left us, and some she hadn't left at all. We noodled and we improvised. We went out on a limb. We played swing and jazz. We even tried some rock 'n' roll. And all the time the dogs were barking and barking out on the screened porch. It was two hours of holy noise.

When we stopped, no one spoke. We were stunned. We had come together as a few disparate musicians doing a favor to friends, and that elusive thing had happened. We had the stuff. We had that intangible thing that a million bands will strive for and never achieve. We clicked. Philip sat behind his drums. Nervously he fingered the drumsticks in his hands. Deb was standing drenched in sweat. Her whole body was depleted. She hadn't just played every tune; she'd danced them. I looked at Mikhail and he looked at me.

"You guys," I whispered. "We could charge money."

"I wish we'd charged money already," said Philip. "We shouldn't be playing this wedding for free."

"They should at least pay us something," said Deb.

"No, no, they're our friends," I said. "Anyway they brought us together!"

"They were the instruments of fate," said Mikhail.

"After this, we're charging," Deb said.

"No kidding," I said. "A thousand bucks a pop."

"That's all?" said Philip. "I was thinking a thousand bucks a person."

"Whoa," Deb said.

We all contemplated that.

"But there's one thing we need for starters," I said.

"Which is?" Philip said.

"A name," I said.

"Of course! A name!" said Mikhail. *"Bashert,"* he said.

"No way," said Philip.

"It should start with *klez,* since we're a klezmer band," said Deb.

"We are not only klezmer," Mikhail objected.

"Yeah, but you have to think marketing. You have to think, the Jewish wedding market."

"There's a lot of good examples out there already," Deb said. "Klezmagic, the Klezmaniacs . . ."

We were still brainstorming on names when Beth and Josh came home.

"Klezmaggots?"

"Klezmagma?" I suggested.

"How did it go?" Beth asked.

"Klezmagnets?" said Deb.

"These names are all too much the same," Mikhail said.

Beth and Josh looked at each other.

"We could go scriptural," I said. "We could do Joyful Noise. As in: Make a joyful noise unto the Lord."

"That's good," said Deb.

"Can I tell you how much I hate that?" Philip said. "I'd rather just go off and shoot myself."

"Maybe it sounds too Christian," Mikhail suggested.

"You're right. You're right," I said. "It's got to say Jewish. It's got to say folk. It's got to say Old Country."

"It's a band," said Philip. "It's got to have an edge."

"Hello?" Beth was calling us.

I was deep in thought. Just staring at Mikhail, deep in thought. "The Refusniks," I said.

"Woooo, baby!" screeched Deb.

"That's okay," said Philip.

Only Mikhail looked unconvinced, because as he told me later, to him the connotations of Refusnik were of bureaucracy and paperwork, rather than Old Country rock 'n' roll. Yet already Deb and Philip were high-fiving me on the name. I knew I could talk Mikhail into it.

OUR debut at Beth and Josh's wedding was fraught with some disasters. First off, we did end up playing the processional too fast. It was the classic problem of art versus life. We envisioned *"Dodi Li"* flowing right along, like a clear running stream; yet Beth had a whole long wedding gown to contend with and elderly parents taking her down the aisle. The three of them just could not keep up. However, our recessional was a big hit. When the ceremony ended we exploded into our klezmer riffs and brought down the house. Everybody was milling around and clapping with us as we started improvising and hot-dogging. We had our own miniconcert right there in the sanctuary, so people didn't even realize they were supposed to go off into the social hall already.

Then during the meal, instead of playing soft dinner music, we were still so excited we kept playing klezmer sets, and Beth came over and had a hissy fit, and Philip said a few things to her that he probably shouldn't have, given that she was the bride and all! I had to go patch things up. However, once I'd patched things and we began playing the dance music we started getting requests for songs and dances that we didn't know, and we got really embarrassed and ended up repeating the stuff we did know, only twice as loud, which didn't go over well with some of the guests. But as happens all the time with new ventures, these dilemmas turned out to be incredibly valuable, because from these experiences and some others we together as a band derived a whole mission statement for our organization, which went like this:

1. *The mission of the Refusniks is to create great music, grow together individually and as a group, and make money.*
2. *The wedding is the customer.*
3. *Do not feud with the customer.*
4. *Sharon is the manager.*
5. *Sharon will be the liaison between band and customer. See number 2.*
6. *When hearing requests, do not roll eyes, make derogatory statements, etc.*
7. *Do not use the f-word to members of wedding party. See number 3.*
8. *Do not play weddings for free anymore. Ever.*

It took a while for us to get another gig. However, we did get one through my boss Telemachus to play a wedding up at a B & B in Maine. And gradually, all through the spring we accrued more experience, and practiced and jammed together with various pieces of borrowed equipment, until by the summer we got a couple more opportunities. We rehearsed until our sound was so smooth we could play softly as well as loudly, tenderly and slow for the processionals, and peacefully enough that people could eat their meal during the reception. When we started we were raw and brash, but now I, being the manager, was steering us in a more refined direction. I had to take the leadership role because I was dealing with three musical geniuses who hated compromising their vision. Philip, Deb, and Mikhail were actually happier playing for themselves than for the customer. They didn't want to think their art was actually a service business!—so I thought about it for them. And, in fact, I became something of a guru on the formalities and etiquettes of the whole traditional Jewish ceremony. Brides and grooms actually came to me for advice on the proper music, and the order of the relatives marching down the aisle, and the timing of the blessings—which was kind of funny, since my own wedding had been this last-minute civil ceremony after Mikhail and I ran off together. But now that I was fronting our Old World–style band, people really looked to me for answers—so, of course,

I had to provide them, and when I didn't know the protocol for some-thing, and the rabbi didn't care, then I'd just make up a few little new tra-ditions along the way.

Our musicality was definitely making inroads, and the Boston Jewish folk music grapevine started working in our favor. By summer's end we'd played Chatham, and the Arnold Arboretum, and the Armenian Cultural Center. We each got two hundred bucks a wedding—which meant four hundred for Mikhail and me, which at times seemed almost unfair, being that civilization rigged the economy that way—where you got twice as much just for the pleasure of being married!

The day after Labor Day, Mikhail and I had enough money to move. It was a stifling hot day, and I was just about nine months pregnant, and I wore a giant-size T-shirt over maternity shorts, and I felt for those guys with the humongous beer bellies, because I finally understood what it was like to have your shorts sliding down the curve of your ro-tundity, and having to tug them back up until they started sliding all over again. We were driving our new preowned Honda Accord, and the seats of the car burned our flesh, because the vehicle, although it was in fantastic shape, had no freon, which was how we had afforded it. Sweat trickled down our faces. But there we were, moving out to Sharon. We drove right out on the pike, and down past the Crescent Dairy's white ice-cream-packing building, which had a whole row of little windows where you could drive up and buy ice cream. And we drove down-town, which was something between a main street and a strip mall. A little ways off there was a beach at this tremendous lake, Lake Mass-apoag, where you could go and sit, and bring your kid. And there was a community center, and over hill and dale, all these ranch houses and lit-tle white saltbox houses abounded, and Cape houses with yards, which we couldn't afford, yet someday we were going to buy one. And then we'd finally have our cat, and our dog, and chickens (we were consider-ing raising our own, in a chicken coop in our yard).

In the meantime we drove around the rotary right in front of the Gulf station, and there it was: Sharon Garden Apartments. There were no gardens, but there was parking. There were numbered spaces. We pulled in and just sat a moment. We didn't talk; we didn't have to. We both felt the same way. Mikhail carried a lamp and a suitcase, and slowly, we walked up the outdoor cement stairs. We came to number twenty-four, and I turned the key. There it was. A living/dining area with royal-blue wall-to-wall carpet. There was the wall for our new Yamaha upright piano, and the pass-through to our own galley kitchen with white Formica. I opened up the freezer and stuck my head in just to feel the cold. I opened the refrigerator and it was sparkling white.

It was good we didn't own much of anything, since it made moving in so much easier. We didn't have really any kitchen stuff, except a couple of pots Aunt Lena had given us. Apart from the piano, we had no heavy furniture. For a bed we were just planning to spread out a *buton* on the floor. The baby's room was all set. The band, i.e., Philip and Deb along with us, had chipped in to buy us this incredible white combination crib, changing table, and dresser. And it turned into a youth bed when the kid grew older!

In the master bedroom there was a built-in air conditioner. It was built in right under the window. So, of course, immediately, we turned it on. We just stood there in the cool air in that empty room.

I have to say, in a lot of ways the whole thing was mundane and bourgeois, yet at the same time, standing in that air-conditioned bedroom, it was such a spiritual moment. It was such a high point in my life. I would compare it to arriving in Jerusalem. I would put it up there with my rebirth. And actually, it was better, because I wasn't doing it alone. Mikhail and I were coming to this whole new plane together.

WHEN you get to a certain size, you start to feel invincible. You get pregnant enough, and you feel as though armies would have to fall away before you. That was how big I was. I'd gained sixty pounds. Mikhail mentioned to me that maybe I should scale back my hours at Fresh Squeezed, but I scoffed at the idea, I felt so good. My legs were like tree trunks. My belly was no island anymore; it was a whole globe unto itself. My breasts overflowed. My hair rippled all down my back, it had such a sheen.

The bride at our Saturday-night gig in Cambridge was taken aback when she saw how much I'd grown. I guess when she'd hired us back in June I hadn't looked so large, and I'd been somewhat vague about my actual due date, which to tell the truth was the day of her wedding, yet I hadn't wanted her to feel any additional jitters on her special day! So

Mikhail and I and Deb and Philip were unpacking all our equipment at Temple Beth Shalom, and the bride was standing with her parents getting photographed, and all of a sudden this look of alarm passed over her face when she caught sight of me in my black, plus-size gown.

"Excuse me," she said to the photographer. "Excuse me." And she came rushing over in her wedding dress, which was pink, and flapper style, and with one of those transparent wrappers, as if you were a movie star in a silent film. I thought, Now, that is a dress. I thought, Now, how come there weren't any dresses like that at the Bialystoker wedding library?

"Cheryl. Hey, you look gorgeous!" I said to her. And I looked down and I saw she had silver lamé sandals on her feet. "Far out!"

"Are you gonna be all right?" she said. "Is she going to be okay?" she asked Mikhail.

"We can cover for her," Philip said.

I shot him a look.

"I didn't know you'd be so far along," Cheryl said.

"She's really not so far along. She carries 'uge," Deb insisted in her New Jersey accent.

We were all a little bit tense, warming up, since this was a more formal wedding than the ones we'd done so far. The temple was one of those gorgeous old buildings with the vaulted ceiling and the red velvet curtains at the front. Above the velvet curtains there was a decorative ceiling scooped out and scalloped like the inside of a shell, and painted in sunset colors to look like clouds of glory. And there were dark wood pews, and marble steps leading up to the front dais, and an actual aisle. At the end of every other pew was a bouquet of hot pink lilies, and the chuppah was decorated with lilies too. When the guests and relatives started filing into the sanctuary, the guys were all wearing suit and tie. And not that we liked to count the house, but there must have been two hundred people there. I turned around to face the band. "Hey," I whispered.

"What!" Philip said, startled. He looked absolutely terrified of me.

"Oh, my God," Mikhail said.

"I'm fine," I whispered furiously. "I'm fine, okay? I'm speaking to you as your manager. Nothing else! You people have to loosen up here. This is about beauty. This is about grace. This is about exposure!"

I turned around again to face the audience. I shook out my music. "*Dodi Li*," "*Hinach Yafa*," "*Eruv Shel Shoshanim*." All music I knew from dancing, wedding lyrics from the Song of Songs. I signaled for the first relatives to start walking down the aisle, and began to sing.

> Dodi li, va ani lo
> Ha roeh . . .
> *My beloved is mine, and I am his.*
> *He feeds his flock. . . .*

That was when I had my first contraction. Still, it was barely a contraction. Just a twinge. It barely registered the tiniest quiver in my voice. Only Mikhail looked over at me. Only he noticed.

All through the ceremony, which was kind of long, I sat and focused on the gardens in the music, and grapes on the vine, and hills of spices. Twinge! Another contraction. I bowed my head as if in prayer. But a great smile was covering my face. I couldn't help it. Even though, in the short term, it was going to be a little bit sticky holding out through the rabbi's sermon, not to mention the four-hour reception, all I could think of was Baby! You're almost here.

You know the wonderful thing about our job—by which I mean weddings? Once the ceremony is done, no one even cares what's going down. You can have the most detail-oriented bride in the world. You can have Cheryl herself, but as soon as the glass is smashed, the details fly out the window. The bride and the groom race off down the aisle, and all the relatives fall in, at ease. Once she and Jonathan tied the knot, Cheryl never gave me a second thought. And that was a good thing, since by the time we got set up again at the reception around the corner in the Dante Alighieri Cultural Center, I had to walk around in circles every once in a while with my hand on the small of my back. I found myself staring up quite often at the life-size portrait of the great poet Dante in his robes and Renaissance-style hat.

Philip said to me, "Why are you starting up on 'Romania' again? We just did that one."

"Oh, yeah," I said. I was a little bit distracted.

We took a break. We huddled at a back table with our chicken breast stuffed with wild rice.

"I am worried," Mikhail said.

"I'm fine," I told him.

"Admit it, Sharon," Deb said. "You're in labor."

"Labor!" Philip drew back like it was catching. "What's the plan?"

"What do you mean, the plan?"

"The plan," he said. "The exit strategy."

"What do you think this is, some kind of fire emergency? I'm telling you I'm fine."

The three of them glared at me. "And what if your waters . . . what if they break?" Mikhail demanded.

"They're not breaking," I said. "Didn't you read the book? Don't you even remember it is a rare occurrence for a woman's waters to rupture before she reaches the hospital? We're playing till the end."

And, by God, we did play until the end of that wedding, and we got our money—by which time I had such hideous gut-wrenching cramps, Mikhail and I didn't even help pack up the equipment. We just took off for the hospital.

We got there, and it turned out everybody else in Boston had gone into labor that night, too, and every other couple of child-bearing age was crowding the ward. And, even if you screamed, other people were screaming louder, because they'd been there longer. If you groaned, or looked like you were going to be sick, no one even gave you a second glance. Laboring women were everywhere. Red-faced women, bruise-faced women, women with IVs on wheelie poles were staggering through the halls.

When I finally got into the nurse's station I had the chills. I was shaking with cold. Whereas before I was powerful and I was smiling, and giving my whole band what for, now all I could feel was this huge baby's head locked in battle with me, bruising my bones, and clawing at my flesh. And I was shivering, because I hadn't known there was such a monster inside of me. And I was lying on a table, and there weren't any labor rooms free. And I thought, Let me die. Let me die right here in my blue hospital gown. Draw all the curtains around the bed. Just let me die.

But then the contraction would pass and I'd open my eyes, and I'd come to. And I'd say, "Mikhail?"

"Yes!"

"Don't crack your knuckles."

"Okay, all right."

"It's really bad for your fingers, Mikhail!"

"Okay."

"Owwwwwwwww!"

"Another one?" He bent over me.

I put my hand up and pushed him away as hard as I could.

"Sharon!" he said.

"Ohhhh . . ." I sobbed. And my poor husband was looking at me so upset, and all I could think of was *Good!* All I could think of was hate and bile and spite, until the pain subsided again.

And this went on for I don't know how long, and then I got wheeled to another room, and I got a so-called bed to writhe on, and I screamed, and I cried, and I tried to walk around and breathe. I tried everything except anesthesia, because I was having a natural birth. That was what Mikhail and I had decided. We would have had a midwife at home if we could have afforded it, but our insurance only covered hospitals. So because of the medical-industrial complex I was there in the ward. Yet I wasn't giving in to epidurals and drugs and needles.

So this went on hour after hour, but when the new doctor came in, it turned out our baby was stuck inside of me, and the head was jammed in like a cork inside a bottle, and the baby was in distress, so I was getting an epidural whether I liked it or not, since I was about to have a C-section.

"Please don't feel that you've failed," said the doctor.

"Fuck you!" I screamed. All I could think of was, I've gone through all that natural childbirth for nothing! Hour after hour after hour. Now in two seconds this interventionist prick zipped me open, and brought forth a nine-pound baby boy.

I was all spaced out. Somewhere far below me the doctor was stitching me up, and then up around my head Mikhail and the baby were floating, and he was carrying on about how the kid was perfect, and he was beautiful, and I said, "Good!" since I'd just decided he was going to be an only child.

I slept the most delicious sleep. I slept on clean white sheets. My soul was calm. My clenched-up muscles all at peace. My pain stood at a distance like a little cloud, since the nurses gave me codeine. And when I woke up I had that blurry wondering feeling that something had happened, but I couldn't quite remember, and then I did remember, the baby was here. What a relief! Then I went back to sleep again.

All the next day I slept and woke and ate anything they put in front of me, and then I slept some more. People came to see me. Aunt Lena came, and Philip and Deb came with one of those balloon bouquets. But mostly it was just me and Mikhail and the kid.

He had tiny red hands and no hair. He knit his brow, and when he looked at you he stared so hard you could not look away. His eyes were dark. They were almost black. He was completely uncompromising.

I said to Mikhail, "He's one day old and I feel like he's already criticizing me."

"He has wisdom," Mikhail said.

"What do you think he knows about us?" I asked.

"Everything!" said Mikhail. "Only when he was born he forgot much of what he knew."

"Maybe it's better not to know everything right away," I said. "Maybe that's a good thing. Mikhail?"

"Yes?"

"He sneezed!" I said. "He sneezed at me." I had never seen such a tiny sneeze in my life.

We stared at the kid in his tiny knit hospital cap and his flannel hospital blanket. He was all wrapped up tight with just his face staring out, solemn and worried when he was awake, and then tiny and shrunken up when he was sleeping. We stared until Mikhail went home for the night, because sleeping in the chair in my room hurt his back. He had to go home, but I got to stay in bed. Something like five days, I got to stay, and have my sheets changed and live in a haze, as if I were lying in a sleeper car on a train. The world was flashing by outside the window.

I didn't keep track of the days or the visitors or anything. Between my exhaustion and my pain meds, and my great relief, I lay there in a dreamlike state. In the distance I heard Mikhail talking on the phone. He was organizing a bris. He was calling people and inviting them. In the most surreal way he was telling people the directions to the Sharon Community Center. He was actually speaking to my father's wife on the phone. It was like something out of a dubbed late-night movie.

Mikhail saying, "Cathy, yes, I agree. To him he will be a grandson to his grandfather. Of course, it will be important for him to see."

Was this my husband, planning and organizing a whole large-scale event? Was this Mikhail speaking to my stepmom whom he'd never met—talking strategy about how to land Dad at the naming ceremony for his own psychic good? Normally I would have been startled, but as it was, my peace of mind was so great that all I did was beam at everyone who came by. I lay against my pillows and beamed at the nurses. I beamed at Philip and Deb. I watched their bouquet of balloons float up toward the ceiling. Mikhail reached for the ribbons to bring those "It's a Boy" balloons down to earth. "Let them be," I said. I radiated peace. "Let them be."

Dreams passed over me like cool cloths on my forehead. I loved convalescence. Everything was wavy and soft. Everything was infantile. It was the world on drugs, but in a good way, because you were in the hospital. Because you deserved them.

I dreamed my mother was at my bedside and she was wearing crinkled cotton lavender robes, and her straight silvery hair hung down around her shoulders, and she was bringing me assorted loose teas, and telling me that she was proud of me.

"But it's so hard to keep my eyes open," I said. "Do you know what I mean?"

"Oh, yes," she said.

"Do you know what you look like right now?" I asked her.

"What?"

"You look like the lilac fairy," I said. "Am I sleeping?"

"No, I think you're awake," she said.

Then I remembered I was awake. At least half awake. I wasn't dreaming about my mom at all. She was standing right there. "You can still be a fairy if you're a witch, right?" I said.

"I only practice part time," she said modestly.

"But you have some powers, right? I wish you'd have some powers." Then I had an insight. "You knew about the baby, didn't you?"

"I knew after Mikhail called me," Mom said.

"Oh," I said. "I thought you just knew."

I was holding the baby, and she bent over us. "Oh, he's beautiful."

"Are you going to make a wish?"

"All right."

"It's just you keep reminding me of those fairies who come to make a wish."

"He doesn't have any hair at all," she murmured.

"Is that a wish?"

"Isn't that something? You had a whole head of hair."

"I know," I said. Then I felt confused, because I didn't know. I'd been told, and I'd seen pictures. So was that knowing?

"When your brother was born, he had a whole head of blond hair. When I saw him . . . They put me out completely, I think. In those days they put you out, you know, and then you came to, and they had the baby all washed and dried and clean, and like a little angel. Just like you!" she said to the baby. "Aren't you? Aren't you? What's your name?"

"We're going to name him at the bris," I said.

"Oh, yes. You're getting your name at the bris. Poor baby! It's not easy being born!"

I looked down at him, busy sucking at my breast. "He knew everything about us," I said. "He knew everything in the whole world, and all the alphabets and all the languages, and the laws of physics, and then when he was born he forgot. An angel stood at the gates. She put her fingers to his lips. Now he has to go back to school. Now he has to go back and learn the hard way. Which, if you think about it, is why he didn't want to come. Did you ever think about that? How it's so warm in there, in the womb, and red? Mom, tell me the truth. Am I awake, or am I asleep? I'm feeling a little bit in between, you know?"

"That's all right. Do you want a little more light? Do you want me to open the curtains? Here, I can open the curtains. It's so beautiful out. Do you know there was one tree on the way here that was completely red? . . ."

She was still talking, but I fell silent. I sat in the bed and I saw that the baby had fallen asleep sucking. His eyes were shut. His head was down. His tiny cap had fallen off. I picked him up, and I held him in the crook of my arm. His head filled the palm of my hand. That's how I was holding his head. Right in my palm. "Mom?"

"What is it?"

"He's asleep."

"Oh, is he sweet."

"Mom?" I said again.

She looked at me.

"Could I close my eyes now?"

"Oh, sure. Is that too much light, now? Do you want to rest?"

"I like the light," I said.

"Do you want to put the baby back in the nursery?"

"No, I like it like this, holding him," I said, settling back. Maybe I had been awake before, but I still didn't think so. But then if you were sure you were asleep and dreaming, could this really be a dream? All my thoughts were loose around me. Only my arms firmly held my baby boy. I said to my mother, "How could you have left me?"

Mom started back.

"I thought you'd left a note. I was looking everywhere. I looked through the whole house. I was sure you'd left a note."

"A note!"

"You probably weren't thinking in terms of notes. I thought there'd be a note explaining the whole thing, and when you'd be back—and if I could just find the note . . ."

"Well," she said, and then she started to cry.

Then I knew this was no dream, or shouldn't be. I swallowed. My hands tightened around the baby, as though I'd lost my balance, and he had been about to fall. "Wait. Wait." I shook myself. I forced my eyes open. "I'm sorry. No. Wait. No, see, I'm not thinking about that now," I said. "Please don't think about that now. I just didn't understand then. I was thirteen—how could I? You were sick, Mom. You couldn't help it. Alcoholism is a terrible, terrible disease! You were in the grips of a terrible, terrible thing. How can I blame you for what happened when you were so sick? I don't," I said. "I really, really don't."

"All right," she said, just to appease me.

"And you believe that, don't you?"

"Yes," she said, in a small voice.

But I did blame her. I held the baby and I blamed her with all my heart, and she knew it.

"Good," I said. "Okay." I took a deep breath. "Because, I'm just saying, I'm actually at a more enlightened place than I sounded like back there."

"You are. No question you are. Enlightened, and everything else.

Jewish! Who would have thought?" My mother's mouth twisted. Her mouth was covered with fine lines. All her face was lined from sun and trouble, but her mouth especially. All around her lips. More than anything I wanted to go back and be asleep again, or at least half dreaming. More than anything I wanted to forget our whole conversation. Where was that angel of amnesia? Too busy attending births and making babies ignorant. Now I was wide awake, and there was my mother, and she was oblivious a lot, but she was not stupid. She was crazy, but she had feelings. I'd hurt her, and I didn't know how to fix it. I didn't know what to do.

Dirty sunshine shone all over the room. It must have been clean sunshine outside, but the windows needed to be washed. I thought awful thoughts. I wished my mother would go away, far away down the hall. I wished that having disappeared before, she knew how to disappear again. I wished her dead because it made me so sad to look at her.

"Do you want to hold him?" I said at last.

"Me?" she said. "Could I?"

"Here." I gave the baby to her. Asleep as he was, curled up in his blanket. She held him for a long time, and she whispered to him. After a while some happiness came back into her voice. "Look! Look!" she was telling me. But I couldn't. I guess I just wasn't enlightened enough.

22

—

Prodigal Sheep

MAYBE within one lifetime a person lives several lives. Maybe people have that in them, similar to cats. So you can say—those other times I was confused, but then I was reborn. Or, that time I was reborn—that didn't work, but give me eight more births, and I'll get it right. Definitely. Just give me all my chances, because how can you know while it's happening which way your soul might grow? Whether it might sprout seed leaves, or whether it would rather tunnel under all alone in the dark like a root vegetable. You might be born with temporary wings like some of those termites and flying ants, and then your wings fall off. But if you get a chance to start all over again, maybe next time you could fly better, and you could, spiritually speaking, be more of a bird.

But on the other hand, you might say, No! That's not right! It's a continuum who you become. Not first you're one thing and then another, but rather, your whole experience is woven together like a single golden thread. Because who am I to say the person I used to be was mixed up or wrong or somehow inferior? Who am I to judge anybody? Least of all myself. You look back and see all your mistakes, but what if, actually, they were all part of God's design? People always say to themselves: I was young then. I was foolish then, and I'm so much wiser now. They say: I had a change of heart. But your heart is the same now as it was then. It's always been the same heart beating inside of you.

So actually I have two theories about one's being, and I've gone back and forth a million times between them trying to figure out which one is right until now, the only thing I can think of is that maybe they're both right. I mean, why can't you be a person with many different lives *and* a person with just one thread? Why can't life be both a wave and a particle? . . .

It was three o'clock in the morning, and I was sweating it trying to finish my letter to the baby that I'd been working on ever since Telemachus had told me that when he was born his parents had written a letter to him with all their thoughts and hopes and dreams for him, and now it was one of his most treasured possessions. So there I was sitting on the floor scribbling for all I was worth, and the baby kept waking up and wanting to nurse and scream and be carried around. "You're defeating the purpose of your own letter!" I kept telling him.

"Sharon, you must get some rest," Mikhail said.

"I have to finish!"

"But, Sharon," Mikhail told me, "tomorrow is the bris. . . ."

"That's the whole point!" I said. "I have to write him the letter now, because tomorrow it'll be too late."

"How can it be too late when it is just eight days he is here in this world?"

"But he'll be named!" I said. "He'll have a name, and then he'll be a completely different person . . . because he'll have this public persona—he'll be part of a social contract—do you know what I mean?"

"No," Mikhail said, as he strode up and down with the baby in his arms.

"He'll belong to everyone else," I said, looking at the baby's little bald head. "And now—he's just ours." I admit, I choked up a little bit.

"But he will always be ours," Mikhail said. "Even if you finish the letter tomorrow."

"It won't be the same," I said. "It'll never be the same!" And then I started writing some more, but then I lost the whole thread of my argument, and I meandered, and my head ached, until finally I threw down my pen. "What's the use! It's hopeless. Throw it out," I told Mikhail, and I thrust my whole yellow pad at his free hand.

"But, Sharon, you are writing page twenty-three!" Mikhail exclaimed, looking down at the scribbled pages.

"Just throw 'em out," I said. "They're no good. They're all about me, not him. They're all about my dreams and my hang-ups, not his. God, I'm so selfish."

"Sharon, Sharon," Mikhail said. "Isn't it natural to write more about yourself than about him, since he's only one week old? Isn't it normal that you, the parent, have more hang-ups, because you have lived a longer time?"

"I just don't want to make a mistake," I said. "I just don't want to do this wrong, and I'm already messing up. I've already messed up the letter."

"Where are the rules to write a letter?" Mikhail asked.

"I wrote too much!" I said. "I already overdid it. What I wrote was overkill. It was pure self-indulgence! You're going to have to write it," I told Mikhail as he dragged me off to bed. "*You're* going to have to finish it."

Mikhail said, "You are a very serious mother."

I *was* serious, which is why I didn't do too well at the bris. I mean, at the business end of the bris. The rest was beautiful.

We had this mohel who drove up in a car with the license plate MOYL, and he made jokes all the time—or, rather, not so much jokes, but he talked in a jokey way, like he kept calling the baby young man, as in "Come here, young man, let's have a look at you." And he took our precious baby and undressed him, and opened up his diaper to check him out, and said in this cheerful voice, "I think he's in the top fifteen percent already!"

And I thought, Go ahead, baby, pee all over him. How dare he talk about you like that!

The mohel was into putting people at ease, usually at the expense of his patient. This mohel's name was Steve, and he was also a doctor. He was clean shaven, and about fifty, and very, very short, and with wry smiles, and a million personal anecdotes, and he wore a suit and tie, and aftershave, and as I said, was jocular and relaxed and he had a piercing tenor voice, so that when he laughed he had that slightly manic girlish laugh that really high obnoxious tenors have. I hated him right away.

People were congregating at the Sharon Community Center. The bris fell out on a Sunday, so the parking lot was filling up with all our friends from work, and from the Havurah, and from the music community.

Everybody brought a vegetarian dish and laid it on the table, and Telemachus and Chris brought gallon containers of our Fresh Squeezed organic apple juice, so we had quite a feast. There was spinach lasagna, and zucchini lasagna, and rice pilaf, and Waldorf salad, and tortilla chips, and salsa, and guacamole, and pita and hummus, and baba ganoush, and I don't know what else. Aunt Lena was organizing the food. She was wearing a black-and-white suit in an oversized houndstooth check, and she had a black patent leather purse and pointy little black patent leather pumps. Her whole face was full of joy. Everyone was congratulating her. People were congratulating us too. They were mobbing Mikhail, who was holding the baby, and crowding around me, asking about the birth, but I was almost too distracted to notice. Both my mom and dad had come.

My mother came in and kissed me on the cheek. "This is my mom," I said to everyone who happened to be standing next to me. She gave me a big flat tissue-paper-wrapped present, which I later found out was one of those Native American dream catchers to hang above the baby's crib.

Then my father came up with Cathy, and not to be outdone, they both kissed me too. And they gave me a box professionally wrapped with blue ribbons cascading in corkscrew curls. When I opened it later I saw it was a little tiny navy-blue sleeper with red trim, and red pompoms on the toes. Cathy must have picked it out.

And I said to both of them, "Thank you so so so much for coming!" as if they'd come from far away, which they had, and they shook Mikhail's hand while Steve, the mohel, was calling everyone to order.

"People, if you would gather over here . . ." Steve was saying.

Still, I couldn't take my eyes off my parents, standing there in the same room like that. I was just in such awe, watching them, and their total politesse. The way they glided near each other, and nodded their heads.

"Hello, Milt."

"Hello, Estelle. How are you?"

And they smiled, and they inclined their heads, and then they proceeded in their separate, translucent, shining spheres.

"*Baruch habah,*" Mohel Steve sang out. "Blessed be he who enters! For those of you who haven't been to a bris before—and for those of you who have, but don't remember—or don't want to remember—I'll be translating as I go along, and explaining. The first thing is—does the cutting hurt the baby? Just for a moment, just for a bit. Does it traumatize him? Will he be in agonizing pain? Absolutely not! One little cut—one drop of blood, on the eighth day of this young boy's life, to symbolize his covenant with his God, and with his people, Israel. This might in fact be the *easiest* Jewish ritual he has to undergo—especially when you remember that Abraham, the first Jew, circumcised *himself*. When he was ninety-nine. So think about that, men, as we proceed.

"*Zeh kiseh shel Eliahu. . . .* This is the chair of Elijah. . . ." Steve's voice pinged through the community center. "As tradition has it, this chair here symbolizes Elijah's throne, and the time when the prophet will return to bring forth the Messiah. It's also the chair where our *Sandek* is going to sit. *Sandek* means 'with child'—this is the guest who has the honor of holding the baby on his lap, for the circumcision. Okay, who's going to sit on the hot seat?"

"Mikhail. Go up there," I whispered.

"All right, Papa," said Mohel Steve. "You're not going to drop him, now! Take this pillow and we'll just put this young man on your lap, and now we'll say this blessing. . . ."

Tears were already welling up in my eyes. Telemachus stood on one side of me, and Deb on the other.

My tiny baby was screaming. He was turning bright red, and screaming with all his tiny might. Mikhail sat still as he could, as if he were afraid to move. And Steve took out his glittering instruments, and after that I couldn't even look.

The screaming just went on and on. That one moment Steve had talked about stretched out, it seemed, for hours.

"Are you okay?" Telemachus whispered.

"No, I'm *not* okay," I sobbed, and I buried my head on Deb's shoulder.

"She's not okay," I heard people murmuring.

"Sharon's not doing so well!"

The baby kept on screaming. I didn't even realize the mohel was finished. Mikhail was chanting a blessing in Hebrew and in English. "Blessed art thou, Lord our God, King of the universe, who hast sanctified us with thy commandments, and commanded us to introduce my son into the covenant of Abraham our father."

Steve was telling everyone to join in saying: "*Even as he has been introduced into the covenant, so may he be introduced to the Torah, to the marriage canopy, and to a life of good deeds.*"

But I still wouldn't look. All I heard was blessing after blessing, and my baby screaming, and then a dull thud.

"What was that?" I gasped.

"It's Philip!"

We all rushed to his side. Philip was lying crumpled on the floor. All six and a half feet of him. He'd fainted dead away! He lay in a little clearing of the crowd—just like a felled tree.

Telemachus and Deb and I rushed to his side. Telemachus lifted Philip in his arms. As he dragged him off, Philip's eyes opened, and then closed again.

"Blessed art thou, Lord our God, King of the universe, who didst sanctify beloved Israel from birth, impressing thy statute in his flesh . . ." Steve was chanting, "and marking his descendants with the sign of the holy covenant. . . . Just go ahead and give him a drink, and he'll be fine—happens all the time—it's always the guys. . . . Because of this, for the sake of the covenant . . ."

So we dragged Philip off to revive him, and we sat him down on a chair in the back, where he slumped ashen faced, and while we were doing that the baby got his name.

"Let him be called in Israel *Zohar ben Michayel*. Zohar, son of Mikhail."

"What did he say his name was?" everyone was asking.

"What's his name?" Deb asked me.

Still, the baby was screaming.

"Here you go, Mama," Mohel Steve told me, and he handed me the baby, and he said, "I gave him a drop of wine—that usually puts them to sleep. . . ."

"You gave him *wine?*" I said. "At eight days old?"

"He didn't want it, so you should probably nurse him."

I lifted up my top, and the baby started sucking for all he was worth. "Poor little guy. You were hungry," I whispered to him. "And nobody was listening. And when you wanted milk, they gave you wine. What kind of place is this?"

Zohar gobbled down his milk so fast he wore himself out. My other breast was fairly bursting, and Zohar was fast asleep. So I had to take off his socks and tickle his toes just to get him to take a few sips on the other side, and even then he sucked with his eyes closed. Whether it was the wine, or the milk, or the covenant on his flesh, Zohar slept and slept. He lay curled up inside his car seat with his cheeks plumped out and his mouth in a tiny disapproving yet angelic frown. "Don't worry," I kept telling him. "You'll never have to see Mohel Steve again."

Meanwhile we were all sitting down at long tables with paper tablecloths decorated with teddy bears, and we were having our festive potluck meal. I have to say, Deb's spinach lasagna was starting to revive me, especially since by now it was something like noon, and I'd forgotten to eat any breakfast that morning, we'd been so busy trying to get out of the house for the bris. Mikhail had been looking pale, too, but now he was laughing, and he was singing, and he rolled in an old upright piano that they had there and played Jewish tunes, and Bialystoker nigguns, and Israeli folk songs.

I said to Deb, "I'd get up and dance if I weren't afraid of busting up my stitches."

"I didn't know you danced," she said. "You should come dancing at MIT sometime."

"At MIT!" I said, "Deb, believe me, I've been dancing at MIT. I mean I was one of the—I was in the—I haven't been dancing there in probably twenty years! I wouldn't even know the dances anymore. My whole repertoire is probably stuck back in the seventies."

"Come to Oldies' Night," she said.

"What, is that when all the old fogies come back?"

"Yeah, they play all the old dances," she said. "They have it every year."

"It sounds depressing," I said.

Mikhail was calling me. "Sharon! We must have our speech."

So Mikhail and I got up in front of the crowd, and we hauled the baby in his car seat up with us. Philip, who was sort of convalescing in a Naugahyde armchair that we'd dragged in for him, shocked everyone by sitting up for a second and giving off a piercing whistle to quiet the crowd.

"All right," I said, "Mikhail and I have written letters to the baby about his name and who we hope he might turn out to be, and . . ." I looked down at the baby sleeping. He was so beautiful I almost choked up again. I didn't know then he was just resting up so he could scream all night. "So here goes," I said, and started reading.

Dear Zohar,

Your name means radiance, splendor, and light. When I think of your name I think of starlight and sunlight and the way light shines on the water. It is the kind of light that you see on the ocean. It is the kind of light that fills the night sky when there are so many stars they look like dust. It is the light that comes from God. It says in a poem that God's light is "a shining like shook foil." That's the idea I had when we named you. Not that we expect you to shine all the time, but we hope you will take your light and join it to everything good. And take your inherent sparks, and let them fly upward as far as they will go. That was our idea—that your name would be a little reminder to you all the time—because it's so easy to get bogged down in life. In fogs, and darkness, and shadows. It's so easy to live in caves. Yet remember your name. That you are made out of light.

I turned to Mikhail. He was in a reverie. He didn't realize I was done. "It's your turn," I whispered.

"Oh!" He rustled his ripped-out notebook papers.

Did you know, dear son, that you are also a book? You are named for the *Zohar*. The Book of Splendor, which is the mystic Jewish book of Kabbalah. It is written in the *Zohar*: "Every living thing in the world has a pair of stars in the heavens corresponding to it. Each tree and plant, even every blade of grass." When you were born, a star descended from the upper heavens into our own firmament. When you are awake that star watches over you. When you sleep that star ascends above, and a different star comes down to guard you. All throughout the universe the stars stand in their appointed places. The Lord has appointed them to their tasks. He has set them all in order in their degrees, and in their shifts during the day and during night. Therefore, dear Zohar, do not cry or fear, because you also have watching you from the heavens your own stars. And truly in life, there is nothing else you will need. . . .

"Except," I said, "if by some chance you do need something else— we'll always be there for you."

Then Mohel Steve said, *"Yasher koach!"* meaning more power to you. "Spoken like a true Jewish mother!"

So, of course, as soon as he called me a Jewish mother, everybody started laughing. I thought, Why is everybody laughing? That's what I am.

"Great name," said Telemachus afterward, when everyone was milling around, gathering to go.

"I love the name," said Mom. She gave me a kiss. A little bit timidly she said, "I have to admit, I thought you were going to name him after Andrew."

"I thought so too," Dad said slowly, coming up to the other side of me.

I was just stunned to hear them say that. So many thoughts were running through my head. First of all, the thought that for Mom and Dad it was still all about Andrew. Everything began and ended—mostly ended—with him. There were my parents, one on each side of me, and they'd both come with exactly the same idea and the same hope! So of course in that moment I was filled with guilt that this had never even occurred to me. I had never once thought of naming the baby after my brother. Of course that's what I should have done. That was the real Jewish tradition, wasn't it? And there were Mom and Dad, after all those years, still with their sorrow. How could they not feel it? You would feel it forever, losing your son. I had never even realized a sliver of how they must have felt until just that moment. And meanwhile, after all these years, even now, I'd still managed to do the wrong thing. I didn't know whether to laugh or to cry.

"I love you guys," I burst out, and I threw my arms around both of them, both my mom and dad, and I drew them together into my fat postpartum, invincibly strong unconditional arms. And I held them, and I held them, and they stiffened up, and they shrunk back from their royal spheres' crushing like that and smushing together in my iron grip. But still I held on to Mom and Dad. I held them until they were really uncomfortable. I held them as if they were my own prodigal sheep returned into my fold.

And afterward my father had to wipe the condensation from his glasses, and my mother had to gasp for breath. They were both so shaken up—we all were, all three—but I wasn't sorry. Not one bit.

23

Oldies' Night

WHEN you get older and start taking stock—when you start looking back and maybe even revisiting the so-called scenes of your youth—you can't help feeling torn between nostalgia and foreboding. That's how I felt about going back to dancing again. Deb kept working on me to come to Oldies' Night when spring rolled around, but I couldn't make up my mind to do it. I dreaded getting there and seeing how everyone had aged, and youth had fled, since that's what youth does—and you can chase her all you want, yet you'll run in circles. You'll end up in vicious circles, unless by some chance you are dancing on a painted Grecian urn, and John Keats writes your story, and then your mad pursuit will be about infinite beauty, rather than futile attempts to relive the past, and your dance will be truth, rather than consequences. The consequences being that youth flees, and grace puts on weight, and gravity comes to the quick. So I concluded that I'd rather remember dancing the way it was than go back now. Then curiosity got the better of me.

I came to Oldies' Night with Mikhail, and Zohar riding in a backpack on Mikhail's back. Our little boy was nine months old, and his face was perfectly round. His cheeks were so big and soft they jiggled and

shook as we walked along. His cheeks were so big that from certain angles you couldn't see his ears. His eyes were dark, almost black. He had
only fuzz for hair, but he had dark eyelashes all fringing his eyes. And we
walked into the MIT student center, which had a bank, and a barber
shop, and an ice cream store, and Zohar said, "Ha!" which meant, This is
very interesting.

We went to MIT's student center and found an enormous room
called the Sala de Puerto Rico. And it had air conditioning and a polished tile floor, but no people at all. I said, "I thought it was today." I
rummaged through my bag. I tried to remember the date.

Then Mikhail saw the note taped on the wall. Dancing Outside.

So we walked out to the lawn on the other side of the student center,
and there on the grass were dancers, something like a hundred of them,
and they were old. They were middle aged, and they'd brought their
spouses and their children. And they were wearing cutoff shorts and
faded T-shirts. The guys were bald, and they had beards, and serious bellies, and hairy legs. The women were wearing sweats and athletic shoes,
no Indian gauze skirts. They had perms and they had gray hair, and (like
me) hips. But meanwhile, the music was blaring from the speakers; the
same old dances I used to know. My feet just started jumping. Slowly I
started twirling. "Mamamam!" Zohar said. "Mamamam!" He kicked his
bare feet.

"Shall you come out?" Mikhail was asking him.

I was already a ways off. Without thinking I'd begun to dance. "This
is for you," this one bald guy said. He'd brought over a fancy name tag,
a white circle like a moon, and it said OLDIE on it and there was a space
where you could write your name, and how many years you had been
dancing, and I took a black marker and I wrote, "Sharon." Then I had to
laugh at myself a little bit. I wrote, "22 Years."

I didn't recognize anybody from back in my era. And yet a lot of people looked familiar. Maybe it was just taking a while to place them. Or
maybe I hadn't ever known these people, but they were the kind of people I had known. Maybe they were just the same ilk. I took Mikhail by
the hand, and he held Zohar, and I called the steps to them, and they followed, so we formed our own little unit there outside the circle, and we
took turns holding Zohar and dancing, and then resting our arms and
our backs, until all at once someone came up to me, and stared at my

face, and came a little closer and kept staring. He was a guy just arrived in a jacket and tie, and with gray hair, and a neat little gray moustache.

"Sharon?"

I knew his voice, and suddenly I recognized his little blinky eyes behind his glasses. I stood stock still. "Gary!"

"I can't believe it." He took my two hands in his. "What are you doing here?"

"I'm just—I'm dancing," I spluttered. "What do you mean, what am I doing here? This is my husband, Mikhail," I said. "This is my kid, Zohar."

Gary shook Mikhail's hand. He looked at Zohar. He looked at all of us. "Sharon," he said to me, slowly. "Wow." He kept shaking his head. "This is good. This is really good to see you again."

"What's up with you? What's with the suit?" I asked.

"I came from work," he explained.

"You work in Boston now? You work here?"

"Is that strange?" he said a tiny bit defensively.

"Well, I mean, of course not. It's just I always had you pictured in my mind at Torah Or, and becoming a rabbi, and living in Jerusalem, and all that. So that didn't happen?"

"Well, I'm living in Newton," he said, "I work for the federation."

"The federation of what?" I asked.

"The Jewish Federation," he said.

"No kidding."

"I'm involved in their adult programming. I don't know if you've heard of the program Partnership for Lifelong Learning?"

"Nope."

"I think I have heard of it," Mikhail said politely. "Yes."

"Well, that's a program I codesigned."

"Neat," I said. "So you're still into Judaism, just over here, instead of over there."

"Well," Gary said, "that's one way of looking at it. The way my thinking evolved, I came to realize that outreach was my particular area— outreach to the assimilated, and to the intermarried. Outreach to the children of intermarriage. Outreach to those in the population who are totally unaffiliated. And, much as I love Israel, America is where the need is greatest. America is where the ignorance and the identity crisis is just—it's staggering."

"That's great that you're turning that around," I said.

Gary folded his arms and he sighed in his dissatisfied patronizing way, and at that moment he was so much the Gary that I once knew that my hands flew up to my face. "Sharon," he said, "if it's anything I've become, it's more pessimistic."

"Really!"

"We've only just begun to see the fallout from two generations of assimilation."

"Well, I guess that makes your job more interesting," I said. "So now you're married and living in Newton?"

"I've been married," Gary said.

I couldn't get over how his hair had turned gray. Even his moustache was gray. But those eyes. He still had those same furtive brown more-sensitive-than-thou eyes.

"I think now I take a much darker view," Gary was telling me.

"What do you mean? You always had a dark view," I said. "Remember the honeycreepers? Remember how Hawaii was spoiled already by the time you got there? You were always a pessimist. You *loved* being a pessimist."

"And what about you?" Gary asked.

"The opposite!"

"I meant, what are you doing now?"

"Oh!" I said. "We're living in Sharon. And Mikhail is a pianist, and we have a band. But actually he's a classical pianist. If you ever have a fund-raiser," I said, "he does fund-raisers. He could do a concert for you. If you ever want to come out and hear him play, he can play any music. He's an incredible musician."

Mikhail was turning red. He didn't like me to boast, but I couldn't help it. Since one of Mikhail's main problems professionally was that he didn't publicize his own work, and since I was so proud of him, any chance I got, I tended to toot his horn. "And then we're taking care of Zohar, along with Mikhail's aunt Lena."

"So you've ended up in the sandwich generation."

"What's the sandwich generation?"

"The one in the middle, managing both child care and elder care," Gary said. "I'm going through that with my mother."

"No, I meant, Aunt Lena is taking care of the baby too. And I'm managing an organic juice store in Brookline, and I'm studying for my HN—to be a licensed herbal nutritionist. Jewishly w e're in a Havurah."

"And you've found what you've been looking for?" Gary asked.

"Well," I said, "to be honest, I'm not crazy about the discussions at our Havurah, since people are so long winded, and anybody can talk as long as she wants about whatever issues happen to occur to her, whether or not it's relevant to the text, so that aspect isn't so great. But the singing is good. The singing is really really nice. Oh, did you mean, in my life? Did you mean, in my life in general?"

"I think he's hungry," Mikhail said to me.

"Okay," I said. "But get his bib. In general in my life, you know what the thing is? I stopped looking. The thing I realized was I didn't need to go on looking anymore, and learning this and reading that and taking classes, because God was actually looking for me! So I've decided to be a receptor. I've decided to be more of a listener, and a sounding board who is open to God in all the ways he might come—visions, dreams, prophecies, music—in all his myriad forms. Do you know what I mean?"

Gary shook his head at me. I think, but I'm not completely sure, I saw him roll his eyes. He said, "You haven't changed at all."

"Oh, I have!" I told him. "How can you say that?" But maybe when enough time passes, people can't even see the changes in you anymore. Maybe after a certain point their memory of you is so strong they can't shake it. I couldn't hold it against him for remembering me as that flaky, self-absorbed person he used to know, since, after all, I remembered him the same way!

The evening was mellowing into this sea-blue. We oldies huffed and puffed. We wove in and out of circles. Swung in lines. Sweat dripped down my face. No question I was out of shape. Yet, as I danced, I felt a calm come over me. I wasn't conscious of how I looked or how I moved. I barely noticed Gary, or anyone else at all. I wasn't conscious even of the steps. My feet were in a trance; they moved by themselves, remembering everything. So I danced, and I was not in this time or that. It was like, so you're forty pounds heavier. So what? So you're twenty years older. If you were aged, you could be ripe. You could be vinted. Cured.

My feet got so hot inside my shoes, I took them off, and also my damp socks, and I danced with the grass tickling my soles. We all danced on the grass, and people's children ran around or crawled around the edges. And

Zohar sat and looked for small rocks that he might swallow, and Mikhail and I had to pry them loose from his hands. A few summer-school students were standing around watching. A little ways off knights-in-armor were running at each other with fake lances tilting, while fair ladies in long satin gowns and cone hats were applauding from lawn chairs. It was a chapter meeting for MIT's Society for Creative Anachronism.

The sun began to set, and *"Hinach Yaffa"* started up. That old dance I'd taught back at the temple in Honolulu. I said, "Hey, Mikhail, this one's easy."

The old song floated out through the air. Those lyrics from the Song of Songs where that poor girl is searching and searching for her lover and she can't find him. I understood those verses. What it was like wandering all around, searching, desperate. It was the feeling you got from loving God, yet loving him from this totally unenlightened place; loving him with this intense, unrequited love. Well, that was being a pilgrim. I'd been there. That was burning up inside with being young.

Now here we were outside on the green field, and the words were passionate, but the music was cool and slow. The music was soft like the soft grass.

> Hinach yaffa raiti . . .
> Hinach yaffa aynayich yonim . . .
> Shiniech keader haketzuvot shelu min harachtzah. . . .
>
> Baleilot bikashti et sheahavah nafshi . . .
> Bikashtiv vilo mitzativ . . .
> Mitzuni hashomrim hasovivim ba ir. . . .
> Et sheahavah naphshi raitem?

> *Behold, you are beautiful, my love,*
> *Behold, your eyes are like doves behind your veil;*
> *Your teeth are like a flock of ewes, all paired. . . .*
>
> *By night I sought him who my soul loves;*
> *I looked for him, but I did not find him;*
> *The watchmen of the city found me.*
> *"Have you see him who my soul loves?"*

Mikhail and I, and Zohar in the backpack, were dancing along among the couples, and the dance really was easy. Unlike my ladies Lillian and Henny and Estelle, Mikhail had no trouble with the steps. We were dancing the choruses and the last verses. The tape was winding down. Only then I realized that very quietly, without even intending to, I'd been singing along. And it was Hebrew poetry on my lips, but I understood exactly what I was singing. I knew all the words.